# Four Ways to Pharaoh Khufu

# Four Ways to Pharaoh Khufu

## A Novel

Alexander Marmer

PARTRIDGE

A Penguin Random House Company

Library of Congress Control Number:    2015959283
ISBN:         Hardcover            978-1-4828-5498-5
              Softcover            978-1-4828-5497-8
              eBook                978-1-4828-5505-0

Print information available on the last page.

**To order additional copies of this book, contact**
Toll Free 800 101 2657 (Singapore)
Toll Free 1 800 81 7340 (Malaysia)
orders.singapore@partridgepublishing.com

www.partridgepublishing.com/singapore

FOR MY BELOVED CHILDREN
ANNA and DAVID

# Acknowledgments

First and foremost to **Anatoly Vasiliev**, the persona extraordinary, who devoted more than 40 years of his life to studying and virtually exploring the Great Pyramid of Giza. Although never himself has visited Egypt, Vasiliev developed one of the most astonishing theories about the creation and purpose of the Great Pyramid and whose zeal and persistence caused this book to be written. I personally met Anatoly back in 1996 in his Moscow apartment and that meeting cardinally changed my perspective about the Great Pyramid constructive methods and made me to look afresh at the "known facts" about the Great Pyramid. He was a proud veteran of World War II where he was wounded in the head. This book is dedicated to the blessed memory of Anatoly Vasiliev who untimely succumbed to his wounds.

I wish to thank **Saveliy Kashnitskiy**, a close friend of Anatoly Vasiliev who helped me to arrange my meeting with Mr. Vasiliev in Moscow in 1996 and his contributions to my inspiration and knowledge in creating this book. It was with great sadness that I learned of Saveliy's sudden passing.

I cannot fully express my gratitude to **Katie Belle**, the dedicated momma of her homeschooled three children. Katie's editing skills are superb, she really knows the way with words by dressing up a text, putting a little lipstick on it and delivering it ready to mesmerize.

The most sincere praise goes out to **Dan Brown** and his eminent "The Davinci Code," which inspired me to write my own novel. Dan Brown's widespread use of trivia facts throughout the entire novel made his book for me the most enjoyable piece of reading material I've ever read.

Words cannot express my gratitude to **Samantha Smith**, an American youngest Goodwill Ambassador from Manchester, Maine, for her desire to write and to show that even a ten-year-old can make a difference in the world. Her visit to the Soviet Union in 1983 created worldwide media attention and changed the way Americans viewed Russians and vice versa. Gone too soon but not forgotten.

I would like to extend the utmost gratitude to the most sincere, honest, helpful and hard-working Egyptian tour guide, **Ahmed Hamed Yousif**. His dedication to work is unparalleled. He always goes the "extra mile" to make his clients satisfied and beyond. The dangerous trip to the City of the Dead was the best example of the level of the dedication this devoted tour guide possesses.

Special thanks to **Mustafa Khaled**, the chauffer for Bravo tours in Cairo, Egypt. His masterful driving skills of navigating safely and with precision through the bustling streets of Cairo and Alexandria were truly splendid. His intimate knowledge of roads and dedication to safety were the ultimate factors that kept me and my wife safe and unharmed.

Many thanks to the fellow scribe **Sascha Zamani** whose keen eye and meticulous attention to the details helped me to avoid some embarrassing moments later. She did an extraordinary editing job on the big chunk of the chapters and I sure hope for the continued collaboration.

And last, but not least, special thanks to my wife **Cristina**. Her loving pessimism and skepticism in seeing this book ever completed, let alone published, was the driving force behind my augmented motivation and perseverance in getting this "seems never-ending" project finally complete.

Let down from heaven, untouched by human hands
Strabo, the ancient Greek geographer and historian describing the
Great Pyramid


What is history but a fable agreed upon
Napoleon Bonaparte

# Fact:

**The Great Pyramid,** the oldest and largest of the three pyramids in the Giza Necropolis in Egypt. It is the only remaining monument of the engineered ingenuity of the original Seven Wonders of the Ancient World.

**Pharaoh Khufu**, also known as **Cheops**, was the pharaoh of Ancient Egypt's Old Kingdom and reigned from around 2589 to 2566 B.C. Khufu, the second pharaoh of the Fourth Dynasty, with the help of his architect HemIwno built the Great Pyramid of Giza. Khufu's mummy and treasures were never found.

**Medjay**, a group of desert tribesmen originated in Nubia, devoted to the perfection the art of war that served during Egypt's Old Kingdom and guarded the temples of ancient Egypt.

# Prologue

The Great Pyramid, Giza Plateau, Egypt
Monday, September 18
9:24 a.m.

German design engineer Günther Schulze, a graying, heavyset man with wire-rimmed glasses, stood gazing up at the Great Pyramid. Even at this hour the top button of his fading khaki shirt was undone, exposing his white undershirt. A slight breeze lifted the edges of his safari vest, cooling the perspiration spots around his collar and under his arms. Slowly he began his ascent, hefting himself up the stone stairs until he arrived at the entrance. Stopping to catch his breath, he relished the fresh morning air before he had to enter the stuffy monolith. He looked down at a group of excited American tourists entering the Great Pyramid's other entrance—a secondary one that had been forced open in the early ninth century A.D. by a determined man named Al-Mamun. The pyramid itself had been closed to the public for the past year for restoration. And today was its long-awaited re-opening.

Schulze lingered, admiring the mesmerizing panoramic view of the Giza Plateau. As another group of tourists noisily approached the lower entrance, he turned his head to observe, listening carefully. *They must be Europeans, either Polish or Ukrainians,* he decided.

Carefully holding the handrail, he turned and stepped inside. This was the original entrance to the Great Pyramid, and it remained closed to tourists even after the Great Pyramid's long-awaited re-opening.

Schulze was not a tourist. For the past five months, he had been involved in a project sponsored by the Egyptian Supreme Council of Antiquities, which was responsible for doing the restoration work inside the Great Pyramid. A French ventilation company, AirCo, had installed a new ventilation system in the pyramid's inner chambers. AirCo had donated the aeration system to remove the buildup of humidity from the ancient structure, which was needed to preserve its integrity. The system was installed in one of the pyramid's airshafts in order to increase the flow of fresh air. As a part of this process, Schulze had been brought into the project as a German subcontractor, helping to design and install a small vent unit on the top of the Great Pyramid's ventilation channel.

Schulze strapped his headlamp onto his head and switched it on. Then he made his way slowly past a pivoted door into the most immense structure ever erected by humankind. He could hear the two tourist groups entering the secondary entrance located several feet below—their chatter drifting up the narrow passageways.

It was pure professionalism that brought Schulze back to the Great Pyramid today. He wanted to personally check the functionality of the air vents that he had installed inside the King's Chamber. At this point he knew the inner pathways of the pyramid like the back of his own hand. This entrance was angled at 26 degrees alongside the Descending Passage, which led to the intersection just above the pyramid's original bedrock foundation. From there, the Ascending Passage rose at the same angle to an intersection of three passages. Continuing up the Ascending Passage and going past the Horizontal Passage, he could enter the so-called Queens Chamber or continue toward the Grand Gallery. A corbelled passage then ascends the antechamber and leads straight into the third chamber: the King's Chamber. It is in this final chamber that Pharaoh Khufu's mummy was once entombed.

Schulze started down the Descending Passage. The air was already hot and humid. Thinking of his newly installed dehumidifier, this concerned him. Deep in thought, Schulze glanced up to see a man with bushy Afro-styled hair running up toward him. When the stranger pushed past him, Schulze was jarred from his thoughts. *Ouch!* He felt a sharp, penetrating pain in his left arm. *What was that?* Schulze turned around in slow motion just in time to watch the man disappear into the darkness of the tunnel.

"Excuse me?" Schulze asked the empty passage. *That's unbelievably rude. He didn't even apologize for running into me.*

Schulze lifted his arm and tried to pinpoint the location of the pain. Despite the enormously painful throb, he could only find a tiny red dot seeping into his shirt fabric. *Maybe it had been a mosquito? Darn it, it hurt!* Schulze had never felt that kind of pain from a mosquito, but surprisingly, an Egyptian mosquito had never bitten him.

The intense pain began to fade away. Rubbing his arm, Schulze resumed walking down the rough-hewn stone passageway and soon fell in line behind the American tourists. When they reached the beginning of the Ascending Passage, he became aware of a growing, sharp pain in his stomach. *What is going on?* Schulze leaned against the wall for a few seconds until the pain seemed to evaporate. *Was it something I ate at breakfast?* He realized that he felt slightly dizzy as well. He decided to keep walking.

When he entered the Grand Gallery, Schulze suddenly felt short of breath. He stopped and tried to take a deep breath. *I need to catch my breath!* He watched the American tour group walk away from him. He bent over, trying to breathe deeply. *Why can't I catch my breath?* It was painful to breathe. Sweating profusely, Schulze struggled to focus on his thoughts. *Wait! That wasn't a mosquito. I suddenly felt pain and then...* His mind raced. *... That man!* The sharp pain deep in his belly was getting more intense. *He must have pricked me with a needle! Have I been poisoned?* The humid, claustrophobic air was suffocating. *But why?*

*Oh my God! They've finally caught up with me!* Schulze hazily tried to remember every single detail from the past week. *Who saw me carrying it away? So, that's why they broke into my hotel room.* Realizing he was about to faint, he attempted to conserve the strength still left inside of him. He tried to stay on his feet by grasping the handrails and propping himself against the corbelled limestone walls of the Grand Gallery. *They'll never find it!* Abruptly, he slumped to the floor while still desperately clinging to the handrail.

"Help! Help!" Schultz squeezed out as loudly as he could manage. But his strangled voice was quiet and quickly absorbed by the thick walls. The American group, led by one of the local guides, had already left the Queen's Chamber and was at the far end of the Grand Gallery, moving toward the King's Chamber. Below him, he could barely make out the voices of the European tourists as they took their turn entering the Ascending Passage. *I need to tell her! She needs to know!* His mind unnerved and his body weak, Schulze's eyes swung desperately back and forth. But nobody was there. *I don't want to die here, especially with nobody knowing.* Now slumped against the wall of the Grand Gallery, Schulze focused on opening his mouth to take in the thick air. His belly pain pulsed and screamed for relief. He was dying alone in the middle of the Grand Gallery. He shivered uncontrollably.

"Help!" He wrenched out a desperate cry, "Help!" His vision dimmed. A few moments, seemingly hours, passed by. Not a single soul appeared to be in sight.

"Sir, excuse me sir, are you OK?" Schulze heard a man's voice; it sounded like it was coming through a cloud. He struggled to open his heavy eyelids. "Sir, are you feeling all right?" asked the same voice.

Schulze struggled to speak, but this was already an almost impossible task for him.

The man was bending down next to him, "Sir, are you OK?" Schulze felt the man's hand on his shoulder.

"Can't. Breathe." Schulze choked out.

"Somebody, anybody speak English?" the man bellowed at the European tourists entering the Grand Gallery. Almost instantaneously, quite a few tourists replied, "Yes!"

The man spoke authoritatively, "This man is having trouble breathing. I need someone to run back to the entrance for help and to call an ambulance." Several of the European tourists immediately turned and dashed back to the entrance.

"Sir, I need you to lie down and try to relax. You will be okay." Schulze could hear the man fall to his knees. The man spoke calmly, "I know CPR and will try to help you restore your breathing. What's your name, sir?"

Schulze relaxed his grip on the handrails and fell into the man's arms. "Günther Schulze," he whispered through barely moving dry lips. The stranger quickly rolled Schulze onto the stone floor, tilted his head back to open his airway and started performing CPR. Despite all of the man's efforts, Schulze's physical condition continued to deteriorate. The poison had reached his major organs and his body was shutting down.

Feeling his life slowly slipping away from him, Schulze fought to stay conscious. *I need to let her know what happened to me.* He opened his eyes and found kindness in the Good Samaritan's eyes. He saw that the man could be trusted. Summoning every bit of his remaining senses and strength, Schulze reached inside his jacket pocket and removed a white business card. The man paused his CPR and leaned down, his ear to Schulze's barely moving lips. "Promise... call her," Schulze whispered. "I was ... poisoned... Beware ...dark man...Afro..." The man nodded and grabbed the card, stuffing it inside his jeans pocket and resuming his CPR.

Schulze's thoughts were breaking up. He reached up and feebly patted his vest. The Good Samaritan stopped and pulled out the notebook for him. Schulze nodded weakly. "Find four ways..." Schulze's lips contorted, but the rest of his speech was incomprehensible. As Schulze's eyes rolled back into his head, his body finally went limp.

The Good Samaritan expertly felt Schulze's pulse. There was no beating.

# Chapter 1

EgyptAir JFK to Cairo
Sunday, September 17
4:35 p.m.

Michael Doyle, a twenty-nine year old software engineer from Orange County, New York, awoke suddenly when the airplane started shaking violently. The EgyptAir aircraft, en route from New York's Kennedy Airport to Cairo's International Airport, was passing through turbulence yet again. Yawning, Michael adjusted his grey hoodie donned over his favorite New York Yankees T-shirt and peered at his wristwatch. Its digital display showed the time as 16:35. He had owned the watch since his army basic training days when life existed in twenty-four hour time. Now a civilian, Michael still kept his watch on military time, as it made sense to him.

Thinking about his destination, Michael quickly did the math to determine the time zone changes. *So, it's gotta be 10:35 in the evening in Cairo now. Hopefully we're not going to have that same problem with the gear again.* Michael winced, thinking about the airplane's mechanical troubles during takeoff. While he was not an overly anxious person—the military had removed any predisposition for that—he was still a bit unnerved by the experience. He was a tall man, just over six feet, and had to adjust his legs yet again in the allotted space by his seat. When standing, he had a tendency to hunch his shoulders as the result of an Iraq War injury. His black hair was cut in a fairly short military style but tended to curl slightly on top. Large, light-green eyes and a large mouth, ready to smile at any moment, were the focal points of his face.

Even with his general friendliness as a whole, Michael gave the impression of being a serious and quiet man. After honorably serving six years in the US Army, including a twelve-month tour of duty in Iraq in 2003 during the invasion, Michael was accustomed to assuming responsibility and doing difficult things, as this is the way of those in the military. He was naturally at ease in the presence of any high-ranking officer because he understood that every officer, above all, is human. Michael's friends would depict him as earthy and friendly. They also knew him as a sincere, quick-witted, charming man with a laid-back and open-hearted attitude that allowed him to easily get in touch with anyone, anywhere. Whether Michael was on the street, in the military or in the corporate world, people seemed to gravitate towards and trust him. Whenever this friendly, quiet, sincere man had a request, people readily responded to him. In return, Michael always quietly bestowed them with one of his charming smiles.

Seconds after taking off from Kennedy Airport, the aircraft's motors had suddenly powered down. A few seconds later they had hiccupped back on, only to power down again seconds later and then repeated the process. It was as if the pilot could not keep the motors going at full throttle, and the plane itself was protesting his efforts. A strange shuddering noise filled the cabin. There were unnatural vibrations, as if something was loose or had been left open. As the plane started rapidly losing altitude, Michael's heart leapt into his throat. *This is definitely not something a plane should be doing! We certainly don't have a lot of altitude to lose.* Michael's insides twisted up as mental pictures of the plane crashing into the ground flashed through his mind. *This is definitely going to be the worst day of my life! And, for that matter, perhaps the last day.* The co-pilot came on the intercom and ordered the flight attendants to remain in their seats. Michael gritted his teeth. *After so many years of dreaming to see the pyramids and now this is happening!? Come on, give me a break!*

He focused his mind on remembering the miraculously safe landing of an airplane on the Hudson River in New York City in 2009. Captain Chesley Sullenberger, also known as Sully, had successfully landed that US Airways plane. At that moment, Michael tried to visualize Captain Sully as the captain of his flight. He imagined Captain Sully expertly landing the shuddering plane and being hailed as a hero, yet again, for successfully landing a crashing plane without any major injuries or fatalities.

Michael had been jarred out of his escapism as a nervous, elderly lady sitting in the back started screaming, "What's going on? I don't wanna die!"

The passengers responded with pure panic. Young children started crying. Even though Michael felt the same unease, he twisted around in his seat and attempted to get the panicked lady's attention. Speaking firmly, he called out to her, "Ma'am, listen to me!"

He took a deep breath and spoke in his best officer's voice to the passengers around him, "You are not going to die! Nobody is going to die!" The passengers around him started quieting down and staring at him wide-eyed. With large green eyes that contrasted sharply with his military style black hair, Michael was a handsome man. He looked at each of them sternly. "Everything will be fine!" And they believed him.

The flight leveled out and the flight attendants were now out of their seats, walking up and down the aisles trying to quiet down and soothe the passengers. All of a sudden, Michael was struck with the memory of the ill-fated Flight 990 from New York City to Cairo in 1999. That flight had 217 people on board and just thirty-two minutes into its journey, it had plunged into the Atlantic Ocean off Nantucket Island. *I hope nothing will happen this time.* Michael took another deep breath; he definitely did not want to let fear overwhelm him. As he settled back in his seat and adjusted his legs again, he observed several people praying. *That's an excellent idea,* he thought as he joined them.

After a few minutes, which seemed to stretch on for much longer, the noises and shuddering stopped. The pilot made a short announcement over the intercom and explained that one of the landing wheels had not retracted properly, but that he had successfully gotten it to go back into place. The flight would proceed as usual.

But even after everything had calmed down, Michael could not help but be haunted by the worry that the wheels would not extend successfully when the plane attempted to land in Cairo. He turned on a movie and tried to settle himself. Despite the commotion and his nagging thoughts, Michael began to calm down. And as the airplane hummed along to Egypt, he thought about how nice it was to be in a business-class seat. The complimentary upgrade was a great perk.

*At least if the plane had crashed, I would have crashed in style!* He smiled, finding that his positive outlook was returning. He was looking forward to the sights that awaited him in Egypt.

He turned and smiled at his seat companions, hoping to talk about the pyramids with someone, but everyone was either engrossed in a movie or sleeping. One businessman worked intently on his computer. After being honorably discharged, Michael had landed an office job as a software engineer in midtown Manhattan. Right now, it felt good to be free from a computer. So he adjusted his legs again, settled back and finished his own movie.

Soon the airplane was descending into the Cairo International Airport. Michael grinned as the other passengers cheered and applauded enthusiastically when the wheels touched the tarmac. The aircraft had successfully landed, much to everyone's great relief, even though a fire truck was waiting nearby.

The flight attendant's pleasant voice came over the intercom, gently informing the passengers that the local time was midnight. After the plane had taxied to the terminal, Michael grabbed his carry-on luggage and eagerly headed for the gate.

At passport control, Michael marveled when his visa stamp was literally licked onto his passport. *What a country!* After passing through customs, Michael and his fellow passengers headed to baggage claim. Baggage from their flight was delayed due to some technical difficulties, but this did not faze Michael at all. He stood next to the empty conveyor belt, still struggling to grasp the reality of his situation – he was finally in the land of the pyramids! *After so many years, I've finally made it here!* His childhood dream had become reality. *I can't believe Jason stood me up! Wow, just because he had a fight with his girlfriend.* Jason had passed up the opportunity of a lifetime with a simple, "Hey, Mike, I know I promised to go with you on that trip, but man, my girlfriend suddenly realized she would be left alone for a week and that was way too much for her." Michael shrugged. *Typical Jason – always backing out. But, I'm here at last and that's what counts.* While having a friend along would have definitely been more fun, nothing was going to ruin this adventure for him.

As he waited for his baggage, Michael paused to reflect on the path that had led him to this remarkable country. After learning about

Egypt in elementary school, the thought of Egypt mesmerized Michael. To be more precise, it was the pyramids that fascinated him. However, everything had truly started when as a freshman at Pace University he chose to take Ancient History 101 as his elective.

Anyone who has ever studied the history of ancient Egypt is aware of the veils of mystery shrouding Egypt's past. It is filled with images of pharaohs with boundless authority, temples guarded by castes of priests and ancient secrets locked away in hieroglyphs. Public relations were differentiated with a strange juxtaposition of the absolute despotism of secular and spiritual authority on one hand and the slavish humility of the common people on the other.

Northeast Africa and the adjoining areas was the cradle of ancient civilization, and within Egypt was formed one of the first class societies in the history of a mankind. From the beginning, Egypt's progress was constantly accompanied by infinite bloody wars and aggressive campaigns. Entire nations were destroyed as Egypt grew in strength and expanse.

Egypt reached its great blossom during a period called the Old Kingdom, which occurred after the first pharaoh of the Third dynasty, Djoser, had unified Upper and Lower Egypt into the largest slaveholding despotism, conquered a portion of Nubia and moved Egypt's capital to Memphis. During Pharaoh Djoser's rule and under the direction of Imhotep, his lead architect, an extensive civil development effort resulted in ornate temples being built, the dykes along the Nile's threshold being strengthened and the first pyramid's construction. This pyramid was constructed to the West of Memphis, in Saqqara, where the tombs of the other pharaohs of the First and Second dynasties resided. This marked the beginning of the construction of the pyramids, which reached its apex during the Fourth dynasty, mainly during the reign of the pharaoh Khufu at the end of the twenty-eighth century B. C. The Great Pyramid bearing his name was constructed entirely during his life and reign. This enormous structure represented a riddle that has stumped even the most renowned Egyptian scholars and proven impossible to figure out.

Yet, there was one amusing point that stood out in Michael's memory above everything else. Michael had always been immensely sympathetic to his contemporaries growing up in the mysterious "country of the pharaohs". After taking an American History class, Michael was always commenting, "It must be difficult for the Egyptian students to learn their country's long and intricate history. Our own history is so "short," just a few centuries, and yet, so difficult to dismantle."

Upon meeting an Egyptian exchange student, Mahmoud, Michael had asked him how he managed to keep track of his country's history. At first Mahmoud was taken aback, but then he had burst into uncontrollable laughing. As it turned out, Egyptian students are not taught about ancient Egyptian history. They are not required to know the pharaohs' names or even the dates when the Old Kingdom started and the Middle Kingdom began. To contemporary Egyptians, the history of Islam and the related events of the twentieth century were sufficient! Upon learning this fact, Michael's sympathy for Egyptian students had evaporated at once.

Ten years had passed since that point. The new century added one more memorable event for contemporary Egyptian students: the Egyptian Revolution of 2011 that overthrew the regime of the President Hosni Mubarak. Despite Michael's disillusionment with the Egyptian school system, his dream to see the Egyptian pyramids still lived on as strong as ever. He smiled as he pulled his bags off the conveyor belt and exited the terminal into the warm, arid Egyptian air.

Seated in the back seat of a taxi, Michael peered out at the slumbering Cairo, enjoying the city wrapped by the night's silence. He tried to imagine how tomorrow morning would bring about an entirely different picture during the bustling daylight hours. *I can't wait finally to see the pyramids.* He was within a mere ten miles of the pyramids, and yet the pyramids were still out of reach for him. He was growing more impatient the closer he got to his goal.

As the taxi zipped through the dark, moonless night, Michael started thinking about a lecture he had attended several years before at Columbia University. The lecturer, a heavyset man in his 60s, spoke slowly and quietly with a monotonous voice during the entire lecture as the audience sat in respectful quiet. It was when he spoke about the Great Pyramid that the lecture got particularly interesting. "The biggest pyramid in Egypt, the Great Pyramid, still disturbs researchers who are trying to understand its many mysteries. The Great Pyramid of Khufu is shrouded in coverlets of great secrets and many archeologists devote their entire lives to unearthing even a few of them. There is still no unanimous opinion about how this gigantic pyramid was actually built. Both thieves and scientists have extensively searched for the pharaoh's tomb buried inside the pyramid with, of course, different purposes. The mummy's location still remains an open question even today."

Intrigued by this mystery, Michael glanced around at the remainder of the audience to determine if they were similarly intrigued. No one seemed to move. "For simplification's sake," the lecturer continued slowly. Michael quickly returned his concentration fully to the lecturer. "We shall focus on the mystery of the Great Pyramid and consider all the existing statements connected to it. John Taylor, the author of the 1859 book, *The Great Pyramid*, argued that the Greek numbers Pi and Phi may have been deliberately incorporated into the design of the Great Pyramid of Khufu as the Great Pyramid's perimeter is close to two Pi times its height. Since its hypothesis, this theory in Pyramidology was supported as well as expanded upon by Charles Piazzi Smyth. Then, in 1880, an Egyptologist Professor, Sir William Flinders Petrie, and a British structural engineer, David Davidson, have added some key specifications to the studies of the aforementioned authors."

"Is it true that Khufu's mummy was never buried inside the Great Pyramid?" A heavy-set man, sitting in the second row, suddenly interrupted the lecturer.

The lecturer peered down through his thick eyeglasses at the man, visibly unhappy at being interrupted from his prescribed presentation. "As I said before, that is still unknown," he said, switching to his next PowerPoint in dismissal. "The Great Pyramid has been considered one of the miracles of the world since the ancient times and has always been surrounded by a shroud of mysteriousness. When workers of Caliph Al-Mamun forced open an entrance into the pyramid in the search of treasures in the ninth century A.D., they found an intricate system of internal passages that interconnected the chambers."

"Was it true they found some human remains inside the Great Pyramid?" interjected the man from the second row, now sitting on the edge of his wooden seat.

Pushing his large glasses up, the lecturer frowned and shuffled his notes. "I don't have anything about that in my slides." He sighed and continued in his grating monotone, pausing briefly from time to time to glance at the audience. "The system of seemingly incomprehensible tunnels and hollows inside the Great Pyramid became the new mystery. In order to solve that mystery, researchers proposed a number of hypotheses, beginning with the assumption that these tunnels were made by ancient tomb robbers. They then modified this view to hold the common consensus that these hollows, on the contrary, were traps for potential robbers."

"So, which one is right?" asked a young man with a goatee seated in the third row, his arm up slightly as if to respectful.

"That is still debated," said the lecturer sharply before clicking to his next PowerPoint. "There are two chambers inside the Great Pyramid. These are so-called the chambers of the King and the Queen, and they are located above the horizon. There is a third chamber located beneath the pyramid itself. In addition, there is a sarcophagus located within the King's Chamber that presents a sequential mystery, as this sarcophagus could not have been brought into the chamber through the smaller entrance passages."

At this point, a whole series of questions were thrown at him. The lecturer grimaced as it became apparent that he would not be able to continue reading the remainder of his prepared PowerPoints. He stood quietly, waiting for the wave of them to end. However, the flow of the questions seemed endless and the lecturer had to knock several times on the microphone to bring the hall back to order. "Ladies and gentlemen, I need order in the auditorium."

The audience went quiet, and the lecturer continued. "Researchers answer these questions differently. There is no unified response that can explain the entire construction process or how all the engineering problems were solved. Nevertheless, the very fact that the Great Pyramid, which has stood for nearly five thousand years, has not had any collapses in its system of hollows likely means that the hollows were constructed according to a well-designed plan."

"Come on," argued the thin, middle-aged man sitting next to Michael. "This is just a waste of time. He doesn't know anything about the pyramids. It's basically just guesses on top of more guesses." He got up from his chair, slipped past Michael and headed towards the exit. Bit by bit, the crowd followed his example and began to trickle out. *There's no point in sitting here.* With a sigh, Michael got up and headed towards the exit himself.

The blaring sound of many cars honking brought Michael back to the present. He looked out at the street his taxi had turned down. *Definitely better than that lecture, but I can't believe there is this much traffic at this time of night!* Slamming his fist into his horn repetitively and waving his arms out the window, his taxi driver managed to weave his way through traffic. Then they wound up stuck behind a mass of gridlocked cars and trucks. Gradually, the traffic jam dissipated and soon thereafter Michael's taxi was in *Midan Tahrir*, or "The Liberation Square," a focal point of the Egyptian Revolution of 2011 that toppled the presidency of Hosni Mubarak. The completely empty square, which resembled a large traffic circle, was enormous. The surrounding street poles flooded the scene with bright lights.

The taxi stopped outside Michael's room at the Cairo Downtown Hotel, just around the corner from the world-famous Cairo museum. Despite his desire to start exploring this mysterious city immediately, the jet lag combined with his fatigue took their toll on his ambition. The man at the desk gave him his key and motioned him toward the elevators. After quickly making his way through the darkened hotel to his room, Michael locked the door behind him. In minutes he was sleeping blissfully under bed sheets made of the finest Egyptian cotton.

# Chapter 2

Mennefer, Kemet, Egypt
1225 B.C.

T he ancient Egyptians called the land, Kem-ta or Kemet, meaning
"black land." In time, Kem-ta became the name of the country. A
narrow strip of fruit-bearing soil, it edges the reddish-brown sands of
the boundless desert while sheer cliffs border its west and east sides.
Kem-ta owes its existence to the holy river, the Nile.

The Nile, living up to its ancient personification of the holy bull
Apis, obstinately and imperiously breaks through the desert bringing
life-giving waters. Jutting inland among the thickening waves of the
sandy sea, Apis opens the way for the treasured waters into this narrow
strip of black land. Benefiting from the Nile's biannual floods, Kem-ta
receives the Nile's nourishing silt, which gives life to the harvest and,
ultimately, its people.

To the west, within the taciturn melancholy of the Arabian Desert,
also known as the country of the dead, seethed the mysterious city,
Mennefer. Although history is not clear, it is thought that Menes, a
pharaoh of the First Dynasty, founded Mennefer.

Within Mennefer resides the temple Hewet-ka-Ptah. From the roof
of the temple, the Hor-em-akhet or "Horus in the horizon" can be seen in
the distant rays of the violet evening sun and the flaming red of the early
dawn. Carved into the limestone cliffs in the distance, Horus is depicted
as a Sphinx with the head of a man and the body of a lion. The Sphinx is
manifest among the cliffs as the sunset strikes it, becoming visible above
the three large and nine small pyramids rising out of the sand below.

As the day slowly turned towards evening, the far away limestone
cliffs took on a faint violet hue. The heat would drop any minute now.

Looking like a young god who had just left the lotus flower, a dark-haired youth stepped thoughtfully along the dusty limestone street. He was shadowed by an intimidating figure.

"I, Amset, the full-fledged inhabitant of the city of Mennefer, will today know the secret of Horus, living and great, ruler of both Upper and Lower Kemet! Yes, live you forever!" While repeating his mantra in his mind, the youth paused from time to time to raise his face to the heavenly sun's burning heat and levitated praise to him – the life-giving sun god Horus.

Quite possibly, the youth repeated his prayer out of habit alone. His thoughts about the secret, however, filled his heart both with happiness and fear, as he was well aware that it could be both excellent and terrible at the same time. This mixed feeling frightened the youth. He truly felt that the unknown excellent was not better than the unknown terrible. There was no way for him to know which would appear first.

What he did know for certain was that today the supreme priest of the Hewet-ka-Ptah temple would reveal to him one of the great mysteries of Khufu's pyramid. Only a selected few became the guardians of Pharaoh Khufu's mystery. He had aspired to be worthy for years for this honor and duty to be bestowed upon him. Now the moment had finally come, and Priest Ur Senu had called Amset for the declaration of the secret. He was the chosen one and it made his mind tingle with anticipation. Finally, it was the time for him to begin the initiation process.

Amset was of noble origin. His full name was Amset Ba-Pef. While he was a native of the city of Mennefer, he was not allowed to take a single step without the careful eye of his Nubian guard, Jibade, who followed him as consistently as his own shadow. Jibade was a thirty-three-year-old man with curly dark hair arranged in a conspicuous bushy Afro. He usually dressed in a long, white, cotton cloak. He took his duty very seriously and was never seen without a crusader-type sword and his polished, but dented, round shield. Jibade was a Medjay. 'The Nubian warrior,' was what Amset liked to call him. Amset had known Jibade for as long as he could remember. They had never been apart. For the Medjay, it was the greatest honor to serve and protect Amset's life.

Soon, Amset arrived at the sandy boundary of the city where the Temple Hewet-ka-Ptah stood. After pausing reverently at the threshold, he entered into the temple's shaded, eternally cool court filled with columns. The columned court was the portion of Hewet-ka-Ptah where anyone could enter to render praise to the gods.

As Amset waited, surrounded by sculptures of gods and bronze vessels filled with fragrances, his Medjay guardian stood right behind him. They stood in front of several priests in long white robes with leopard skins over their shoulders that were holding rolls of papyrus and reading the sacred texts. On both sides of Amset were others in prayer, either drawn to full height chanting the sacred texts or inclined in a reverent, low bow. The majority of the people gathered to offer prayer were of average wealth: "those, who feed by fish" as high priests called them. These people were not allowed further than the column court. Amset turned and observed as two priests slowly walked in front of the people that were praying to the god sculptures.

Amset, as a privileged, had the right to pass further, deep inside the temple to the Cherished Hall. The Cherished Hall was the holy of the holies where the statue of the god Ptah resided. Only one supreme priest had permission to enter the Cherished Hall twice a day. His job was to open the Gates of the Horizon in the morning and to shut them tightly at the end of the day. The temple personified the tendency to seek the divine but, at the same time, the impossibility to fully understand the deity.

Amset always lingered in the columned court to offer prayer before passing further into the temple's mysterious halls. The quiet coolness, lack of deliberateness of the priests and stately silence of the gigantic columns depicting papyrus stems all gave the temple a reverent and mystical aura. The grandeur of the temple and its sculptures, the sublimity of its forms, and the rationality of its plan appealed greatly to him. Like the very creation of gods and the invariability of the world's order, everything within the temple had to personify the sublimity and the rationality of the world. Amset imagined this would not only strike the imagination of his contemporaries but also even the imaginations of his distant future descendants.

As Amset raised his eyes from his musings, he saw in the depth of the ornately decorated hall the one who had asked for him: the supreme priest, Ur Senu. Dressed in flaxen, white clothing, a cap with a gold top and the overhanging leopard skin that signified his rank, the old priest was standing alone, praying next to the alabaster sacrificial table. The sacrificial table was set with the viands brought to the gods: fried geese and pigeons, vessels with honey, onion, cucumbers, breads, figs and grapes. Amset waited for the right moment before walking up, raising his right hand to rest on his opposite shoulder and bowing to the supreme priest. "You called me. I arrived. And, I questioned my heart . . ." the words of prayer flew to Amset's lips.

High Priest Ur Senu turned to face Amset, wordlessly pointed his hand to the Cherished Hall's entry and then walked slowly towards it. Amset hurried in his wake, shadowed silently by Jibade. Where Amset went, he went. This was his unwritten law and Jibade followed it precisely, regardless of the occasion.

Once they had entered, the supreme priest greeted Amset silently by majestically raising his priestly baton – the top a carved cat's head, the symbol of the goddess Bastet. The priest then gestured at a door in the wall, asking Amset nonverbally to follow into the inner courtyard. The supreme priest, Amset, and the Medjay guardian moved slowly along the winding path of the internal garden.

The group paused for a moment. "We have an important task for you," announced the supreme priest in a hushed but imperious voice. Even while speaking to Amset, the priest looked past him to somewhere far beyond. "Amset, you have reached your sixteenth birthday, and I must now carry out the will of your father." It was as if he spoke not to Amset, but to someone behind him, far behind him, or perhaps, to someone at an elevated level, far beyond this earthly plane. "You have reached adulthood, and now you must learn the truth. Prepare yourself."

The simple, yet dread-inspiring words of the priest agitated Amset and with but a glance, Jibade understood the depth of it. Looking at the majestic figure of priest Ur Senu, Jibade understood Amset's apprehension. The supreme priest was a heavyset man with powerful arms. He had a strict face with narrow, small but penetrating eyes. The priest always held his head elevated and stuck out his torso majestically. He was the embodiment of the inaccessible itself.

"Follow me," commanded Ur Senu and the three began walking again. As they neared the stairs that led to the gates, Ur Senu removed his gilded cap. His hairless, round head gleamed in the sun. Suddenly, Amset's heart started beating frantically. From above the gates, he witnessed a breathtaking view of the valley of the great Nile River, the Libyan Desert, the Eastern Ridge, the dam of Delta, the green fields of barley, and the majestic pyramids among the reddish-brown sands of the desert to the south. Throughout his sixteen years, he had been privileged only once to stand above the gigantic gates of the temple and not for very long. On that day, from the top of these gigantic gates, he had seen the gigantic Sphinx sculpture for the first time in his life. The Sphinx had subjugated his young imagination. From that time onward, keeping the experience at the surface of his thoughts, he had worshipped to it.

As all three men slowly climbed the stairs to the top of the gate arch, they reached a wide, open area where a cool Northeastern breeze wafted. It was refreshing. The day tended towards its close, so the scorching heat of the sun had dissipated to a bearable level. Ur Senu slowly turned his head and pointed towards the infinite plain of sand dunes that stretched out before them in the glowing amethyst light. Moving towards sunset, it doused the reddish sands, the silhouettes of mountains and the pyramids in its violet twilight. The wind that blew heavily throughout the day began to calm as a quiet fell over the desert.

"Take a look," Ur Senu spoke solemnly. "Over there is the country of the Dead, the country of the West." Amset turned to gaze in the direction Ur Senu was pointing. The desert and the pyramids appeared to be an azure color.

"Take a look," repeated the old priest. "Here are the pyramids: the great tombs of the pharaohs, our living gods. Their stones are blessed. They are the embodiment of the highest godly validity. The pyramids will remain standing for all eternity. Do you see the colossal sculpture of the Sphinx?"

The priest turned his head slightly towards Amset. "The Sphinx's forms are majestic. The years will pass and the stone may begin to crumble. But, the Great Pyramid will not be destroyed. Time itself is not imperious on it. Only an outside evil force could destroy it, but no such force is in existence nor may ever be. All three measurements of the Great Pyramid are in the equilateral construction. Its sides are the faces of the world; the Delta connection on the equilateral basis is the law of the world. The formula of the relationship of the sizes was given by the gods and was given once and for all. The world was created once and forever. That is why the Great Pyramid will always remain standing."

Amset scrutinized the majestic structure of the Great Pyramid from afar. Ur Senu turned and began to walk along the stone barrier above the gate. Amset and the Medjay followed the priest along the southern edge.

"You know," the great priest continued, "Khufu's pyramid, the largest of all, was built over only a few decades period because the gods themselves participated in the erection of the Great Pyramid. Without the aid of the gods, men could not create so perfect a construction. Men could never have created the Great Pyramid, if they were not inspired by the godly will, if they did not act upon the words and the call of the gods, and if men's hands in reality were not the hands of the gods. While the cruel pharaoh Khufu was not the gods' favorite, Khufu was destined to create the symbol of the invariability of life, and he completed the task laid upon him by the gods."

Amset paid close attention to the supreme priest's words. Outwardly he stood in a silent, patient reverence; but deep in his heart, he desperately wished to hear the secret of the Pharaoh Khufu. Amset's eyes were shining and his heart was pounding so loudly that Ur Senu soon sensed a visible tension in Amset.

"You are anxious to hear the secret, correct?" Ur Senu asked rhetorically before continuing. "The biggest mystery is that Pharaoh Khufu was entombed deep within his pyramid, and the gods were merciful to his soul since he obeyed their orders. Khufu erected the pyramid to glorify the gods, and therefore, for this the gods were in debt to him. His body was buried in a secret chamber inside the pyramid known only to the gods themselves. All who participated in the burial proceedings were sent to their death one way or another. No witnesses remained."

Subjugated by the force of the supreme priest's words, Amset began to experience a rise in his anxiety. Suddenly, the story told by Ur Senu seemed too close a reality as they descended the stairs and reentered the chamber below.

"No mortal knows the true location of Khufu's mummy as it is guarded by the gods themselves," continued the priest. "Only we, the heirs of the pharaoh know his true resting place – the location of his burial tomb. We have in our possession the stele handed down to us by the great God Ra himself."

The supreme priest paused and looked at Amset meaningfully. "Are you ready to take on the sacred mission of guarding the stele?"

"I was born ready," answered Amset honorably, pushing any lingering anxieties from his mind.

"Remember that the integrity of the stele cannot be compromised. Were the stele to fall into the wrong hands, this would lead to irreversible consequences. Gods do not forgive."

"Supreme priest, I will do what it takes. The secret will remain safe with me."

Satisfied by Amset's devoted response, Ur Senu walked towards the sacrificial table in the corner as Amset and Jibade silently followed him. Pushing on a carved glyph, the priest reached deep down into the revealed secret compartment, removed the stele, and reverently handed it to Amset.

"The meaning of it will not be revealed to you yet," said the priest quietly. "However, the time will come."

"I understand. It will be my honor," replied Amset as he bowed before the supreme priest.

The priest acknowledged him with a slight nod and continued, "The great wisdom of life consists of the fact that the world is inviolable and constant. The world is inviolable as long as it follows the order given to it by the god Ra and remains protected by the feather of Ma'at." Ur Senu raised his wand of Bastet, the sacred daughter of Ra. "We guard these laws! We will not let anyone disturb them. This is why we need to protect the resting place of Khufu. Kemet is still alive because of this secret and it will remain so."

The priest stood silently for a long period of time, prompting Amset and Jibade to remain silent as well.

Suddenly the priest broke the silence in a low tone of voice. "I will tell you the legend of the Pharaoh Menkaure. He was the grandson of the great Pharaoh Khufu. The pyramid of Menkaure is located to the left of the others."

Amset nodded, as he was quite familiar with its location. "The legend states that the Pharaoh Khufu was a cruel person, as was his son, Khafre, whose pyramid is in the middle of the triad. During the reign of these pharaohs, the land of Kem-ta underwent great calamities such as droughts, bad harvests and diseases. Nevertheless, by the order of these pharaohs, the temples were closed down and the people's labor was used entirely on building the pyramids. Indeed, it was necessary to transport stones and clear the sands. But, when Menkaure, the son of Khafre and grandson of Khufu, became pharaoh, he opened all the temples again. He freed his tired people from their burdens, allowed them to go back to work the fields and into the temples for the offerings. Menkaure was also the most righteous judge and a far more respectable pharaoh than all those that preceded him. The people of Kem-ta were grateful to the gods for providing such a righteous pharaoh.

However, our most gracious pharaoh, Menkaure, was suddenly struck by three terrible misfortunes: the death of his daughter, the treason of his friends, and an ill-fated prophesy of the gods. This prophecy stated that he had six years to live and on the seventh he would move to the Duat country, or the afterlife. The Pharaoh Menkaure was thrown into a great grief and in desperation he sent his priests to the oracle of the goddess Ma'at. His priests appealed to Ma'at, the goddess of world order, "Oh great Ma'at! Both father and grandfather of the great Menkaure locked down the temples and suppressed their people, however they satisfactorily lived to an old age. Why must the most righteous Pharaoh Menkaure die in six years? Is this righteous?" And, Ma'at answered the priests, "Menkaure is a good and righteous pharaoh. But, for this very reason, I reduced his lifespan. He has not completed what had to be completed. Kem-ta had to undergo the calamity for one hundred fifty years. Khufu and Khafre understood this, but Menkaure did not."

"Does that mean that I'm doomed as well?" Amset quietly asked.

Ur Senu smiled almost softly as he replied calmly, "The legend has a continuation. The priests brought the oracle's answer back to the pharaoh."

"What did the pharaoh do? Did he follow in the footsteps of his father and grandfather? Were the temples shut down? Did he begin to suppress his people?" Amset interjected questions in rapid succession.

"No, he remained the same," answered the priest. "Menkaure decided to deceive his fate. He gave the order to prepare one hundred thousand torches and to ignite them at night. In this way, the night would turn to day. The pharaoh ceased to sleep. At night, as in the daytime, he drank wine, played games, and delighted himself with the dances of slaves. By converting the remaining nights into the days, he attempted to expose the oracle in a lie. Menkaure wanted to convert his six remaining years into twelve. He thought he could cheat his fate, but he did not succeed."

"What if Menkaure had stopped being nice to people?" asked Amset in astonishment. "What if he had become as ruthless and terrible as his grandfather and father? Then what?"

"Then, Ma'at would have possibly abolished his death sentence."

"Why is it that righteousness must always be held with less respect then evil? Is cruelty legitimate?"

"We cannot know what is correct and what is not. The gods decide this. Because cruelty and evil exist in the world, it means it is convenient to the gods for it to remain. The story about Pharaoh Menkaure indicates that it is not possible to deceive fate, but that it is necessary to entrust oneself to fate. Menkaure destroyed nights and thought that he would prolong his years. Nevertheless, his fate triumphed."

"Is that what awaits me?" Amset asked, almost in a whisper.

"Calm down, my dear boy. The goddess Hathor has not determined your fate yet. You have not learned enough yet: only the method of the accomplishment of fate. Leave unexpected contingencies alone and it is quite possible you will live to reach an old age." He motioned to Amset for the stele. Amset carefully placed it into the old priest's hands. The priest reached deep down into the table's secret compartment, reverently placing the stele back into its hiding place. "That is all I have for you currently."

"Old age," repeated Amset to himself as he slowly walked away, his guard behind him, leaving the old priest alone in the chamber.

Ur Senu once again ascended the stairs to stand above the gates and gaze out to the west towards the desert. The sun was setting rapidly below the desert. The violet light of evening became thicker as it spilled on the sands. The shadows became more drawn.

A disconcerting anxiety crept into the heart of the supreme priest. What would the god Ra deliver in the morning to the old priest? What would be awaiting him along with the crimson light of dawn, the singing of the birds and the sparkling transparency of the air? What if dawn brought with it the information of the boy's death? Would his soul be able to reconcile the fact that this death was just fate and that the great goddess Hathor stood guard over the highest legitimacy? Ur Senu sighed with helplessness.

\* \* \*

Thirteen days later, Jibade stood over the lifeless body of his sovereign while the women wept and wailed around him. Amset had contracted a mysterious illness at the temple of Hewet-ka-Ptah. Unfortunately, it had progressed far too quickly before anyone could intervene. He had been only sixteen years of age.

Although stunned by complete disbelief, Jibade knew deep in his heart what a heavy burden had suddenly been placed in his arms. He knew he would never compromise the secret of the stele. He owed that much to Amset. Fervently, he vowed that the integrity of the stele would die with him.

# Chapter 3

Sahara Desert, Egypt
Wednesday, September 6
10:25 a.m.

Wearing a long white cotton cloak, Jibade sat on his snow white horse at the top of a sandy dune. The Sahara stretched out before him in never ending miles of sand dunes sculpted over time by the powerful desert winds. The heat from the sand rose up to meet the pale blue sky in the quiet afternoon. As the fifty-five-year-old Chief of the Medjay tribe reflected on the immensity of the desert that surrounded him, the wind slowly waved his curly hair, which was arranged in a distinct Afro style. Off in the distance, Jibade's tribesmen patiently waited on their horses for the return of their leader.

Disquieted, Jibade pondered his predicament. The Medjay tribe had valiantly maintained guard over the ancient holy stele throughout the centuries. The stele itself had been carefully passed down his family line, as the tribal leaders, from one generation to the next. But now it was in the hands of a foreigner. *That German paid the ultimate price for his godless action. But the stele has not yet been found.* He frowned, furrowing his brow. *The tribe must not know. And the stele must be returned to its place. That is the gods' law.* Nobody in his tribe, besides the ruling triad, knew about the disappearance of the stele. He planned to keep it that way by all means possible.

Despite his distress, Jibade looked younger than his age. He was a Medjay, the desert Nubian. His high forehead and black eyebrows set off his dark eyes, shining with intellect and slyness. High cheekbones and a square jaw line intensified the masculinity of his looks. As all Medjay, he favored earrings worn in a pierced lobe and crafted of silver wire formed into hoops with overlapping ends. Jibade had broad shoulders and long, muscular arms that ended with strong hands and long fingers. By relying on his fighting skills and leadership abilities, he had become the warrior he was today. But now his tribe's oath had been compromised by the theft of the stele. It was time to check the trustworthiness and steadfastness of his tribe.

Staring out at the unending desert, he contemplated several thoughts. Did he feel useless now that the stele had disappeared? Did its disappearance mean that his tribe would have nothing to do? Certainly, that was not the case. There were still many necessary tasks for the warriors of the tribe: to guard against the neighboring tribe's constant thieving and pillaging from them for one. Yet tribal wars had been going on for centuries and would likely continue long after he had gone onto the afterlife in the Duat country. His mind wandered as he envisioned his future: repelling attacks from the neighboring tribes, marrying a worthy wife, having children, watching them grow up, and watching himself becoming old and dying.

He must find the stele by any means possible. Otherwise, he saw no meaning in his life. The stele was like a bridge that spanned the celestial sky connecting the mortal world to the immortal. It would bring him, as well as all of his potential future descendants, a step closer to their gods. Jibade waited for answers in the hot desert sun: none came.

Growling in frustration, Jibade wheeled his horse around and galloped back to his men. He signaled for them to follow and headed home. The Medjay tribesman needed no landmarks to guide them back to their village. An hour later they were riding down into their small valley, lined with numerous tents and children playing.

As the warriors arrived, they were greeted with a cheer. It did not matter whether they were returning from fighting the enemy or merely re-supplying their stocks, the celebratory greeting had become routine. It was, however, a ritual that seemed far out of place to Jibade under the current circumstances. As he brought his white mustang to a thundering stop beside his tent, Jibade swung his leg over the back of his stallion, dismounted and handed the reins to a waiting horse wrangler. "Take a good care of him." The youth bowed before walking Jibade's horse into the corral to attend to it.

Glancing over the village quickly to make sure nothing was amiss, Jibade entered his tent. He had only taken a few steps inside when he heard a familiar voice coming from the corner. "I finally took the time to come over and greet you myself."

Jibade instantly turned and saw a familiar old warrior sitting calmly in a shadowy corner. He had grayish hair and was wrinkled with age, but his eyes still sparkled in the darkened tent.

"You delight in my anguish," Jibade said coolly, as he leaned his ancient crusader sword against the table. "If I die, it will be from you giving me a heart attack."

The old warrior chuckled in amusement, "Is that how you greet your own uncle?"

Jibade sighed, "Good afternoon, uncle."

"Such a heavy sigh. Am I to understand that the responsibilities of the tribe are too great for you?"

Jibade sat down cross-legged on the carpet and slowly leaned back against a large pillow as he closed his eyes to gather his thoughts. After a few moments he opened his eyes and looked firmly at his uncle. "No, uncle." Despite his attempt, he could not disguise the frustration in his voice.

"Then what?" asked the old man, staring keenly at him.

*He doesn't know?* His uncle was a very powerful man and always received information firsthand. Jibade put his hands behind his head and closed his eyes again.

"I feel emptiness inside of me, a loss . . ." Jibade frowned, unable to continue.

"The oath of the Medjay is an ancient responsibility borne by our people, one that has kept our tribe going. But you, as their leader, have failed it. Now, a heavy burden will descend upon us."

Jibade's eyes flew open. "How did you . . .?"

"I have my sources. You weren't planning to keep this from me, were you? Don't you trust your own blood?"

Jibade groaned. "The stele will be found. It's only a matter of time. The wicked soul of the one who stole the stele has already been fed to Ammit, the devourer."

"And the tribe?" asked the old warrior.

"Nobody besides the triad knows, and I trust them with my life," Jibade replied proudly.

"Yes, let's keep it that way. We don't need to start a panic now," the old man agreed, gazing out the tent's narrow window. "Our people look to you to keep our nation strong. If they were to learn of this, they would be at a terrible loss of direction and faith."

"Yes, dear uncle," Jibade exclaimed vehemently. "The stele will be recovered."

His uncle gave a curt nod, "Any progress on finding it?"

"Asim, my fearless warrior, and Police Inspector Suliman, whose services we've used in the past, are working on that as we speak. I should hear from both of them tonight."

"Keep me informed." The old man stood up and walked over to his nephew, bending down to kiss his forehead. "May peace be upon you," he whispered before stepping outside the tent. Lost in his thoughts, Jibade watched him through the small window as he departed.

# Chapter 4

City of the Dead, Cairo, Egypt
Wednesday, September 6
9:50 p.m.

F or the past two excruciating hours, Asim, a hulky thirty-year-old
fearless warrior from the local Medjay tribe, had been searching
for a makeshift tomb-turned-into-house in the City of the Dead, located
in Cairo's outskirts. Over six feet tall and donned in a long white cotton
cloak covering a crusader-type sword slung behind his back, Asim did
not blend into the crowd. In fact, the locals were staring cautiously at
him and his curly dark hair, which was arranged in distinctly bushy
Afro style.

Asim had long strayed that afternoon among the ancient, unkempt
tombs and mausoleums. In his hand was a crude map that his chief
Jibade had scrawled on a crumbled, torn piece of paper. It was very
little help. Uneasy and turned around, he strode up and down the
haphazard streets, puzzling over his map with its crude pencil-
scratched directions and comparing it to the few signs he found.

As night fell and darkened the shadows between the living and the
dead, his heart filled with dread. He had heard many ill rumors about
this place. He had never been to the City of the Dead before, nor had he
ever had any inclination to visit such a place. But, tonight was different;
he was on a secret mission. His great chief's orders compelled him into
the heart of the City of the Dead; a place known to the people of Cairo
simply as *el'arafa*, meaning "the cemetery".

Brimming with tombs and mausoleums, the City of the Dead
was a magnificent centuries old necropolis that was spread out in an
immense hodgepodge fashion at the base of the Mokattam Mountains.

Its foundation dates back to the Arab conquest of Egypt in 642 AD. When the Arab commander Amr ibn al As founded the first Egyptian Arab capital, the city of Al Fustat, he also established his family's graveyard at the foot of the al Mokattam Mountains. Now it is a four-mile long cemetery that stretches from the northern to the southern part of Cairo. Paradoxically, the City of the Dead thrives with its own robust life and intriguing activities. Amidst the marble headstones and crypts, people live and work amongst their dead loved ones and ancestors in the slummy makeshift town. It has everything from barbershops to cafés and even a bazaar that takes place on Fridays.

Two hours later, Asim stopped in front of a rotten, two-story, makeshift edifice constructed over two adjacent mausoleums. It looked like an old military barracks made of crumbling, plaster walls. He glanced at the chief's directions and found that the street and the number coincided at last: Ebn Roshd Street, number 19. Relief appeared across the Medjay's drooping face. Ascending the old, creaking stairs, Asim was baffled that the chief's famous expert, a legendary chemist, lived in such bestial conditions. *Who would've imagined?* He thought, wondering what would possess a man to live in a hovel.

At the top of the dark flight of stairs, Asim found a brown door bearing the name of "Nassar" elegantly engraved on a faded, dull metal plate. Asim leaned forward, pressing his ear firmly against the door. He could not hear anything, only the eerie silence and the omnipresence of dead corpses. He knocked resolutely. Soon he heard a rustling from within. The door gradually opened until it was stopped by a thick metal chain. A stooped, gray-haired old man with a large nose and glasses peered from behind the door.

"To what degree would I oblige your visit?" His voice was very hoarse as he spoke, his small eyes blinking behind the thick lenses of his glasses.

"*As-salaamu aleyka*, Nassar," Asim quickly answered. "I have come to you under the direction of my great Chief Jibade, who is familiar with your very alluring business."

"Lately people have not come to me on matters other than the non-alluring," the old man replied solemnly, carefully studying every single detail of his late-night visitor. Satisfied, he unlatched the door chain and beckoned him inside.

"I feel honored to be recommended by the great chief," announced Nassar as he quickly closed the front door, twisted shut the three deadbolts and fixed the heavy chain behind his visitor. Asim was surprised to see three deadbolts on the door. *Something of great value must be hidden behind these deadbolts.* Glancing around surreptitiously, Asim could not imagine what of any value could possibly be hidden in this shack. The only thing he could imagine being housed here were long departed souls.

The main room, which looked like the old man used as both his bedroom and dining room, smelled of dampness and mold. Taking up the majority of the room were two massive tombs that doubled as makeshift tables, the tops covered with various books and manuscripts. Stretched between these tombstones was a clothesline with the old man's laundry hanging on it. In the far corner of the room was a large, modern wooden cabinet with glass doors. Asim could see that it was crammed with various jars, bottles and flasks.

Chief Jibade had explained to Asim that Nassar was considered an eminent and brilliant poison expert. For that matter, there probably was not a single contact, gas or ingestible poison, natural or synthetic, that he could not reproduce or analyze in his laboratory. Several years ago he had suddenly retired to the City of the Dead and was now living over a tomb in a wooden, makeshift house fit for a peasant. The only people who visited the old man were individuals such as Asim: strangers with very alluring problems.

Nassar broke the silence, "How can I be of service to your great chief?"

"My name is Asim," the visitor introduced himself. "I'm Medjay."

"I noticed that," the host replied quietly. "I knew that you were Medjay the moment I saw you at my doorway. I notice a lot of things, young man," he added, chuckling softly.

"May I ask you a question?" asked Asim.

"Please, call me 'Chemist,'" the old man replied quietly, nodding. "And please, have a seat."

Asim sat. "I was just wondering why with your position, title and reputation do you choose to live here in the slums of the City of the Dead?"

The chemist nodded his head thoughtfully and sauntered over to a worn sofa where he sat. "My home was constructed more than a hundred years ago by my grandfather. My father was born and raised here. I spent the majority and the best part of my life here. Indeed, I could be living in a mansion in downtown Cairo, but here, in the City of the Dead, is where my life began and where I intend to conclude it. The two massive tombs you see in front of you are indeed the graves of my beloved grandfather and father," he said, sighing deeply, a small smile finding its way to his lips at a distant memory.

His smile faltered as he continued, "My late father was poisoned for a measly five Egyptian pounds. Justice was never served as his killer was let go because of a lack of evidence. That is why I left to study poisons. I am the best, which has led many people to use my potions and knowledge." Nassar paused and looked at Asim firmly, "As a toxicologist, I am the best. You were sent to me for something?"

Slightly concerned that he had insulted the chemist, Asim sat up straighter and spoke respectfully, "Our great chief knows that you are an expert on poisons, that there is no equal within your field. He also understands that you have amassed a unique collection of poisons, many of which are very difficult or in some cases impossible to identify."

The chemist nodded his head gently.

"My chief says that from time to time you, so to say, 'help people' by supplying them with a means to get rid of certain problems. Am I not mistaken?"

The chemist paused. "You are not mistaken," he answered somberly. "I can supply a poison, if the cause is just. Despite my age, I have not become a humanist. I do understand that taking a life is sometimes the only way to solve a vital predicament. However," he added, steadfastly looking at Asim through his thick glasses. "I do not provide poisons to whomever so desires them, and I certainly do not help everyone with every situation. I believe in taking a life only for the good of society. I do not condone murder. However, if a society finds itself unsuccessful in punishing bastards such as murderers, rapists, tyrants and torturers, then I provide a means. That's also partly why I live here in the City of the Dead. I wish to be acquainted with death in a way most people wouldn't comprehend."

Asim gave the chemist a surprised look.

The chemist continued, ignoring his startled expression. "But, the motive is very important to me. If it's compelling enough, I would never refuse my expertise."

"Chemist," Asim spoke solemnly, "your help is vital to my people. There is no other way out for us. The great chief is willing to pay any amount of money for a reliable and swift poison that cannot be identified."

"First, young man, I do not take money for my services. Secondly, each poison I supply to my clients is unique. None of these poisons can be identified by modern medicine yet. Even the best pathologist will diagnose it as a heart attack, an insulin shock or anything else you would like, but never a poisoning. Thirdly and most importantly, I repeat that it is necessary for me to know the motive of the poisoning." The chemist got up from his comfortable position on the shabby couch and stood in front of Asim's armchair, straighter than Asim would have imagined possible for such an old man. "Therefore, Asim, either tell me why such a poison is necessary to you and your chief or leave. I must warn you that I have no difficulty in distinguishing a ruse from the truth."

Asim was not ready for this, as he had imagined his conversation with Nassar would be swift: pay the price; receive the merchandise and leave. But now this old man demanded to know the most sacred loss the Medjay had suffered at the hands of the foreigner: the loss of the most sacred stele in the whole of the Medjay's long history. *Perhaps, I should invent fake stories about bandits or quarrels with other tribes. But I have not prepared such a story and doubt it would ring true.*

After a long pause, Asim surprised himself by speaking the truth. He told the chemist everything he knew about Günther Schulze, the German engineer who had stolen their sacred stele.

As the entire story unfolded, the chemist listened quietly with his hands behind his back and his eyes averted.

"…This foreigner has dishonored us in the face of our mighty gods and must answer on the merits of the larceny of our sacred stele. We wish to get rid of him so the secret of the stele dies with him and to restore the honor of the Medjay. I beg you, chemist, please help us! Name any price: only give me this poison. I want him to suffer for his crimes before his death as I would have suffered and never revealed the secret of the stele!" Asim's eyes were glowing with unmasked pride.

The chemist was silent for a while. He examined his visitor: the well-kempt, young-looking, muscled fellow with a distinctive bushy Afro hairstyle wearing a long, white cotton cloak. He could tell from the bulge in the back of Asim's cloak that he was armed. Finally, after a long pause, the chemist spoke. "Well, you have convinced me, warrior. I shall give you what you ask. In exchange, I will not take a single piaster (Egypt's smallest coin denomination) from you." Asim gleefully moved forward. *So simple! The Chief will be so pleased.*

"But first," Nassar paused, smiling faintly, "I wish to offer you a *shai.*" Considered to be Egypt's national drink and a sign of great hospitality, shai, or tea, holds a special place in the heart of every self-respected Egyptian. The Medjay had internally frowned, but managed to keep the expression off his features. He had already wasted a lot of time finding the nutty old man's house, explaining the situation to him, and now he would have to drink his tea. Afraid to frighten off his success, however, Asim nodded in agreement.

Soon the chemist was holding up two small cups as he squeezed through the narrow hall from his kitchen back into the living room. He presented his visitor one of the cups and settled into a lounging position on the sofa across the room.

Asim was not partial to the *Saiidi* shai, which is more common to this area. Saiidi shai is prepared by boiling black tea with water for five minutes over a strong flame and had an extremely heavy taste. Asim took the cup and drank it to avoid offending his host. As he drank the dark tea, it tasted peculiar to him. When his cup was empty, Asim looked impatiently at the old man.

"So, chemist, when will you give me the poison?"

Nassar remained silent for a long time, testing Asim's patience. He spoke slowly and carefully, "You have already received it, Asim. I added a strong, reliable and very rare poison to your cup of Saiidi shai. By the look on your face, I presume that its bitter taste was definitely not to your liking." The chemist chuckled, "I see that you are more accustomed to drinking the *Koshary* shai, but Koshary is too sweet for me."

Asim stared at the chemist in horror.

29

"Throughout the years I have assisted society rid itself of villains," said the chemist as he slowly rose from the couch. "I have helped defenseless women suffering at the hands of their monster-husbands, innocent young girls brutally raped by pedophiles and businessmen who have been cornered by extortionists. The reasons they all came to me were crystal clear. But your case is special as this is the first time I have come in contact with it. Vengeance is a very nasty motive for murder; therefore, I have decided that *you* are the true danger to society. So, the poison for which you requested to kill a defenseless foreigner is already in your stomach."

"Is this a sick joke?" snapped Asim. His mouth had started to dry and he could feel a metal taste on the tip of his tongue, which he could only assume was the poison taking its effect.

"This is not a joke," the chemist answered coldly. "Soon you will feel an indisposition, then a pain in your stomach, and then you will die from a heart attack. Your near future is not a pleasant one, but it is the one you have earned and is no less than what you deserve."

"I will beat the living shit out of you. You lousy old bastard!" Asim jumped up and rushed towards the chemist, reaching for his concealed sword. He suddenly stopped short as he came to his senses. "Nassar, what have you done?" he asked, breathing heavily despite his best efforts to control his lungs. "Am I going to die?"

"Without any doubt," the chemist said quietly, remaining absolutely calm. Asim looked at him in disbelief. "However," the chemist added slowly. "The outcome of your fate depends entirely on you now. As promised, you have received the poison from me, free of charge." He paused, a dangerous smile playing across his lips. "But you will have to pay for its antidote. A unique chance to survive," he paused, his smile gone. "Your only one."

The Medjay's eyes glowed dangerously, unable to mask his fury. His forehead dripped with sweat as his internal temperature began to fluctuate wildly. "How much?" exclaimed Asim forcefully, as dizziness overtook him. "Just name your price, and you will receive it."

"I repeat, money has no interest for me. Your payment for continued life will take another form." The chemist paused for a moment, his dark eyes boring into Asim through his thick glasses. The Medjay looked back at him, puzzled.

"If you wish the death of another person, no matter the motive, I believe you must suffer the same as the person that you wished to kill would have suffered. You must fully grasp what you have wished upon another. You claimed, without a second thought, that you would suffer the same way the German engineer would have suffered were you to poison him, in order to protect your stolen relic. If I were to assure you that I would make sure the greedy foreigner met his death swiftly, would you accept your own death as a part of this grandiose design?"

"It would be an honor!" Asim exclaimed as he sank to the floor. He proudly raised his head as all sense of anger drained from his body. "I'm a Medjay warrior in my heart and in my soul. If you assure me that Schulze will die, then it will be a great honor for me to die knowing that the secret of the stele, preserved throughout the ages by my fellow Medjay, will die with him."

\* \* \*

When the door was closed and bolted securely behind his nocturnal visitor, Nassar stored the remainder of the antidote potion in his locked safe. Approaching the small makeshift slit window, he watched Asim's silhouette fade away amidst the shadows and spirits of the mysterious City of the Dead. He smiled to himself, knowing justice had been served. *What a noble people are the Medjay. Nowadays it is impossible to find a more trustworthy and fair people.*

# Chapter 5

Giza Plateau, Egypt
Monday, September 18
8:00 a.m.

The Pyramids! Michael Doyle stood at the edge of the Giza Plateau enraptured by the most magnificent creation erected by the ancient Egyptians. Michael's lifelong dream to see and touch the pyramids with his own eyes and hands was finally reality. At that moment, nothing else seemed to matter at all.

His arrival at eight o'clock in the morning proved to be fortuitous, as he soon discovered that the tourist masses did not begin so early in the morning. He seized the unexpected opportunity to take unobstructed and stunning photographs. He worked his digital camera Nikon D3100 non-stop as he captured the unforgettable, breathtaking views of the Giza Plateau.

He walked over and positioned himself next to the plateau's entrance, trying to imagine what it might have looked like 4,500 years ago, the theoretical time of the Great Pyramid's construction. In the time of the pharaohs, the white outlines of the pyramids must have shone brilliantly in the rays of the ancient sun. Their apexes, covered with thin gold plates, must have blinded the eyes of all those who gazed out across the desert at them. Michael stood there for another twenty minutes thinking about the many different theories that attempted to explain how the pyramids had been constructed. He enjoyed trying to imagine which theory he thought was more likely to be accurate.

As his eyes scanned the horizon, he focused on a nearby livestock stand. Horses, donkeys and camels awaited their tourist-riders for prices of mythical proportion. He chuckled as the guidebooks had warned him away from such excesses. The books had also claimed that the best site from which to observe the pyramids was where he was currently standing. Happily, he had to agree. The pyramids played tricks on the visitors' imaginations by appearing smaller than they really were and taking much longer to reach than expected.

While he could not be sure of how the Giza Plateau had looked in ancient times, presently, it was a lifeless plateau with pyramids rising out of its sands. Michael imagined that this barren sight likely contributed to the idea that the stone blocks used to build the pyramids were transported along an artificially created sand mound. This theory held that the mound was increased in height in equal proportion to the increased height of the pyramid. Using the sand mound theory, Michael assumed that it would be quite possible to raise blocks weighing several tons. It seemed, however, impossible to him that such a method would allow for lifting blocks weighing tens or hundreds of tons, especially since the Great Pyramid was 487 feet in height. He doubted any sand mound was capable of holding that kind of weight without starting to crumble. In addition, this theory could not account for the criticism of the assumption that these blocks were transported along the masonry. From his studies, Michael had to agree that the masonry simply would not be able to sustain the block's prolonged movement and would begin falling apart during the construction process, meaning there had to be a more reasonable approach.

The longer Michael stood there, the more he fantasized about how the Great Pyramid could have been built. It seemed to him that none of the current theories made any possible sense. *There had to be another way. And perhaps I will discover it,* he mused. Then his thoughts took on a darker tone as they led him to imagine what would happen if the multi-ton pyramid mass suddenly crumbled to the ground in millions of pieces. This thought caused his breath to catch in his throat, suddenly bringing back the painful memories of the terrorist attacks on September 11th, 2001, that had led to the collapse of the New York City Twin Towers. Those memories were still fresh and vivid in his mind.

Despite the passage of time, he could recall those images just as if it had happened yesterday. His father took him to his office that fateful morning. After the first plane had hit that morning, his father's workplace, located in a midtown office building on the Avenue of the

Americas, had immediately closed and everyone had been dismissed. After leaving the building, his father and he started walking toward the Brooklyn Bridge to go home. But then Michael got an idea. He stopped at a corner store and purchased a disposable camera. He and his dad left the shop walking quickly but, realizing the danger around them, started to jog and then run. Meanwhile, every once in a while, Michael would pause and take a photo of the disaster exploding all too near them. Despite being in the midst of all of the chaos, he had managed to snap multiple, unforgettable photos of the dying Twin Towers: thirty-six to be exact.

Those thirty-six images, taken on the worst day in American history, were one of his most prized possessions, despite their low resolution. On their canvas, the pulverized concrete and shattered pieces of the steel perimeter columns, which had been thrown out of the towers during the horrific stages of the unimaginable collapse, were forever immortalized. The debris ejecting and the immense volume of crushed materials generated from the collapsing towers could only be compared to an explosive volcanic eruption. A pyroclastic flow of debris could be clearly traced in some of his photos as he had literally raced away from the collapsing structure and down the street to relative safety. He recalled his journey to work that fateful morning as seeming so peaceful: much like this day. The horrific flashback of devastating images and chilling thoughts were juxtaposed inexplicably with his memory of that otherwise sunny, cloudless and ordinary September day in 2001. These disturbing thoughts kept Michael lingering on the Giza Plateau for another few minutes before he could shake them off and a smile found its way back onto his lips.

He began walking toward the pyramids and his dreams. The closer Michael got to the pyramids, the more immense they appeared. The Great Pyramid was amazingly beautiful in the light of the morning rays. It seemed as if its apex, abutted against the sky, burnt out to the brightest blue. Its surface appeared to merge with the very desert sand as its exterior mirrored its color so closely. The pyramids were like a mirage sailing along the hot air.

*Man fears Time, yet Time fears the Pyramids.*

Michael had memorized this old Arab proverb from one of the countless pyramid books he had read. As he arrived at the foot of the magnificent structure, he could finally understand the proverb. The Pyramid of Khufu, though not the oldest in Egypt, had become a symbol of long lasting durability. For this reason, the Great Pyramid was chosen as an icon on the reverse side of the U.S. dollar bill.

Michael timidly bent down to touch the pyramid's granite bedrock foundation. Trembling with excitement, he began his climb up the external carved-in-limestone stairs that led to the entrance. His head rushed with scraps of thoughts and facts about the pharaoh's curse of terrible diseases and impending death that was supposed to pursue anyone who attempted to disturb Khufu's final resting place. He figured that if that were truly the case, there would be a lot of sick and dead tourists, so he was probably safe.

In spite of a timid feeling brought about by the pyramid's majestic sublimity, he stepped inside the Great Pyramid. As soon as he had fully entered the pyramid, he stood in reverent awe of having fulfilled a lifelong dream. A fitting inscription found inside King Tut's tomb in the King's Valley came to his mind:

*Death will slay with his wings anyone whoever disturbs the peace of the pharaoh.*

This threat, which seemed to be soaring around the pyramids in a whispered warning to all the unsuspecting visitors, did not seem to deter them in the least or lead them to be wary of what awaited them inside. Like those who had come before him who ignored the forewarning inscription, Michael made his way to the inner entrance. He found it necessary to crouch over and bend his legs to keep his head inclined away from the low ceiling. This was difficult to do, as he had to try not to slip on the wooden steps that were nailed to an inclined wooden plank that served as the stairs.

Once completely inside the pyramid, Michael heard a familiar American-English dialect coming from a group of tourists ahead of him. Michael approached the group. Their tour guide, despite his typical American name, Steve, was in reality one of the local Arab guides that had been assigned to the group. Unable to go around them, he lingered nearby. *I should have signed up to take a tour as well,* Michael scolded himself slightly as he started paying attention to Steve's speech.

"The Great Pyramid at Giza is the only one of the original seven wonders of the ancient world still standing. It was built as a tomb for the fourth dynasty Egyptian pharaoh, Khufu, or Cheops, as the Greeks called him. This pyramid was constructed over a 20-year period and has an estimated 2.3 million limestone blocks. These blocks were transported up and over a mound of sand constructed next to the pyramid," Steve lectured.

*Ok, time to go,* thought Michael, deciding that the tour guide's speech was useless.

The tour guide started rushing the group through the pyramid with a rocket's acceleration. Always with a keen eye to the tiniest details, Michael usually took a long time to examine things. He did not plan for this exploration to be any different.

While Michael was still examining the Queen's Chamber, the American group was already quickly making its way up to the King's Chamber. Without warning, a man in a white cloak brusquely rushed by Michael and almost knocked him to the floor. Startled, Michael steadied himself, observing a tall guy with a distinctive bushy Afro hairstyle hurrying away. *What arrogance! He didn't even say excuse me,* thought Michael as the stranger glided down the stairs and disappeared. *I hope he had a real emergency,* he thought with disgust as he turned to continue his journey.

Next, he began following along the horizontal passageway that ended at the entrance to the Grand Gallery. As he approached, a marvelous view appeared before his eyes, and he wished that cameras were allowed inside. The design of this long gallery, with its incredibly high ceiling, was ingenious. Its walls consisted of thoroughly connected stone blocks. These limestone blocks were packed so that each subsequent layer covered a portion of the previous layer. Lost in his thoughts, Michael was completely consumed by the Grand Gallery as he scrutinized every detail of its grand corbelled ceiling. *Somewhere there it's gotta be. . .*

"Help!" The cry was barely audible but unmistakable. Curious, Michael glanced down the Ascending Passage and observed another tourist group that was making its way up. *That scream was too weak. It definitely didn't come from down there. So, where did it come from?* He had just convinced himself that it was just his overactive imagination when it sounded again.

"Help!" Again, the same hollow call echoed faintly through the Grand Gallery. This time Michael knew for certain that he was not imagining it.

*It definitely came from the top,* Michael decided as he searched with his eyes. About thirty feet away, in the middle of the Grand Gallery, he finally made out the silhouette of a lone man collapsed against the wall, barely visible in the looming darkness. Michael sprinted forward as the man slumped into a crouched position despite trying to support his body weight against the handrail.

"Sir, excuse me sir, are you OK?" Michael asked upon his arrival. The man struggled to open his droopy eyelids. Michael bent over the man, "Sir, are you feeling all right?"

The man struggled to lift his chin up, and fought to choke some words out.

Michael placed a hand on the man's shoulder, "Sir, are you OK?"

"Can't. Breathe," the man choked out.

Michael turned and bellowed at the top of his lungs toward the group that was entering the Grand Gallery "Somebody, anybody speaks English?" His deep baritone voice echoed thunderously throughout the Grand Gallery and into the chambers beyond. Even minutes later he could still hear his voice reverberating throughout the interlocked blocks of the Grand Gallery.

Almost instantaneously, several tourists replied, "Yes!"

Michael spoke quickly, "This man is having trouble breathing. I need someone to run back to the entrance for help and to call an ambulance." Several people immediately turned and dashed back towards the entrance. Michael turned back to the stricken man, "Sir, I need you to lie down and try to relax. You will be okay. I know CPR and will try to help you restore your breathing. What's your name, sir?" Michael reached to check the stranger's pulse, but at that moment the man collapsed into his arms. The man wheezed that his name was Günther Schulze. Michael held no doubt that Schulze was German: the accent and the name never lie.

Michael immediately knelt down, rolled the German onto his back, and began performing chest compressions. He looked into Schulze's face and saw that his eyes were partially open. Schulze reached up and Michael paused his CPR efforts. The man fumbled inside his jacket pocket, removing a white business card. Michael leaned his ear to Schulze's barely moving lips. "Promise... call her," Schulze whispered "I was poisoned. ... Beware ... dark man ... Afro ..." Michael nodded and grabbed the card, stuffing it inside his jeans pocket. He resumed performing CPR. But the German was not about to give up easily. Again, he reached for an inside pocket of his vest. Michael put his hand inside the man's vest and felt a small notebook in an interior pocked. He pulled it out. Schulze nodded feebly. "Find four ways..." Schulze's lips contorted, but the rest of his speech was incomprehensible. As Schulze's eyes rolled back into his head, his body went limp. Michael placed the notebook on the ground and continued to perform CPR as he waited for the ambulance to arrive. Each minute was desperately counted as Michael watched the seconds on his "Timex" watch slowly roll forward. It was a long and desperate wait.

A pair of local paramedics made their way into the Grand Gallery, loaded Schulze's body onto their hand-held gurney, and fighting the narrowness of the passageways, rushed back to the entrance. Michael picked up the notebook and stuffed it under his arm. He followed the paramedics, trying to tell them what had happened, but he was not sure if they understood a word he was saying. Finally, they were in the open air and the paramedics were preparing to load Schulze's motionless body into the ambulance. Schulze's arm twitched and Michael reached out to take his pulse. To his relief, he felt a slight pulse. Schulze was still alive!

Despite the commotion, Steve the tour guide had also made his way out and attempted to assist with the language barrier. Michael asked Steve, "What hospital are they taking him to?"

Steve inquired and then interpreted the paramedic's Arabic response, "The Anglo-American Hospital, Zohoreya." The ambulance doors were slammed shut and it sped away, leaving a cloud of sandy dust behind it.

"What happened to that man?" worried one of the tourists.

"He was having difficulty breathing inside the pyramid," Michael replied.

"Oh, claustrophobia. That happens to many people," Steve said nonchalantly. "Some people have no idea how claustrophobic they are until they actually step inside the pyramid. I am sure he will be fine." *Yeah, right. Claustrophobia. The man was poisoned!* Michael scoffed to himself. He had already decided not to mention anything that Schulze had told him inside the Great Pyramid. He did not want to start a panic.

Visibly satisfied by the tour guide's explanation, the crowd slowly started to disperse. Soon, Michael was left standing alone at the entrance of the Great Pyramid. Now that the crisis was over, he struggled to absorb what had happened. *What did he mean by poisoning? Who poisoned him? Why? It doesn't make any sense.* Michael felt consumed by his numerous questions. It seemed that the pyramid's mysteries could be fathomed more easily then the circumstances that he now found himself embroiled.

Rubbing his forehead, Michael pulled out the business card business card and examined it carefully.

| | |
|---|---|
| **Anna Schulze**<br>gesetzlicher Sekretär<br>Florrenstrasse 201<br>10719 Berlin<br>Deutschland |  |
| **Telefon: 30 649901-0**<br>**Fax: 30 649901-31** | **www.GRCAnwälte.de** |

*Who is Anna? Hmmm . . . she has the same last name. Maybe she is his wife or daughter.* Michael glanced at the city listed on the card. *Well, she is German – that's for sure. I need to give her a call. After all, I made a promise to a dying man.*

He turned the business card over. On the reverse side, in the upper left corner, Michael saw a four-word phrase neatly written in pink sharpie. It was obviously German, so he did not know what it meant. "Zu meiner lieben, Papa!" He read the phrase aloud a couple of times.

*Well, Papa definitely means Dad,* he concluded. *That's a universal word.*

Along with the business card, Schulze had given him a pocket notebook. Michael slowly started flipping through it. *Why would he give me his notebook? What is in here that would be important?* Michael did not find anything in the notebook besides some names, phone numbers, and phrases in German, which he could not understand.

*What else did he say?* Michael paused for a moment, trying to concentrate. A few minutes quietly passed by. *Oh, that's right. Find four ways!* He considered the authority of so-called dying declarations, a principle that originated in the medieval English courts – *Nemo moriturus praesumitur mentiri* – a dying person is not presumed to lie.

In order to shed some light on the matter and put an end to all his unanswered questions, Michael decided that he would pay Schulze a visit in the hospital. Surely, there was a rational explanation. He also decided that he should call the lady named on the business card after he stopped by the hospital, so she would know how her either father or husband was doing. After all, Michael was traveling alone and if he had gotten into trouble, he would appreciate someone helping him out.

Taking one more glance at the pyramids, Michael decided that they would still be here after he had sorted this out, but it did pain him to leave such a picturesque view. From the Giza Plateau, the perfect chain of pyramids seemed burnt out to the whiteness below them, like a natural continuation of the sand dunes. They were harmonious barrows for the ascension of the godlike kings to be closer to the sky and the sun.

*True pharaohs' tombs rose high above the perishable and so vulnerable mankind,* Michael quoted to himself as he walked to the road to catch a taxi to the hospital.

# Chapter 6

Giza Plateau, Egypt
Monday, September 18
9:44 a.m.

The hot sands whipped into a heavy cloud behind the Red Crescent ambulance as it rushed to the hospital with Günther Schulze strapped onto a gurney in the back. As the ambulance made a sharp turn toward Giza Square, the paramedic riding in the back braced himself as he pulled out his cellphone and pressed a speed dial button. Almost immediately the paramedic started speaking rapidly in Arabic with the person on the other end of the call. A couple of moments later, the paramedic barked at the driver to pull over at the intersection of El-Malek and Faisal Bridge, next to Giza Square. The driver complied. After a brief stop the ambulance slowly merged back into traffic with a new passenger on board: Asim. Asim looked hard at Schulze's body on the gurney. As the driver navigated the ambulance through the hectic and notorious mid-morning Cairo traffic, Asim spoke briefly to the paramedic while handing him an envelope. Slowly and purposefully, Asim made his way to Schulze's gurney, his bushy Afro waving with the ambulance's jerking and swaying. Keeping his icy eyes fixed on his victim the entire time; he quickly disconnected each of the tubes from Schulze's body.

*You will die! That's what you deserve!* The thoughts that ran through his mind did little to calm him, as he still did not have the stele. Schulze took his last breath and his eyes rolled over. Asim sat next to Schulze and began a slow and meticulous search of his lifeless body.

But all he found was a wallet. Opening it, he found a German driver's license, several family pictures, 120 euros and 100 L.E. *It*

41

*can't be! There's gotta be something ... some kind of clue!* Asim slowly inspected Schulze's clothes. He first inspected the dead man's vest, sticking his hand in the pockets. After a close inspection of the dead man's shirt and undershirt he found nothing unusual. The dead man's trousers were then inspected with the same effort. In the end, Asim's search of Schulze's dead body had produced the same fruitless result as the search of Schulze's hotel room the previous day. Hanging onto a strap, Asim stood up in the rocking ambulance and took an overhead view of his prey. He let out a deep, anguished sigh.

*What am I going to say to the chief?* In a fury, he kicked the gurney, but Schulze's spirit was already too far away to feel it. However, it did prompt Schulze's left foot to fall off the gurney. Startled, Asim looked at the dead man's exposed black sock. He braced himself against the swaying ambulance and bent over to pick up the man's foot. He yanked off the shoe, tossing it aside. Then he grabbed the top of the sock and began pulling it off. And as he pulled, a white piece of paper was revealed. Curious at the unexpected discovery, Asim carefully pulled out the thin white piece of paper with a familiar logo, three capital red letters on a yellow background: *DHL*, a division of the German logistics company, Deutsche Post.

Asim felt triumphant! The white piece of paper he was holding was a postal receipt dated September 12th. The Medjay glared down at Schulze's body. *That was six days ago*, Asim thought. *He must have mailed our sacred stele six days ago.* The thought of their stele being shipped to a foreign country gave him a sinking feeling in the pit of his stomach. "Oh Horus, living and great, please no!" He sobbed in a whispered wail. The crackling sounds of the ambulance radio muffled his desperate cry of prayer.

As the ambulance made a sharp turn onto El-Tahrir Street in front of the Jordanian embassy, it suddenly came to a complete stop. The ambulance was stuck in the city's infamous traffic, despite being only a dozen street blocks away from Cairo's public hospital, Anglo-American Hospital Zohoreya. The ambulance's wailing siren had no effect on the traffic clogging the El-Galaa Bridge as it crossed the Nile. Nobody moved and nobody even attempted to pull aside to let the emergency vehicle through, which is typical for Cairo traffic.

Asim quickly examined the postal receipt. *Mailed from 38 Abd El-Khalek Tharwat Street in Downtown, Cairo*, he read silently. Below the heading, he observed that the item shipped weighed one kilogram and that 200 Egyptian pounds was paid for DHL Express Worldwide delivery.

*Wait*, he thought. Relief flashed across the Medjay's face. *Our stele certainly didn't weigh a mere one kilogram.* For a brief moment Asim drifted back to a memory from fifteen years before, during his Right of Passage ceremony that signified his passage into manhood. That was the first and last time he had ever seen or held the sacred stele. Even though he was merely thirteen at the time, he clearly recollected lifting the weight of the stele physically onto his shoulder at the same time he ceremoniously shouldered the heavy weight and honor of protecting it.

A ton of weight dropped off his shoulders as Asim realized there was no way the German could have mailed the stele through DHL's Express service. *But what does the receipt mean? It must be important for him to have hidden it so.*

*I need to let the Chief know.* Asim pulled out an outdated version of a RAZR cell phone. At least he had something to report.

"My great warrior, may Horus always be with you," answered the firm male voice on the other end as he had recognized Asim's number on the incoming call.

"May Horus always be with you, Great Chief."

"Tell me the good news," commanded the Chief.

"I carried out your will, oh Great Chief!"

"That's definitely good news. I know Ra will be merciful today."

Asim thought that the Chief sounded pleased and boasted, "The deceiving thief is gone to the distant place from where nobody returns."

"I assume you left no witnesses. The risk is too great."

"He died inside Khufu's Great Pyramid," Asim paused before adding solemnly, "The very place he had defiled."

Asim relayed all of the earlier events of the day to the Chief. He meticulously reported following Schulze from his hotel to the Giza Plateau, slipping inside before Schulze entered the Great Pyramid, and how he had patiently waited with the small syringe filled with the chemist's poisonous liquid. Even though he had not the slightest clue what fate was waiting for him, the German engineer, Schulze, had been doomed from the very moment he had stepped inside the Great Pyramid. In the very place he had defiled.

"Yes, the very place he had defiled," repeated the chief somberly. "Anubis, the guardian of the underworld will not be pleased with his soul so weighted down in sin. Schulze's heart will outweigh Ma'at's feather, and his condemned soul will be given to Ammit, the crocodile-headed devourer of souls." The chief exhaled calmly and engaged in a barely audible prayer.

There was a long pause, during which Asim could hear chief's muted pleas to the guardian of the underworld before resuming the conversation. "Then, I presume you found what he stole from us and what we so vigilantly guarded for generations."

"Great Chief, be Horus my witness. I searched his entire body," Asim gave Schulze's body another disgruntled glance. "I found a DHL postal receipt on him that showed he mailed a package six days ago."

The chief exhaled loudly, agitation creeping into his voice. "There is no way he could've mailed the stele."

"You are correct, Great Chief. The weight of the package was a mere one kilogram," Asim responded quietly. "But the postal receipt is the only clue. I searched his entire hotel room, but nothing was found there either," Asim concluded with frustration and anger apparent in his voice.

"My fierce warrior," the chief's voice interrupted him, sounding composed again. "We are the Medjay. We will never quit until righteousness triumphs and what was stolen from us is returned to its rightful place. The stele will be found at any cost. I have confidence that the German didn't smuggle it outside of Egypt. And while it is still inside the country, it is within our power."

Asim knew the stakes were great and eagerly awaited the next set of instructions from his Great Chief.

"Don't call me; I will initiate the next call. Are you on the way to the hospital?" asked the Chief.

"Yes, we are stuck in traffic."

"How predictable," the Chief chuckled. "I will make all the necessary arrangements. The cause of his death will be unsuspicious." The Chief's confident tone eased Asim's mind, after all, his Great Chief was a man of his word.

Right as Asim was about to end the call, the chief hurriedly asked, "What was the date on the DHL receipt?"

Glancing down at the receipt, Asim answered, "September 12th."

"Very well, Asim, my fierce warrior," the chief seemed satisfied. "You've done well. Just make sure you place the postal receipt inside the German's wallet."

Asim was surprised to hear that request, but knew he would strictly follow it. Asim flipped his cell phone closed and tucked it back into his cloak. *I'm still at the mercy of the Chief!* He grabbed Schulze's wallet and put the receipt inside. After stuffing the wallet inside Schulze's vest pocket, Asim began the task of reinserting the tubes into the German's lifeless body.

The traffic finally gave way with a roar. The ambulance rushed along the streets before slamming to a halt in front of the emergency room entrance of the Anglo-American Hospital Zohoreya. As they opened the back door, Asim gave a silent nod to both paramedics, exited the ambulance and slipped away unnoticed. The gurney supporting Schulze's body was lifted out and as the triage team ran out to greet them, the paramedics started shouting medical stats. Unobserved, Asim walked away from the scene snickering to himself. *What's the rush? He's dead. Anyone want to take a wild guess? May I suggest...a heart attack?* His own recent near-death experience at the hands of the chemist Nassar was still fresh in his mind. *My "dear old menacing friend" predicted that would be the findings.*

# Chapter 7

Cairo, Egypt
Monday, September 18
10:14 a.m.

M ichael Doyle was sitting in the back seat of a taxi on his way to the Anglo-American Hospital Zohoreya. He checked his watch. His young driver, Ahmoud, was busily navigating his way through Cairo's crowded streets, but the trip to visit Schulze in the hospital was taking longer than Michael had anticipated.

Despite being eager to continue his long-awaited Egyptian vacation that he had fantasized about exploring since his early teenage years, Michael felt it was necessary to follow up and make sure nothing untoward had occurred. Deep in his heart he hoped to find Schulze well. He was also hoping that all his talk about being poisoned had been a vivid figment of Schulze's heat-addled imagination.

His first surprise took the form of Cairo's infamous traffic. For a big city, such as Cairo, traffic is a major issue and even a typical day's navigating is not an easy procedure. Considered the largest city in Africa, Cairo is home to at least eighteen million people. As its streets are already clogged with stop-and-go traffic, it is good news that not every family has a car.

Abruptly, Ahmoud made a right hand turn and sped down a narrow street where all the other headlights were pointed the wrong way. When he looked in the rear view mirror and saw Michael scowling, Ahmoud laughed and pointedly reminded him that while many streets are marked as one-way, this rule is not always respected. Further, as Michael soon observed, red lights do not necessarily mean "stop", or for that matter even "slow down." Cars flooded through the red lights with their horns blaring to warn anyone foolish enough to consider getting in their way. In Cairo it is the worst of mistakes to believe that a green "walk" light indicates it is safe for pedestrians to cross the road. Michael shook his head as a couple of tourists almost learned that lesson the hard way. He realized that the overriding rule seemed to be for everyone to make use of every bit of available space. Many of the streets lacked lane markers, but the ones that were there were simply ignored. The only time a driver seemed to stop is when there was absolutely no way to squeeze around whoever was in front or to either side of them.

If Schulze had any chance of surviving, he would have needed to be transported to the hospital within the so-called "golden hour," the first hour after a trauma where a majority of critical patient's lives can be saved if definitive medical intervention is provided. As he stared out his smudged window at the gridlock of packed, honking cars, Michael had a dismal feeling. The one-hour time frame sounded like it would have necessitated a miracle.

Michael was snapped out of his musings when he realized his taxi was driving between two lanes of stopped cars. Blasting his horn and gesturing, Ahmoud laughed again at Michael's panicked expression. "This is not considered rude or in any way out of place," the native Egyptian stated with irony. "Nobody respects the traffic regulations. Everybody simply goes his own way. It takes hours and hours to go anywhere. But don't worry! I'll get you there in one piece."

As Michael's cab driver turned his attention back to the road, he was able to edge the cab forward a few more car lengths before becoming trapped once again. Ahmoud leaned out his window and began having a lively conversation with a driver in the neighboring vehicle. Michael's thoughts started drifting away from his current plight of being stuck in traffic. He was happy at finally being in Egypt and seeing the pyramids, even if it was a bit briefer than he would have liked. However, the morning's incident was seared into his thoughts. He could not shake the strange statements Schulze had made to him nor the lingering sense of unease. Something was not right, but he doubted he had even half the pieces of this puzzle. Hopefully, Schulze would survive and would be able to shed some light on this morning's events.

As the taxi inched along, Michael thought about how he had performed CPR that morning. While he was stationed at Camp Shelby, Mississippi, he had trained during the Iraqi war pre-deployment Combat Life Saving Course. But today was the second time he had performed CPR in a real life-or-death situation.

In March 2003, his unit was one of the first to deploy in support of Operation Iraqi Freedom. His deployment had occurred near the end of his military days; for six years he had been enlisted in the U.S. Army before retiring at the rank of Sergeant. It was that one-year deployment, "the twelve months boots-on-the-ground," that had taken a great toll on his mother's health, as he was her only child. He knew there was not a single day that passed without her fearing for the worst.

It was in July of 2003 when his mother's worst fears nearly came to pass. Michael was one of the five soldiers inside a Humvee. They had assumed a nearby vehicle was merely parked until a rocket-propelled grenade was launched at them from it. Then it immediately sped away. Michael was the luckiest of all due to his position on top as a gunner. He received only a few non-life-threatening injuries from the blast, while it killed two of his comrades instantly. The soldier sitting next to the driver had been thrown through the window and knocked unconscious. The driver was saved by Michael's swift actions. His training kicked in when he saw the driver's left arm severed and bleeding heavily. He quickly applied a tourniquet and tirelessly began performing CPR while waiting for the rescue helicopter. Thankfully, his buddy had lived to go home. And now he hoped that Schulze would as well.

The taxi crawled its way to the hospital. He looked up at the overpass of El-Tahrir Street. It looked peaceful with only several people walking and a parked vehicle. Suddenly Michael's body shook from the abrupt explosion; his eyes discerned a fire spreading throughout the vehicle as a sharp, penetrating pain ripped up his right leg. "We're hit!" His shout came automatically. The Humvee tilted heavily to its left but miraculously avoided rolling over as it was counterbalanced by the weight of its fifty-caliber gun. While the gun turret, located on the top of the vehicle, swayed from side to side, Michael clung to the gun as the vehicle settled. Michael's breath caught in his throat as he realized that had the muzzle of his .50 Cal been turned the other way, a rollover would have been imminent. The chance of any of them surviving would have been slim to none.

Michael managed to pry open one of the damaged upper armored doors and crawl outside the burning vehicle. He instinctively pulled and crawled himself away from the fire-engulfed vehicle, dragging his injured leg behind him. The first thought that came to his mind, *I'm alive!* was soon forgotten when he turned back and saw the remains of the medium-sized RPG penetrated halfway through the right side of his Humvee. Michael rushed back to burning vehicle.

"Preston! Are you all right?" Michael yelled as he yanked the door open and pulled the driver out of the burning vehicle. Private First Class Preston, fresh out of Basic Training and a country boy from Boise, Idaho, had no response. Seeing that Preston had lost an arm in the blast, Michael dragged his body to safety. Ripping off his belt, Michael quickly tied a makeshift tourniquet around the bloody remains. Then he looked at Preston's chest. To his horror there was no motion or any other signs of breathing. Falling back on his training, Michael immediately started the CPR process. Soon he felt the rising and falling of the driver's chest.

"So, how do you like Cairo?" the driver asked abruptly, glancing back at Michael. Blinking the glaring sun out of his eyes, Michael glanced at him in disbelief. *What? But...how? A minute ago, he had no signs of life, and now he's asking this nonsense? Egypt?"*

"My friend, hello," Ahmoud was now giving Michael a lop-sided smile in the rearview mirror, "you like Egyptian traffic?"

Michael looked through the side window and refocused on the Nile River they were crossing atop the El-Galaa Bridge. "Nnn o," Michael stuttered. *Oh my God!* It took Michael a couple seconds for his mind to refocus. He was in Cairo, not Baghdad. He took a deep, shaky breath of hot Egyptian air and gritted his teeth. *These flashbacks, I can't keep having them. It's over and I'm safe now.*

Once the taxi crossed over the Nile, which surrounds Gezira Island, they emerged at the entrance to the island. Almost instantaneously, the traffic faded away. Michael caught a glimpse of the outlines of the Cairo Tower, the famous freestanding concrete TV tower located in the Zamalek district on Gezira Island. At 187 meters, the Cairo Tower is 43 meters higher than the Great Pyramid of Giza, which stands some

15 kilometers to the southwest. The distance, however, felt a lot farther considering the amount of time they had been trapped in traffic.

The cab made a sharp left turn onto Om Kalthum Street and passed the Cairo Opera House. The splendid Opera House complex housed multiple galleries, including the Museum of Modern Art, a variety of restaurants and concert halls. The funds for the Opera House were a gift from the nation of Japan to Egypt after the Egyptian President Hosni Mubarak visited Japan in April of 1983. Michael was excited to see the Opera House in person as he planned to see one of its productions during his vacation. "Swan Lake," a ballet composed by the Russian composer Pyotr Tchaikovsky about Odette, a princess turned into a swan by an evil sorcerer's curse was indisputably Michael's favorite.

The taxi finally pulled over at hospital. He exited the cab, giving Ahmoud a tip for safely navigating him through Cairo's crazy traffic and then made his way into the emergency room entrance.

The registration clerk looked up when Michael reached the counter. "I'm here to visit a patient, Günther Schulze," Michael said. The clerk checked the files and politely asked Michael what his relationship was with the patient.

"He is my friend," replied Michael. He paused and added, "Well, he's not really my friend. I just met him today."

"Ok, mister . . ." the clerk paused for a second, looking at him expectantly.

"Doyle," said Michael.

"Yes, Mr. Doyle," the clerk paused and then gently apprised him, "Unfortunately, Mr. Schulze passed away."

"Oh my God, really?" exclaimed Michael in a state of shock. *I was hoping for a miracle. But he did have a pulse when he was loaded inside the ambulance.*

"Can you please tell me how he died?" Michael asked.

After checking the hospital records, the clerk said, "Heart attack."

"Heart attack?" Michael was shocked and confused. Even though he had mentally prepared himself for the worst news possible, it had not seemed like a heart attack at the time.

"Yes, sir, definitely a heart attack," confirmed the clerk. "That's exactly what it says in our records," he looked up at Michael, his eyes soft with compassion. "I'm sorry, sir."

*How is that possible?* Michael gripped the counter in disbelief, trying to grasp the meaning of the clerk's words and the reality of the situation. He retreated into his thoughts, trying to recall the details from earlier. *Where the hell did a heart attack come from? Schulze clearly told me he had been poisoned. Was he hallucinating? I don't think so. Something is definitely not right.*

"Mr. Doyle," the clerk called Michael's name, bringing him back from the labyrinth of his thoughts. "The family has been notified and his wife is flying in from Germany, but that is all I know."

From the depths of his heart, Michael wished to inform the clerk that Schulze had told him that he had been poisoned. But he decided not to start a panic or, even worse, suspicious questions. After all, they were doctors and definitely knew more about medicine than he did. *I didn't know this man at all, and I am not gonna to get myself involved in any dirty games being played—whether by Schulze or the hospital.* Michael was not about to waste any more of his long-awaited vacation. But all the same, he felt he should at least talk to Schulze's wife to let her know what had happened.

"Can you please give his wife my phone number?"

"Yes, certainly sir."

Michael quickly scribed his hotel's phone number on a piece of paper the clerk offered him. Thinking she might want to meet with him, he added his room number as well and handed the paper to the clerk. In a fog of thoughts, he turned and slowly walked out the entrance and sat down on a nearby bench. His mind was back inside the Grand Gallery of Khufu's pyramid.

"I was poisoned!" Schulze's whispered voice echoed over and over again throughout the Grand Gallery. *And, now they say it was a heart attack?* Michael tried in vain to come up with a possible explanation for the discrepancy. *Well, I'm sure there are poisons that fool even well trained doctors.*

# Chapter 8

Cairo Police station, Egypt
Monday, September 18
12:30 p.m.

Visibly satisfied, Inspector Suliman of the Cairo Police Department hung up the phone after a call from his old friend, Jibade, the Chief of the local Medjay tribe. The Medjay Chief's news had made his day. If he were to recover the missing stele, a prized ancient Egyptian artifact, it would be the highlight of his career. Known as a hunter, not only within the police department, but also among the criminal elements, Suliman had chased and successfully recovered numerous ancient Egyptian artifacts throughout his time on the force.

"Egyptian heritage belongs to Egypt" was the motto that gave purpose to his law enforcement career. He had spent the last fifteen years preserving Egyptian heritage by catching smugglers of antiquities. His otherwise stellar career with the Cairo Police had been sullied over the last few years due to a corruption scandal involving a large portion of the top brass. Even though there had been no evidence of the inspector's involvement, it was hard for him to dodge all of the allegations directed at him by a few influential individuals. The inspector had a reputation for being a ruthless interrogator, which usually had advantageous results. In this instance, however, the accusations, combined with his interrogation methods, put a dark blemish on his admirable career. To avoid unwanted attention, Inspector Suliman had stepped away from the spotlight entirely and begun leading a secluded life. He no longer involved himself in trials that made front-page newspaper news, but instead devoted himself to routine police work that involved petty cases and everyday criminals.

He had waited patiently in the shadows for a case that would restore his career to its limelight.

Finally, it had come knocking on his door: the case of a lifetime. The Medjay chief's phone call was the opportunity for which he had been waiting all these years. The chief had assisted him on a previous case involving a missing tribesman, and they had become friends. And now the chief was calling and asking him for a favor. He needed the inspector's assistance in finding the missing stele that had been safely guarded by the Medjay tribe for generations. The Medjay chief decided not to go into all the details surrounding the mysterious way the sacred stele had initially gotten into the Medjay hands, preferring to give the explanation that stele had been used in Medjay traditional ceremonies for the last several thousand years and retained substantial spiritual significance to the tribe. The words "several thousand" made a distinct and lasting impression on the inspector, who had jumped at the chance. The Medjay chief had then explained that he believed a German engineer by the name of Günther Schulze was at fault and that he believed the German had a DHL receipt on him that might be important.

As soon as he got off the phone, Inspector Suliman started with the lone suspect, German engineer Günther Schulze. He and his right-hand man, Chief Detective Ashraf Hussein, began extensive research immediately. Deaths of foreigners were always reported to officials, and soon they were able to confirm that Schulze had died of a heart attack earlier that day at the Zohoreya Hospital.

The Inspector slowly rubbed his hands together. This was starting to get interesting. The lone suspect in the case was dead, and the inspector certainly did not believe in the cause of death for a moment. His gut told him that Schulze's death was not a coincidence. Dispatching several of his best detectives to the Zohoreya Hospital, Inspector Suliman instructed them to probe deeper into Schulze's sudden death.

The Inspector gave last-minute instructions to his Chief Detective Ashraf Hussein. "I don't believe those medical records for a second. Search everything you can and explore every possible lead."

About an hour later, Detective Hussein called from the hospital and informed his superior that the German engineer's death was confirmed as a heart attack. Nothing suspicious or even interesting was found among his belongings besides a DHL postal receipt. The Inspector was amazed. He wondered how his friend, the local Chief of the Medjay, could have possibly known about the postal receipt inside Schulze's wallet.

Detective Hussein also reported that based on the accounts of the paramedics who had delivered Schulze to the hospital, the German engineer reportedly had difficulty breathing before collapsing inside the Great Pyramid. His condition then deteriorated significantly on the way to the hospital where he was pronounced dead on arrival. In addition, the detective noted that someone had attempted to visit Schulze at the hospital, an American tourist by the name of Michael Doyle.

"Who is Michael Doyle?" demanded the Inspector.

"He came to the hospital after Schulze's body arrived and asked about him."

"Are they related?"

"No, Inspector, they are not. According to the hospital staff, the American said that Schulze was an acquaintance that he met earlier today."

Inspector puzzled. *Earlier today*, he contemplated. *That's kind of peculiar... hardly a long enough acquaintance to warrant a hospital visit...especially since the German died shortly thereafter. So, the American was the last person to see Schulze alive. Yet another doubtful coincidence!*

"Detective Hussein, you need to find this American. He was the last person to see Schulze alive and could be connected to the theft of the stele," Inspector Suliman paused briefly. "Now that I think about it, Schulze and the American probably stole the stele, quarreled about the money and the American killed him for it."

"It is possible, Inspector," Detective Hussein replied questioningly.

Inspector Suliman continued verbally running through his thoughts. "Or, maybe the American found out that Schulze stole the stele, confronted him and then killed him."

"Inspector, the diagnosis of Schulze's death is a heart attack. I doubt a heart attack warrants foul play," reminded the detective.

"Right ..." the inspector said pensively. Deep in thought, he preferred the first version of his own story. Regardless, he suspected that the American was involved in the theft of the stele—either directly or indirectly. However, the idea that appealed to the Inspector was where they quarreled about the money. "How can we find that American?" He barked.

"Inspector?" questioned the detective.

"Can anybody provide his description?" Inspector Suliman continued speaking over his subordinate, seeming not to hear him.

"Inspector, the American left his hotel information."

"What?" the inspector was incredulous. "Why would he do that?"

Detective Hussein replied slowly and deliberately, "Inspector, the American is staying at the Cairo Downtown Hotel in room number thirty-six."

Rubbing his hands together with satisfaction, the inspector smiled widely and shook his head. He could not believe it would be that easy. His only possible suspect was within his reach. *The American may or may not have the stele.* The Inspector, however, did not want to start an international incident, especially while he was still suffering from the fallout of the accusations from the smuggling incident. Since the American had so kindly left his coordinates, catching him was not his immediate concern. He would have time for that after he followed up on his other lead.

Locating the stele before it left the country was key or the chances of recovering it would go from slim to none. Not wanting to waste any more valuable time, Inspector Suliman directed his detective to go the post office listed on the receipt and get as much information as possible.

Soon thereafter his loyal Detective Hussein called. "The clerk at the DHL post office remembered Schulze when I showed him Schulze's picture ID that I got out of his wallet. The clerk remembered him because at the time he was privately amused that Schulze was mailing some papyruses; actually just cheap imitations made out of banana leaves and commonly sold at the local souvenir shops. He recalled Schulze commenting that he was mailing the souvenirs to his daughter back in Germany. I've got a copy of the confirmation slip with the destination address listed as Berlin, Germany," Detective Hussein slowly concluded his oral report.

# Chapter 9

Cairo Downtown Hotel, Cairo, Egypt
Tuesday, September 19
6:00 a.m.

Michael Doyle's hotel room phone rang loudly. Michael was cuddled up in the finest Egyptian cotton sheets, relishing a deep sleep. The events of the previous day had taken a great toll on him, and the night's rest was much needed.

The phone rang again.

Awakening was unexpected as if somebody had turned on a TV. First appeared a color picture and with it the sounds, the smells and the feeling of presence. Michael looked around the room. The hotel he was staying in was a renovated old colonial building from the British era. He was in a large, concisely furnished room with very high ceilings and a beautiful polished wood floor. One wall had a set of three small windows covered by elegant burgundy drapes. In the middle of the wall between two of the windows was a door leading to an iron balcony. Next to the door was a rickety antique-looking armchair. The twin-sized bed was adorned with two side tables; one had a telephone, a clock and a lamp. These simple furnishings completed the room's decorations.

Still only half-awake, Michael reached over and turned on the lamp. The hands on the old table clock displayed six o'clock. The phone rang again as Michael stared at it in disbelief. He rubbed his eyes several times, trying to adjust them to the amber light coming from the bronze antique-looking lamp. *Who would be calling me on this phone? Nobody even knows the number.* Although more coherent thoughts were gradually crawling into his sleep-addled mind, none could explain this unexpected, early-morning phone call.

Suddenly the phone went silent.

Michael wearily sat on the edge of his bed. A minute went by without the phone making any sound. Everything stood still. Glancing at the phone, Michael let his body plunge into the soothing layers of his bed. Ten seconds later, as if somebody had kept the exact count, the damn phone rang again, just as loud and jarring as the first time. His curiosity won out. Supporting the weight of his body with his left elbow, Michael reached for the phone, "Yes," he said quietly.

On the other end of the line, a hoarse male voice with a strong Arab accent asked, "Mr. Doyle?"

"Yes," Michael replied, curious. "Who is this?"

"Cairo Police. This is Inspector Suliman," the voice stated firmly. Before Michael could interject anything else, the Inspector continued, "Mr. Doyle, I need you to come to the police station to clear up a few formalities."

Michael suddenly realized what this was all this about.

"Is this about the German who had difficulty breathing inside the Great Pyramid?"

"Yes, precisely," the Inspector replied immediately.

Michael felt uneasy. *What do they know? Had they finally discovered that he had been poisoned? Do I really wanna be involved in that mess?* Still unsure what the police knew, Michael decided to play it safe and not to disclose anything Schulze had told him before becoming unconscious inside the Grand Gallery. At least, not until Michael could shed a light on what was really going on.

"How did you get my number?" asked Michael, puzzled.

"From the hospital," the inspector immediately responded.

*Oh, yes, that's right. I left it there for Schulze's wife. Damn it.* Michael felt that now, with the irony of fate, his dreams of walking in the steps of the ancient pharaohs were slowly slipping away from him.

"Mr. Doyle, I need to ask you a few questions," continued the Inspector, oblivious to Michael's shattering dreams. "A police car is already on its way to your hotel."

A thought came to Michael's mind and he blurted it out, "I need to contact the American Embassy first."

"There is no need for that formality," said the inspector. He paused for a moment before slowly continuing in a soft, calm voice. "This is not an interrogation; I just need to clarify a couple of details about the German engineer. That's all. It's really just a formality."

*That's all?* Easier said than done. A trip to the Cairo police station was not exactly in Michael's sightseeing plans. Throughout the years, leading up to his visit, Michael had heard plenty about the famous Egyptian police and their unorthodox activities through newspaper headlines. The Cairo police uniforms are white: clean and pure. But unlike their uniforms, the same cannot be said about the force. For that matter, virtually every local newspaper stains the uniform with articles about police brutality. Almost every Cairo citizen has a story about the police, be it of bribery, abuse or even torture. Several months before his trip, three officers were investigated on murder charges for allegedly beating a man to death. Naturally, all of the charges were dropped. In another incident, a fourteen-year-old boy died after being detained by the police. The boy's family claimed he had been badly beaten, although officers denied any misconduct. Human rights groups mirror the claims that Egyptian police abuse is prevalent, however, the government says that such claims are exaggerated. That being said, Michael had read that most people in Egypt are, if not scared, then certainly wary, of the police. Nobody wants to get on the wrong side of the law.

"OK, I will get ready," Michael sighed and hung up the phone. He heard heavy pounding on the wooden door of his hotel room. "Mr. Doyle, police!" The voice behind the door stated imperiously.

"Yes, yes, I'll be right out," Michael answered irritably. *Wow, that was quick! These guys don't play around.* Suddenly, he realized that during his entire conversation with the inspector, the police were already inside the hotel and standing outside his room. Michael donned his favorite blue HBO Sopranos T-shirt and a pair of grey shorts with cargo pockets. He had barely pulled on his blue Nike sneakers before the heavy pounding behind the door resumed. *Unbelievable! That guy has no patience whatsoever!*

Michael opened the door while crouching in a continued attempt to lace up his Nikes.

"Are you Mister Michael Doyle?" inquired the middle-aged, overweight, balding policeman in a heavy Middle-Eastern accent as he stood over Michael in the doorway.

"Yes," said Michael and then with a smirk he added, "Wow, everybody knows my name around here. I'm famous in Egypt."

The face of the policeman remained unchanged and completely devoid of emotion.

"I'm just trying to make a joke," added Michael. However, in truth, joking was the last thing on his mind at this moment. If somebody knows your name, that means you are in trouble, a piece of insight he had picked up from day one of his U.S. Army Basic Training course. The old but true aphorism 'out of sight, out of mind' proved to be the best notion. Michael assumed the same would be true here as well.

"You spoke to my inspector, right?" asked the policeman, despite the fact that both knew that the conversation had taken place moments before.

"Yes," Michael answered, trying to play along, even though his explicit unwillingness was hardly masked.

"Good. I'm Chief Detective Ashraf Hussein, and I will give you a ride to the police station."

"Yes, sure," Michael said, "looks like I don't have much of a choice now, do I?" He followed the detective out of the hotel and got into the back seat of the waiting scratched and dented police car.

The crisp, fresh morning air whipped through the open window of the old Chevy as it accelerated through Midan Tahrir square. As it passed the famous Cairo museum, Michael mused, *that would have been a much better place to be headed.* He could not help but feel like a prisoner as he sat in the back seat of the vehicle right behind the detective. The only thing missing was a pair of metal braces tightly cuffed around his wrists behind his back. An uneasy feeling captivated Michael's entire attention. He realized that it had most definitely been a bad idea to not contact the American Embassy, but realized that it was far too late try to convince his driver to transport him to the American Embassy instead.

It was just thirty minutes past six in the morning, but the streets of Cairo were already in full motion. Two of the most popular Egyptian tour destinations are Cairo and the Great Pyramid. Even so, Cairo itself is somehow lost in these tours because the city seems too dusty, hot and noisy. The Cairo museum is the only part that truly receives constant admiration. That being said, in reality Cairo is an interesting city.

Although one must get accustomed to it, Old Cairo, the birthplace of Cairo, is worth spending a lot of time exploring as well. As the Chevy penetrated the old city, Michael admired the ancient architecture through the back window of the derelict police car.

Wanting to remain calm, Michael let his mind wander by watching the passing scenery. The boundaries of the old city were clearly outlined by ancient crumbling walls. Two preserved towers of the Roman fortress Babylon towered above them. On this very spot, at this subjugated fortress, the Arab conqueror Amr ibn al-As erected the city Fustat in 641, the roots of modern Cairo. Cairo's official name is Al-Qahira, although the name informally used by most Egyptians is "Masr" which is derived from the original name of Egypt's first Arab capital Fustat, Misr al-Fustat: literally, the city of the tents.

Cairo was a grand city when many of the world's largest metropolises were still in their infancy. Yet, even as the years have passed, Cairo still remains a city shrouded in excitement and mystery: full of dark secrets and bright celebrations. Cairo definitely can be called the city of contrasts as it often mixes the many cultures of the world with the many ages of the world. Travelers are greeted by French cuisine, German new age culture and American enterprises, all while embracing Egyptian heritage stretching from the dawn of civilization. Cairo mixes modern religion with ancient traditions as easily as her streets accommodate modern Mercedes and donkey-drawn carts.

Early morning was the perfect time to get around the city without getting stuck in the bustle of the notorious city traffic. Michael assumed this was probably the reason the police inspector had sent a car at that early hour. Michael rubbed his eyes warily. "Do you know the reason why the inspector wanted to see me?" he asked, focusing on the back of the detective's head.

"No, my orders were to bring you to the police station," the policeman firmly answered.

When they reached a large bazaar, Detective Hussein was forced to slow down. Located in the center of the city and not far from the Cairo museum, the Khan el-Khalili, the oldest and largest market of Cairo, blared and screamed. The Detective struggled to navigate through the sprawling market. He laid on his horn, but the market vendors completely ignored the police sedan as they wheeled out their colorful merchandise. Leaning out his window, Detective Hussein began barking several orders at the locals. This maneuver seemed to be working, as the vendors finally and slowly moved out of the way. Soon the battered police car was skimming through the bazaar at an accelerating rate.

Despite his current predicament, Michael was enjoying the view as he peered through the smudged side window. The market exuded a truly amazing atmosphere with its labyrinth of bustling alleys lined with merchants displaying bright traditional crafts. Michael imagined himself wandering behind the shop fronts into the concealed cramped workshops, where craftsmen produce lanterns, inlaid boxes, water pipes and brassware using traditional techniques. Khan el-Khalili merchants are masters at the art of haggling, and even the locals joke that they can never get *the local* prices.

Finally, the police sedan pulled over and stopped. The detective opened his door, pulled his bulky frame out and opened Michael's door, waving him out. As Michael exited the vehicle, the detective pointed to an old, rusty metal door attached to the building they had parked beside.

"That's the entrance. The inspector is waiting for you."

# Chapter 10

Alexandria, Egypt
Tuesday, September 19
1:45 a.m.

A dark, clear night hung over the city of Alexandria, the "Pearl of the Mediterranean" as the locals call it. Founded by Alexander the Great in 331 B.C., Alexandria is the second largest city in Egypt. Its ancient status as a beacon of culture was symbolized by the Pharos, the legendary lighthouse, once lauded as one of the Seven Ancient Wonders of the world. Today, however, Alexandria is a dusty, seaside Egyptian town with an overinflated population of about five million. Fortuitously, its current status as Egypt's leading port keeps business buzzing. Tourists still flock to its beaches during the summertime and explore the Citadel of Qaitbay, built in 1480 with the Pharos' last remnant stones.

Beneath its dark blanket of sky, the city slept as Asim sat in the back seat of a distinctive black and yellow Soviet-era Lada taxi. The sleeping city was of little concern to Asim as his entire focus was on the screen of his Personal Digital Assistant, which Chief Jibade had personally given to him. It was an earlier version of the PDA, so it did not have Internet capabilities; however, it was preloaded with maps, pictures and several text files. The Chief explained that he preferred to use the older PDAs because they lacked Internet capabilities, preventing them from being traced or, even worse, hacked. Thus, the outdated equipment guaranteed the security of the information stored on it.

The street where Asim's driver, the Chief's personal chauffeur, chose to park their taxi was empty at this hour. A lone traffic signal intermittently blinked its amber yellow light. As they listened to the muffled, traditional Middle Eastern music on the radio, the driver slowly fell half asleep. Asim glanced out the windshield. The Alexandrian Library's distinctive design, a tilting disc rising from the ground, could be made out from several hundred meters away. Intended both as a commemoration and an emulation of the original library, the Bibliotheca Alexandrina was inaugurated in 2002 near the site of its ancient world famous predecessor. The original library, founded by Alexander the Great in the third century B.C, housed as many as 700,000 manuscripts: the whole mass of knowledge accumulated by all the ancient philosophers, scientists, and poets. Some of the ancient sources suggest that Julius Caesar accidentally burned the library down during his visit to Alexandria in 48 B.C.

Satisfied the street was empty, Asim shifted his eyes back to his PDA screen that clearly displayed two men's faces and their respective names: Günther Schulze and Karl-Heinz Fischer.

One of the faces Asim already knew well: Günther Schulze. For the past couple of hours, Asim had reminisced about poisoning Schulze and savored his thoughts about the excruciating pain Schulze had experienced before his death. While he was pleased with this victory, at the same time Asim was disappointed that no traces of the stele's whereabouts had been found. Asim had never met the man in the second picture. He hoped this meeting would go as well as the one with Schulze.

After relaying the information about Schulze, his Chief had commanded him to go to Alexandria. The road trip from Cairo through the desert to Alexandria had taken three long hours. True to its name, the Desert Road literally crossed the desert. It was both faster and less crowded than taking the Agriculture Road. Asim could not understand why he had to travel all the way to Alexandria, of all places, considering the theft of the stele had occurred in the Great Pyramid near Cairo. But as a loyal follower of his chief, Asim always executed his commands without question. If the chief directed him to be here, then Asim must be here.

Asim opened a text file attached to Schulze's photo and began to read:

*Günther Schulze: male, 52 years old*
*Home address: Friedrich Ebert Straße 23, Berlin, Germany*

*Last known place of work: French company, AirCo. Engineer. Suspected of stealing an ancient artifact.*

Asim next turned to the text file for Karl-Heinz Fischer and read his personal information:

*Karl-Heinz Fischer: male, 60 years old*
*Home address: Sohnstraße 15 D-20173 Düsseldorf, Germany.*
*Last known place of work: French company, AirCo. Engineer.*
*Suspected of being an accomplice to Günther Schulze.*

Asim whistled through his teeth. *The same company!* Now, it was becoming clear to him why Fischer's profile was displayed next to Schulze's.

When Asim finished reading, he leaned back in his seat and grinned. These two were on a slippery slope indeed, engaging in the business of theft. It would make sense that Fischer was Schulze's accomplice—they were both Germans and worked for the same company. Already one of them had paid with his life. Asim imagined that he would be eliminating the other one, as soon as he received his chief's call to fill in the necessary, missing details. *Well, they both have chosen their own destiny,* mused Asim as he switched off his PDA and gazed back out the window.

While Asim was admiring the illuminated facade of the Bibliotheca Alexandrina, his cell phone's ringtone broke the silence. Looking down at his phone, he smiled as he recognized the number. *Finally!*

"Yes, Great Chief."

"We have finally located the place in Alexandria where Karl-Heinz Fischer is staying," replied his chief. "I believe you have already arrived in Alexandria, right Asim?"

"Yes, Chief. I am waiting for your instructions."

"Excellent. This German, Fischer, was Schulze's friend. They both worked for the same French company in Cairo. This company, AirCo, is currently engaged in some business in Alexandria. That's why I have sent you there."

"Yes, Chief. Your will is my command!"

"The hotel where Fischer is staying is the Darison Blu Hotel, room 219. How long will it take you to get there?"

Asim quickly alerted his sleepy driver and asked him to turn on the portable GPS. Once the GPS had calculated the shortest path to the hotel, Asim turned his attention back to the phone call. "Chief, I can be there in twenty minutes."

"But, Asim, remember that we need information this time. Make sure you get it from him first. His death won't solve anything. Schulze is dead and we're not a centimeter closer to getting our stele back." Chief Jibade frowned and paused to catch his breath.

"Great Chief, I will get the information we need, even if I need rip him apart."

"Yes, yes, but do it quietly. We don't need any publicity. Just remember, they are both Germans and worked together on the same project in the Great Pyramid. He must know something!"

"Chief, you will not be disappointed."

"Keep me informed. Don't forget, his room is 219."

Asim clicked off the cellphone and alerted the driver. The streets were empty so they made it to the hotel in less than twenty minutes. Leaving his driver, Asim stepped out into the night air and opened the side door of the Darison Blu Hotel. His steps echoed in the stairwell as he made his way up the stairs to the second floor. He paused and looked at the number on the first door: 201. He strode soundlessly down to the end of the long, dimly lit hallway. Knocking firmly on the door with the number 219, Asim momentarily considered pulling out his gun, but decided that he could probably resolve the issue without it.

The door opened a bit and a sleepy, heavy-set man with a swollen face appeared in the doorway. Asim recognized his face from the PDA photo file. His gray hair bristled and stuck out in all different directions. He wore a white T-shirt with a faded Dusseldorf red lion mascot that stretched to his knees and almost hid his gray linen shorts.

"Is your name Karl-Heinz Fischer?" asked Asim as he stared down the yawning man in front of him.

The man stared at him as he squinted and stared at the late night intruder, "Yes, and who are you?"

"The plague," Asim answered abruptly, shoving the man backwards into the room and slamming the door. He forcibly grabbed the man by his shirt and dragged him toward the desk chair by the window.

"What is the meaning of this? I'm a German citizen. You don't have the right—"

"Shut up!" Asim muttered decisively, shoving Fisher.

"This is outrageous! Get the hell out of here before I called the police—"

Asim did not wait for the end of Fischer's tirade, but instead nonchalantly grabbed him by the shoulders and pushed him down. Fischer toppled into the chair with his arms waving ridiculously as he fell. Although its wooden legs desperately creaked, the chair survived the perturbed German's rough landing.

"Get out of my room!" Wide-awake now, Fischer attempted to get up, but Asim immediately threw him back down into the chair.

Asim thrust his face into Fischer's. "Sit down and stay down!" he commanded with quiet intimidation.

Now that he was finally able to see the face of his late-night intruder clearly, Fischer's anger vanished only to be replaced by fear. As soon as he met his intruder's opaque gray eyes, his chest began to swarm with clammy dread. *He will kill me. God, this guy will kill me!* More intuitively than consciously, Fischer obeyed, deciding it was better to follow his visitor's commands than to die in a hotel room. "What do you want?" Fischer asked warily, looking up at the strange, tall man standing over him. "Do you want money? Jewelry?"

Sitting on the edge of the rumpled bed, Asim leaned forward and calmly studied Fischer, who quietly moaned as he backed himself further into his chair.

"I see that you are ready to talk, am I correct?" Asim asked politely a few moments later.

"What? It's two-thirty in the morning! Tell me what the hell you want and get out!" Fischer spoke brusquely; but his heart was racing so hard it was about to burst.

Asim shook his head slowly, his eyes fixated on Fischer's.

"Do you want me to break something?" Asim asked thoughtfully, making a show of slowly considering Fischer's soft body in its disheveled, white T-shirt. "Perhaps your arm or your leg?" he added coldly.

Fischer went silent. Looking up into Asim's cold eyes, he pictured himself lying on the floor with unnaturally twisted arms and legs in a puddle of his own blood that slowly spread out from under his head.

"OK, just tell me why you came," Fischer said meekly in the hopes of getting rid of his terrible visitor with the least amount of bodily harm.

Asim's calm eyes flashed with satisfaction. He was ready to use more drastic measures, but that did not appear to be required at the moment.

"Schulze," Asim pronounced the name carefully while staring intently at Fischer's face. He noticed that Fischer's face immediately became an obstinate mask. Asim added sharply, "Do not deny that you were familiar with him. Schulze stole the holy stele belonging to my tribe." He watched Fisher expectantly.

Fischer remained silent.

"In some countries, like Turkey for example, in ancient times they used to cut off a thief's hand." Asim grinned, as a mental picture of chopping off Fischer's hand came to his mind. *But, Fischer is not a thief – at least not yet. He might be an accomplice though.* His eyes sparkling dangerously, Asim collected himself and continued, "But in my country we punish thieves by death. So I just have one question for you: Where is our stele now?"

Fischer's face tightened instinctively as his brain worked feverishly. *This crazy bastard looks like he knows a lot. But how?* Fischer decided to play the fool. "I don't know anything about this. Schulze is dead. Unfortunately, he died of heart attack, otherwise you could have asked him."

Asim laughed menacingly. "He didn't die of a heart attack. I poisoned him," he announced coldly.

Losing his poise, Fisher blathered rapidly, "Why should I tell you about them? What guarantee do I have that you won't kill me too, even if I tell you?"

Asim's predatory grin caused a chill to run down Fischer's spine. "There is no guarantee."

"But if I tell you then they will kill me!"

"Who are you talking about? Who are they?"

"The antiquities smugglers."

This time the chill ran down Asim's spine. He suddenly remembered hearing about an antiquities smuggling ring on the news a couple of days before. It consisted of four men who had allegedly smuggled a multitude of ancient Egyptian artifacts out of the country over a two-year span. According to Egypt's Minister of Antiquities, this was one of the most significant cases of antiquities smuggling in recent history. Asim recalled that the indictment alleged that a prominent New York collector of Egyptian antiquities had conspired with three antiquities dealers—two in the United States and one in Dubai—to steal sarcophagi, Egyptian boats, limestone figures and thousands of ancient coins. The stolen collection was estimated to be worth on the order of 2.5 million in U.S. dollars. Asim could not recall if had heard about any steles being smuggled on the news. The very thought was Asim's worst nightmare.

"Tell me all that you know, or I will kill you right now!" Asim commanded perilously.

"Günther was going to sell the stele to the smugglers. He told me he needed money to pay off some gambling debts he had back in Germany."

"Did the smugglers get the stele?"

"I don't know," said Fischer quietly. "All I ever did was to accompany Günther on his first meeting with them." Fischer slowly shook his head. "I told him not to get involved in that shady business. I told him those people were dangerous. But he didn't want to listen to me." Fischer shook his head again and sighed. "We met with them late one evening several days ago. Günther was negotiating the price, but I stood aside not wanting to get involved. So, I don't know what they settled on."

"Have you seen the stele? Did he have it with him?"

"Oh no, he didn't have the stele with him. He never did show me the stele either, even though I asked him many times to show it to me. I have no idea where he got it." Fischer paused, thinking. He thought at this moment that it was probably for the best to pretend that he had not seen the stele. That way no one could accuse him of aiding and abating the thief of an ancient artifact.

"Where did you and Schulze met with the smugglers?"

"No, I will not tell you!" *That would be equivalent to putting my head inside the hangman's noose!* His mind and body were engulfed in terror, "They will kill me!"

"That's not my problem. And soon won't be your problem either." All the color drained from Fischer's face as Asim pulled out an Egyptian Helwan 9mm Parabellum pistol and coolly switched off the safety. The 9mm Parabellum was the Egyptian police's standard service pistol. It was a copy of the Italian M1951 Beretta, which was developed shortly after World War II and incorporated a pivoting locking block inspired by the Walther P.38 pistol. The pistol, like the earliest Italian-made guns, had a short slide from which a short section of muzzle protruded. As Asim pointed the pistol at his captive's face, Fischer noticed the pistol's serial number was scratched out.

"Wait!" Fischer cried desperately. "I will tell you, just put away the gun!" While he was afraid of the smuggler's retaliation from revealing their location, the gun in Asim's hands scared him much more. The thought of Schulze being killed by this merciless stranger was already haunting him as he choked on the bile rising in his throat. "We met at their warehouse, in the village of El Alamein. In a small, grey building. It had a sign with a small pyramid that had the all-seeing eye inside it. That's all I know."

Asim stared at him sternly. "You better not be bullshitting me."

"I'm telling the truth, I swear. That was all Schulze. I had nothing to do with it."

"If you have lied to me, I know where to find you," Asim stated flatly as he slowly got up from the bed's edge. Fischer shook his head, feeling like he might survive this ordeal after all. *And to hell with the smugglers, as long as this moron with the icy eyes leaves me alone. Perhaps they will kill each other,* thought Fischer.

As he watched Asim rise from the bed and head for the door, the only desperate, screeching thought in Fischer's mind was *Go away! Go away!* Only when the door clicked shut behind the stranger, did Fischer allow himself to get up from his chair and stagger to the portable fridge as relief started to flood his body. While he poured out the Rumple Minze Schnapps, the bottle intermittently pounded and clinked on the edge of a low-cut glass. *Death itself came after you, Karl-Heinz.* He swore he heard a squeaky voice in his head. *Death itself, Karl-Heinz.*

Gripping the slippery glass, he hissed forcefully "Go back to hell!" He steamily drew it to his trembling lips and drank.

Bang! The door flung open and Asim reappeared in the doorway, his unsheathed crusader sword glinting in the moonlight. "I've got a better idea," he barked, resolutely striding inside. Fischer's stomach lurched. "I don't trust your words," Asim growled menacingly. "You will show me the way." Fischer's heart sank as he shakily set down the Schnapps.

# Chapter 11

El Alamein, Egypt
Tuesday, September 19
4:55 a.m.

Seventy miles later, the taxi arrived at the Porta Marina on El Alamein's outskirts. From there it did not take long to find the old, grey warehouse with the sign depicting a pyramid with the all-seeing eye. Asim instructed his driver to park around the corner and be ready for a swift departure. Fischer lay captive inside the trunk. Asim had gagged him and bound his hands tightly behind his back with a rope that snaked its way around his torso and pinned his arms to his sides.

Giving a nod to the driver, Asim stealthily exited the cab and crept in the shadows toward the warehouse. As he approached the front door, the sign's all-seeing eye stared back at him, prompting him to glance around several times. The old building had large double sash windows on both sides of its front door. Upon closer inspection, Asim realized the door was slightly ajar. He stood there for a moment and listened. Deciding that there was no noise coming from inside, he decided to cautiously push the door open and take a step inside.

Zing! A chain whizzed over Asim's head. Fortunately for him, it was aimed too high. *I should have anticipated that*, Asim scolded himself. Moments later the end of the chain came whistling through the air toward him again. He called upon his warrior training and accelerated his perception of his surroundings. Narrowing his eyes, Asim carefully watched the chain as it approached his face. As he steadied his breathing, time drew itself out as he watched the chain's end coming closer and closer. With lightning reflexes, Asim's hand shot out and grabbed it, the metal links quickly wrapping around his fist. Summoning all of his strength, Asim jerked his fist to himself. Not expecting such a response, a stocky man rolled out from around the corner, following the whiplashed chain. The man dropped the chain and quickly jumped to his feet.

"Who the hell are you?" the chunky, red-haired man demanded.

Holding onto the chain, Asim remained composed, watching the man carefully. He stepped fully inside the building, steadily and resolutely striding toward the man. "I came here for the stele you received from the German, Schulze. Where is it?"

"I don't know what you're talking about." The man huffed in anger.

"Oh?" Asim's eyes gleamed angrily. "Let me explain it to you then!"

Asim launched himself at the stocky man, but he was more nimble than he looked and managed to dodge Asim. Thrown off balance, Asim stumbled forward, knocking an antique-looking ceramic oil lamp off a nearby shelf. Recovering quickly, he managed to catch it just before it crashed to the floor. Steadying the oil lamp on the shelf, Asim appraised the situation; his red-haired opponent was surrounded on both sides by metal shelving filled and piled high with cardboard boxes.

It did not take the stocky man long to realize he was trapped, but this did not prompt him to give up. On the contrary, his face darkened and filled with rage as he looked around for an escape route. Asim calmly pulled his Helwan 9mm Parabellum out and pointed it at the redhead.

"Don't even think about shooting in here!" the man shouted. "Don't you know what's inside these boxes?"

Asim kept his eyes and pistol trained on his opponent.

"Ancient statues and sarcophaguses! If you miss, you will destroy ancient Egyptian heritage!"

"I never miss," Asim replied calmly, keeping his pistol steadily aimed at the man. As the red-haired man had determined correctly, Asim cherished his Egyptian heritage and would take every precaution not to destroy any artifacts. Keeping an eye on the smuggler, Asim cautiously looked around. His eyes jumped from some alabaster statues on a top shelf to a pair of sarcophagi with hieroglyphic writing, unceremoniously leaning against the shelving. Three small animal beds, various chests and even a few thrones adorned the room. On the far right side of the dimly lit room, Asim could make out a golden canopy shrine, various chests and a golden cow's head. The spacious room was eerily silent, as his opponent seemed to hold his breath.

"Where is the stele?" Asim demanded again.

Suddenly grinning, the redhead responded, "Try to find it," as his eyes shifted to something behind him

Instinctively Asim bent sharply to the ground. Seconds later, Asim heard a muffled whistle as a bullet passed where his head had been. The bullet clanged off a metal beam and ricocheted away with a loud clatter.

Spinning around to face his new opponent, Asim saw a tall bald man aiming and preparing to fire again. Asim managed to dive between some cabinets as the new man fired another shot.

"Don't shoot, you idiot!" the redhead shouted at his friend as he fled between the shelves and hid behind some high steel boxes. "Don't let him escape!"

Momentarily distracted by his boss, the tall bald man did not notice as Asim seized his opportunity, carefully taking aim and shooting him in the leg. The bald smuggler fell to the concrete floor, writhing and howling in excruciating pain, "Help! Help me!" he howled. Asim's bullet had inadvertently penetrated his femoral artery, and he was unconscious within seconds.

The redhead bolted out from behind the steel boxes like a raging bull. Producing a short-barreled gun, he aimed it directly at Asim's chest.

They fired simultaneously.

The bullet leaving Asim's pistol tore a chunk out of the redhead's palm but did not prevent the shotgun from spitting out a short burst of its own. Asim felt a burning sensation in the lower right side of his torso. Glancing down, he noticed a bright red spot spreading on his white cloak. Gritting his teeth and ignoring the pain, Asim looked up and fired again. The second shot did the trick as it hit the redhead in the shoulder, forcing the shotgun out of his hand. Asim watched as the redhead slowly collapsed on the floor.

Kicking the abandoned shotgun away, Asim found some rope and quickly tied the injured redhead's wrists together and then dragged him over to his wounded friend. Ignoring the dizziness that attempted to cloud his mind, Asim positioned the redhead next to the bald guy and then bent over to tie him up completely. When the bald guy gave a deep sigh, Asim looked over and realized that the man was sitting in a widening pool of blood. Asim reached down and grabbed his wrist: dead.

The redhead suddenly moaned, summoning his strength in an attempt to get up, "I'll kill you!"

Asim punched him in the face without hesitating. With the heavy blow the smuggler slipped into unconsciousness. Asim carefully stood up and was watching the men carefully when he found himself swaying slightly from side to side. Swinging his cloak open, he determined that the bullet had merely grazed him. Even so, his side was torn up; fresh blood was leaking out with every heartbeat. Trying to staunch the blood flow, Asim used his cloak to press down firmly on the wound while glaring at the unconscious men lying on the floor near him. Staring at the pools of blood surrounding their broken forms, Asim gave a satisfied smirk as he gradually turned to view the warehouse.

The morning sun found him thoroughly searching the warehouse. He had carefully investigated every box and ransacked the little office when he realized something: the stele was not there. Either they had already shipped it out of Egypt or the smugglers had not received the stele after all. He nervously flipped open his RAZR cellphone, *What will I say to the Great Chief?*

"My fearless warrior," the Chief responded softly after receiving the latest news about Asim's ordeal. "You accomplished your mission and I praise you. I will immediately give a call to the Inspector and inform him about this warehouse. As for the stele, I truly believe it's still in Egypt and soon will be ours again. Start making your way back to the tribe."

Back at the waiting cab Asim woke up the driver and opened the airless trunk. Although sluggish, he dragged a bound and frightened Fischer out onto the pavement. With a few precise strokes of his sword, Asim skillfully cut the ropes binding his captive.

Fischer stood quietly, his breath catching in his dry throat, preparing himself for the worst. However, Asim waved him away and turned his back to the German.

Fischer fled.

As he escaped his nightmare, Fischer was filled with the terror of the ordeal and relief that he was still alive. He had no idea of anything but the simple pleasure of being alive.

It was not physical pain that troubled Asim's heart as he leaned heavily on the cab door. Whilst fresh drops of blood slowly trailed down his cloak, it was the thought of his tribe's sacred and beloved stele hidden in the belly of a ship sailing away from the Alexandria's docks that sank his heart.

# Chapter 12

Police Station, Cairo, Egypt
Tuesday, September 19
7:20 a.m.

The police station looked like a shed. Its dirty, mottled windows seemed permeated with misery and depression. Once Michael stepped inside he saw that the interior differed little from the exterior. The small, dimly lit room was sparsely furnished with a couple of chairs and a moth-eaten sofa. A lone, beat up desk, with an old-fashioned black rotary dial telephone, was placed at one end of the room. A dulled nameplate, bearing the name, 'Setkufy Suliman, Police Inspector,' was seemingly the only indication that he was indeed in an actual police station. A tall, heavy-set man with a balding pate sat at the desk.

Peering over his old-fashioned, black-framed glasses, the man curiously studied Michael. "I'm Inspector Suliman," he declared imperiously without rising from his chair. "You are Michael Doyle, correct?"

"Yes," Michael answered uneasily, still on edge about this unexpected meeting that had dragged him out of bed so early in the morning. *I should have contacted the American Embassy. This could go very wrong.* The inspector motioned for Michael sit down on the rickety chair in front of his desk. "That's all right, I will stand. Hopefully this won't take too long."

"Mr. Doyle," the Inspector said quietly. "You can relax now. This is not an interrogation," he flashed a short-lived smile at Michael, attempting to put him at ease. "This is just a friendly talk."

Realizing this meeting was anything but friendly, Michael decided to go with the flow. He nodded quietly and set his chin. *Wow, I don't think I'm going to enjoy this little talk one bit.*

The desk phone rang just then, and Michael found himself with a brief respite, as the Inspector was inclined pick up the receiver and bark imperious orders and instructions. He obviously relished being in charge. Michael glanced around the room. The wobbly ceiling fan was spinning rapidly, but the room was progressively becoming hotter and dustier. Michael was already starting to sweat profusely. The inspector unplugged the phone jack from the receiver and pulled out a notebook from a drawer, slapping it on the desktop. "How long have you known the German engineer Schulze?" the Inspector asked, flashing a not entirely sympathetic smile.

"I don't actually know him at all," Michael replied.

The Inspector folded his hands under his chin and arched his eyebrows questioningly. "What do you mean? You went to the hospital, no?"

Michael nodded awkwardly before answering, "I didn't know Schulze before yesterday. He was having difficulty breathing inside the Great Pyramid. I found him and gave him CPR until the paramedics came."

"I see," said the inspector, unmoved. "What were you doing inside the pyramid?"

Michael's facial expression mirrored his disbelief. *Hello! We're in Egypt! Are you seriously asking me what I was doing inside the pyramid?* However, he restrained himself, "I'm a tourist," Michael explained patiently. "I arrived in Egypt two days ago." He watched as the inspector jotted down notes. "This is my first time in Egypt. I was on a tour to the pyramids. While I was inside, I saw the man suffering from a health problem. I intervened and tried to help. Was that the wrong thing to do?"

"No, no, of course not. Mr. Doyle," the Inspector smiled genuinely. "You acted like a gentleman and did the right thing." He paused and asked, "Did you call the ambulance?"

"No, another tourist did."

"I see," said the inspector, writing something in his notebook. "You went with Schulze to the hospital?"

"No, but I went to see if he was OK later that same day."

"And, what happened at the hospital? Did you get to see Mr. Schulze there?"

"No, by the time I got to the hospital, he was already dead."

The Inspector sighed deeply and wrote something else in his notebook. "Yes, unfortunately he had a weak heart and being in a claustrophobic space such as the Great Pyramid didn't help." As he spoke, the Inspector avoided Michael's eyes, which left him feeling ill at ease. Since he had entered the room, he had felt the constant, cold, penetrating gaze of the Inspector's brown eyes. "Mr. Schulze is accused in the theft of an ancient artifact, and you were the last one who saw him alive."

Michael was startled, "Are you saying that Schulze was a thief?"

"Yes, and we are working hard to establish the safe return of what was stolen."

"What did he steal?"

The Inspector paused, looking at Michael carefully, "A very important ancient artifact: an ancient stele. That is all I can tell you. This is a private matter and we want to keep it that way."

"I understand, Inspector."

"Mr. Doyle," said the Inspector, and Michael felt that penetrating look again. "Did Mr. Schulze say anything or give you anything?"

Ever since his brain had woken up on the way to the police station, Michael had anticipated this very question. As much as Michael was afraid of the question, at the same time, he had been eagerly waiting for it. At that moment he knew that his answer to this very question could change everything. "He only said to 'find four ways,'" Michael answered quietly.

The Inspector's eyes widened as he sat back, his chair creaking and groaning in protest. "Find *four ways?*" the Inspector repeated the phrase with a surprised and puzzled look. "What does that mean?"

"Inspector, your guess is as good as mine."

Inspector Suliman sat up and quickly wrote the phrase in his notebook. After taking a moment to study the phrase, however, the inspector looked as confused as before. "Did he say anything else?"

"No, unfortunately, his condition got worse. After that, the rest of his words came out as gibberish."

"That's too bad," sighed the inspector.

Turning away from Michael, he shouted something in Arabic. Suddenly a young officer donned in a crisp white uniform appeared in the doorway. Inspector Suliman barked some instructions and moments later the officer, tightly clasping the sheet of paper torn from the inspector's notebook, ran out the door.

As soon the door shut behind the departing officer, the Inspector said, "Mr. Doyle. You were a great help. That phrase might help us expedite the safe return of the artifact. Every street and traffic policeman is already on the lookout for the stolen stele."

Michael had no doubt about that. He had seen thousands of police officers in their crisp white uniforms since arriving in Cairo. He had read that Cairo had more police per capita than any other city in the world, and just walking down the streets of Cairo confirmed that statistic. His thoughts wandered slightly. It seemed white was an unfortunate color in a city where pollution, dust and sweat made for a disadvantageous combination.

That combination had clearly gotten the better of Inspector Suliman's uniform as he dabbed his brow with a handkerchief he pulled out of his pants pocket. He pulled a few blank sheets of paper out his notebook and handed them to Michael. "I need you to write down the statement you gave me. Just a tiny formality...you understand?"

Michael took the offered paper and sat down in the chair in front of the Inspector's desk. He took the Inspector's pen and carefully began writing. He could feel the Inspector's cold hard stare on his every word. Everything about Schulze claiming to be poisoned, the business card and notebook were left out as planned. There was definitely foul play involved in this case, and Michael was not about to risk losing the rest of his precious vacation by getting involved in the criminal proceedings of a foreign country.

Once Michael finished, Inspector Suliman took the papers and began transcribing the statement into Arabic, his hand slowly shuffling across the page, leaving behind a trail of stylish script. Once two copies had been written out, as there were no photocopiers in the office, he sat back in his creaking chair, let out a long sigh and admired his handiwork.

"Mr. Doyle, thank you. Here is a copy for you," the Inspector handed Michael one of the papers and got up from his chair.

Michael grasped his Arabic-translated statement and stood up, "Thank you, Inspector. I'll find my own way back."

"Mr. Doyle, I hope you understand the need to keep all of this private."

"Yes, absolutely." Michael nodded as he turned to head for the door.

"We'll be in touch in case we need anything else," added the Inspector. Michael nodded and stepped out of the police station into the bustling streets. *Schulze is a thief? I can't believe that. He looked like a very respectable and considerate person to me.*

Michael wracked his brain in an attempt to come up with a possible explanation. Everything seemed strange: the sudden death of Schulze, his phrase "I was poisoned," the hospital report that he had died from a heart attack and now the weird conversation with Inspector Suliman. Considering all the facts he knew, all Michael could determine at present was that something was really fishy, and it was likely bigger than it had initially seemed.

Back in the small, dusty police station, Inspector Suliman was already on his rotary phone.

"Chief, the American claims to have heard the German say 'find four ways' when they spoke inside the Great Pyramid."

"What does that mean?" asked the guarded voice on the other end.

"I can't come up with an explanation. My men are working on it as we speak."

"Good, good. Hopefully it will lead us to the stele. Did you search Schulze's hotel room yet?"

"Yes. Unfortunately the stele was not found."

"We need to find it as soon as possible." The voice was thick with frustration. "The faith and livelihood depends on it! Keep monitoring the American."

"It's already done," Inspector Suliman paused for a second. "I have a feeling that the American didn't tell us the whole story. I will have my men following his every move."

"Good, good."

"We are also tracing Schulze's activities from the past few days. Hopefully we will turn up another clue."

"This ancient stele was safeguarded for many generations, so we must expedite its safe return. I know Allah will be great to you, and what the foreigner stole will be returned safely," said the voice, sighing deeply. "Inform me of any progress that occurs. Thank you, my friend."

# Chapter 13

Berlin, Germany
Tuesday, September 19
4:20 p.m.

The phone had been stubbornly silent for the past three days. Picking up the phone the German lady listened to the dial tone for a moment before angrily slamming it back onto its base unit. *He should have called*, she thought. The phone squeaked compassionately but refused to jingle its familiar ringtone. She rewarded it with a look of distain, and then shoved it across the desk.

Anna Schulze, age twenty-five, sat inside her Berlin apartment staring at the phone, her big, green, almond-shaped eyes glistening with tears. Anna's beauty laid precisely within her eyes, in the vitality of her manners and in her facial expressions. A person's eyes are the mirrors of their soul. They are the only part of the face that nothing can disguise. You cannot paint over them or even sprinkle them with golden dust: they will always remain windows.

Her basic personality traits were not as easily recognizable. While she came off as cool and kept a low profile with most people, they saw her goodness and sincerity in her eyes. Although she did not have many friends, she was ready to give anything that was required. With her close friends, she was usually cheerful and enjoyed playing practical jokes. It was well known that she never put up with lies and hated hypocrisy the most.

Anna pulled the phone cord out of the jack in the wall and opened up the drawer in her nightstand. She shoved the entire thing, handset, base unit and long cord, inside with a disdainful look. "I don't deserve your silent treatment!"

While Anna was addressing her phone, this poignant speech was in actuality addressed to her new boyfriend, Seth. They had been dating for about a month, and she could not believe he could not find the courage to apologize. All it would take is three simple words: 'I am sorry.'

They met at a party thrown by one of her work colleagues. Seth's Middle Eastern accent and his 19th century Spanish toreador look had definitely cast a magic spell on Anna. She found him staring at her from across the crowded dance floor, and before long he was next to her, asking for a dance. After several whirling dances Anna felt exhilarated and breathless, delighted that his gorgeous eyes followed her every move. When they danced to a slow sweet song, he confessed that when he had caught sight of her, he had been overtaken by a giddying belief that he would spend the rest of his life with her: the most beautiful girl he had ever seen. He said it so beautifully; his eyes so mesmerizing, that Anna had stepped into his spell willingly. He found her a drink and they walked away from the crowd and onto the balcony, the city lights and noises sparkling and echoing around them. They ended up spending the entire night chatting until the morning sun began to peek up in the sky. Prior to meeting Seth, Anna had thought that the idea of love at first sight was a load of rubbish. Yet, as soon as she met Seth, she knew she had to be with him.

Anna opened the nightstand drawer and stared at the mutinous phone. Sighing, she pulled the base unit and phone out of the drawer and gently reconnected its cord back to the wall jack. Otherwise, how was she going to find out whether he had called? She listened tensely for its ring as she walked into the bathroom and turned on the bathtub faucet. The phone remained silent. As the water slowly started filling up the bathtub, Anna thought of her magical time with Seth. It did not make sense that he did not call.

Their first days could have been directly lifted out of a fairytale. He met her with a bouquet of freshly cut red roses every day after work, and they would head for the city park where they would walk, chatting and laughing. It seemed like the fairytale romance would never end, but about a week ago Seth's personality had changed literally overnight. One night she asked him about his Egyptian friends who often lurked in the shadows of their relationship. She found it strange that he would not introduce her to them since they seemed to be a big part of his life.

Anna asked if she could accompany him to one of their meetings, but got a fierce refusal. He told her not to bother as they would be talking in Arabic, and that it did not concern her. He was adamant that she was not to meet his friends, which put Anna ill at ease. Two days ago, Seth had promised to call her the next day and clarify everything. He still had not.

"Ring! Ring! Ring!" The phone, of course, chose the absolute worst possible moment to ring. Anna groaned as she sat up in her in her hot, bubbly bath and contemplated ignoring the mutinous phone. But then she imagined how much she would enjoy cursing out her boyfriend for his tardy ways. At this thought, Anna stood up, wrapped a thick pink flowery towel around her and carefully stepped out of the bathtub. She ran down the short hallway and grabbed the phone. "*Hallo?*"

"Hello, can I please talk to Anna Schulze?" Michael asked politely, glancing at the business card.

"This is Anna," answered a pleasant, female voice with a German accent.

"Yes, hi, you speak English, I presume, right?"

This was definitely not the call she was expecting. "Yes," replied Anna. She scurried back to her bathroom, awkwardly pulling off her towel as she held the phone up to her ear. "May I ask who is calling?"

"Oh, hello! I called your company GRCAnwälte …"

"Yes, GRCAnwälte," interjected Anna "that's my workplace." She flopped back into the hot, bubbly water.

"They told me you were on vacation and gave me your home number. I need to tell you something very important," Michael said, catching his breath. "I want you to sit down and listen to me carefully."

"Yes, please continue."

"I'm not gonna continue until you tell me you are sitting down." Michael paused for a couple of seconds. "Are you sitting down?"

"Yes," said Anna, sitting comfortably in her bubblicious bathtub. "I can assure you I'm sitting down."

She sounded relaxed, so Michael figured this was as good of a time as there could be to continue. "Do you know a man named Günther Schulze?" He asked.

"Yes, of course. He is my father," she responded immediately, a tone of uncertainty creeping into her voice. "Why?"

"Unfortunately, I have bad news about your father."

"Who are you, and how do you know my father?"

"My name is Michael." He cleared his throat. "Michael Doyle. I'm an American on vacation in Egypt. I met your father inside the Great Pyramid yesterday."

"Oh? What do you mean you have bad news?"

Michael spoke gently, "I'm sorry to be the one to tell you this, but he died yesterday."

"What?" Anna nearly shrieked into the receiver. "What are you talking about? It can't be! How did he die? Where? What happened?"

"I don't know exactly how he died. That's what I'm trying to find out. Apparently I was the last one who saw him alive."

Anna sobbed. "Are you sure?" She asked after a short pause.

"Yes, I'm sorry, but I'm quite certain. I performed CPR, but he died in the ambulance. Again, I'm sorry for your loss. He handed me your business card and made me swear to contact you. So I am doing my best to honor his last wish."

"But how is this possible? What did the doctors say?"

"Heart attack. Apparently, they think your father was claustrophobic."

"Claustrophobic?" She screamed at the top of her lungs, causing Michael to wince on the other end of the line. "That's not true at all. He was a healthy man for his age and definitely not claustrophobic. He worked inside the pyramids almost every day. There has got to be some other explanation."

"Well, he told me he was …" Michael paused for a moment and lowered his voice almost to a whisper, "poisoned, but at the time I thought he might have been hallucinating. But later on, it actually made perfect sense."

"Poisoned? What? Why? And by whom?" Anna's shocked voice sounded paper-thin.

"I don't really know, but the Cairo police inspector involved in the case thinks that your father might have acquired some type of ancient artifact."

"What kind of artifact?" Michael could tell that Anna's puzzlement was genuine.

"I don't know. I was under the impression that you knew about it." Michael paused for a couple of seconds to wipe the sweat from his forehead. "Do you know anything about the phrase, 'find four ways'?"

"No. I don't know what you are talking about. Find what four ways?"

"I have no idea. But that was the last comprehensible phrase I heard from your father. He said something about finding four ways."

"Well, we haven't been close for the past couple of years. He left my mother for a younger woman almost my age, and I never forgave him for that. I have barely spoken to him since then. He has tried to reach me on several occasions recently, but I always refuse to talk to him or see him."

Michael did not know what to say, so he fell back on the only thing that he could think of to say, "I'm sorry."

Anna sobbed. "The last time he called me was about a week ago. He said he was on the verge of some great discovery, but I was in a huge hurry to go somewhere so I interrupted him and ended up hanging up on him. You know, I got a package from him today."

"Was there anything in it that mentioned four ways?"

"No, I don't think so." She paused for couple of seconds. "But . . . he did mail four Egyptian souvenirs to me."

"Souvenirs?"

"Well, actually papyruses."

"Really?" Michael uttered as Anna's last phrase captivated his full attention. "Real ancient papyruses?" he asked enthusiastically.

"Of course not, don't be silly! They are imitations of the real ones. Every time he traveled to Egypt, he always brought me back some type of papyrus. That was our thing ever since I was a little girl."

"Are you sure they are imitations?" Michael asked, still intrigued by the possibility.

"Yes, I'm sure. I'm sorry; I don't think I can help you."

"Well, I'm sorry your father died. I believe he was a noble man."

"Thank you."

"In case you need me, I'm staying in Cairo for another week, and you can reach me at the Cairo Downtown Hotel in room number thirty-six."

"Ok. Thank you for calling and letting me know. It was kind of you to do that for a stranger. Bye Michael." She hung up the phone, reached over and set it down on the edge of the sink. She sat very still for a long time, deep in thought, as her bath water slowly cooled off. When she finally dragged herself out of the tub, she caught a glimpse of her face in the mirror and burst into tears again. Her normal, everyday life was shattered.

The doorbell rang, startling her. She clutched her towel and stood quietly, dripping bath water. She simply could not deal with anyone right now. Suddenly she yearned to be home. Running far away from Berlin and its memories sounded good. She thought of her grandmother and her sunny cottage in the country. She wished she were eight years old and curled up by her grandmother's side, her eyes closed as she listened to her grandmother's gentle voice telling her a story.

# Chapter 14

El Alamein – Cairo route, Egypt
Tuesday, September 19
8:15 a.m.

After releasing his prisoner, Asim had the driver return to Cairo via the long route. El Alamein, with all of its pristine beach resorts, was soon far behind them and replaced by shepherds grazing their herds on the street curbs. The innumerous sand dunes, tiny Army outposts and villages chaotically situated alongside the road flew past. On the horizon, dark chestnut-haired camels scampered through scattered palm gardens that surrounded frugal villages made up of trounced huts.

The long drive back to Cairo was not an easy one. As El Alamein was slowly swallowed up by the desert expanses, Asim huddled in the backseat tightly holding his cloak against his bleeding wound. The blood had started soaking through the cloak, and it was not long before Asim realized he was losing too much blood. One hundred and thirty miles was way too long to wait in agony and risk his life from blood loss or infection. His chief needed him, predominantly now, as it truly was the darkest time in the Medjay's long, proud history.

Asim was gazing out the cab's dismally smudged window to keep his mind off the pain when he caught sight of some tents. He recognized them instantly as Bedouin villages. His chief's wise words ran through his mind. "Asim, if you are ever in trouble, make your way to the nearest Bedouin tent. They are nomads like us and will always help you in your darkest hour." Asim decided to test this hospitality. After all, it was likely the only place where he could get help and no one would ask too many questions.

The taxi slowed down for the tiny army outpost. Once the outpost disappeared from view and he saw a narrow paved road ahead, Asim signaled the driver to pull over. Giving him explicit instructions to wait for him, no matter what transpired, Asim gingerly stepped out of the vehicle. He made sure his crusader sword was still slung across his back, pulled his cloak tightly around him and slowly began his journey into the desert, merging into the vast landscape of dunes.

Asim made his way on the narrow, paved road that eventually turned to sand. After trudging through the sand for a while, the path then narrowed down and turned into a hard, little path, bordered by tufted grass that could hardly conceal a single person. The sun stood high overhead, banishing the morning chill. Asim ran his tongue across his parched lips, realizing the blood loss made the heat even more deadly. Fortunately, he did not have that much further to go. As the trail began to climb steeply, rising between the cliffs of chopped red sandstone, Asim could already make out the silhouettes of the Bedouin's tents more clearly now as they spread across the vast horizon. The red sandstone cliffs gradually yielded to a dull-white, weathered limestone. He paused. The silence was so abundant around him that it sounded like some strange, primeval roar.

Peering over the cliff's horizon he spotted the nearest Bedouin tent about 100 meters away. Although his body was becoming heavy with exhaustion, he quickened his pace. He methodically followed the meandering curve of the little path around the base of one of the cliffs. As soon as he reached the side of the cliff, Asim found himself almost nose-to-nose with a Fellah with a dagger raised high above his head. The warrior was wearing a traditional *dishdasha*, an ankle-length blue robe with no collar and wide, free-cut sleeves. His headgear consisted of a *kufiya*, a square cotton scarf, which was held in place with an *igal*, a doubled rope-like cord made of camel wool.

Astonished by the man's presence after his solitary journey, Asim slowly raised his hands in surrender. The Fellah seemed to be studying Asim's attire closely but made no move to speak. A few moments later Asim took the initiative. "*As-salāmu `alaykum*. My name is Asim. I'm a Medjay and have come from the great tribe of the Great Chief Jibade. I've been badly hurt and need help. If you can help me, I will greatly appreciate it, and if not, I will seek help somewhere else."

"Wa 'alaikum salam," the Fellah lowered his dagger. "I am called Zaid Al-Hilali, and I'm Bedouin. We are people of the desert, and our long history with the Medjay goes back hundreds of years. A Medjay is always welcomed in my home. I would not think to turn you away." Together they walked to his dwelling, a traditional Bedouin tent made of goat and camel hair panels stitched together. While the tent felt very hot to the touch on the outside, it remained blissfully cool on the inside. Asim welcomed the cool, dark tent after such a hot, dusty walk in the bright, blazing sun.

Offering Asim a seat on a rug, Zaid barked several phrases toward the female side of the tent. Within seconds, a middle-aged lady, covered from head-to-toe in a black robe appeared. As she peered cautiously at Asim, he stared at the curtain of gold and silver coins that was secured at her hairline and cascaded down her face. Zaid barked another order and the woman quickly ran outside. "To summon a medicine man," explained Zaid.

In the meantime, Asim was offered a delicious glass of *badawi shai*, a special blend of tea prepared over an open fire right outside the tent. As Asim drank it, his host explained that the tea had multiple healing effects from its many herbs, and that it would help him relax and regain his strength.

Asim was already semiconscious by the time the old Bedouin medicine man arrived. He wore a goatskin *kaftan*, a front-buttoned, long sleeved overdress reaching the ankles. Many handkerchiefs and ribbons symbolizing serpents were embroidered on the kaftan. Some ribbons were shaped like a snake's head with an open mouth and eyes. The larger snakes forked their tails, and a trio of snakes had one head. The kaftan also had several iron objects attached to it, including some small bows and arrows, designed to scare the evil spirits. Attached to the back were several copper circles and various animal skins. The collar was decorated with a fringe of flamboyant feathers.

After quickly looking at Asim's bloody cloak, the medicine man wordlessly pulled a few supplies out of his bag. He laid some herbs, scissors, a needle and some thread on a white handkerchief. A candle and matches were brought out, and he proceeded to light the candle. He pulled a bottle out and opened it, pouring a specially prepared liquid solution into a small bowl. After saying a few connotation chants, he placed the thread in the bowl. He picked up the scissors and neatly cut the rip in Asim's cloak larger. He looked at the wound and then gently applied several herbs to it. In a few short seconds, the whole area was numb. Running the needle through the candle's flame several times, he then began to slowly stitch up Asim's torn side. When the job was done, he tied a knot at the end of the thread as tight and close to the last stitch as possible. The Medicine man then chanted a few closing connotations. He blew out the candle and gathered his items into his bag, instructing the Bedouin host to give Asim a specially prepared medicinal drink. He got up, nodded to those watching and quietly left the tent.

Asim woke up a few hours later and glanced down at his wound. There were no blood spots anywhere. Zaid pointed to the cup placed nearby and Asim sipped slowly despite the taste being a bit bitter for him. A thin smile found its way to his lips as he thought of the chemist Nassar. It was, after all, nowhere near the worse thing he had drunk recently. Once he had reached the bottom of the cup, Asim felt an incredible relaxation spread throughout his muscles as well as a burst of energy. Shortly, the stiffness around the wound disappeared. Zaid's family rejoiced and organized a festivity in honor of their healed Medjay visitor.

That evening, Asim sat outside the Bedouin tent, in the middle of the majestic desert, under the endless, starry, Egyptian sky. The crackling fire warmed him as he was nourished with traditional Bedouin dishes: pita bread; *mensaf*, rice with lamb meat; and fresh, delicious, cardamom-spiced coffee. Soon after the food was consumed, musicians started playing *shabbabas*, small lengths of narrow metal pipes fashioned into a flute of sorts, and the *rababa*, a versatile, one-string violin. Zaid's wife and three daughters and some other women from nearby tents sat in rows facing each other and engaged in a sort of sung dialogue that was composed of various mysterious verses. The instruments and voices dramatically intertwined, glided away in the night air and then echoed back in whispers over the open expanse of the desert.

# Chapter 15

Berlin, Germany
Tuesday, September 19
7:00 p.m.

The doorbell rang loudly again, bringing Anna out of her reverie. Mystified, she quickly threw on some clothes as the doorbell sounded again. Anna jerked open the front door. On the threshold stood a pretty young woman of Middle Eastern descent. As an early autumn chill swirled into the apartment, Anna shivered, taking in the unknown woman's appearance. She wore a blue silk dress and elegant dark blue sandals with high heels. On her shoulder hung an expensive white purse covered with lacquered leather. Her dark brown hair fell smoothly and stylishly across her large forehead, resting lightly on her shoulders. Beige sunglasses with tiny, multicolored rhinestones crowned her head. The woman put her hand on her hip, causing the multitude of silver bangle bracelets on her wrist to tinkle and clang. Her big brown eyes stared at Anna, cold and hard.

"Hello, Anna," she hissed in a low voice with a Middle Eastern accent. "I'm Layla, Seth's wife."

*Seth's wife? Did she hear that correctly?* "Excuse me?" Anna stuttered as the floor seemed to wave and sink beneath her. While she hesitated to find the right words, Layla immediately took advantage of the situation. Smirking, she put her foot in the door and pushed Anna aside, boldly entering the apartment.

"Can I please come in?" Layla asked mockingly as she sauntered down the hallway. Glancing from side to side, her heels clicking on the wood floors, the newcomer seemed to be soaking in her surroundings.

"Come . . . Ah...Go straight down the corridor...into the living room," Anna stammered as she rapidly shut and locked the front door, hurrying to catch up to the intruder.

Layla strode into the living room and sat theatrically in the loveseat across from the coffee table. When Anna arrived, Layla was stretching her long, perfectly toned legs out in front of her and crossing them at the ankles. Her dress came to her mid-thigh, its sky blue color underlining the golden tan of her skin. She glanced up at Anna as she pulled her beautiful handbag onto her lap.

Layla expertly reached inside her purse and pulled out a pack of Virginia Slims cigarettes and a tiny gold lighter. "Allow me to smoke," she stated, not even waiting for Anna's permission as she lit up. Strangely enough, Anna recalled Virginia Slims were first introduced in the late 1960s and were marketed to the young, professional women of the time. She caught a whiff of the smoke, but bit back her response. When she recalled their infamous slogan, "You've come a long way, baby," she decided it perfectly suited her unwanted visitor.

Layla's eyes slid tenaciously across the room, studying every detail carefully. Nothing seemed to escape her watchful and curious eyes. First she scanned across the burgundy loveseat she was lounging on and then at the matching queen sleeper sofa opposite her with solid lodge pole wood frames, the faux chenille throw and coordinating pillows. Anna's heart sank as Layla's eyes moved to the wall behind the sofa where three framed Egyptian papyruses, gifts from her father, were hung. After the momentary rush of Seth's wife's appearance, the loss of her father gripped her heart once again. Her losses seemed unbearable: in the past few minutes her father and now Seth, her fairy tale prince, had been abruptly ripped away from her.

Anna did not realize her eyes were closed until she opened them to observe Layla staring at the other side of the room, her eyes flitting between the room's other major accents, including a wall rug, framed artwork and a large, dried flower wreath made by Anna's mother that hung over the large fireplace. She then turned her attention to the round, pine coffee table that stood in the middle of the seating area. A ceiling fan remote; a crystal candy dish, which Anna had gotten on her trip with Seth to Vienna; some newspapers and a distinctive yellow-and-red colored DHL Express envelope cluttered the low table.

Anna could not help feeling like Layla was appraising her threat's worthiness.

Layla released a plume of a fragrant smoke and then laughed, albeit slightly forced. "You probably don't know anything about me. It shows on your face so, please, have a seat." She indicated the burgundy sofa across from her.

Stiff with anxiety, Anna obediently sat on the edge of her own sofa, vaguely realizing that she must be in shock. "Seth specifically told me he was not married," Anna could not wait any longer. "If he were married I would have definitely known about it."

"And, how long *exactly* have you known Seth?"

"About a month," Anna replied sheepishly.

"Exactly! I rest my case," Layla laughed again, searching inside her purse. "I think you will be even more amazed to learn that we had our wedding just two months ago. We spent an unforgettable honeymoon in the French Riviera. If you have any doubts, take a look at our honeymoon pictures." She casually tossed several photographs on the table between them.

"I wonder why Seth never said anything to me," Anna pondered out loud, breaking the awkward silence.

"Apparently, he did not think it was necessary," Layla replied coldly.

"But, if you just got married, then I guess he kept a secret from you that he was seeing me as well?"

"I'm pregnant."

Anna cast a look of disbelief at her visitor.

"Well, you must know … from the beginning, Seth's family was categorically against me. When Seth told them he wanted to marry me, they would not hear of it. But we were in love! So we went ahead and got married. When I found out I was pregnant, Seth thought it would help smooth things over and informed his family. They became enraged and insisted that I have an abortion. Of course, I refused. This has alienated me even more from his family." She paused for a second and took another puff from her cigarette. "But, Seth loves me and that is the only thing that is important to me." Layla paused and moved her fingers across her hair, slowly brushing it out of her eyes and across her forehead. "But lately it is becoming more and more obvious that he is treating me differently than before."

"What do you mean differently?"

"Hard to say. Some strange people were coming in and out of our apartment at ridiculous times. Then Seth started making lame excuses to leave with them, regardless of the time of day. Then I found out about you." She paused and stared at Anna.

Anna sighed, "You know what? Seth was acting weird when he was with me as well."

Layla carelessly extinguished her cigarette butt in the crystal candy dish. Anna frowned, but her uninvited guest did not interpret the signal correctly and obliviously continued, "I guess I'm not the only one that was irritated by his unpleasant behavior."

As Layla went on describing her life with Seth in gory details, Anna desperately tried to make sense of the situation by studying Layla's photographs. *How could he do this to me? I've lost my father and now my boyfriend is suddenly married to a pregnant wife?* She looked closer at the picture in her hand. Something did not add up. *Wait a second! Seth doesn't have an anchor tattoo on his left arm!* Anna picked up another picture and closely examined it. The face was definitely Seth's—there was no doubt about that—but he did not have a tattoo like that. *What is going on?*

"When was this photo taken?" Anna abruptly interrupted her visitor's sob story.

Layla glanced at the photograph with a surprised expression. "This photo?" she asked in a tone of voice that seemed to be a bit calculating.

"Yes, this photo."

"Well, on our honeymoon," mumbled Layla. "Beginning of," she paused and looked up at the ceiling fan rotating slowly overhead. "August. Yes, the third week in August."

*What a liar!* Anna wanted to scream at her exasperating intruder but held herself in check. She knew Seth did not have an anchor tattoo. As a matter of fact, the only tattoo he had was on his shoulder and consisted of the word Peace written in Arabic. She closely examined the photograph one more time. *The photo was photoshopped!* There was no doubt about it. Seth's face was imposed over somebody else's body. Flipping through the other pictures, she realized they all had Seth's face on top of somebody else's body with a similar build. Anna looked carefully at her smoking visitor, suspicion growing inside of her. *Why would she go through all this work to make fake photos of Seth and her together? Could she be an ex-girlfriend trying to get revenge?* Sure, Seth's behavior as of late was a concern to Anna. But what was of far more concern to Anna at the moment was the real reason this stranger had made this unsolicited visit.

"Do you think I'm lying?" Layla asked suddenly, as her beautiful face distorted in anger.

Anna blushed, "Yes, I think so."

"Well, that's your choice. But, food for thought, Seth confessed everything about you to me and even gave me your address. How else do you think I found you?"

Actually, that was a very good question. "And, how exactly did you find out—"

"Excuse me," Layla suddenly interrupted her as she rose from the sofa and pointed to the three papyruses hanging on the wall behind Anna. "Is that a duplicate of the papyrus of Ani found at Thebes?"

Shocked, Anna turned to the wall behind her. "Are you talking about the one in the middle?"

"Yes."

"No, that's a papyrus of Kha found at Deir el Medineh. The original is on display at the museum of Torino." Anna's mind scrambled to fathom what was happening.

"Is that Osiris sitting on the throne?" Layla asked.

She was surprised Layla knew so much about ancient Egyptian life. She certainly did not know where this intruder was leading with this sudden interest in her papyruses, but Anna decided to go along with it, hoping it might shed some light on the situation. She smiled wistfully as she gazed at them, remembering how her father would always tell her the captivating and intriguing stories behind each work of art. These were treasured memories, so Anna definitely remembered the stories behind each papyrus very well.

"This papyrus depicts the deceased Kha and his wife kneeling before Osiris, the great God of the Dead, who is seated under his canopy in the Afterworld." Anna replied as she turned back to face her visitor.

Layla was studying her nail polish and seemed absolutely uninterested in the story, but Anna continued anyway. At that moment, talking about her papyruses brought a small measure of joy into her heavy heart. She felt like she could tell their stories all night. "The tomb of the architect Kha and his wife was discovered intact in 1906 at a place called Deir-el-Medineh," stated Anna, proudly glancing at her visitor.

Layla offered no praise, instead remaining as cryptic as ever. "I ask you only one thing. Call me when you are sure that I speak the truth. What I want to tell you is very important for the both of us."

"OK, then tell me now." Anna's frown deepened to furrow her brow. "If you want honesty, then stop trying to show me photoshopped pictures of Seth! Do you really know Seth or did you just get his picture off Facebook? And, yes, please tell me the real reason you came to see me. Who are you? Honesty begets trust: not these games."

"First, I must be confident in you. Everything is serious, very serious." Layla repeated mysteriously while looking fixedly into Anna's eyes. "Very serious and extremely dangerous. You don't even have a clue what you have gotten yourself into."

Exasperated, Anna snapped, "Then tell me, and stop playing cat-and-mouse games!"

"I will," Layla paused dramatically. "When the right time comes. And now is not that time." She paused again, "Not yet." She laughed mischievously.

Layla's gaze and intonation gave Anna goose bumps. Suddenly, her enigmatic visitor stood up, turned and briskly walked to the door. Reaching for the doorknob, she hesitated momentarily to catch Anna's eye before offering her parting statement, "We will meet again."

As her intruder briskly descended the stairs, Anna locked the door and walked back to the living room in complete bewilderment as an uneasy feeling welled up within her. She grabbed the fan remote from her coffee table. After only two cigarettes, the room held a smoky aroma and she wanted to turn the fan up. Suddenly, she realized that her father's DHL envelope was no longer on the coffee table. Finding that odd, she bent over to look under the table as it might have been blown off by the ceiling fan. The envelope was not there. That did not make any sense. Puzzled, Anna thoroughly searched the entire living room in vain. Only her father's DHL envelope was missing.

*That's bizarre,* Anna thought. *Why would she take my father's envelope?*

# Chapter 16

El Alamein – Cairo route, Egypt
Wednesday, September 20
6:35 a.m.

As the early dawn painted the desert in light reds and oranges, Asim warmly thanked the Bedouin family for their generous shelter and care. Feeling strong and refreshed, he walked briskly back to his taxi. He smiled down at the basket he was carrying. His new Bedouin friends had filled it with various fruits for his trip. The Bedouin truly were a noble tribe.

Thankfully, his cab was still parked in the same spot where he had left it the previous day. He opened the door, quickly situated himself in the back seat and instructed the sleepy driver to continue to Cairo. When Asim's phone rang, he looked at the phone number and realized instantly it was his chief. Asim's heart sank with worry. However, his chief's soothing words made him realize that he would remain on the stele's trail. Chief Jibade's friend, the Inspector, had used the information Asim had provided about the smugglers' warehouse to not only successfully seize the pillaged artifacts, but also apprehend the ringleader.

"Inspector Suliman takes his job very seriously," said the Chief. "The ringleader confessed that he had not received the stele from Schulze."

Asim was relieved. This meant that the sacred stele was still most likely in the country.

"Of course, in order to find the truth," the Chief chuckled, "the inspector would have employed all manner of extreme measures."

Asim himself had implemented some extreme interrogation measures before. One event, in particular, came to mind. Asim had assisted the Chief with the questioning of a thief who had stolen from the Medjay tribe. Based on the advice from this same police inspector, his Chief had decided to implement both the electric shock and waterboarding techniques. The waterboarding method had proven to be extremely enlightening. Once the use of electric shock was implemented as well, the thief had quickly confessed. *We should've used one or both of those techniques on Schulze*, Asim mused.

The chief continued, "So, this is good news. It means the stele is still in Egypt."

Asim sighed in relief, glad that the chief thought so as well.

"Also, Inspector Suliman discovered Schulze did mail a DHS package to his daughter in Germany. Obviously, he didn't mail the stele, but the Inspector thinks Schulze may have put some indication as to where to find it inside that package."

"How can we get that package?" questioned Asim, uncertainty creeping into his voice. "It is probably in Germany by now."

"Don't worry, my fearless warrior," the Chief answered calmly. "We already have our operative in Berlin working on that."

"That's great news!"

"Now, once you get back you will receive all the necessary instructions and your passport. You are booked on the first evening flight to Germany."

"But, Chief?" asked Asim, "I don't even have a surname."

The Chief burst out in a long laugh. "Well, my brave warrior, how about the name Jabari? In the mighty language of our ancestors it means 'brave warrior.'"

Oh Great Chief, I do like that name."

"Dear Asim, from now on, you will be called Asim Jabari, the brave protector!"

"The brave protector," repeated Asim proudly before hanging up the phone.

The remainder of the journey to Cairo was tedious, but Asim did not mind. He smiled to himself as he considered the great compliment his chief had bestowed upon him.

* * *

Asim stared at the plane impatiently as he waited at his gate at the Cairo International Airport. Once he had picked up his passport and tickets from his chief's contact, he had raced to the airport. However, his flight had been delayed due to mechanical difficulties. He glared at his reflection in the terminal window. *I look ridiculous*, he grumbled to himself. The brown hoody sweatshirt that his chief had picked out for him was pulled over his tribe's signature white cloak. He was not going to doubt his chief, but he was still uncertain.

"You will blend in easily," his chief had reassured him.

"But, Chief—"

"Do not argue Asim. We want to make sure nobody recognizes you there."

After an hour of delay, Asim boarded EgyptAir Flight 2573 traveling from Cairo to Berlin. As he buckled himself into his seat on the weird flying contraption, he reminisced about his crusader sword which was normally always behind his back. He had been forced to leave it behind in the chief's tent.

Asim looked out of the window as the plane made a smooth take off, slowly gaining in altitude. He glanced down at the receding ground before briskly pulling down the window shade. It was his first time on board an airplane and even though he would not personally admit it, flying truly unnerved him.

# Chapter 17

Berlin, Germany
Wednesday, September 20
7:30 a.m.

Anna was sleeping deeply when her telephone finally started ringing. Jarred awake, she answered it, her voice sleep-husky, "Hello?"

"Anna, I hope I did not wake you up," Seth's voice filled her ear with what seemed like mock concern.

She glared at her alarm clock, "No." Taking a deep breath, she allowed a bit of anger to creep into her voice, "Seth, do you know who came to visit me? How dare you even call me?"

"Dear Anna," Seth's voice was soft and apologetic. "I know about Layla's visit."

Anna snapped, "Oh really, so you just *forgot* to mention that you were married?"

"Anna, listen to me. I'm not married. Layla is *crazy.*"

"Oh, really?"

Seth spoke rapidly, "Yes, she made all that up because she's trying to break us up."

"Why would she want to do something like that?"

"Layla was my fiancé, but I caught her cheating on me. She's been trying to win me back ever since."

"That's the truth?" Anna felt hopeful despite herself.

"Yes. But, trust me, it's never going to happen."

"Suppose I want to believe you," Anna started tearing up. "But it doesn't explain why you didn't call me for four days."

"Our relationship is important to me. Can you meet me for lunch today?"

"You'll explain everything?"

"Of course!" Seth exclaimed. "Trust me, Anna."

Irritated, Anna relented, "Okay. But this had better be good."

"Of course." Seth replied calmly. "Do you remember where we had our first meal together?"

Despite herself, a faint smile came to her lips. Anna could hardly forget that cozy Turkish restaurant with its delicious, exotic food. "You mean *Defne*?"

"I was afraid you had forgotten," Seth joked.

Anna shook her head. How would it be possible to forget that cozy place? She felt herself melting. "OK, Seth, but I have plans for today. Maybe tomorrow?"

"Anna, I want to clear everything up between us today. I can't leave us like this for another moment."

Anna remained quiet, thinking.

"Please?"

"All right," she said, giving in, "What time do you want to meet?"

"How about noon?"

"Alright."

"Excellent, I already made a reservation," interjected Seth.

This took her by surprise. "Wow. Ah … how did you know I would say yes?"

"Pure male intuition," he replied playfully.

"Sure. I'll see you at noon." Anna hung up the phone and allowed herself to daydream. She was looking forward to his hopefully romantic apology. Yet, she had a nagging suspicion that refused to go away.

Anna leisurely showered and then took her time fixing her hair and choosing her outfit. She carefully applied her makeup and tidied up her vanity. Darting down her steps to the street, Anna felt sharp in her trendy trouser suit and her new matching boots.

The rain's mist seemed to hang in the chilly air, but the freshness invigorated her. Anna was in an excellent mood as the gusting winds swished her perfectly curled hair. Settling into her white Audi, she patted her hair back into place and started the car. It was getting close to the lunch rush hour and combined with the foul weather, it took almost an hour to arrive at her romantic destination.

\* \* \*

On her way home from *Defne*'s the rain began to furiously pelt her windshield. She took a few cleansing breaths and concentrated on driving well. As she drove, her confusion and frustration began to bubble into justified anger. When she was almost home, her cell phone rang inside her purse. Fumbling to get it out, she glanced down at the screen while attempting to keep her Audi on the stormy road. Seth. Anna let out a puff of anger and growled in frustration as she turned on the phone.

"Anna!" Seth's voice squealed through the speaker, "Where are you? I've been waiting for the past 30 minutes."

Anna let his lie hang in the air for a few moments. "You know Seth, I'm not gonna play this sick game with you," she snapped. "I'm almost home, and I'm done." Then she added sarcastically, "By the way, thanks a lot for the wonderful lunch."

"Let me explain—"

"Don't," Anna cut him off immediately, "I'd really like to know how you made reservations at a closed restaurant. That must be quite the feat." She paused to catch her breath before snapping, "I don't want to see you anymore, Seth. I'm sorry, but you're an ass." She ended the call and held her cell phone tightly. Her jaw was clenched; she just wanted to get home. A second later, her phone rang again. She held up the phone and looked at the screen before turning it on, "And, don't call me again," she screamed as she cut their connection and hurled the phone somewhere in her car.

As she pulled into her parking lot, tears were quietly pouring out of her eyes. Something was really wrong. She parked her car, pausing to think. Not only had she lost her boyfriend, but she also doubted he had ever been her friend at all. Even worse, she was scared that she was caught up in something really dangerous. *I miss my Dad so much. My life doesn't make any sense.* Her car was starting to cool down, so she found her phone and gathered up her tissues and purse. She was shaking. And hungry.

Taking the stairs two at a time, Anna unlocked her door and then bolted it behind her. As she walked inside, she felt something in the air. When she entered her bedroom, she nearly jumped when she saw her spilled makeup bag lying on the floor. She walked to the window and cautiously looked out. After firmly shutting the drapes, she frantically searched her room for any other disturbances before a slip of paper caught her eye. Clutching it in her hand, she desperately started dialing the international operator. She got connected to the Cairo Downtown Hotel in Egypt and asked for Michael Doyle's room. After several rings, his answering machine picked up.

"Michael, it's Anna Schulze. I don't know where else to turn and I really need to speak to you." She swallowed hard and tried to slow down her speech. "Please call me back. Weird things keep happening to me." Panic and fear were escaping her firm hold on them. She could not breathe. "I know somebody was inside my apartment just now ..."

"Hello, hello, Anna," Michael bellowed, trying to talk over the answering machine recording. "I'm here, don't hang up!"

"Michael, thank God you're there. I'm so scared." She let out a shaky breath.

"OK, hold on. I just walked into my room. What happened?"

"I think I'm starting to lose my mind," sobbed Anna. She could no longer hold back the tears.

"OK, tell me exactly what happened," Michael tried to sound as reassuring as possible.

"Yesterday, this lady barged into my home with ridiculous claims and then my father's DHL envelope went missing right out of my living room. Then, today I got manipulated into leaving my apartment and ran into that same strange lady. And now I think someone broke into my apartment when I was out."

"Did you call the police?"

"No, nothing's missing. I've already checked, but I know somebody was here because things were moved. I'm scared Michael," Anna's voice was starting to border on hysterical.

"Anna, please just calm down. Is it possible you are just imagining it?"

"Michael, I've got a feeling deep in my gut that somebody's after the package my father sent me. And if someone poisoned him," Anna's head started to pound painfully, "I could be in real danger."

"But, I thought you said it was missing already?"

"Yes, she took the envelope but not the contents of the envelope. I took extra precautions and the contents are safe," she paused. "Really safe." She took a deep breath, trying to calm herself down.

"Wow, that's really smart," Michael said proudly. "You know what," he paused, thinking. *I must be crazy.* "Let me see if I can still get tickets for today's afternoon flight to Germany. Together we can work out what would be the best course of action to keep you safe."

"Really, Michael?" Anna was shocked that he would even consider coming to help her.

"Yes," he said firmly. This definitely sounded like an adventure. He reasoned that if somebody was trying to steal her father's package, then it must have had some valuable information in it. *I'd never forgive myself if something happened to her because I did nothing.* Army's famous motto, *Leave no man behind*, was on his mind.

"Anna, do you have any friends in Berlin?"

"Yes," she answered, obviously confused.

"I mean the kind of friend that you could go and stay with for a couple of days?"

"Oh, I see, yes, of course," she said as a bit of strength crept back into her voice.

"Ok, I'll book the earliest flight I can get and let you know when I will arrive. In the meantime, just get out of your apartment. Don't return until I get there."

"Yes, Michael, thank you so much for helping me." She was started to feel better. "I will meet you at the airport. I can't begin to explain how much this means to me."

Anna hung up the phone and pulled out her travel bag. As she began packing, she called a friend from college.

"Irma, hi. How are you? It's me, Anna. Hey, would you mind if I spent a couple of days with you?" she asked, trying to neatly toss her things into the bag.

She peeked out the window as Irma sympathized, "Did you break up with your boyfriend again?"

"Please? I will explain it to you when I get there. Just say yes."

Irma laughed, "Sure, I'll get some rocky road ice cream, and we'll have you sorted out in no time."

"Rocky road sounds like an excellent idea," a smile slowly spread across Anna's face. After she ended the phone call, she quickly opened her door and locked it. She ran down the stairs, trying to look at her surroundings discreetly. She knew she would not feel safe until she got into her car and locked it. Still shaking, she unlocked it, heaved her things into the passenger seat and jumped inside. She could not lock her doors fast enough, but she managed to do it and start the engine as well. She edged into traffic, still looking to see if anyone was following her. Then she forced herself to think of the chocolate, nut and marshmallow ice cream in store for her. As she loved history, it soothed her to recall that rocky road had its origins in 1853 Australia, as a dessert to represent the brave gold miners there.

# Chapter 18

Tegel International Airport, Berlin, Germany
Wednesday, September 20
10:55 p.m.

Lufthansa flight 2311 made a graceful touchdown at Tegel, Berlin's international airport. Located in the northern borough of Reinickendorf, the airport is only five miles northwest of Berlin's city center. Michael Doyle exited the plane and followed the signs, written in both German and English, to customs. He was pleasantly surprised at the short walking distance; about 100 feet from the aircraft to the terminal exit, and marveled at the architectural feat.

Forty-five minutes later, after passing through an efficient customs passport control booth and claiming his luggage, Michael was skillfully navigating his rolling camouflage duffle bag along the airport's pathways.

Following Anna's exact instructions, he stopped at the Schnell-Imbiss, a local snack bar. It was not hard to miss, as it was a repurposed, colorful railway car that he recognized by its kitschy vintage sign reading "Die EsS-Bahn." He understood "EsS-Bahn" to be a German pun on S-Bahn and "essen", the verb 'to eat.' Michael ordered a cup of hot chocolate. As he stood a few feet away and slowly sipped it, the whole situation began to sink into his mind as one of absurdness. *What am I doing in Germany? Why did I get involved in this? I don't even know this Anna.* Michael sighed as he finished his drink. He was supposed to be enjoying his hard-earned vacation in sunny Egypt. Furthermore, he was supposed to be exploring the pyramids, his childhood dream. Yet, even a continent away, he could close his eyes and be transported to the Grand Gallery. He could hear Schulze's trembling, fragile voice echoing through his mind over and over again: "I was poisoned! I was poisoned!" A mystery shrouded the truth. It dawned on Michael that it was the mystery itself that was steering his course. After spending the last few minutes of the man's life trying to help him, he believed he owed it to Schulze to determine what had happened to him. After his experience with the Cairo police and the Inspector, he doubted the Cairo police were interested in determining the truth. He knew he would not be able to let it go until he solved the riddle. He supposed it would make one heck of a story when he got back home. Besides, he smiled to himself, he felt like a spy on a covert mission.

*What really happened there? Was Schulze really poisoned or was it just a figment of his imagination? Was he really a thief or just being framed? Even if he were a thief, he hardly deserved to die from it.* Michael shivered slightly as he recalled his unpleasant conversation, more like an interrogation, with Inspector Suliman. He was becoming more and more aware that something else, something much bigger, was at stake here. Now that he was aware of Schulze's package to his daughter, he believed that its contents contained an important piece of the puzzle.

"Hello," a pleasant female voice with a German accent swiftly broke Michael out of his contemplations. "Michael, I presume, correct?"

Twisting his head in the direction of the friendly voice, Michael took in the slim, attractive and stylishly dressed brunette woman in her early twenties. Anna's long hair framed her large, beautiful green eyes. Her outfit consisted of a low cut, ruby-red argyle sweater that reached her mid-thigh and was worn over a button down light pink Oxford dress shirt. Combined with trendy light gray argyle leggings and a pair of dark brown classic Australian Uggs, her fresh look and slightly defiant composure reminded Michael of a prep school student. The light-pink *Chloé* leather drawstring purse, which neatly hung on her right shoulder, told Michael that she must be reasonably well off and fashion conscientious. He thought her most memorable feature was by far her dazzling smile.

"Yes, I'm Michael," he smiled. "And you must be Anna, right?"

"Yes, I'm Anna Schulze," she said firmly, nodding her head.

"Great, nice to finally meet you," he said, extending his right hand to her.

"OK, Michael," she stepped closer, closing the distance between them to a mere foot. The expected handshake did not follow. "How do I even know that you saw my father?"

Michael reached inside his leather jacket pocket, as Anna's bright green eyes cautiously followed his every move. He pulled out the business card Schulze had given him and displayed it. Anna eyes brightened as she plucked the card from his fingers. "Is this what I think it is?"

Michael just shrugged, watching her examine the card.

Anna stared in awe at her own business card before flipping it over. There was her message to her father: *To my lovely Dad*. She had given her dad that card three years before on a sunny, summer afternoon when she had first gotten her job as a legal secretary. It was one of the last positive memories she had of her father before their relationship had become strained. She looked up at Michael happily, every doubt in her mind erased.

"I'm sorry Michael," she said quietly, brushing her bangs out of her face. "I've been under so much stress the last few days. So much has happened, and I don't know what's going on." She took a deep breath before continuing slowly. "I used to live in a world that made sense, but now ..." she raised both hands up to her face and then dropped them in despair.

Not sure what to say, Michael remained silent. Anna continued, "Ever since you called me with the terrible news about my father, strange things have started happening to me. My boyfriend started acting weird. Things have started disappearing in my apartment. It feels as if I've been trapped in some kind of endless twilight zone." Visibly shaking, she walked over and sat down on a nearby bench. Michael followed suit, rolling his duffel bag behind him. He sat down, resting his hand on her shoulder in a comforting manner.

"I'm sorry about what happened to your father, but trust me when I say this," he looked gently into her eyes, "the circumstances surrounding his death are not right." Michael paused, watching Anna. "I don't know what exactly, be it the will of destiny or God's hand, but something connected me to your father at the moment he needed help the most. Anna," he paused, taking her hand, "I did everything in my power to save him, but I couldn't bring him back to life. An injustice has been done to your father. I don't know how I'm certain of this, but ..." he said, dropping his gaze, "I just know it."

"I don't know what to do." Anna leaned back against the bench, shaking her head in frustration.

"I believe your father's last words about being poisoned. And I have more bad news," Michael paused. "The Egyptian police are accusing him of stealing an important artifact." Anna gasped, staring at him. "I personally don't believe he is a thief. I firmly believe that a person should be presumed innocent until proven guilty."

Anna nodded her head slightly as tumultuous expressions played their way across her face. He squeezed her hand, "We will solve this puzzle together, and I promise I won't let anything happen to you." Anna's face brightened, prompting him to add, "As one wise man said, 'a trouble shared is a trouble halved.'"

"Thank you, Michael, for coming to Germany," Anna replied, a spark of hope shimmering in her eyes. "You seem like a really nice guy, and it comforts me that you were the one that was there during my father's final moments."

Suddenly, Michael's eyes caught a glimpse of a bizarrely dressed man. Standing about a hundred feet behind them, he seemed to be watching them intently. The peculiar man made Michael feel both apprehensive and curious at the same time.

When Michael released her hand, Anna noticed an apprehensive look cross his face. She asked curiously, "Michael, are you all right?"

"Shhhh."

"What's wrong?" She hissed sharply, turning her head to mirror the direction Michael's eyes were looking.

"Don't look back!" he whispered emphatically. "It could be dangerous!"

She spun back to face Michael, "What is going on? Don't keep me in the dark!"

Michael's eyebrows furrowed. "I don't exactly know yet, but that man standing next to the escalator seems really familiar to me. I have a gut feeling that he is bad news."

"Can I take another look? Maybe I've seen him before," her curiosity was gnawing away at her self-control.

"Yes, but make it look natural, so he doesn't get suspicious. He is about a hundred feet behind you and slightly to my left."

"But there are dozens of people in the terminal."

"He has a dark complexion and a thick, black, bushy Afro hairstyle. He's wearing a brown sweatshirt with a hood. You can't miss him!"

"And, what's so special about him? For your information guys often stare at me."

Michael gave her an expression of disbelief, biting his tongue.

"What? It's true!" snapped Anna as if reading his mind.

In an attempt to get her refocused, Michael decided to appease her. "Anna, I have no doubt that many guys find you very attractive, but ..."

"So, do you find me pretty?" She looked at him innocently.

Cornered, Michael had no choice but to respond, "Yes, I do."

Anna's eyes sparkled mischievously.

"I have no doubt guys admire your beauty," Michael said seriously. "But, please, now is not the time for this." She gave him a quick flirty smile, but he continued without hesitation. "You see, I'm pretty sure I saw him back in Egypt inside the Great Pyramid, when your father died."

Anna froze. She took a deep breath and asked, "Are you sure?"

"Very sure. He almost knocked me to ground in his big hurry to get out of the pyramid. And I'll never forget those ice cold eyes or his distinctive appearance ... especially that hairstyle," Michael's confidence was draining from his voice. "There's no way his presence here is a coincidence." Anna started to turn back to look at the stranger, but Michael stopped her by impulsively reaching out and brushing his hand through her hair. "Not like that," he scolded in a whisper, looking directly into her eyes. "More discreetly. Do you have a mirror?" he asked, looking pointedly at her purse.

She paused, "I've got a better idea," she said, looking rather pleased with herself. Reaching into her purse, Anna pulled out a compact and a tube of lipstick. She flipped open the compact and pulled the top off the lipstick, slowly applying it to her lips. After replacing the top on the lipstick tube, she dropped it. "Oops! My goodness! Butterfingers," Anna announced loudly as the lipstick bounced against the bench before dropping to the floor and ricocheting underneath. Smiling, she slid down onto her knees and crawled beneath the bench until her upper body was concealed from view. Michael watched the whole enactment in awe. "OK, now tell me where the guy is," she ordered from under the bench.

"He's standing next to the escalator. He's tall—do you see him? He has a big bushy Afro."

"I see him! I see him!" She exclaimed in an excited whisper several seconds later. She fixed her eyes firmly on the stranger; he could be her father's killer.

"Okay now … remain calm, please," Michael whispered as Anna emerged from under the bench. "I don't think this guy is in Germany on a sightseeing tour. Perhaps, he is spying on me," he paused. "Looks like the Cairo Inspector that brought me in for questioning didn't believe my story. Maybe he still thinks that I'm involved in the disappearance of the Egyptian artifact. Hmm … so maybe he sent one of his people to spy on me," he paused, considering the possibilities. "Actually, he might be spying on both of us." Michael paused, thinking. "You did say that somebody broke into your apartment," he added a moment later.

Anna looked up from putting away her compact and lipstick in her purse. Her brows furrowed as she gave Michael a worried look.

"Don't be surprised if they know about the package your father sent you," he said, reading her expression. "With their resources we better assume anything is possible. Whatever artifact is involved, it must be very important to some very powerful people."

Exasperated, Anna sighed. "So, basically, expect the unexpected, right?"

"Yes." Michael nodded solemnly.

"Well, why don't we just summon the police and have them arrest the guy?" She asked. "After all he killed my father."

"We don't have any proof of that," he argued quietly. "The Cairo police's official investigation concluded that your father died from a heart attack. So, without further proof, we unfortunately only have speculation with nothing to back it up."

"So, what are we going to do?" Anna asked, visibly confused.

"First things first. Let's try to leave the airport undetected and lose this guy somehow. We certainly don't want him to follow us. He may have accomplices here in Germany that could be armed. So, I think our best option at this point is to run."

"Agreed."

"Good, then how are we leaving the airport? Taxi, bus, subway?"

"I have my Lady parked outside the terminal," Anna said with a smirk that put a sparkle back into her vivid green eyes.

"Lady?" Michael raised an eyebrow. "Is there anybody else here with you?"

"Don't worry," a smile slipped across her face. "That's just what I call my Audi."

"OK, you could've just said that," Michael said, chuckling and rolling his eyes.

# Chapter 19

Tegel International Airport, Berlin, Germany
Thursday, September 21
12:05 a.m.

G rabbing his duffel bag, Michael stood up from the bench and walked briskly to the exit with Anna trying to keep up. As soon as the terminal's double-sliding door hissed opened, both rushed discreetly out of the building and into Berlin's chilly night air. Michael increased their tempo with Anna remaining closely behind him. Swiftly peeking back over his shoulder, Michael spotted the Egyptian spy jogging in their direction.

"Come on, he's following us!" Michael practically barked, "Where's your car?"

Anna found herself panicking slightly in reaction to his demeanor as well as to the danger. She fumbled around in her purse as she tried to keep walking quickly. "Hold on. I'm looking for my keys." Yanking the keys out, she started pressing the remote's button, frantically pointing it in every direction. Anxiety welled up into her throat, "It's got to be somewhere around here!"

Meanwhile, the tribesman was through the double-sliding doors and quickly gaining on them. Soon he would be close enough to grasp Anna's stylish argyle sweater. Hoping the tribesman was alone, Michael mentally prepared himself for a fight.

A shrill alarm pierced the silence of the parking garage. "There she is!" Anna shrieked. Pointing to a white, two-seater Audi R8, Anna sprinted forward. Given the circumstances, the Audi's remote starter proved handy.

They had barely thrown themselves inside the vehicle before Anna breathlessly floored the gas pedal. Fortunately there were no vehicles in front of them; otherwise, the sporty little Audi with its 4.2 liter V8 engine that goes from 0 to 60 mph in just 3.2 seconds would have had a violent collision. As it was, Michael's door was still ajar. His right hand frantically gripped the dashboard while his left hand clutched his rolling duffle bag, still halfway outside the car door. Anna gunned her Lady and as they tore past the building at 50 mph, Michael finally managed to wrestle his bag inside and shut the door. He spun around in his seat to peer out the back window and caught sight of the tribesman throwing his hands up in desperate rage.

"We lost him!" Michael exclaimed satisfactorily as he buckled himself in.

"That's great!"

"Hopefully he stays lost."

"So, what are we going to do now?" asked Anna as they blew through the deserted traffic light at the airport's exit.

"Well … I guess you should probably drop me off at my hotel. It's pretty late," Michael glanced at his watch, "tomorrow we can come up with a plan."

Anna nodded. "Did you reserve the one I recommended to you?"

"Yes, I believe the name of it was Amadeus, as in Wolfgang Amadeus Mozart, I presume," Michael said, mesmerized by the glittering storefronts passing by his window.

"Yes, that's exactly right," she grinned, "named after an incredible composer of the Classical era. It also has the notable benefit of being just a ten minute drive from my friend's apartment."

Soon the lighted storefronts yielded to dull and bleak scenery as they made their way across the countryside. A blistering wind appeared out of nowhere and tossed a drizzling of rain violently against the windshield. As they drove further into the night, Anna let herself be transported back to a rainy morning three years before, when her father's car had gotten stuck in the woods on a long-awaited fishing trip. He typically worked long hours and was often away from home, so Anna had relished their time together. They had been happy on the trip, despite the car troubles, and at the time it had seemed like nothing could darken her cherished moments with her father. How naïve she had been.

That night her life had changed. He confessed that he was having an affair and leaving her mom. As she sat in her father's car, Anna looked straight ahead, attempting to hold back her tears. She willed everything to disappear, to become oblivious to her surroundings and especially to her father so she could bear to absorb his words. She calmed and cocooned herself in her mind, alone in the dark and under the cold raindrops so no one would be able to hurt her. Since that night some invisible force pulled her away from people, and it was impossible to resist: until she met Seth. She did her best to erase her father from her life as if he had physically died. He had been dead to her for the past three years; at least that was what she thought she had convinced herself. But when the news about his actual death broke into her protective fantasy, Anna had felt the pain of losing him all over again.

"You became unusually quiet," Michael remarked, bringing her back to the present.

"The truth of the matter is that my father died for me three years ago. He cheated on my mom and left us for another woman. We really hadn't spoken since then. He tried, but I didn't want it. He betrayed us by breaking apart our family. I could never forgive him for that."

Anna pulled over into the Amadeus Hotel parking lot. She slid into a parking space and put the engine into park. The September night was chilly, and the heater kept the car comfortable.

"Well, some men have mid-life crises," said Michael, weakly attempting to soothe her, now that her father was actually dead.

"Don't give me that mid-life crisis bullshit," she snapped. Looking down at her beautifully manicured hands holding onto the steering wheel, she sternly added, "Nothing will ever justify his actions."

"I'm sorry," Michael said quietly, slightly embarrassed.

"What was done ... was done. But," she said, calming the tremble from her voice, "five days ago, my father called me from Egypt and said he was on the edge of some great discovery. Strangely enough, he claimed he was being persecuted by some mysterious tribe."

"Did you just say tribe?"

"Yes, that's what he told me. And at the time I told him that he was probably having hallucinations after working so long in the desert, and then I hung up on him."

Michael became quiet.

"So, what do you think?" Anna asked thoughtfully.

"You know, when I first saw the man that chased us, he was inside the Great Pyramid. He pushed right past me and the first thing that came to my mind was 'tribesman.'" He looked at Anna's eyes to gauge her reaction. "Let me pose this to you: what was your first impression of that man?"

"You aren't suggesting that he's a wild tribesman from Egypt, are you?" She stared at Michael. "He did have peculiar hair, but that's about it."

"He didn't look as much like a tribesman to you because you didn't see him in all his glory!"

"What do you mean by that?"

"Back in Egypt he wears a long, white cotton cloak and carries a crusader-type sword slung across his back."

Anna arched her brows and pursed her lips.

"That's exactly what he looked like inside the Great Pyramid."

"Wow," she exhaled deeply. "Then, what's the name of his tribe? Do you think it could be 'Four Ways?'"

"Quite possibly. It doesn't sound like a tribal name, but how should I know?"

"So, what's your point?"

"My point is about your father's statement that a tribe was persecuting him. I don't know if the name of the tribe is called Four Ways, but it looks like they really were after him. Now it appears they are after us."

Anna shook her head in an attempt to clear it. "But, why are they after us? What have we even done?"

"You said that your father told you he was about to make an important discovery, right?"

She nodded.

"So, they must think that you have something they want."

"But, I don't have anything particularly valuable. Definitely not valuable enough to kill for," she spread her arms out in despair.

"Nothing besides that package your father mailed you."

Frustrated, Anna explained, "There was nothing valuable in that package. I even took the papyruses to several antiquities dealers, and they all assured me that they were made in modern times from banana leaves and only worth a few euros each."

"Then maybe what the papyruses' depict have a double meaning or are a clue," he said leaning forward to rub his head into the palms of his hands. "We need to examine the contents of your father's package—but in the morning. I'm completely jetlagged and won't be much use until I get some sleep."

"Ok, we'll do it tomorrow. We can retrieve them as soon as you wake up."

"Please don't tell me you left the papyruses in your apartment!" Michael's eyes widened.

"Don't worry, Michael, after the incident with the envelope, I placed the contents of the package in a safe place."

"What incident?"

Anna briefly summarized the mysterious woman's unexpected visit that had led to the disappearance of her DHL envelope. However, Anna decided not to mention anything about her ex-boyfriend, Seth, or his connection with Layla.

"Aha," Michael exclaimed rapturously. "You see, I was right. There was something inside that package that they wanted. And it appears that we now have at least two people in Germany that are after your father's package as well as you," he said, shaking his head. After a moment's thought, he added, "Actually, after us now."

"OK, Michael, it's late, so I'm going to let you get some rest. I will pick you up tomorrow morning around … hmmm," she thought for a moment, "nine, nine thirty. Does that work for you?"

"That would be fine, thank you."

"No problem," she smiled warmly. "Believe me, I'm eager to get to the bottom of this mystery."

"I'm intrigued as well. That's why I'm here in Germany," he said, catching her eye before adding gently, "with you."

"Thank you, Michael, I really mean it."

"No problem. I'll see you tomorrow morning around nine," he said, opening the car door. As heavy raindrops began to invade her Audi, Anna barely had time to shout "Good night!" before he pulled his duffel bag out and shut the door.

Michael made a dash through the rain to the hotel entrance. He turned and waved goodbye before stepping into the lobby. After checking in and making his way upstairs, Michael's only thought was the hope for an uninterrupted, deep sleep. Rain was falling heavily on the city as the eventful day came to its long awaited close.

# Chapter 20

Amadeus Hotel, Berlin, Germany
Thursday, September 21
9:05 a.m.

The grey morning skies poured out a steady rain as Michael approached the hotel's front door. He was glad to find Anna's Audi idling right outside and quickly entered the warm vehicle, shutting the door to the chilly morning rain. Anna saluted, *"Guten morgen,* how did you sleep?"

*"Mir geht es gut, danke,"* Michael replied warmly, feeling completely refreshed.

"Wow, impressive! You never told me you know German," she exclaimed, national pride creeping into her voice.

"Well, I never told you I didn't," he smirked. "So, don't start saying bad stuff about me in German, like in that Nicole Kidman movie, Birthday Girl. Not sure if it was popular over here."

Maneuvering her car out of the parking lot, Anna smiled, "Yes, my favorite scene was when the British guy ordered a Russian mail-order bride only to discover that she didn't speak any English."

Michael grinned, "Yup, that's the one."

*"Sind sie giraffe?"* Anna laughed.

"Wait a second, are you trying to test my language skills like in that movie?"

"Yep," she winked.

"No, I'm not a giraffe," Michael guffawed, trying to hold back tears of laughter.

"I didn't think so, but one can never be too sure!"

As they drove through the winding streets, passing homes and an assortment of small shops, Michael fell silent, absorbing the city's historical treasures. Anna slowed down, "This is where I live," she remarked, parking behind a grey, three-story apartment building. "WolfStraße 57." She smiled at him, "I need to get some more clothes and things. I thought it would be safer if you accompanied me. Besides, you wouldn't want me coming here by myself, would you?" she asked with a cute smile, giving him puppy dog eyes.

Michael nodded, nervously glancing around as he exited the vehicle and followed her to the back entrance. After walking up three flights of stairs, Anna pulled out her house key and was inserting it into the lock when the door swung inward. "What on earth?" she murmured. Undeterred, she started to step inside, but Michael grabbed her arm, firmly pulling her back.

"What?"

"I'll go in first," Michael whispered as he silently removed his Schrade U.S. Army fixed-blade knife from his belt sheath. Anna held her breath, remaining still as she watched. He played the black coated, high-carbon steel 5.7" blade in his hands as he listened. Not hearing anything, he stepped quietly and cautiously inside, as he had been trained. Despite her fear, Anna discreetly glanced around to see if anyone was observing them.

Michael slowly crept around, exploring each of the rooms in the apartment. As he carefully pulled back the bathtub curtain, he noticed some toiletries strewn inside the bathtub. Otherwise, the apartment was tidy. He caught Anna's attention and motioned to her. To his surprise she immediately ran to the refrigerator. *Huh?* Michael was confused. *You have a break-in, and the first thing you check is whether or not your groceries are still there?*

Anna flung open the freezer door and dug deep into the ice cube maker before pulling out a frozen plastic bag. As Michael stepped closer, she quickly opened it and removed four Egyptian papyruses. As she unrolled them carefully on the kitchen table, Michael recognized the familiar images that illustrated life in Ancient Egypt.

The first papyrus was an image of two large cats flanking an Egyptian cartouche.

Seven people engaged in a procession were on the second.

The third showed a married couple.

The fourth displayed the feeding of a king.

"Are these what I think they are?" he asked curiously as Anna nervously watched him.

Carefully placing them inside the bag, she replied quietly, "Yes, these are the papyruses my father mailed to me."

Surprised, he asked, "I thought you removed them from your apartment?"

"Well, I found a good hiding place instead," she answered.

"Well, you're lucky they were still in the ice cube bin!" He looked at her sternly, "I would like for you to carefully look around your bathroom and let me know if anything is out of place."

She disappeared into her bathroom and returned almost immediately. She shrugged, "Everything seems okay to me."

Shaking his head, Michael looked at her keenly, "Is your stuff supposed to be scattered inside your bathtub?"

Anna returned to the bathroom and a few seconds later Michael heard a meek, "probably not."

"I don't understand why somebody would be after these modern papyrus imitations," he said, holding up the cold plastic bag as he walked into the living room where Anna joined him. "I'm confused. These fake papyruses probably cost five dollars each."

"Is it because of them that my father was killed?" asked Anna, giving the papyruses a puzzled look. "It doesn't make any sense."

"I don't think so," he said, pacing the room. "I agree, it doesn't make any sense," he stopped next to the window. Deep in thought, Michael pressed his forehead against the glass and looked through the rain to the street below. "Actually, on second thought, it might just make perfect sense!"

Anna moved so she could look at what Michael was transfixed by. Looking across the street, she saw the tribesman who had chased them at the airport standing outside der Kaffeefreund, a small coffee house. He was in a heated discussion with somebody inside the café. When he threw a quick glance in the direction of Anna's apartment, Michael barked, "Don't let him see you!" as he scooted away. Anna stepped away from the window as he barked again, "Try to conceal yourself!"

"How did he manage to find us so quickly? Did he follow you from the airport?"

"Of course not," Anna replied, confusion slipping into her voice. "After dropping you off at the hotel, I went straight to a friend's house."

"That's strange. It can't be a coincidence that the same tribesman is right outside your window." For the first time Michael was seriously frightened. They stared at each other wide-eyed, hearts pounding as they both tried to absorb the realization that the stranger who had poisoned Anna's father now knew exactly where she lived.

"Do you think he noticed us standing in the window?" Anna suddenly exclaimed.

"He may have seen me, but I imagine he would have reacted somehow. It looked like he just kept talking." He paused and then continued with what was on his battle-trained mind, "Of course, if he saw me and started coming up here ... well, it makes me think he is capable of some nasty things."

"I do not know what is going on here, but I would really like to find out." Anna stuffed the bag with the Egyptian papyruses deep inside her spacious purse.

Michael was deep in thought. "Should we call the police? After all, he did break in to your apartment." Anna remained silent, her eyes on the scene outside her window. "Actually, we really don't have any proof that he's been here. He might have left fingerprints, but that's a long shot," he decided sadly.

"Precisely!" exclaimed Anna. "Let's go over there and figure it out." Michael stared at her in utter disbelief. "I'm going to do it!" she announced as she walked toward her bedroom.

"What?" Michael was astounded and more than a bit concerned. She looked back at him, "That tribesman saw you in Egypt would definitely recognize you."

"What about you?" Michael asked, watching her disappear into her bedroom. "He saw you at the airport as well, and ...well, there's no telling what he might do to you." He paused, listening to her rummaging around. He continued authoritatively, "He's responsible for your father's death, and I'm not gonna let you approach him alone." He waited. Was she ignoring him? "It's not safe," he pleaded.

Anna appeared at her bedroom door, some clothes in her arms and a determined look on her face. "Trust me, Michael, I took acting classes in college and performed in several plays." With a confident nod, she declared, "I just need a few minutes in the bathroom and even my own mom wouldn't recognize me." She quickly went into bathroom and closed the door behind her. Michael, both fascinated and surprised, gave up and decided to sit on her couch and wait.

# Chapter 21

WolfStraße 57, Berlin, Germany
Thursday, September 21
10:15 a.m.

Anna opened the bathroom door, leaned against the doorway and struck a pose. Michael was bewildered. The woman he saw in front of his eyes was not the same woman who had walked into the bathroom. Pushing off the doorway, Anna sashayed down the hallway, striking another pose at the end of her imaginary catwalk. Employing a British accent she asked, "What do you think?"

Michael was stunned, not sure where to look first. Anna had transformed from a sophisticated, professional woman into a genuine Goth clubber. Her stunning appearance started at the floor with tall, strappy black boots, torn fish net stockings and a red pinstripe mini skirt with a spiked belt encircling her waist. She sported a black leather jacket, ornamented with dozens of zippers placed in different directions. Her face was made up white with black lips and raccoon-like decorative eye makeup. He hoped her various piercings were not real but stuck to her skin with adhesive. She wore a wig, the long jet-black hair parted down the middle.

If he had crossed paths with her on the street, Michael would never have believed this gothic, creepy-looking teenager was indeed the charming, suave Anna he knew. He realized his jaw had dropped at some point. "Wow."

"Thank you," a smile flirted across her face. "Don't worry!" She laughed heartily, "It's a Halloween costume."

"Then, I'm safe," visible relief showed on his face.

"So, back to our plan," Anna's tone became serious. "The tribesman will have no idea who I am. And besides," she narrowed her eyes as she cast a menacing glance out the window, "My country, my rules." "It's your show."

"I think this will be safer with you," Anna handed him the bag of fake papyruses. Michael nodded and put the bag into his jacket's inner pocket. A slight chill ran across his chest, as the bag was still ice cold. They walked out the door, down the three flights of stairs and into the building's lobby. Anna went directly to a window facing der Kaffeefreund and peeked outside. Turning, she whispered, "Stay here, I'll be right back." Michael nodded as she opened the door. In just a few moments she had crossed over the street and disappeared behind der Kaffeefreund's door.

Michael paced a bit while waiting. He checked his watch and sighed: six minutes. *What is taking so long?* Time stood still. Two minutes later he checked his watch again. Having completely exhausted his patience, he decided to find her. Opening the door, he attempted to casually walk down the street, holding his knife discreetly by his side. His heart and his pace quickened and quickened.

As he neared the café door, Anna came flying out of it. She grabbed onto his jacket, her face almost colliding with his. Grabbing his hand, she started pulling him down the street. "This way!" she ordered frantically, dashing into a small grocery store.

They hid behind a wood produce bin, still breathing heavily from their desperate sprint. Breathless, Anna blurted, "Watch over there!"

"What happened?" Michael whispered frantically, keeping his attention on the window and unconsciously gripping his army knife.

The door to der Kaffeefreund was opening. "They're coming out!" Anna whispered back.

"They?" Michael hoped she had used the wrong pronoun in the excitement. "I thought there was only one." He grimaced as the tribesman and another Middle Eastern man exited the café and walked into the middle of the street. They were looking up and down the street.

"I know that guy," Anna suddenly announced, her grip tightening on the bin in front of her.

"Yeah, me too, remember?" Michael looked at Anna strangely. "That's the guy I saw in Egypt. He was at the airport."

"No, not him," Anna replied weakly.

"What do you mean *not him?*" Michael gave her a quizzical look. "That's the same guy. I'm good with faces."

"I meant that I know the *other* guy."

"Really?"

"Yes, his name is Seth," Anna lowered her head and spoke under her breath, "He is twenty-eight years old, speaks German and Arabic fluently, likes Turkish food, dances well and has a fear of heights."

"Well, nice to meet you Ms. Sherlock Holmes," Michael stared at Anna. "Your detective skills are impeccable!"

Anna muffled a laugh, "Actually he was my boyfriend up until five days ago."

An older gentleman appeared, speaking politely in German, "Excuse me, can I help you find something?"

Anna looked up, smiled sweetly at the grocer and replied in German, "Hans, it's me, Anna!"

The grocer looked stunned and then burst into laughter. "Oh! Anna! What is going on? Do you need some help?"

"Actually, yes, please. I just broke up with that guy out there and I don't want him to see me. Would you mind if my cousin and I hid here until he left? He makes me nervous." Anna's puppy dog eyes were in full force as she looked up at the grocer's familiar face.

The grocer's eyes grew understanding. He walked over to the front window to get a closer look. He turned, "No problem. I have a back room where you and your cousin can sit comfortably until they leave."

Michael looked at Anna curiously as they stood up and moved to the back of the little grocery store. He did not understand what they were saying, but was happy to assume the man was trying to help them.

"So, this is your cousin?" Hans chatted familiarly with Anna as he took them to the back storeroom.

"Yes, this is Michael, he's from America. I'm so sorry, but he doesn't speak a bit of German. Thank you, thank you so much Mr. Schneider. I can explain it to you later."

With a small flourish, Mr. Schneider ushered them into a small, dark storeroom and pulled on the overhead light bulb. "I will let you know when they have cleared out," he promised with a smile as he shut the door behind him.

Michael stood in the little room, amazed at their good fortune. Now that they were alone and could talk, Anna knew it was time to confess. Sitting down, Anna took a deep breath and started from the beginning. She recounted her short-lived romance with Seth, the strange meetings with his Egyptian friends, his sudden disappearance, the late-night visit by his so-called wife Layla, and finally Seth's strange phone call about meeting at the restaurant that was closed for renovations. A few tears kept interrupting her, as it struck her how kind and protective Michael, a complete stranger, had been to her. It was if an emissary from her dear father sat next to her. Michael remained quiet throughout her entire story and was deep in thought when she finished.

"Well, now we know that the tribesman knows about the package," he said. "You may not want to hear this, but I think Seth was dating you in order to get what he was really after."

"That's probably true," Anna said softly as she dropped her watering eyes to gaze at the floor.

"I'm thinking that because he didn't succeed, the tribesman was sent here for reinforcement, assuming he's their henchman."

Just then, the door opened and an older, blonde woman appeared with a basket on her arm. She smiled at Michael as she wrapped Anna in a hug. Reaching inside her basket she pulled out some freshly baked pretzels wrapped in a worn dishtowel and placed them on a nearby crate. Their heavenly scent filled the tiny room. Michael said, "*Danke*" as he picked one up and began tearing into the treat. Anna and the woman spoke rapidly in German. The woman turned to Michael and spoke in heavily accented English, "Welcome to Germany." She waved good-bye and exited the door the same way she had entered.

Anna sat down with a pretzel, "That was Mrs. Schneider. I've shopped here for a few years. She has daughters my age and understood what was going on." A small smile played across her face. "She thought I was clever to disguise myself to see if he was with another woman." She popped another piece of the large, warm pretzel into her mouth. "Oh! These pretzels are delicious! They are such wonderful people." She paused to finish eating. Looking up at Michael, her face started to crumple, "I can't believe I was so naïve."

"That's all right," Michael soothed, gently taking her free hand between his hands. "You had no reason to suspect him." He paused to collect his thoughts. "There could be more of them that we haven't seen yet. So, we have to act quickly if we don't want them to get their hands on this package," he said, firmly pressing a hand against his jacket pocket, making sure it was still there. "How did they recognize you in that outfit?"

"Not me," Anna looked at Michael, "you."

"Huh?"

"They saw you through the window."

"Oh. What were they talking about?"

"They were speaking in Arabic, but it sounded like they were quarreling about something. They had a map of Berlin. Then Seth went up to the bartender and asked for directions."

Just then the door opened and the kindly grocer entered with his smile. "Those two men just got into a black Volvo and took off. I don't think either of them saw you," he reassured her, patting her arm.

"Thank you so much! You and Mrs. Schneider are so kind. And I need to get this outfit off! Thank you for the delicious pretzels," Anna gushed happily.

Waving good-bye to their protectors, they hustled out of the grocery store and into the street to Anna's apartment. Even though they knew all was clear, they could not help but look around cautiously.

Anna stopped short. "Wait for me here!" She grinned before turning to jog back to der Kaffeefreund. Michael was stunned. *Now what?* Minutes ticked by before she reappeared. "Are you out of your mind?"

"I asked the barista how often those two came by," she replied with a shrug.

"And?"

"Well, Seth has been hanging around for the past three days."

"That's disturbing. So, it's safe to assume they've been staking out your apartment. I'm glad you went to your friend's house instead of your apartment."

Anna interjected tersely, "They know what hotel you are staying in."

"What?"

"Seth asked the barista for directions to it."

"Wow, they seem to know everything," he sighed deeply.

"It doesn't make any sense," Anna shook her head as they walked back to her apartment building. Michael looked at her oddly. "OK, they know what hotel you are staying in, so? That doesn't prove they're criminals. You know, maybe it has nothing to do with my father, you being here in Germany or anything else related to Egypt!" she bowed her head as if doubting her own words.

"So, what do you think happened to your apartment?" Michael raised his voice in frustration. "A simple break-in?"

"Yeah!" Anna locked eyes with Michael. "A simple break-in!"

"You can't be serious! Come on, they're after your father's package and you know it!"

"I'm just so confused. I just saw my boyfriend Seth with the tribesman from Egypt. I ... I just can't wrap my mind around it." She stopped and closed her eyes for a moment. "Ok, what do you suggest we do, then? I'm still in shock about Seth knowing the Egyptian tribesman."

"I think the best course of action would be to analyze these papyruses. They might contain some hidden information or clues."

"How?"

"We need to find an expert on Egyptology. There must be something we don't see," he paused before adding, "yet."

Anna gave Michael a determined look. "I think I know the right person. And luckily for us, he is here in Berlin." Her mouth twitched, "Of course, I need to change back into myself first." They both started laughing at that.

After they climbed the three flights of stairs and unlocked her apartment door, Anna headed straight for the bathroom. Michael waited for her on the couch again. About ten minutes later, Anna strode out into the living room looking like her normal self.

"Damn it," she patted down her pants pockets. "I left my cellphone at der Kaffeefreund. Don't go anywhere," she said before disappearing out the front door, "I'll be right back."

Michael remained sitting on the couch, astonished, still amused by her transformations.

# Chapter 22

Berlin, Germany
Thursday, September 21
11:45 a.m.

"I have nothing to say to you, Seth," Anna's angry words seemed small and ineffective as she stared in frustration out the tinted window of Seth's black Volvo. She realized her words were futile at this point. The rainfall outside grew heavier. Her stomach twisted as she pondered how she had gotten herself dragged into this dangerous game, the meaning of which she could not comprehend.

Moments earlier she had been compelled by the mad tribesman and his sharp knife to get inside the tactically parked Volvo. In the minutes before his surprise assault, she was blithely crossing the street as the rain clouds began to open up again into another storm. Nearing the der Kaffeefreund café to retrieve her cell phone, her eyes and mind were focused on avoiding the small puddles collecting near the sidewalk. The tribesman silently appeared out of nowhere and discreetly grabbed her. Anna almost screamed before realizing he was pressing a sharp metal blade against her stomach. Its enormous size stunned her.

The developing rainstorm had sent everybody scrambling for shelter. Even if she screamed, she doubted anyone would hear her and come to her rescue. Instinctively she realized that by screaming she would find her death right there on the empty street, ironically only a few feet away from the safety of her home. Still in his grasp, Anna glanced up at her window, hoping Michael might be watching. Unfortunately the window remained dark, her white curtains framing its emptiness.

When her attacker gestured for her to get inside the Volvo with its running engine, Anna resisted, knowing that if she was inside the vehicle it would be far worse than remaining outside, where the tribesman would at least have to keep his weapon concealed. Inside the car, he would have the luxury and freedom to use it in any way he so desired. Her attacker knew she was stalling and pressed the blade painfully.

At that moment the driver's side window slowly opened, revealing a familiar face: her ex-boyfriend, Seth, his face grim and demanding. He gestured sharply for her to get inside the car. Surprised, Anna obeyed, seeing his presence as an improvement. As soon as she got into the car, the tribesman had shut her door firmly, opened up the back door and taken the seat behind her. Seth had promptly stomped on the accelerator pedal, steered the car into the steady rain filling the empty street and taken a sharp left into an alleyway.

Michael was not only oblivious to the dramatic scene unfolding in the street below, but also getting weary of relaxing on her couch with nothing to do. He glanced at his watch and shaking his head, slowly stood and walked over to the window. As he neared, the Volvo was making a sharp left turn, escaping Michael's casual glance. He stood observing the rain's powerful escalation. With only a few passing vehicles below and a lightning storm off in the distance, Michael sighed when he saw nothing of interest. Michael collapsed onto the sofa, wondering how long a female's perspective of "be right back" really took. He imagined her laughing and chatting away with the barista inside the warm *der Kaffeefreund* café as the rain poured noisily outside.

The Volvo drove two blocks away, stopped abruptly and pulled off the road. Seth turned and barked something in Arabic to his partner-in-crime. To Anna's profound surprise, the tribesman unquestioningly obeyed by opening the door and stepping into the rain that pounded the car.

"I did not want to lie to you," Seth stared firmly at Anna who was trying her best to ignore his once adored countenance by staring blankly in front of her. "But if I had told you the truth," he continued "it would have scared you away and exposed me to unwarranted risk."

"No, you pretty much used me," Anna snapped angrily. "I thought you were in love with me, but your whole elaborate scheme was to get closer to me in order to get the information you needed. Isn't that right?"

"It wasn't in my power. If I hadn't complied, the tribe would have killed me," he paused for a moment. "The tribe did me a favor in the past, and I was in their debt."

"So, what do you want with me? I need to know the whole truth."

"Unfortunately, you were set up. It's not your fault. The tribe wanted to get to your father. To them, you were just a way to get back what belonged to them in the first place," he replied matter-of-factly.

"And then they killed my father in cold blood because he did not have any more value?"

"I can assure you that I had no part in killing your father. Trust me, I was shocked by the news." Seth studied Anna's expression. "The tribe gave him a chance to return the object that belonged to the tribe, but he refused."

"I do not know anything about that," Anna replied angrily.

"I believe you. Your father was not one who would trust anybody with his plans," he paused for effect, "even his own daughter."

"So why did you just kidnap me?" Although tense and afraid, she was sure Seth and the tribesman did not intend to kill her: at least not yet. It occurred to her that she needed to play along. "What do you want from me?"

"Every day lots of people disappear ... without a trace."

"Is that a threat?" Anna retorted angrily. "I don't know anything about my father," she protested before adding in a more desperate tone, "I haven't been in contact with him for a couple of years. Look, I don't know anything."

"The tribe made a mistake and left their most prized possession out in the open. The ancient artifact disappeared with all traces pointing to your father. The tribe tried to negotiate with him in vain. Everything could have been different, but your father wouldn't cooperate with the tribe and, thus, predetermined his fate. So, as long as you cooperate and help the tribe to retrieve the artifact, nothing bad will happen to you or your new American friend."

Anna stared at him in disbelief. She got to keep her life if she helped some foreign tribe find their trinket? Suddenly, she understood with absolute clarity the full terror of her situation.

"Yes, we know about the American," said Seth spitefully, misunderstanding her reaction.

Anna sighed deeply. She did not know anything about this tribe, but realized she was being forced into signing a contract with Satan himself. While her deal might appear beneficial for the time being, her value would drop dramatically in the end, when she would most certainly pay with her life. Clenching her jaw to keep her fear from dripping out of her mouth, Anna inquired quietly, "So, you want me to work for you and find this ancient artifact that I know nothing about?"

"Not for me—but together with me!" Seth exclaimed with a widening smile. Anna forced a smile to her face. "I'm just a small link in this chain. If you cooperate, the tribe will give you another chance at life." Seth leaned forward, his eyes piercing Anna's. His voice dropped menacingly, "You can pretend you are safe, but the truth of the matter is that the tribe can eliminate you like that," Seth snapped his fingers in front of her eyes, causing Anna's breath to catch in her throat.

He paused and sat back, studying Anna's expression intently. He wanted to give her time to digest all of what he had said and for the reality of her situation to sink in fully. Contemplative, she remained silent while succeeding at keeping her face calm. The situation seemed so strange and out of place. The Seth she had known from before this moment in time was full of fun and enthusiasm. But now, in front of her, he had morphed into an entirely different person: menacing and deadly.

"Come on Anna, your father was never there for you. And what did he do? He literally dragged you into trouble by stealing an artifact that belonged to the tribe?"

"My dad didn't steal anything!" she objected forcefully. "He is not a thief!" She choked back a sob before suddenly asking, "What kind of artifact are you talking about anyway?"

"I can't tell you that and don't ask me again," Seth chuckled, although there was no mirth in his eyes as they drilled into her.

"If you can't tell me, and I can't ask you, then how am I going to help you?" The entire issue was becoming more absurd and impossible.

Thunder struck nearby as the raindrops dropped bigger and heavier onto the car windows. Anna could not help but think about the tribesman who was patiently waiting in the pouring rain for the outcome of their conversation. Seth stared out the window, and began meticulously planning her unfortunate fate.

Although the whole predicament of her present situation bewildered Anna, she desperately racked her brain for a way out. *What should I do?* Then a bright flash of insight struck her. All she had to do was *pretend*. It would be foolish for her to try to escape, but as she realized with dawning hope, pretending to go along with them until she had an opportunity to escape was her best option for survival.

Back at the apartment, Michael had no idea what had happened to Anna. After pacing back and forth inside her living room and constantly checking the time, he searched her desk drawers and found some tape. He taped over the front door's latch mechanism to prevent it from automatically locking itself as he shut it and walked down the stairs.

Once out of the pouring rain and inside the warm and cozy cafe, the barista politely informed him that Anna had indeed left her cellphone but had never come back for it. Bewildered as to where she might have gone or what could have happened, Michael asked the barista to call the police. Shaking his head, the barista calmly replied that the police would not even respond, as Anna had not been missing for more than twenty-four hours. In fact, the barista tried to assure him, Anna had probably seen one of her friends, gotten carried away and lost track of the time. While Michael doubted this, he nodded in agreement. He politely thanked the barista and pocketed Anna's cell phone. Putting his hood up over his head, Michael exited the café and stepped into the pounding rain.

Lingering by the café's empty tables and chairs, he rapidly scanned the street, looking for any clues. The street, however, was deserted with the exception of several passing vehicles; none of which were Volvos. Michael stood on the sidewalk in front of the der Kaffeefreund for a few more minutes before heading back up to Anna's apartment, hoping that he was overreacting to her disappearance. After all, the Volvo was long gone before she left the apartment to go back to the café for her phone. Maybe the barista was right. *Women: can't live with them, can't live without them,* he thought as he untaped and relocked the apartment's door. Shedding his soaked jacket in the entryway, he decided to simply stand and observe the neighborhood from the window.

Meanwhile, inside the Volvo parked several blocks around the corner, Seth had lost almost all hope of ascertaining anything of worth from his victim. He taciturnly informed Anna that the man standing outside the vehicle was a ruthless killer from the Medjay tribe who harbored no pity toward his victims. Having said that, Seth signaled the drenched Medjay to enter the vehicle. Upon his entry, the Medjay and Seth exchanged monosyllabic phrases, none of which Anna could understand, not even what language they were speaking. The Medjay tribesman made certain that Anna saw him stare her down with an evil, predatory look that gave her no doubt that he had anything but the worst animosity for her.

Anna was feeling physically and emotionally drained. She leaned against the door, folded her arms and closed her eyes. While the raindrops outside were sleep inducing, thoughts of her father dying a terrible death at the hands of the ruthless killer sitting behind her kept her firmly awake.

"You wouldn't dare try to run away from us now, would you?" asked Seth as he noticed her moving closer to the door.

She opened her eyes partway and looked sideways at him. He gave her a false smile.

"I have nowhere to go," she gloomily responded, feeling her heart start to tremble. *I do not want to die.* She watched the raindrops run together on the window she was leaning against. "I did get a package from my father recently. I will give that to you."

"OK, now we're talking," he sounded genuinely cheerful.

"The American has the package. If you let me go I will bring it to you. I have no interest in it as it's completely useless and meaningless to me."

Seth leaned forward, locked eyes with her and spoke menacingly, "If I do decide to let you go, don't even think about calling the police." He paused for effect, "we will find you. My partner, the Medjay, will kill both of you before you can even squeal." Seth sat back in his seat, "I hope you understand that this is a one-time deal: you bring the package and you will never see us again. I promise."

"Yes, I'll bring you the package," she replied meekly. "I have no interest in it."

Seth exchanged several foreign phrases with his Medjay counterpart, turned on the engine and drove back to Anna's apartment. As he parked in front of Anna's building he turned to her, "We'll be waiting around the corner," he warned, flipping the switch to unlock the car doors. "Don't be stupid."

# Chapter 23

57 WolfStraße, Berlin, Germany
Thursday, September 21
12:40 p.m.

The apartment door opened abruptly. "What happened?" Michael exclaimed.

Anna stood dripping in the tiny entryway, "Get your jacket and make sure you have the papyruses." She quickly leaned over and grabbed her raincoat from its perch on the bathroom doorknob. "I'll tell you on the way!" she promised, frantically yanking on her coat while turning back to the stairs.

Michael snatched his jacket, made sure the bag of papyruses were safely tucked inside and started after her. To Michael's surprise, Anna was running up the next flight of stairs instead of down. Pulling on his jacket, he shut her door and ran after her, catching up just as she started climbing a ladder to the rooftop. Anna quickly informed him that she had been kidnapped and her captors were close behind.

She forced open a metal hatch leading to the roof. Rain and wind swirled down on them as Anna climbed the last rungs of the ladder and stepped onto the roof. Hunching over, she ran to the other end of the building as Michael quickly flipped the hatch shut and did the same. She wrested open a similar hatch, jumped inside and started climbing down a ladder situated in the building's opposite stairwell. Amazed at her ingenuity, Michael climbed down the ladder as well, pulling shut the hatch door behind him and racing down the four flights of stairs after her. They paused as Anna peeked out the lobby window. Just then, a taxi rolled up and dropped off one of her neighbors. Anna pushed open the lobby door, grabbed Michael's hand and sprinted to the taxi. Shoving Michael inside, she squeezed in next to him, both automatically slouching down.

As their cab pulled away from the apartment building, Anna directed the cabbie to take them to Berlin's city center. She nervously looked one way and then another out the windows for Seth's menacing black Volvo to appear. Keeping an eye on their surroundings, she told Michael a little bit about what had happened.

As they neared Berlin's city center, Anna directed the cabbie to take them to the Deutsches Archäologisches Institut. She explained to Michael that it was an international scientific research organization founded in 1829 whose employees were responsible for performing excavations and research in the field of archeology.

The sky was still leaden and dripping rain when the cab dropped them off in front. The old sandstone exterior was welcoming, almost like a mansion, with its wide, creamy shutters and warm red roof. The wide, covered walkway from the street to the building itself was a majestic refuge from the weather, with multiple pillars and ancient potted ferns. Before they reached the front door, Anna turned to Michael, "The man we need to see is David Krüger. Back in 1993, David and my father were part of the exploration of the two shafts leading outside the Queen's chamber inside the Great Pyramid."

Michael's eyes lit up, "Oh yes, I remember that."

The receptionist at the grand wooden reception desk greeted them warmly in German.

Anna replied in German.

The receptionist nodded, speaking again.

"Anna Schulze," Anna replied.

The receptionist paused, smiled wider and picked up the phone. As they walked over to one side to wait, Anna turned to Michael, "So, how do you know about my father's exploration of the Queen's Chamber?"

He smiled, "Easy. I've been fascinated by the Egyptian pyramids since I was a teenager."

She replied thoughtfully, "Fair enough."

"They had a robot go inside the Queen's Chamber, that's exciting stuff. I remember they discovered a small door set with metal pins, right?"

"Yes, there's speculation that those pins were door handles."

"Anna!"

"*Guten Tag, David*," Anna greeted a man approaching them. "*Wie geht es Dir?*"

"*Hallo, Anna*," David gave Anna a big hug. They spoke in German, but then switched to English when Anna introduced Michael. David turned to Michael, "So sorry, I didn't know that you don't speak German."

"Americans, ha," Anna smirked. "One universal language: English."

"That's all right," Michael said to David before giving Anna a sideways smile and adding, "*Ich bin nicht Giraffe*." They burst into giggles. After the intensity of their morning, the laughter helped to lift their spirits. As Anna hurried to explain the joke to David, Michael glanced over at the receptionist, concerned that their loud chatter was disturbing her work. He was surprised to find her steadfastly observing them. He met her eyes and smiled at her. She graciously smiled back at him and then politely looked down at the papers on her desk.

"I knew Anna's father, Günther, well." David spoke to Michael, pausing somberly. "We worked together preparing a robot to explore the air shafts of the Great Pyramid. And that was at the beginning of . . . let me see . . . 1993?"

"Yes," Anna replied softly,

Taking ahold of Anna's hands for the moment, David said sadly, "Anna, how nice of you to stop by. I was so sorry to hear about your father. It was a real tragedy both personally as a close friend and to the Archaeological Institute as well. He really was a valuable asset to both the fields of archaeology and Egyptology. This is truly a really big, big, loss ... to the world," David concluded, struggling with his tears.

"Thank you so much, David, I'm truly touched," Anna replied, a small, sad smile playing across her lips. "Michael is from New York. He tried to save my father's life inside the Great Pyramid in Egypt."

"Yes, I learned basic CPR back in my military days," interjected Michael, "but, unfortunately, I wasn't able to save him."

Anna looked solemnly into his eyes, "You did everything you could. More than most people would."

"You did a truly noble thing." David added. "I heard he had a heart attack inside the pyramid."

Michael gave Anna an odd, questioning look before glancing back to David. "Well," Anna replied cautiously. "That may not be entirely true."

"What do you mean?"

"There might be another explanation related to my father's death, but it is irrelevant right now because we don't have proof. In fact, we need your expert opinion on some items my father mailed to me from Egypt. I have them here with me. Do you have time to take a look?"

"Sure, no problem. I have a little bit of time before I have a teleconference, so please, follow me to my office."

As they walked up the stairs to David's office, Anna and David reminisced about Anna's father. Meanwhile, Michael's emotions were brimming over. Logically, he should not be in Germany. He should be in Egypt, enjoying the trip of a lifetime; yet, his heart had taken the lead. At present, he could not wrap his mind around his incredible fortune: he was meeting with an archeologist whose explorations and discoveries were well known within the small world of Egyptology.

David's office was cluttered with an eclectic collection of artifacts. Michael's eyes gravitated to a poster lying on top of David's desk.

*DEUTSCHES ARCHÄOLOGISCHES INSTITUT*
*Proudly presents:*
**The Bronze Age Egypt**
*A lecture by Dr. David Krüger*

*Well-known archaeologist, participant in a multitude of archaeological projects, author of several books on Egyptian archaeology, contributor to various magazines and frequent guest on television shows, Dr. Krüger presents findings from his latest expedition to Egypt.*

Carefully placing the Egyptian papyruses on the table, Anna explained, "David, these were in a package my father sent to me just before he died. Can you tell us anything about these four papyruses?"

"Please," David gestured for them to take a seat in one of his office chairs as he sat down in his own. Anna quickly sat down, her eyes focused on the papyruses. Although Michael sat down, his eyes and mind were exploring David's office, soaking in his surroundings. "Very interesting," David examined each of the four papyruses for a few moments before setting them down.

After locating his magnifying glass, David switched on a high intensity lamp and carefully picked up one of the papyruses. Adjusting the glaring light of the lamp, he held his magnifying glass over the papyrus and studied it for a few moments.

He spoke quietly and deliberately as he described what he saw. "This papyrus depicts two cat gods with a cartouche between them." He looked up at the both of them and smiled, "It basically signifies that Egypt is a heaven." He carefully placed the papyrus aside, picked up the next one and studied it for a few minutes.

"This next papyrus has a scene from the Book of the Dead. It depicts a scene from an "opening of the mouth" ceremony. The ancient Egyptians believed that in order for a person's soul to survive in the afterlife, it would need to have food and water. This symbolic animation of a mummy was a ritual that they believed would bring sensory life back to the deceased form. In other words, it would enable the deceased person to see, smell, breathe, hear and eat in the afterlife, and thus partake of the offering foods and drinks brought to the tomb each day."

Anna leaned back, "It always amazes me how sophisticated the Egyptians were in everyday life, yet they believed in such fantasy." Michael nodded in agreement as he was eagerly waited to hear what David would say next. David set aside the papyrus and picked up the next one.

"This one displays Osiris, the god of the underworld with his wife, Isis, the goddess of magic." David smiled briefly at both of them before setting the papyrus aside and picking up the last one.

"The last one depicts a sacrificial ceremony of offerings to the god Horus, the Egyptian god of the skies. He was the son of Osiris and Isis," he said, returning the last papyrus to the pile.

Anna felt stumped, "Anything unusual you can tell us about these papyruses?"

"No, nothing unusual," said David, prompting Michael and Anna to both sigh sadly.

"Well, Michael was thinking that since my father sent these to me right before he died, that they were significant in some way. Perhaps my father had a secret message hidden on one of them," Anna said adding, "Strangely enough, some people have tried to steal these papyruses twice already."

"Really?" David shook his head in confusion. "That doesn't make any sense."

"Well, maybe one of them is a *real* ancient Egyptian papyrus and worth lots of money," Michael suggested optimistically.

David laughed, "No, no." His smile disappeared when he saw their faces. "I'm sorry but these papyruses are merely cheap imitations of the real ones."

There was a knock at the door. A heavyset lady, her hair pulled up into a tight bun, hurriedly opened David's office door, causing a draft to blow the papyruses off his desk and onto the floor. Apologizing profusely in English, David introduced his secretary, who frowned as she rushed to pick up the scattered papyruses.

The secretary handed the scattered papyruses back to David before reminding him that his teleconference would be in *fünfzehn Minuten* (fifteen minutes). She hurried out, closing the door behind her.

Anna rose from her seat, "Well, David thanks for your help."

"I wish I could have been more help," he replied as he shuffled the papyruses back into a neat pile. Suddenly he stopped to stare at the papyrus on top of the stack. "Wait a minute, where did this one come from?" He snatched the questionable papyrus up and flipped it over. The familiar image of Osiris and Isis holding hands was on the other side. He flipped it back over to stare at the other image in shock.

"Look!" he announced, his voice filling with eagerness, "I missed an image on the back side of this one!" Michael and Anna were stunned. Hastily, David checked the backs of each of the other papyruses; however, they were blank.

*I can't believe we never thought to turn them over,* thought Michael, astonished at the how close they had come to missing something. David picked up his magnifying glass and concentrated on the newly discovered image.

Shocked, he declared, "I believe this is Pharaoh Khufu's cartouche. I don't recall ever seeing it before."

"Pharaoh Khufu?" Anna exclaimed.

"Khufu, or Cheops as ancient Greeks called him, was the second pharaoh of the Fourth Dynasty," David explained. "He reigned for 50 years and built the Great Pyramid."

David was closely examining the papyrus again, "That's odd. The drawing appears to be a pencil rubbing from something etched into stone."

Seeing their confusion, David tried to explain, "Basically, it's similar to what people do at the Vietnam Veterans Memorial Wall in the United States. People place a thin piece of paper over the name of their loved one and then rub a pencil over it." He glanced up at Michael. "I'm sure you're familiar with this practice."

"Oh yes, of course," Michael recalled. "Actually, I've visited there and seen people doing that."

Satisfied, David continued, "It looks like whoever made this got only part of it."

"How can you tell?" Anna was squinting.

"We'll readdress that momentarily," David said. "The hieroglyphic text is impossible to read and most of the scenes look difficult to interpret."

Anna sighed in frustration, prompting Michael to put his hand on her shoulder.

"Anyway, we can try and see what we can understand. It is my job after all." David looked sympathetic, "Patience, my dear Anna, patience." He got up from his desk and walked over to a cluttered bookshelf. After looking for a few moments, he snatched a book from a lower shelf saying triumphantly, "This should do it!"

He started flipping through its pages. "Here," he said, pointing at a picture, "Look at this, it closely resembles the picture on this papyrus." Both Anna and Michael had their eyes glued to the book as David continued, "It represents the royal title, Lord of the Two Lands, meaning the Pharaoh of both Upper and Lower Egypt.

The next image appears to be the royal pharaoh cartouche bearing the name of Pharaoh Khufu."

"What have scholars determined about Pharaoh Khufu?" asked Anna, intrigued.

David flipped through several pages in his book before stopping at the desired page and reading out loud:

*Pharaoh Khufu, or Cheops as the Greeks called him (ca. 2585 – 2560 BCE), whose name means 'he who crushes the enemies,' was the second ruler of the Fourth Dynasty, which was founded by his father*

*King Sneferu. Ancient Greek historians credit him with a reign of approximately fifty years. He was known to have had at least four wives, with whom he had several children each. Khufu continued the policies of expansion initiated by his father and extended the Egyptian borders to include Sinai and Upper Egypt. Khufu built the Great Pyramid, a monument that makes him one of the most famous pharaohs from ancient Egyptian history. Supposedly, Khufu was buried inside the Great Pyramid with all his treasures, but neither his mummy nor his treasures have been found. It is believed that the Great Pyramid was robbed during ancient times, shortly after Khufu's mummy was buried within his pyramid.*

"Wow, I wonder what the connection between my father and Pharaoh Khufu could possibly be?" Anna wondered.

"That's impossible to say, but let's look further," said David as he flipped earnestly through the pages. "This scene is from the Book of the Dead and is related to the afterlife and the soul of a deceased pharaoh."

"The Book of the Dead?" Anna looked puzzled. "You've mentioned that before."

"That's the book that explains the procedures that the dead must undergo to reach the afterlife," Michael explained.

"It's the afterlife in today's language, but the ancient Egyptians would have said 'to gain admittance to the eternal realm of the god Osiris,'" David further explained. "This next image also closely resembles one of the scenes from the Book of the Dead; it shows a pharaoh adoring the god Osiris. That's definitely a pharaoh, because he is wearing the crown of the Upper and Lower Egypt.

"Here, look," he added, pointing out another picture, "you can see the crown of the Upper and Lower Egypt much better in this image.

David studied the papyrus intensely for a few more minutes before speaking in a reverent hush, "I would say that based on the royal cartouche bearing his name, this is none other than Pharaoh Khufu himself."

"Wow," exclaimed Michael. "Are you sure?"

"If this pencil rubbing was made from an authentic artifact from that time period, then I would say so with about a ninety-five percent certainty. It would be a difficult thing to make a fake piece out of something as elaborate as this."

Michael and Anna looked at each other wide-eyed. It was possible that Anna's father had been on the verge of some incredible discovery.

"Let me briefly explain ancient Egyptian life and spirituality," David continued. "Ancient Egyptians believed that in addition to the body itself, human beings were made up of different spiritual elements: the body's shadow and two other forces, 'ka,' the divine energy giving life to the body, and 'ba,' a person's unique personality. It was crucial that these elements remain intact for participation in the afterlife. Although Egyptians loved life and didn't want to die voluntarily, it entirely consumed Egyptian religious thought." Sitting behind his cluttered, yet impressive desk, David looked like a college professor giving a lecture.

"Egyptians believed in the afterlife, with death viewed as a pathway into eternal existence. So, they buried their dead with all the tools they might need in the next world. The mummification and burial rituals were designed to preserve the integrity of the deceased."

"OK, then who is Osiris?" Anna interrupted inquisitively.

"He is the god of the underworld," answered David. "He's depicted as a mummy with his hands coming through the wrappings to hold his shepherd's crook and flail. He always wears a tall white crown. Sometimes it has two plumes on either side, but sometimes it has ram's horns." David closed his book on ancient Egyptian life.

Michael took this moment to break the contemplative silence, "Is there anything else you can tell from the pencil rubbing?"

"Unfortunately, that's all I can tell you at the moment." David peered at the papyrus once more. "Actually, if you look here along the bottom, it appears that you can almost see the beginning of another diagram. So, if you were to find the other part of the pencil rubbing or, even better, the original surface from which it was made, it would bring more to light."

"Do you think my father made this?" asked Anna.

David shrugged. "No way to know at this moment, but I can tell you one thing, if this artifact really exists, then it would be the most sacred artifact to ever exist. It shows Pharaoh Khufu's transition into the afterlife."

"Could it be a stele?" Michael asked.

David gasped, "Sure, it could be a stele. The size and shape would definitely correspond."

"What is a stele?" asked Anna, perplexed.

David gave Michael an inquisitive look, "But how did you know?"

"Just an educated guess," Michael replied calmly.

"Well, if you happen to find it, please show it to me. It would be the find of the millennium!"

"We sure will," replied Anna, collecting the papyruses.

"Wait," David said, picking up the papyrus with the etching on the back. "Would you mind if I got a copy of this? I would love to take a longer look at it."

"Certainly," Anna agreed.

"Thank you! This is very exciting!" David hastily opened his office door and walked over to a copier, carefully placing the papyrus on the glass.

David's secretary suddenly appeared from around the corner. When she saw him, her eyes widened, and she started scolding him in German.

"I'm sorry," he looked apologetically at Anna and Michael, "but I need to run." He pulled out a business card from a holder on his secretary's desk, writing something on the back. He handed it to Anna, along with the papyrus. "If you need anything, here's my cell phone number."

Grabbing the copy of the papyrus, he strode quickly into his office, hastily scooping up some files from his desk. Putting his arm around Anna in a fatherly manner he said, "Please, again, accept my deepest condolences."

Anna quietly responded, "Thanks," giving David a hug. Meanwhile, Michael retrieved the papyrus from the copier, put it with the others inside the bag and tucked it back inside his jacket. "David, who are the Medjay?" Anna asked quickly.

"The Medjay?" David looked at her curiously, "They were a group of elite warriors in ancient Egypt, guardians sworn to protect the pharaoh's tombs and temples."

"Do they still exist?"

"I believe so," David said, slowly walking away from them. "I've heard stories that they still exist today," he paused. "Why do you ask?"

"I believe I met one today."

David and Michael stared at her in bewilderment.

"I'm sorry, I'm late for this teleconference," David starting jogging away, "but please call me." He disappeared around the corner.

"Michael, what's a stele?" Anna asked again as they walked back to the staircase leading down to the lobby, "Do you happen to have a PhD in Egyptology that I don't know about?"

"What do you mean, you know a Medjay?"

Anna chuckled. "Well, oddly enough, you know him as well."

He stopped, looking at her strangely.

"The tribesman."

Michael's eyes opened wide. "He's a Medjay?"

Anna nodded, "I had forgotten that part. Do you know much about them?"

"Oh, man," he paused heavily, "we're screwed."

"Not yet. We've got something he wants. As long we keep it with us, we're guaranteed he won't touch us," she said, attempting to be reassuring. "Now, tell me about this stele."

"Well, it's a bit like a tombstone. It's made of stone or wood and has a message carved or painted onto it. In ancient times it was used to give laws or a message." Michael paused, "There is something you should know."

"What do you mean?"

Gravely he put his hand on her arm, causing her to stop and look up at him. He leaned toward her, speaking softly, "Your father is accused of stealing something in Egypt. That *something* is an ancient stele."

Anna stared at him.

"The Police Inspector in Cairo told me." He sighed deeply, "But I don't believe it and that's why I'm here." Astounded, Anna stood shock still, her mind racing.

# Chapter 24

German Archaeological Institute, Berlin, Germany
Thursday, September 21
1:37 p.m.

"How did they find us?" Anna asked, stunned to find herself hiding behind a column. Anna and Michael had just left the building and were discussing their lunch plans when Michael shoved her behind a column without warning. He crouched behind her.

"Shush!" he commanded, discreetly pointing at the menacing, black Volvo parked a few lengths down their side of the street. Noticing the car's open windows, Michael was afraid that any noise would alert the driver.

Anna murmured, "Do you really think it's them?"

"It looks a lot like the Volvo from this morning."

"Yeah, I think you're right." Anna was squinting her eyes, trying to see into the vehicle. "I see Seth behind the wheel," she sighed deeply. "So, it means the person in the back seat is the Medjay." She shook her head, "I can't believe they found us."

"Well, the stakes are high. We are talking about a missing, priceless ancient stele," he glanced at Anna. "They're getting desperate and think we know where to find their stele."

"But we don't know or have anything. All we have is a cheap, imitation papyrus with a pencil rubbing," she replied despairingly.

"Well, there may be more to that pencil rubbing than we know. I think the best thing is to not to let them get their hands on it."

"Good. So, how do we get away from here without them seeing us?"

"As long as they think we are still inside this building, I don't think they will move from their spot."

"Are you proposing we wait here until the end of the day?" she looked at Michael, sincerely hoping this was not his plan.

"Well," Michael had been pondering this thought. They needed to evade the enemy in an urban setting. "If we can't get past them in the open, then we need to make a visual shield in order to evade them." Anna looked at him, stunned. "What? How?"

"Do you know the phone number for the fire department?"

"One-one-two."

"Excellent!" Michael exclaimed.

"Hey! I've got a better idea," she said, an evil grin suddenly appearing on her beautiful face.

"What are you doing?" he whispered as Anna crept back inside the DAI. Moments later he jumped as a thundering alarm blasted from the inside the building. He had his answer. He watched from his hiding place as Seth's head moved back and forth, looking around. Within moments DAI employees were swarming through the front door, scurrying through the columned walkway and flooding the adjoining streets. Sure enough, Berlin's fire trucks and ambulances were quickly approaching the building with their distinctive, two tone signal.

A police car screeched to a stop in front of the building, the officers jumping out to direct the employees and street traffic. Michael could not help laughing as the police officers ordered Seth to move his Volvo out of the way. As the fire trucks and ambulances filled the street, the Volvo crawled away from the scene. Anna appeared at his side. "They made them leave!" he whispered with a grin. They eagerly joined the crowd and started briskly walking down the street in the opposite direction. Merging with the crowd, they walked along the street while trying to inconspicuously look around from time to time. There was no sign of the black Volvo.

The clouds gathered again in the grey sky, and soon the first drops of rain started sprinkling. Umbrellas started popping up, and in that sea of umbrellas, Michael and Anna felt as if they were virtually invisible.

Or so they thought.

The street suddenly ended, so they turned left onto Königin-Luise-Straβe. As they passed by an Italian restaurant, Michael turned slightly and whispered to Anna, "We need to eat, but I think we should put more space between us and Seth." Anna nodded in agreement. They kept walking as the rain formed puddles on the wide sidewalk. They came up to a larger road where Michael pulled on Anna to hurry and cross the street with him. As they turned onto Englealee, the crowd and cars seemed to grow in strength, much to his relief. He knew their anonymity in the crowds was the key to their safety.

Their rain jacket hoods were up, so conversation, at least a private one, was simply out of the question. As they continued walking, Michael enjoyed the beautiful greenery found throughout Berlin. The trees glistened in the rain, making it hard to believe they were in the middle of a large city.

Michael soon realized the cleverness of walking away from the scene, rather than driving. They could turn at any corner, duck into any store and simply hide in entryways. Still, he could not help but marvel at Seth's prowess in finding them. As soon as it seemed like they were lost in the city like two proverbial needles in a haystack, he showed up. Obviously, Seth and the Medjay were not alone in this quest for the stele. *There has to be a number of people involved in this,* he mused.

Soon the sidewalk narrowed and there seemed to be less people around them. Looking from side to side, Michael knew they needed to get to a more crowded area. At first he was tempted to escape into a small park nearby and walk amongst the trees and bushes. Then he realized the park was deserted in the rainstorm. There was no other choice but to keep walking.

After about five more minutes of walking, they reached a larger street intersection. Cars were zipping back and forth as they approached. The cars suddenly came to a stop in front of them, and he made a quick decision. Looking back at Anna, "Let's go over there," he urged. "There seem to be more people." She responded by stepping up her pace and crossing the intersection well ahead of him. He followed her as she strode purposefully.

They fell in with another crowd of people. Soon the street split into two parts. Immediately, Michael felt safer as the traffic was now coming toward them. He knew they could duck into any store and make an escape if needed.

"We need to find a place to eat."

He turned his head slightly and smiled at her, "The next place we see," he promised. As it turned out, Santa Café was the next restaurant.

As soon as he saw the word "café," Michael started to head for the door. He took one last look behind him. *Nothing unusual*, he thought to himself.

"Taxi!" Anna exclaimed suddenly, grabbing Michael's arm and leaping inside a taxi that had pulled over. Astonished by the unprecedented turn of the events, Michael understood the meaning of it the moment Anna pointed out a certain black Volvo passing by on the other side of the street. As the taxi took off, Anna directed the driver to quickly turn down an alley and go in the opposite direction.

As the taxi exited the alley, they slouched deep into their seats. They lifted their heads a little bit and observed some kids on their bicycles hurrying home to escape the raindrops, and two moms urgently trying to cover up their babies in their strollers. Everything seemed normal. Anna directed the cab driver to drive across the city so they could "see the sights."

A little while later they relaxed and started enjoying their ride. They were laughing about the whole ordeal when the cab driver suddenly addressed them. "The driver says that vehicle is tailgating us," announced Anna. Michael turned his head discretely and saw the black Volvo behind them. The face of a Middle Eastern man with distinctive, bushy Afro hair was most definitely looking back at him from the front passenger's seat.

"I'm calling the police," Anna said, looking through her purse for her cell phone.

Michael placed his hand on the top of hers, "We have nothing on them."

"We can tell the police they are following us. Come on, it's got to be something. We're here in the civilized world, not in some tribal-land-wilderness-place," she cried, losing her temper.

"Anna," Michael tried to keep his cool, "if you call the police, the only crime those two would be guilty of right now is following too close."

"Well, that's good enough," Anna approved. "This way, we can get away from them by the time the police finish issuing them a citation."

"Unfortunately, they will not get a citation."

"Ok, they'll get arrested," she said, her face brightening with enthusiasm. "Even better."

Four Ways to Pharaoh Khufu

"They will not get arrested," Michael said, smirking.

Anna sighed deeply. "OK, so what do you suggest we do?"

He thought for a moment, "Tell the driver you are in the middle of a divorce and that your ex-husband is pursuing you."

Anna frowned skeptically.

"Trust me," he said firmly. "It will work."

Anna shook her head but started speaking emphatically with the driver. The driver got a big grin on his face and started laughing. "He bought it," she turned to Michael, trying hard to hold back her laughter as well.

The driver called out, "*Festhalten!*"

Anna quickly interpreted by calling out, "Hang on!" as the cab suddenly lurched forward and accelerated, weaving through several lanes. Even though the driver expertly maneuvered between occupied lanes and sped through lights at the last possible moment, the black Volvo always appeared in the rear window. It seemed to always catch up, lurking behind them like a black panther tracking its prey. The cab driver sped the cab down alleyways and even over sidewalks in a valiant attempt to shake the black Volvo.

As the cab rapidly approached a busy intersection, Michael and Anna glanced at each other with visible horror. Anna screamed, "He's not going to stop!"

"Brace yourself!" Michael bent his body forward, ducking his head low against the front seat. Anna followed his example. The roar of the engine filled their ears as the cab, now at a full speed, entered the intersection just as the light turned green. The driver laughed with bravado.

"The driver says the Volvo is a good distance away," said Anna, sitting up.

Michael sighed deeply and groaned when he looked out the back window. "They can still see us! We aren't out of danger yet!"

It was dusk outside. The cab driver looked back and started speaking again. After a short dialogue with the driver, Anna looked over at Michael and grinned, "Hey, it doesn't matter at this point."

"Why?" asked Michael.

"The cab driver grew up in this neighborhood," she explained. Racing down the street at over a hundred kilometers per hour, the

155

taxi stopped short in a T-intersection marked by the stop sign. Tires squealing, he made a sharp right onto a local street. Turning off his headlights, the driver drove in the semi-darkness through the neighborhood, solely relying on his childhood memories. When they passed a school, he turned into the schoolyard.

"This is his old school," explained Anna as the driver raced through the schoolyard, turned left, drove between two buildings and then turned left again into a dark, inconspicuous nook next to the first building and a volleyball court. He parked his taxi, turned around and gave high five's to Anna and Michael as they whooped and hollered. Besides a few spontaneous thunders and a bright lightning flash, everything was quiet in the vicinity.

They decided to wait before moving out of their hiding spot. As it turned out, the driver's ex-wife had pulled the same stunt when they were getting divorced. It seemed as if divorce was like an invisible power, giving him an unusual burst of adrenaline. There was no other explanation as to how a sleepy cab driver could almost instantaneously become a Formula One auto racer. With a grin, Michael privately thought it would be a good idea to offer that notion to the Formula One committee. But then, in reality, it probably would not work out: before each race, the drivers would have to go through a bitter divorce.

They waited about thirty minutes and then asked their hero driver to drop them off at a good, local restaurant. They were sure to reward him generously for his brave and speedy driving.

# Chapter 25

"This place doesn't look half bad," said Anna as they walked inside Franz's Wirtshaus Bistro, shaking off the raindrops. They made their way to the back where Michael made sure he was sitting facing the entrance, following a technique used by almost every law enforcement officer. The idea is to always face the entrance and not sit with your back to it, as if in anticipation of a dangerous subject walking through the door. Michael's life motto, "prepare for the worst and hope for the best," was always in motion. The German culture's propensity for bright lighting meant that even their back booth was filled with cheerful light.

"I'm starving!" Michael exclaimed, looking at his wristwatch. "Wow! It's a quarter to eight."

The waitress brought their menus. While Anna spoke with her, Michael scanned his menu. *I wish this was in English,* he thought, suddenly feeling tired.

Noticing Michael's expression, Anna leaned forward, "Let me help you out. You might like ... sauerbraten. It's really good."

"What's that?"

"Roast beef. You can get a side order of potato dumplings or mashed potatoes to go with it."

"Sure, that's sounds good. I'll have the mashed potatoes," Michael started to smile. "Is that what you're getting?"

"Yep."

"I'll get a beer, too," added Michael.

As the waitress walked away, Anna leaned over conspiratorially, "So, what do you think? What are we gonna do?"

Michael leaned forward as well, whispering, "Wait for our food."

Anna chuckled, "Oh, come on, you know what I meant."

"Well, two men are chasing us all over Berlin so they can get their hands on a package your father sent to you before he died. These men believe that whatever is in that package will lead them to the ancient stele your father supposedly stole from their tribe, right?"

Anna nodded in agreement.

"After what happened today, I think there are more people involved in this chase."

"You really believe there are more tribesmen here in Germany?"

"Don't be surprised if more people are involved. It depends on how powerful their organization is."

"So, almost anybody here could be a spy?"

Michael leaned forward and whispered conspiratorially, "Take, for example, our waitress."

"Oh, come on, Michael," she started to laugh.

Michael sat back with a wry smile.

Anna reached into her purse. "Can I have the papyruses?" she asked, gently taking out a magnifying glass and placing it on the table.

Michael gave her a puzzled look, but pulled out the bag and handed it across the table to her. "What's this?" He looked pointedly at the magnifying glass.

Anna was busy unrolling and opening the bag. "David let me borrow it," she said softly, not looking at him.

Michael looked at her firmly and cleared his throat.

Anna glanced at him, pulling out the papyrus with the pencil rubbing and placing it on the table. "OK, ok," she sighed. "I took it, but I'll return it to David as soon as we figure everything out." She picked up the magnifying glass and looked through it at the papyrus. "So, what do you think about this?"

"Your guess is as good as mine," said Michael, taking the magnifying glass from her hand. He studied the papyrus, adding, "I think your friend David was right, there is more to it. Here, take a look."

Taking back the magnifying glass, Anna agreed, "Yes, I can definitely see the bottom edge is unfinished."

"Well, there could be two possible explanations: either the person who made the rubbing was scared off and couldn't finish it," Michael said, thinking. "Or that's the only remaining part of the artifact that survived until this day."

The waitress came bustling back to their table, plates in hand. Anna quickly moved everything safely to the side. After she had settled their plates, the waitress smiled at them, "Bon Appetit!"

Anna smiled back at her, "*Danke.*" The waitress hurried away as they started eating. "So, you think this stele was an ancient artifact made during Pharaoh Khufu's reign?" asked Anna, pausing to wipe her hands.

"I'm just assuming that there's a possibility that an ancient stele was found and that the papyrus is the proof of that."

"Do you think my father made the pencil rubbing?"

"Quite possible."

Anna took another bite and chewed slowly, deep in thought. "Do you think he stole this ancient stele?" she looked up at Michael sadly.

"No, I don't think so," said Michael, using his most reassuring tone of voice.

The waitress appeared at their table again, dropping off a pair of beer bottles and tall glasses.

Reaching for a bottle, Michael began pouring the creamy liquid into a glass. He took a sip and set his glass down. "Wow. This is not very cold."

"Yes, that's how we drink it." Anna replied patiently.

"You're right. Sorry. It's fine. OK, you told me your father was helping restore the Great Pyramid?"

"Yes. The last time he called me, he was working with a French company to install a new air ventilation system inside the Great Pyramid."

"OK, here is what I think happened in Egypt. Your father found an ancient artifact by accident. Then he hid it somewhere, not knowing what to do with it. After all, he was an electrical engineer, not an archeologist with permission to excavate. Somehow the members of some ancient tribe found out about it and started blackmailing your father so he'd give it back. He didn't want to reveal its location, so they poisoned him."

Anna listened carefully to Michael's trail of thoughts.

"But of all the places they could poison him, why would they do it inside the Great Pyramid?" she asked suddenly.

"I don't understand that either."

"Hopefully we'll find out one day," said Anna. "I know my father isn't a thief."

"I assure you; I truly believe that too."

Anna nodded thoughtfully, picking up the other bottle and pouring herself a glass. "Okay, then why would he send the pencil rubbing to me?" Anna rolled her eyes. "We weren't that close after he divorced my mom several years ago." Abruptly, Anna's eyes filled with tears. "I didn't wanna forgive him." She lowered her face, picked up her napkin and dried her tears. She blew her nose and took some slow, deep breaths, calming herself.

"Anna, I don't understand why he sent it to you," Michael said sadly. "And quite frankly, I know your father never stopped loving you."

"Michael, I don't know what to think anymore," said Anna, looking up miserably. Michael reached inside his jacket, pulled out a small brown notebook and handed it to her. As she started slowly flipping through the pages, she looked up at Michael in surprise, "This is my father's."

"He gave it to me." He grimaced, "I'm sorry, I wish I had thought of it earlier."

"Me too."

"Do you see anything unusual in there?"

"Well, I'm looking through it right now," she said, carefully turning the pages over. "There are at least a hundred names in here," she said, scanning the pages. "Are you suggesting we start calling every one of them? And what exactly are we going to ask?" She laughed, "Excuse me, did my father tell you about an ancient artifact he found in Egypt?"

"Are there any archaeologists in that notebook?"

"Possibly, but I have no clue who they would be," she paused and gave it some thought. "Actually, all of his contacts could be archaeologists. He always considered himself to be one of them even though he was an electrical engineer."

"Anything related to the pyramids?" he asked. "The Great Pyramid in particular?"

"Not really, nothing about pyramids at all," said Anna closely examining the pages. She stopped. "This could be something."

"What?"

"I just found your mystical phrase." She pointed to one of the lines inside the pocketbook. *Hr. Kirilov — Moskau, Russland —"Vier Möglichkeiten."*

"What does that mean?" Michael asked.

"It's in German, and it says 'four ways.'"

"You mean it's actually written, *'four ways'*? The hairs were standing up on the back of his neck.

"It says Mister Kirilov — Moscow, Russia — 'four ways.'"

"Your father said that to me!" he exclaimed excitedly. "But who is Mr. Kirilov?"

"I have no idea, but we will need to talk to him in order to shed some light on this."

"Is there a phone number for him?"

"I'm looking," she paused, turning the pages. "No, unfortunately no address, no phone number."

"Is it possible to call information and ask for someone in Russia?"

"Sure, I can try," said Anna, reaching for her purse.

"I'm going to the men's room."

When Michael returned, Anna was still talking on the phone. She ended the call, "No luck, his phone number is not listed."

"Well, then there's only one thing left to do," said Michael as he sat down, a thoughtful look on his face.

"Are you suggesting we go to Russia?" asked Anna, not sure whether Michael was serious or joking. "I've never been to Russia and have always wanted to visit. It's an amazing country; I've heard so much about it," Anna chattered happily. She paused, looking at his face. "I still have two more weeks of unused vacation," she added.

"No, that's not what I meant," Michael was looking at her incredulously. "What I meant was that we could Google his name."

"Oh! OK, I can do that," she laughed, a bit embarrassed. She focused on her cell phone, keying in words. "Here," she held the cell phone so he could look at it with her. "Your search – **Kirilov Russia** – did not match any documents," flashed across the screen. "Nothing," she glanced at Michael. "We gotta go there," she added eagerly.

Michael looked at her like she had two heads.

"We're going to Russia!" she exclaimed merrily, ignoring him.

"You can't be serious," he shook his head. "Russia is an enormous country."

"Yes, I am serious," said Anna. "And we can get away from Seth and the tribesman." She paused, watching him. "We're going to Russia!" she exclaimed again.

Michael remained silent, deep in thought.

"What? Don't look at me like that," she pouted. "You hinted first. Come on, say it!" she demanded, a grin eagerly spreading across her face.

"OK," he finally blurted out, feeling pushed.

"*Fräulein!*" Anna called for the waitress so they could settle the bill.

"Visit Russia before Russia visits you," Michael pondered as he absent-mindedly pushed aside his dinner plate.

# Chapter 26

Franz's Wirtshaus Bistro, Berlin, Germany
Thursday, September 21
8:30 p.m.

After paying for their meal, they wound their way through the boisterous crowd to the front door. Looking through the bistro's window, Michael spotted someone running past. He turned to Anna, "Stay here." He jogged to the front door and looked outside. He resolutely looked back and forth, but the person had vanished.

Mystified, Michael opened the bistro's front door. Hearing a loud commotion down the street, he turned and observed a man being chased by an angry crowd. The mob's frenzy was palatable. Just as the man was about to escape, another mob emerged from around a corner, blocking the man's only route to escape. A blood-curdling yell sliced through the evening air, followed by others.

In a few seconds the running man was abreast with the bistro. To his own astonishment Michael suddenly recognized the desperate man. *The Medjay!* The tribesman who had brushed past him in Egypt, the man responsible for the death of Anna's father, the man who had kidnapped Anna herself at knifepoint that very day.

The Medjay stopped short in front of the bistro, winded and helpless. Michael stood still, mesmerized. The Medjay was a foot away from him, within arm's reach. Amazed by this turn of events, he realized he only needed to block the Medjay's way and the frenzied, screaming crowd would immediately have him.

The mob was closing in on their prey, chanting excitedly, seeing their victim's inevitable fate. The Medjay slowly turned, his eyes leveling with Michael's and widening with recognition. Suddenly, despite the fact that Michael's life was in danger from that same Middle Eastern warrior, he grabbed the Medjay's tunic and abruptly pulled him inside the bistro.

The two ran to the back, zigzagging around several tables despite the indignant hollers of the raucous and drunk customers. Still holding onto the Medjay's sleeve, Michael pulled the warrior into the kitchen. They burst through the kitchen door to the amazement of the cooks and through the back door to the outside.

Back at the front door, Anna was speechless. Her mind was confused and reeling from the scene she had just witnessed, but could not believe. *Michael was helping the Medjay escape?!* The roar of the bistro faded into the background as she sat down on a nearby chair.

Michael was disappointed after rushing through back door. He had imagined that it opened into an alleyway. Instead, it was a courtyard with a grassy park, circled by trees and bushes. The foliage was thick and glossy, still dripping from the day's rain. Michael started heading in one direction, but a small glass door happened to catch his eye. He turned and raced toward it. As he neared, he realized it was propped open ever so slightly. He grabbed the handle and flung it open. Sprinting past a surprised family in raincoats waiting for their elevator, Michael headed for a glass door that looked promising. As he slammed through the doorway, he groaned when he realized that it opened into yet another courtyard. Berlin is an old city and although it has orderly streets, Michael was finding it to be filled with nooks and crannies. As he sprinted past benches and tables he could see that the courtyard opened into an alley.

Michael looked to his left and saw that the wide alley ended at another building. He turned right, deftly skirted around a small pickup truck and kept running. He instinctively looked back; the Medjay was on his heels. He turned left onto the sidewalk, not wanting to run back into the arms of the chanting, salivating mob. Relief flooded his mind when he saw they were approaching a tree-filled park. He was not sure how large it was but felt assured of disappearing into the thick stand of trees and overgrown bushes.

The dark and solemn park provided a shadowy cover for Michael and the Medjay as they sped over the wet, slick grass. The large leaves dripped rainwater, and as they brushed past the thick bushes, droplets of water exploded onto them. They raced behind an old stage and only slowed down as they cautiously exited the other side. With no one in sight, Michael headed for a break in the bushes, hoping to find an exit.

Leaving the park, they ran through a maze of interconnecting streets. During the entire run Michael remained ahead, occasionally looking back to make sure that the Medjay was still behind him. To Michael's surprise, not only did the Medjay keep close, but also seemed to be giving him a run for his money.

Michael could hear a buzz of people so he followed the growing clamor to a busy, lighted market area. He slowed down, merging with the crowd. Michael stopped, looking around desperately for the Medjay. The warrior had disappeared. Pleased with himself, Michael turned and slowly jogged back the way he had come.

When he reached the bistro, he found Anna waiting for him just inside the front door. Her arms were crossed and her face was filled with emotion. "You just pulled a *Der Polnische Abgang* Michael!" she said sternly.

"What?" Michael was a bit winded and not understanding her German. He motioned for her to come outside. The bistro had gotten even louder; the air was hot and thick to him after running so hard. He relished the cool, crisp air as he walked over to a tree and leaned against it. "What are you saying?" he asked as she approached him.

"You just pulled what we Germans call a Polish Retreat," she replied irately. He was stretching his legs methodically. "You ran off without saying anything at all!"

He looked over at her, smiling.

"I don't understand why you helped him," she asked, her voice trembling. "He would have been captured and all our problems would have been solved." She went on to grimly inform him that they were in Kreuzberg, a borough populated predominately by Turkish immigrants. Unfortunately, the Egyptian tribesman had stolen something from the wrong kind of people in the wrong place.

Michael remained silent, still focusing on his cooling muscles.

"And," she continued crossly, "it's cold out here!"

He continued to carefully stretch his limbs while deep in thought.

Anna looked at him solemnly, "You don't even know why you helped him, do you?"

Michael stopped stretching and looked Anna in the eyes. "He was frightened," he said quietly. "I couldn't just leave him there to get lynched by that mob."

# Chapter 27

Ostbahnhof Railway Station, Berlin, Germany
Friday, September 22
4:30 a.m.

No other train station in Berlin has changed its name as often as Berlin's *Ostbahnhof*. A plaque on one of the platforms catalogued the station's names throughout its history. Originally opened in 1842, the Ostbahnhof Railway Station was located in a pretty grim section of the former East Berlin, named Friedrichshain. It was one of the city's two main railway stations, the other being the *Zoologischer Garten*.

Michael and Anna's cab pulled up to the station in the chilly, predawn hour. Retrieving their bags, they walked inside the terminal. Despite the relatively early hour, the station was crowded and noisy. The line at the cashier's window stretched and wiggled across the enormous hall. Some passengers were loaded down with huge bags and bales, while others simply had small backpacks. As passengers navigated past clumps of baggage with their own enormous loads, a few arguments ignited. While waiting in the long line, a few cantankerous passengers started fighting. The station's security officers hustled over to the raging passengers, resolving the conflict before it spiraled out of control.

As they got closer to the cashier's windows, the main line divided into two independent, smaller lines. The timetable reshuffled every few minutes. When Anna approached the window, she purchased two one-way tickets to Moscow, paying in cash. After yesterday's incident, they did not want to leave any trace and risk being found. Thankful the wait was over, Michael grabbed his duffle bag and followed Anna to the waiting room, where he was happy to collapse onto a comfortable chair and rest.

Several minutes later, a bell rang and a pleasant female voice on the PA system announced in both German and English the arrival of the next train. A few minutes later, he could hear the gnashing wheels and a loud whistle. Michael watched with bleary eyes as the timetable reshuffled itself again.

The bell rang again and the now familiar voice announced that passengers traveling in the North and Northeasterly directions should report to their platforms.

"Come on," Anna announced happily. She stood up and gathered her belongings. Michael hoisted up his duffle bag and slung it over his shoulder. They moved slowly but steadily with the other passengers down a corridor. Soon they found themselves on platform number three. Boys ran back and forth along the platform selling morning newspapers. Street vendors strolled past the train cars with small carts. Passengers scurried along the platform looking for the right car, some stopping by the little carts.

Anna found their train car quickly. They still had some time before the train's departure, so Anna bought a morning newspaper from one of the boys running along the platform.

The uniformed conductor checked Michael and Anna's ticket, wished them a pleasant journey and let them inside the car. Anna led the way and found the right compartment. Opening the door, they were surprised to find it empty. They each chose lower bunks and stowed their luggage. Finally, Anna and Michael could relax in the relative discreetness of the compartment and wait for the train's departure. Anna opened her newspaper and read quietly for a few minutes. Suddenly, she gasped and pointed excitedly to one of the articles.

"Look! Michael! Here's an article about the incident with the Medjay." She looked at him sternly, "You know, the Medjay you helped to escape."

"Huh. What does it say?"

"Well, apparently, the Medjay robbed a store."

"Wow, robbed?" Michael whistled.

"Yeah," she continued, putting the paper aside.

"Did anyone die?" he asked.

Anna looked annoyed, but shook her head.

"So, for stealing somebody's stuff the Medjay would have been lynched or beaten to death," he said quietly, maintaining his firm eye contact with her.

Anna stared back at him just as firmly.

"Either way," Michael continued, "the punishment would not have fit the crime."

The door slid open. An older man in an expensive suit stood glancing around the compartment. He stepped inside, rolling his elegant suitcase behind him. Shaking their hands, he introduced himself as Rolf. He lifted his suitcase onto the top shelf and sat down at the table across from Michael. His entire demeanor confirmed to them that their new companion was a wealthy man.

"So, are you going to Poland or all the way to Moscow?" he asked in English, a contagious smile on his face. As it turned out later, Rolf spoke five languages fluently, was originally from Germany and owned several hotel chains in Europe. He traveled extensively all over Europe and the Americas on business trips in his profession as a hotel entrepreneur.

Anna picked up on his German accent right away and began conversing with Rolf in German. As they chatted happily, it occurred to Michael that Anna must have been starving to speak German. For the past several days she had no choice but to speak in English with him. Michael did not mind a bit and turned his attention to look out the window at the people on the platform.

A bell rang loudly and overhead a pleasant female voice announced first in German and then in English that the train was leaving the station in five minutes. Michael watched as the people on the platform hastily bid farewell to their departing family and friends. Soon a loud whistle was heard and the train slowly started moving. The tedious sound of the train wheels and the monotonous landscape outside the window soon brought on fatigue. In no time Michael was dozing with his head pressed up against the window. He woke up at one point and despite his body wanting to stay in its position, forced himself to move to his bed. Once there he blissfully went to sleep.

The train shook Michael awake. He glanced at his watch and was surprised to realize it was half past one o'clock in the afternoon. He glanced around and realized Anna was asleep on her bed. Rolf sat quietly at the table working on a pile of some important looking documents. Michael's stomach was aching, and as he slowly became more and more awake, he also became aware that not only had they skipped breakfast that morning, but also he had been asleep for more than seven hours.

"Excuse me, Rolf," Michael said, keeping his voice low so as not to disturb Anna's sleep. "Do you know where the dining car is?"

The man looked up and wearily rubbed his eyes. He checked his wristwatch. "I didn't realize it was lunchtime," he said, looking at Michael kindly. As he carefully stacked his paperwork he offered, "Let's go find it." They quietly exited the compartment and started walking.

After passing through a few cars, they arrived at the dining car. The interior was spacious and pleasant music played softly. There were few customers, so they quickly found an empty table. After ordering his meal, Rolf removed a book from his jacket's inner pocket. He excused himself and began reading. Michael was watching the scenery passing by when he looked at Rolf's book. He could not believe his eyes. Rolf's book had Egypt's Great Pyramid on the front. Surprised, Michael turned his head a little and noticed that Sir William Matthew Flinders Petrie was the book's author. Michael stared at Rolf in disbelief: his compartment mate was interested in Egyptology. He knew the author's name from the countless lectures on the Egyptian pyramids that he had attended. After all, Sir Flinders Petrie's 1880's survey of the Giza Plateau, which included the Great Pyramid of Khufu, was the most detailed Egyptian study ever undertaken by a surveyor.

"I didn't know that you were interested in ancient Egyptian history," Michael remarked.

"Not exactly all of Egyptian history," said Rolf, pulling the book away from his face. "Just the Great Pyramid."

"Me too."

Really?" Rolf put his book down as Michael nodded. "That's interesting. Since when?"

"I've been fascinated with the Egyptian pyramids since I was a teenager," said Michael.

"So it's been a while for you then," said Rolf, chuckling "I got interested in the Great Pyramid about five years ago after one peculiar encounter. In fact, it happened here, on this same train."

"Wow, no kidding."

"Trust me," Rolf said, rolling his eyes. "A first I thought the man was a crazed lunatic after he told me a synopsis of the concept of his theory." He chuckled, "But then I got intrigued and started doing my own research. Surprisingly, I am starting to lean toward that man's explanations."

"You have intrigued me," said Michael, with growing enthusiasm.

"That man intrigued me as well," said Rolf, leaning forward, his eyes shining.

"What was his name?"

"He was Russian ... had one of those typical Russian names. Koralev or something."

"Was it Kirilov by any chance?"

His eyes widened with shock, Rolf replied, "Yes! Kirilov. That's right. But how do you know?"

"You are not gonna believe this," replied Michael, hardly able to believe it himself.

# Chapter 28

"Throughout history there have been countless theories about how the Great Pyramid was built and with what purpose," Michael said as he sat across from Rolf at their dining car table.

"Oh, yes, I know."

"So what is so special about Kirilov's theory?"

"This is what I have been examining. To start, the Great Pyramid is shrouded in many veils of the great mysteries. Many desire to loosen at least some of them. To simplify the task, let's first consider the existing, fairly modern statements regarding the purpose of the Great Pyramid."

Michael nodded, listening intently.

"John Taylor, in his book *The Great Pyramid,* argued that the mathematical number $\pi$ (pi), which is the ratio of a circle's circumference to its diameter and is approximately equal to 3.14159 and $\varphi$ (phi), which is the golden ratio, have been deliberately incorporated into the design of the Great Pyramid. The perimeter of the Great Pyramid is close to $2\pi$ times its height. Charles Piazzi Smyth then expanded Taylor's theories in pyramidology. And in the 1880's they were studied by the famous Egyptologist ..."

"Sir William Flinders Petrie," Michael interjected, smiling widely.

"Right, Professor Sir William Flinders Petrie," Rolf chuckled, pointing to his book. "And finally, David Davidson, the British structural engineer. Despite being a skeptic, he proved Smyth and Petrie's original calculations."

Michael and Rolf barely noticed when their food was brought to their table. "While not questioning and not considering the detailed statements of all of these researchers, whose ideas can be considered common knowledge for all those interested in the pyramids, it would be desirable in the course of these arguments to ask only two questions," said Rolf, carefully cutting his beefsteak into pieces.

"Ok, what are these two questions?" asked Michael as he sorted through his *bratkartoffeln*, a traditional German dish of fried potatoes with diced bacon and onions.

"Firstly, what prevailed in creating the Great Pyramid: a desire to ensure its reliability and stability or the desire to embody mathematical knowledge within its structure?"

Michael paused his eating to think. "Well," he was uncertain, "I would guess both ..."

"Actually the first part dominated. You see, otherwise, the Great Pyramid would have collapsed and all of its inherently intelligent hidden messages in the form of mathematical calculations would have been lost in the ruins."

Michael agreed by nodding.

"And the second question," continued Rolf. "If the Great Pyramid is such an intelligent pyramid, figuratively speaking, then what about the intelligence of the smaller pyramids built right next to it on the same Giza Plateau? Have they also embodied the great knowledge within or were they built based on a tradition?"

Michael shrugged his shoulders.

"Both of these questions are really farfetched," Rolf continued, pushing aside his empty plate. "If the pyramids, which were built by different pharaohs, are connected by one main purpose, then it will be easier to unravel the whole mystery surrounding them. The fact of the matter is that the main purpose of the pyramids was the same: to serve as the burial places of pharaohs. They only differed from each other in proportion and size."

"OK," said Michael pushing aside his empty plate, "what's unclear to me is how did ancient Egyptians transport and stack limestone blocks weighing no less than several tons each?"

"It's true," said Rolf, chuckling, clearly enjoying their conversation, "packed inside the Great Pyramid are blocks that for the most part weigh five tons and up. Certainly such blocks could not be moved or dragged across the sand by a small group of people, as popular modern sketches sometimes depict the Great Pyramid's construction. And don't forget that it was done in a difficult climate under the scorching sun."

"It looks like only Superman could do this kind of job," grinned Michael.

"No Superman existed during ancient times," chuckled Rolf.

"OK then, what about another popular theory that large limestone blocks were dragged over an artificial, man-made sand mound that was built up around the whole pyramid as it was built? At the end of the construction, the pyramid was dug out and the sand removed."

"This theory makes absolutely no sense," objected Rolf, shaking his head, "this is equivalent to saying that the main amount of work had to have another, at nearly the same amount, for its excavation."

"What about the theory mentioned by Herodotus?"

"You mean after the stones were laid out for the base, they raised the remaining stones with a machine made of short wooden planks? That theory is that the first machine raised them from the ground to the top of the first step where was placed another machine, which received the stone upon its arrival and conveyed it to the second step, and so on."

"Yes, precisely," nodded Michael. "So, which construction method does the stranger you met on this train agree with?"

"Neither."

"Really? Neither?"

"You will have to ask him yourself," said Rolf, grinning as he got up from his chair. "All I can tell you is that his theory does not require any assumptions about the Egyptian lifting machines mentioned by Herodotus, from which no trace remained whatsoever, and which would not have been possible to exist under the then-level of productive forces."

Michael got up from the table as well and followed Rolf back to the compartment. Entering, Michael saw Anna was still asleep. Rolf held out his book to Michael, "Why don't you read it for yourself?"

"Thank you." Michael lay on his bunk and started reading. In the meantime, Rolf went back to his paperwork.

Michael did not realize exactly when he fell asleep again, but was awakened by a strange sound, like a clap. For the first few moments, he wondered whether the sound was from a dream or reality. He looked around the dimly lit compartment. Looking up he saw Rolf asleep in the bed above him. Anna was still deeply asleep. Besides Rolf's barely audible snoring and the melodic sound of the train wheels, everything seemed incredibly quiet.

Clap!

Michael quietly and carefully opened the compartment door, stepping out of the tiny room into the aisle. All was dark and quiet. He started walking down the aisle. Most of the windows were curtained except for the last window at the far end. No one was around. All of the compartment doors were closed.

A door slammed loudly at the other end. Michael turned and walked quickly but silently in that direction, stopping short by the vestibule double doors. He attempted to peer through the darkened windows to the door. Just as he was deciding whether or not to open the doors, he observed a tiny spark that blinked for a split-second and then disappeared in the same instant. *Maybe someone is having a smoke.*

Curious, he pushed open the double doors. It was dark and quiet. For a moment Michael wished he had on night vision goggles, the same ones he had used in night raids in Iraq. Walking inside he tripped on something attached to the floor, literally crashing inside the vestibule. To his surprise, nobody was there. Feeling like an idiot, he squatted all the way down to the floor and felt around. He blindly searched for a cigarette butt, yet found nothing in the darkness. Finding this very strange to say the least, Michael returned to his compartment.

During his absence, nothing had changed. Both Rolf and Anna were still asleep. All was dark and quiet. Michael lay down on his bunk and soon was asleep, lulled by the droning sound of the train wheels.

There was a small knock at the compartment door. Michael awoke. *Who would knock so early in the morning?* Someone knocked again, a little bit louder. *Why isn't anyone opening the door?* He wondered. *Am I alone in here?* It turned out that he was, indeed, alone. Neither Anna nor Rolf was in the compartment. Rolf's bed was neatly made and the table was covered with a paper napkin with a plate and cup on top. *Of course, he got off in Poland.* Michael glanced at the napkin and saw something scribbled there in a hurry, 'If you are still intrigued—'

*Intrigued*, Michael reminisced, smiling. He realized the note was from Rolf. He continued reading, 'Mr. Kirilov's address in Moscow: Voronezhskaya Street, building 4, apartment 10.'

Michael was stunned. Here was what he and Anna were looking for: Mr. Kirilov's address! It seemed almost impossible that the very Mr. Kirilov that Anna's father had written about in his notebook was also the 'lunatic' Rolf had met five years ago on the same train. *I've gotta tell Anna, but where the heck is she?*

Abruptly, Michael recalled the knock at the door. He opened the door, but there was nobody there. Whoever was knocking had walked away, apparently tired of waiting.

Soon, Anna walked in. Michael briefly filled her in about his conversation with Rolf. As soon as she saw the message on the napkin, Anna jumped in excitement.

"You may think of me as superstitious, but this is more than just a coincidence." Anna's eyes were huge with exhilaration. "After all, come on, what are the chances of us getting on this train and meeting Rolf? He knew the very person we were looking for—and his address?"

"Yeah," Michael agreed, "the probability of that happening is … well, in order for that to happen..." He rolled his eyes upwards, "It looks like somebody is helping us."

"Michael, I would like to think that this is my father sending us messages from the grave and trying to give us a hand," Anna said quietly, a few tears starting to form in her eyes as she thought of her dear departed father.

Michael smiled kindly and put his hand on her shoulder to comfort her, "I believe you are right. That is a very nice way of putting it."

A bell rang loudly and overhead a pleasant female voice announced first in German and then in English that the train would be reaching their destination in ten minutes. As they packed their bags, Michael decided he should use the bathroom. He walked down the aisle toward the end of the train car, passing a couple of families who were noisily chatting. The window curtains were now open and sunlight was bouncing around the train's interior. So different from the last time he was in the aisle. As soon as he opened the bathroom door, he was facing a mirror attached to the back wall. Suddenly, for just a moment, the dark silhouette of a man painfully familiar to him flashed in the glass.

*The Medjay is here on this train?* The thought paralyzed his whole body momentarily. He turned his head in the direction of the mirror's reflection. The Medjay was not there. He let out his breath. He stared into the mirror, but only the familiar aisle and a few passengers were there. The Medjay had disappeared the same way he had appeared.

Not knowing whether to believe the reflection in the mirror or his sick imagination, Michael walked all the way down the aisle to the other side of the train car searching, just to be sure.

Meanwhile, the train was already in the city limits of Moscow.

# Chapter 29

Belorusskaya Railway station, Moscow, Russia
Saturday, September 23
9:30 a.m.

It was half past nine o'clock in the morning as the Hannover HBF–
Moscow passenger train #447 approached Moscow's Belorusskaya
Railway Station.

"We are now approaching our final destination, the Belorusskaya
Railway station in Moscow, the capital of Russia. Please remain
seated until we come to a complete stop," the pleasant female voice
announced first in German, then in English. Completely ignoring the
announcement, most of the passengers were already standing up and
crowding the aisles in anticipation, eagerly gawking out the windows.

The train pulled slowly into the station. When doors opened the
passengers poured onto the platform into the massive human pool with
everyone swimming to the exits.

After experiencing 'hurry up and wait' throughout his military
career, Michael encouraged Anna to take her time getting packed while
the masses in front of them squeezed through the doors one at a time.
At long last it was time to leave the train, and Michael was jumping
onto the platform.

"Finally," he declared, taking a deep breath of Moscow's morning
air. He reached up to help Anna.

"Yes, finally," she repeated happily as they were carried away by
the enormous, noisy crowd.

Although it was late September, the weather in Moscow was
unusually warm and pleasant. As they bumped their way to the exit,
Michael and Anna attempted to stay together. In reality, this was

a difficult task as passengers were hauling loads of luggage, bags, strollers, carpets and boxes.

There was more room to walk when they got outside. Anna made her way over to an empty bench and collapsed. "That was a real nightmare! Can you believe it?" The Belorusskaya Railway terminal loomed behind her, an enormous mint-green building with gothic towers. As Russia's second largest railway station, the Belorusskaya has seen a lot of history over the years. Its grand opening was in 1870, the same year Vladimir Lenin, the leader of the 1917 Russian revolution, was born. During World War II the first military trains headed to the front lines departed from this station in 1941.

"Well, we need to find Kirilov," Anna remarked as she tried catching her breath. "So let's find our hotel, get changed and track down his apartment."

"Sounds like a great idea," said Michael, getting up to flag down one of the taxis passing nearby. Moments later one came to a stop next to them. "Do you speak English?" Michael asked as he and Anna climbed inside.

The driver, wearing an oversized Kangol wool cap and a long mustache shook his head. He pointed to a small flag hanging from his rearview mirror. It was a white rectangle divided into four parts by a large red cross. In each of the four white spaces was a smaller red cross. *Georgia* was emblazoned across the front.

"Oh," Michael looked over at Anna doubtfully. "He doesn't speak English? And he is from Georgia?"

"Obviously, not the Georgia that you know," chuckled Anna, "He is from the former Soviet republic of Georgia. It is now a sovereign state in the Caucasus region of Eurasia."

Michael looked over at Anna grinning, "I should've known it would be complicated."

As it turned out, Georgia's unwritten rules require Georgian men to wear what is considered the national regalia of a *real* Georgian man: a *Kangol*-style classic wool ivy cap, an impressive mustache and a traditional Georgian dagger. It is believed that the bigger the size of his Georgian cap, the straighter and blacker the mustache, and the sharper the knife, the more respectful and honorable a man is considered among his people.

"Deutsch?" Anna asked hopefully. But the cabbie threw his arms up in surrender.

Michael glanced at Anna with visible frustration. "We gotta find another taxi," he said opening the door and starting to get out of the cab.

"Not so fast," Anna laughed, grabbing Michael's arm and pulling him back inside. She held up her iPhone. "I knew this app would be useful one day," she said, showing him the screen.

Michael looked at it curiously, "OK, let's see what happens."

Anna typed, 'Hello, our names are Michael and Anna, what's your name?' She pressed a button. In a metallic voice, the iPhone translated her words into Russian. Anna and Michael froze in anticipation, looking hopefully at the driver. The driver grinned broadly and nodded, uttering, "Vahtang," and pointed to his chest.

"That's amazing!" Michael exclaimed.

Anna's face was lit up like a kid at Christmas. She typed in the name of the hotel and street name. The cabbie nodded. Next, she typed and asked how long it will take to get there. The moment the voice uttered the Russian words; he nodded again and started looking for something. He found a piece of paper and with a pencil wrote '20' on it. Anna squealed in delight.

The driver flashed another one of his grins. "Hotel," he said happily in heavily accented English. A fresh September wind blew into the half-open windows of the taxi as they sped off into Moscow's traffic.

Founded in 1147, Moscow is the capital of Russia and Europe's largest city with 11.5 million people, the seventh largest city in the world. Nowhere are Russia's contrasts more apparent than in Moscow: antique pre-revolutionary monasteries, soviet era government buildings, one-size-fits-all residential complexes and avant-garde megaliths that stand side-by-side. New Russian millionaires and poverty-stricken seniors share the same streets. For those who live in Moscow the city brings about contradictory feelings: from loving devotion to extreme aversion. People either love Moscow or hate it, thus leaving nobody indifferent to this magnificent and ancient city filled with traditions. It does not matter whether it is your first time visiting or if you are a native; Moscow is a multifaceted, diverse and incomprehensible city that is rapidly changing beyond recognition.

In the post-World War II era, the Soviet Union's Premier, Joseph Stalin, ordered seven huge, tiered neoclassic towers to be built around the city. One of them was placed at Moscow State University. This thirty-six-story tower is by far the largest of the seven and can be observed from miles away. At the time of its construction it was the tallest building in the world, outside of New York City, and remained the tallest building in Europe until 1990. Michael was thrilled when he got a glimpse of the historical tower. As they followed the ebb and flow of traffic, however, it disappeared from view.

The driver suddenly shouted, bringing them back to windows of the cab. With the driver smiling and pointing, they drove past the mammoth Red Square, dominated by the Kremlin and the extravagantly colored domes of St. Basil's Cathedral. Michael and Anna were mesmerized by the breath-taking view. The Kremlin, the residence of the Russian rulers, was one of the finest architectural works in the world. The first of its walls were built back in the twelfth century.

The cab pulled over in front of a high-rise building. "Looks like a nice place," said Michael. As they walked inside the grand entrance, the cab sped away, the driver proudly holding a crisp new 20 EUR banknote.

"This hotel is beautiful," Michael commented as he walked inside the building rolling both his duffel bag and a piece of Anna's luggage.

"Hello, welcome to Holiday Inn Suschevskiy!" Exclaimed the lady at the front desk. "Are you here for business or pleasure?"

"Pleasure," Anna replied.

"I can recommend you visit *GUM*, our supreme department store. Also if you need any tickets to any Moscow's concerts, ballets and shows just let me know."

"Thank you."

After checking in, Michael and Anna took the elevator to the fifth floor to their room. Anna decided she needed to freshen up properly and change her clothes, so she excused herself and went into the bathroom. Michael unpacked his duffel bag, setting aside his toiletry bag and a set of clean clothes for after his shower.

He went to the window and found that it faced so many buildings he was unable to see past them. He spent a few minutes watching the Russian traffic and people. After a while, he sat on the sofa and started slowly flipping through the TV channels. He clicked through channel after channel hearing only Russian, but just as he was about to turn the TV off, his ears heard the beautiful sound of the English language. Strangely enough, it was one of his favorite movies, *The Mummy*, accompanied by captioning in Russian. It was at the part where the two main characters, Evelyn and O'Connell were inside the Hamunaptra, the City of the Dead. They had just found the ancient sarcophagus with the mummy of the high priest, Imhotep. Carved inside the sarcophagus were the ominous words, 'Death is only the beginning.'

Michael had watched that movie many times, but that phrase suddenly made him realize something. He started thinking about Pharaoh Khufu's soul trapped within his sarcophagus, waiting impatiently to get out. The reincarnated mummy in the movie was looking to exact revenge on everybody who disturbed his peace: definitely not a pleasant fate to experience. Michael mused that he and Anna were getting closer to solving one of the greatest mysteries of the Great Pyramid, which meant they would have to disturb Pharaoh Khufu's final resting place. Perhaps the ending result might not be a pleasant one for both of them. After all, at least one person was already dead and now the Medjay and his accomplice were hunting them down.

"Michael!"

Startled and roused from his thoughts, Michael turned and looked up at Anna.

"I think I know what you're thinking," she said quietly.

Michael looked at her steadfastly, not breathing.

"I've watched this movie before. I've heard the stories of the Pharaohs' curses that started when Howard Carter discovered the tomb of Tutankhamun. Most of the people in his crew died unnaturally either from diseases contracted by a mysterious illnesses or by accidents surrounded by strange circumstances."

"You're absolutely right," he nodded solemnly. "Aren't we exposing ourselves to a greater risk by trying to uncover the Great Pyramid's secrets that have been hidden for ages?" He paused, and then continued slowly, "and maybe these secrets should be remained hidden. I mean, after all, your father died inside the Great Pyramid, which most definitely is cursed. In addition, you were kidnapped in Germany, and it's a miracle that you escaped unharmed from those thugs."

"Michael, I understand you are worried. I'm worried. But, if you are afraid of some ancient curses, consider this: Howard Carter died in 1939 at the age of 64 of natural causes, some seventeen years after discovering the tomb, despite being in charge of the expedition."

"Wow, how do you know that?" he asked in amazement.

"When I was growing up, my father told me many stories about the ancient Egyptians," she replied. "Many of his stories and fairytales I have forgotten, but some I still remember. The saga of Tutankhamun, the boy king, was certainly one of my favorites. So, to put your mind at ease and consider this," Anna sat on the couch next to him, "Howard Carter's natural death is the great confirmation that contradicts the idea of a so-called *curse of the pharaohs* that might have plagued his expedition."

Michael remained quiet. "I hope you right, Anna," he finally whispered.

"I know I'm right! Come on, look around," Anna got up and approached the window "here we are in the twenty-first century, for goodness sake. There is little room for superstitions."

"OK, ok," Michael got up and approached the window, "you've convinced me. It's just the events of the past several days combined with the scenes from that movie." His voice trailed off as they both looked at the TV screen where O'Connell was defeating the evil Imhotep by forcing him into the River of Death.

"You know," said Anna grinning, "In every fairytale, good always defeats evil."

"Yeah," Michael chuckled, "that's why they are called fairytales."

Anna laughed, "I think it's time for you to hit the shower."

"Right," Michael replied as he headed to the bathroom with his things. The bathroom was clean, neat and stacked with toiletries. Even though the shower was equipped with a German-made showerhead, Michael got no more than lukewarm water. After only about ten minutes he gave up on getting a hot shower. It felt good to get clean, though.

Soon they were downstairs walking into the restaurant. Once inside, they greeted the hostess in English, hoping she spoke English as well. They were delighted when the young lady, wearing thick glasses and sporting a black-haired ponytail, responded to them in English. Then, she asked them politely whether they had ordered their lunch that morning. Michael and Anna glanced at each other in astonishment. "I'm sorry," said Michael, amazed, but hoping the hostess had misspoken. "Did I hear you correctly?"

To their surprise the hostess had stated her request correctly. They soon found out that in order to get lunch, the restaurant's patrons had to order it during their breakfast. In fact, to get dinner they needed to order it during lunchtime. The hostess was surprised that they were surprised.

"You should have ordered lunch in the morning," the hostess informed them with a tone of strong disapproval as she attempted to impress on them how ridiculous it was to expect a lunch without ordering it in advance. It was only after a lengthy discussion, one which eventually involved the manager of the hotel, that the wait staff understood that neither Michael nor Anna could have ordered lunch in advance simply because they had just arrived to the hotel a mere one hour before.

Michael watched in amazement as the manager used some forcibly spoken words in Russian that quickly persuaded the cooking staff of the restaurant to serve his desirable foreign hotel guests. The Russian chefs had no choice but to fix a simple meal from supplies taken straight out of the refrigerator. Soon Michael and Anna were enjoying chicken sandwiches made in record time. Anna thought that if the representatives from the world famous Guinness Book of World Records were present they would have witnessed a new record in sandwich making history.

"'You should have ordered your lunch while eating your breakfast' is gonna be my new slogan," announced Michael as he and Anna stood in front of the hotel trying to wave down a taxi.

Anna grinned.

"Oh, come on!" Michael laughed at his own witticism. "You know that's even funnier than a Saturday Night Live monologues."

Anna looked over at him and started laughing as well, getting caught up in Michael's contagious laugh. When a cab stopped next to them, Anna dug in her purse for her iPhone with the life-saving translation app, but Michael quickly discovered that the taxi driver spoke fluent English. As soon as Michael showed him Kirilov's address, the cab driver nodded and stepped on the gas pedal. After twenty minutes they were pulling in front of a seventeen-story blue building.

"There it is," the driver announced. "Voronezhskaya Street, building 4."

Commending the cabby for the smooth and fast driving, they quickly emerged from the cab and walked into the sought-after building.

*Could this be it?* was on their minds as they waited inside the lobby for the elevator. When the elevator stopped on the seventh floor, Anna said, "I'll check the left side, and you check the right," as she started walking away.

"Found it," Michael exclaimed ten seconds later. "Number ten, third door on the right."

As Anna approached the apartment door, it was almost as if her heart would jump out of her chest. She stood still for several seconds, catching her breath and trying in vain to slow down her heart rate. Her anticipation was becoming almost too great. Just as she was no longer able to handle her overwhelming feelings, she reached out and rang the doorbell.

# Chapter 30

*Belorusskaya* Railway station, Moscow, Russia
Saturday, September 23
9:30 a.m.

It was half past nine o'clock in the morning as Hannover HBF–
Moscow passenger train #447 approached Moscow's Belorusskaya
Railway Station.

"We are now approaching our final destination, the Belorusskaya
Railway station in Moscow, the capital of Russia. Please remain
seated until we come to a complete stop," the pleasant female voice
announced first in German, then in English. Completely ignoring the
announcement, most of the passengers were already standing up and
crowding the aisles in anticipation, eagerly gawking out the windows.

Seth motioned for the Medjay to come stand by him at the door.
After the long train ride, he now knew the tight-lipped Medjay's first
name: Asim. Asim had located Anna and Michael's compartment
earlier in the trip. He hoped Asim had not slipped up and been spotted.
He watched in disgust as the Medjay rudely pushed past the passengers
and glared at them menacingly. Soon Asim was at the head of the line
with Seth.

The train pulled slowly into the station. When the doors opened,
with Seth and Asim first in line at their door, the passengers poured onto
the platform into the massive human pool with everyone swimming to
the exits. Their first objective was to locate Anna and Michael in the
crowds and follow them to their hotel without being seen.

With some difficulty, Seth made his way to the Information booth
in the railway station. The stoic lady at the window quickly ascertained
that her new customer with the hard face was a difficult one. Seth

attempted to describe Anna and Michael in broken English to her. The lady had no idea what this nasty man was talking about and stopped caring after a few moments. She had a line backing up at her booth and this man was bothering her. After the third attempt, he finally decided that his efforts to find out anything about Anna and Michael were useless. Before stepping away from the window, he angrily cursed at her. Obviously, this had no meaning whatsoever for her as the only language she knew was her native Russian. She deftly ignored him and nodded at her next customer.

As soon as he turned away from the information booth, Seth noticed Asim standing on a bench in the distance, waving both arms in air, trying to get his attention. He began zealously running and jostling his way through the crowd to the Medjay warrior. Asim quickly reported that he had just observed Schulze's daughter and the American get into a taxi. Not wanting to waste any precious time, Seth started briskly pushing through the last of the crowd, his luggage banging into the unlucky people who did not get out of his way quickly enough. When Asim caught up to him, Seth had already flagged down a taxi and was jumping inside. Luckily for Seth, the driver spoke decent German, so Seth was able to instruct him to follow the cab a few vehicles in front of them. They both sighed with relief that it had taken Anna and her American accomplice extra time for their taxi to start moving. Seth began telling the taxi driver an elaborate story about how they had spotted some colleagues from home and wanted to catch up to them as a surprise. As Seth chattered on, Asim began to reflect on the events of the past several days.

His mind dwelled on Thursday, and his hopes for quickly obtaining the package Schulze had sent to his daughter. Initially, the plan was to stay at Seth's apartment for a few days, as this was the amount of time Asim had projected it would take to obtain the package. Seth had reassured Asim that the package would be found that day and that Anna herself would deliver it to them.

As he ate a couple of sandwiches and drank some strong coffee for his breakfast early that morning, he envisioned holding that package in one hand and in his other hand the phone, pressed up to his left ear, with his great chief praising him for the success of the whole operation.

He prepared himself for his mission by remembering the last words of his beloved chief, "Asim, my fearless warrior, trust Seth as he knows everything necessary to retrieve the package." This put his mind at ease. He wholly trusted Seth's logic and intuitions, even though Seth's accomplice, Layla, had returned empty handed and two break-ins into Anna's apartment had also proved to be fruitless. These failures meant only one of two things: either Anna knew everything and was cleverly hiding the package or it was just pure bad luck on Seth's part that the package could not be found.

Relying on Seth's intimate information about Anna's whereabouts, Asim was pleased when he and Seth laid in wait outside her apartment building and nabbed her, completely unnoticed by anyone. The interrogation inside the car was successful. While watching for Anna to reappear out of her apartment, his mind was already returning to Egypt and the tribal life to which he was accustomed. Here in Germany he was a stranger, helpless against the German language, customs and laws of which he did not know or understand. Back at home in Egypt, Asim only relied on himself and trusted no one, except his wise chief. The more Asim dealt with Seth, the more he wished he did not have to rely on him.

After employing his 'smooth interrogation techniques', as Seth defined them, Anna never returned with the package. Worse yet, as they waited for her at one end of her building, they observed a cab arriving and stopping at the other end of her building. Asim could not believe his eyes when he saw Anna and her American friend suddenly leap out from behind a door and escape.

Seth followed the cab at a distance and managed to remain undetected. When Anna and her American friend were dropped off in front of the German Archaeological Institute, Seth parked the car near the front entrance. When Seth translated the welcome sign for him, Asim's heart sank. The word *archaeology* gave him goose bumps. It meant the German female and her American accomplice not only had the package, but also realized its importance. *Her father sent her the map to the location of the stele*, Asim suddenly realized.

After a couple of phone calls, Seth abruptly left Asim in the car, swiftly entering the two-story building. Returning, he informed Asim that the front door was the only entrance to the building. When

Schulze's daughter and the American exited the building, they planned to nab them.

At first, the hot-blooded Asim wanted to go inside the building and forcibly grab the map, but Seth talked him out of it. After all, they were not in Egypt where such activities might be overlooked. Seth explained that since they did not own a firearm, by using Asim's dagger they would essentially be bringing a knife to a gun battle. If the German security guard took into the account Asim's exotic look and outfit, complimented by his traditional white cloak, arrest by the police was exactly what was awaiting both of them at the end of an attempt to a hand-to-hand fight. They had no choice but to wait right in front of the Institute and catch their victims by surprise.

But their decision backfired. Seth caught a glimpse of Anna and her American accomplice as they left the building. Unfortunately, the American caught a glimpse of Seth as well. Seth was just about to leap out of his car when the fire alarm went off. Later, the receptionist at the German Archeological Institute told Seth that she saw Anna walking away from the fire alarm and realized that she had staged a false fire alarm.

But the ruse worked beautifully for Anna and her American friend. The alarm forced everybody outside, not only creating a crowd of people on the sidewalk, but also bringing the police, who forced them to drive away. They lost Anna and Michael.

At that point, Asim grimaced as he remembered how frustrated and angry he was with Seth and the entire situation. As they had driven around looking for Anna and her American friend, Asim became angrier and angrier.

Then they finally spotted Anna and Michael at the entrance of a café getting into a cab. He reported to Seth that the cab was turning into an alley. Seth quickly made a few maneuvers and soon they were behind Anna and Michael's cab. Asim was starting to think that Seth had a special touch to following people when Anna's cab burst into action: they had been discovered. Zipping, turning and accelerating at terrifying speeds, Seth stayed on their tail, giving a spectacular vehicular pursuit. Despite his skills, they were outsmarted by the cab driver, who managed to make his cab disappear. As they hunted the unfamiliar neighborhood that twisted and wound back upon itself,

Asim roared in anger, pummeling his fists against the interior of the car.

Seth stayed on his phone, telling all of his contacts to be on the lookout for Anna and her American accomplice. After hopelessly circling, Asim decided that his beloved chief needed to know what was happening. He needed to ask his advice about any possible clues that would lead them to the whereabouts of Schulze's daughter.

It was then that he picked up his cell phone and discovered the battery was dead. To add insult to injury, the car was running on empty and they needed to find a petrol station. After finding one and filling his car, Seth asked the attendant where the nearest cell phone store was located. It was on one of the main streets leading out of the neighborhood, and they found it easily.

The day that had started out so promising was ending on the worst note possible imaginable. The thirty-year-old Medjay warrior had never experienced this kind of failure in his entire life; especially all packed into one single day.

Greatly discouraged, the Medjay warrior entered the cell phone store. Before he knew it, the cellphone storeowner was screaming at him. Looking back on the matter, Asim realized that the storeowner had misunderstood his actions. The owner thought the Medjay was stealing one of the latest iPhone models from him. In reality, Asim had taken the cellphone battery out and inserted it into his phone, attempting to phone his great chief. Moments later, the bewildered Medjay warrior was being confronted by a street mob lead by the cellphone storeowner. The situation rapidly escalated with the uncontrolled street mob stalking and chasing him down the street. Seth was in his car, waiting for Asim to return. When he saw the frenzied mob on the street pursuing Asim, he simply took off. Asim's glorious life filled with adventures would have ended on the streets of Berlin's Turkish neighborhood by lynching. In the country of Turkey itself, the punishment for stealing was the severing of the thief's hand. It was only the American's unforeseen Good Samaritan gesture of spiriting him away from the street mob that saved the Medjay. He barely escaped. Even though Asim's life was spared, this changed nothing between them in Asim's point of view. The American may have saved Asim's life, but he was still the enemy merely because he accompanied the German engineer's daughter, and the ancient sacred stele was still missing. Seth's obnoxious voice brought Asim back to Russia. The cab they were following was stopped next to a high-rise building. Seth and the Medjay watched with barely contained excitement when Schulze's daughter, accompanied by her American friend, climbed out and walked inside the Holiday Inn Suschevskiy hotel. Continuing with his elaborate story, Seth told the taxi driver that they wanted to prolong the surprise. Seth directed him to wait not far from the entrance and to be on lookout for his colleagues when they exited the hotel.

# Chapter 31

Voronezhskaya Street, Building 4, Moscow, Russia
Saturday, September 23
4:15 p.m.

Anna rang the doorbell again.
"Maybe he doesn't live here anymore," Michael said.
"What should we do?" Anna asked nervously.
"We don't even have his phone number."
"You know what, let's wait awhile …" Suddenly they heard someone approaching the other side of the apartment door. A female voice speaking in Russian could be heard. As they waited, the pleasant voice slowly got closer and closer.

Just as Anna started to reach inside her bag for her iPhone with its indispensable language app, the door slowly opened up, stopped by a metal chain. An elderly, heavyset woman stood in the gap sporting a brightly striped kitchen apron with fresh drops of water on it. She spoke, her words spilling out in a cacophony of syllables and sounds.

Anna and Michael looked at each other silently. Anna spoke in English, breaking the silence, "Excuse me, do you speak English or German?"

"Oh, yes," answered the old woman, proudly speaking in English with a British accent. "I was an English teacher for twenty-five years."

Anna and Michael smiled broadly as the old lady carefully examined her visitors through the small opening.

"Allow me to introduce myself. I'm Anna Schulze, and I'm from Germany." She turned her face slightly and gestured toward Michael, "And this is Michael Doyle, and he is an American."

"Hello Miss Schulze and Mister Doyle," the elderly woman greeted them politely as she nodded.

"Please, you can call us Michael and Anna," said Michael.

The woman smiled and asked politely, "How can I help you?"

"We are looking for Mister Kirilov. Do you know him by any chance?" Anna's heart stopped beating while awaiting the old woman's response. This was the moment of truth: if the lady standing in front of them, barricaded by the chain holding the front door, did not know Kirilov, then it pretty much meant the end of their journey. Anna even shut her eyes tightly in anticipation of the old woman's response.

"You are asking me if I know Mister Kirilov," the woman answered slowly, a smirk on her face. "I'm married to him, so you could say I know him a little," she laughed mischievously.

Michael looked at Anna with a huge grin on his face. Anna suddenly realized her heart was beating again. *Thank God we are in the right place*, she thought with utter relief.

"Is your husband at home?" asked Michael.

"No," she answered right away, shaking her head.

Michael's stomach sank. Trying not to lose hope, he asked, "Do you know when he is coming home?"

"Oh, sure," the old lady responded cheerfully. "Anatoly should be back soon." Both Michael and Anna audibly sighed with relief. "What kind of business do you have with my husband?" she asked them curiously.

"It's about the Great Pyramid," Michael replied.

"I should have known," she said, sighing deeply. "Please come inside. Here, let me unlock the door," she apologized, briefly closing the door. They could hear a rattling sound as she unhooked and removed the chain. The door swung open, "Come in, come in my dears," she gestured to her guests.

Anna and Michael stepped inside the hallway as the old lady closed the door behind them. "My name is Svetlana Aleksandrovna." She paused, smiling at them, "of course, it would be easier for you to call me Svetlana."

"It's nice to meet you, Svetlana," said Anna.

"Yes," Michael added, "thank you so much for having us."

"Here," Svetlana gestured toward a row of hooks on the wall and a soft bench, "you may hang up your coats here. I need to ask you to remove your shoes as well. I have some house slippers you may use."

Michael and Anna dutifully hung up their coats and umbrella. Then they sat down and removed their shoes. Although it felt a bit strange to be putting on someone else's slippers, it appeared that Svetlana had them ready and waiting for visitors. The Russian tradition of taking off street shoes when they enter private residencies has gone on for centuries. Svetlana stood to the side, patiently waiting for her guests to do her bidding.

Michael had gotten the impression that the pyramid business was definitely not Svetlana's favorite subject. "I'm sorry, the Great Pyramid is probably not your favorite topic," said Michael as he stood up.

"Well, if the person you love the most devotes all of his free time on something located in a foreign land more than five thousands kilometers away, rather than his wife, then I suppose you can say that topic is definitely not my favorite."

"I'm sorry."

"Please, don't apologize, after so many years I am used to it," Svetlana answered with a warm smile and the wave of her hand. "Wait until my husband comes home, he will be thrilled." Turning to Anna, Svetlana asked reproachfully, "Did he drag you into this too?"

"Oh no, I kind of dragged myself into this," Anna said apologetically.

"Oh. All right. Now, please follow me to the living room." Svetlana led them into the next room. She added, "It's not big, but it's cozy." She stopped and pointed to the sofa, "Please, have a seat and make yourself at home."

Anna and Michael sat on the worn brown couch.

"For many years we used to have lots of visitors coming to our apartment inquiring about the Great Pyramid. But lately no one ever comes," she paused for a second. "So, I think it will be a pleasant surprise for my husband to see you two here," she said quietly. "If you need anything please let me know. I'll be in the kitchen," Svetlana walked slowly out of the living room.

Michael got up from the couch and looked around the room while Anna checked her phone. The living room was furnished with twentieth century Soviet furniture. In one corner was a large Soviet-made TV resting on a wooden table. In the other corner was a large desk covered with papers. The main centerpiece of the living room was a dressing table accompanied by not one, but three large vertical mirrors. Michael positioned the two side mirrors slightly away from each other and saw multiple images of his own reflection appear at the same time. After a few mesmerizing minutes of gazing at his images, he forced himself to look away and look at the dresser top.

There were several framed photographs displayed. One of them depicted a World War II veteran well into his 80s dressed in a military parade uniform, his chest full of war medals and ribbons. The second photograph was in black-and-white and depicted a group of World War II era soldiers gathered next to a bunker built into a hillside. The third photograph depicted a dark-haired man in his twenties tightly grasping a set of rifles as he stood next to a group of captured German soldiers with their hands bound amid the snowy hills. The last photograph was in black and white as well and depicted a young couple. The man was the same dark-haired man from the previous image. Next to him was an attractive young lady with her hair pulled back into a bun. She had fine facial features with a small nose and a generous, sensual mouth. As Michael looked closer, he recognized the young woman as their hostess, Svetlana, who was busy at the moment washing dishes in the kitchen.

Michael called to Anna and pointed to the photograph.

"Oh! That's Svetlana when she was young," Anna said, smiling at picture.

"That's definitely her," Michael nodded in agreement "and that's gotta be Kirilov," he pointed to the man standing next to her.

As soon as he uttered that phrase, the duo heard the sound of keys rattling in the front door lock. The door opened up and somebody walked inside the apartment. A deep, male voice called out in Russian. Michael and Anna could hear the man removing his overcoat and hanging it up. Then he was sitting down and changing his shoes to slippers. As he stepped into the living room, Michael recognized the man as the veteran with the chest full of war medals in the photograph on the dressing table.

Svetlana stepped out of the hidden kitchen and greeted her husband. Speaking rapidly in Russian to the old heavyset man, Svetlana pointed at Michael and Anna, who nodded politely. Behind his thick old-fashioned glasses, the man's eyes widened in surprise at his visitors as she continued to speak. He was balding with very short grayish hair;

the left side of his head had a deep dent. He wore a striped brown suit jacket over a light-blue checkered dress shirt and a dark-blue tie in a Windsor knot. The sight of this elderly man was calming. His eyes shone with intelligence and confidence. The man addressed Anna and Michael in Russian.

"Tolya, they are Americans and don't speak Russian," Svetlana smirked at her husband.

"Oh! Hello, I'm Anatoly Kirilov," he said, speaking with a British accent just like his wife. "And you are?" he asked, arching his brows and looking directly at Michael.

"I'm Michael Doyle and this is Anna Schulze," Michael replied, shaking the man's hand. "You speak English well," said Michael.

"I had to learn," answered Kirilov, winking and grinning at his wife.

"Mister Kirilov," Michael continued, pointing at the dressing table, "These are great photographs."

Kirilov grabbed one of the black-and-white photographs. "That's us in pre-war Moscow. It was taken two days after we got married and one month before the German troops attacked the Soviet Union back in 1941," he said, sighing.

"Wow," exclaimed Anna, looking at both of them with surprise and admiration, "you've been married for so many years!"

"And what wonderful and exciting years they have been," Svetlana added passionately.

"Except, of course, the year … when I died, remember?" said Kirilov.

"Oh yes," Svetlana sighed deeply. "How can I ever forget that?"

Michael suddenly grasped the meaning of Kirilov's last phrase, "Wait a second. What do you mean by *when I died?*"

"I still have his death certificate," Kirilov's wife answered. "It was mailed to me back in 1943. The letter said my husband 'was killed in the battle of Stalingrad for the Soviet Motherland displaying courage and heroism. He was buried in a mass grave,'" she recited it from memory, her voice shaking.

Kirilov put his arm around her shoulders, attempting to comfort her.

"I'm still here," he pronounced quietly to her.

Svetlana retrieved a handkerchief from her apron pocket and gently wiped her eyes. She looked up at her guests with a smile, "Well, I will leave you here since I have much to do in the kitchen. Would anyone like some coffee?"

"Yes, please," said Anna as Michael nodded in agreement.

"It will be ready in a few minutes," Svetlana walked back into the kitchen.

"As you can see it's still a painful subject for my wife," said Kirilov as soon as his wife's steps faded away "she thought she had lost me."

"Mr. Kirilov," said Michael in low voice "can you tell us what happened there?"

"Oh sure," said Kirilov, "if you are really interested in war stories."

"Absolutely," said Michael. "I was a soldier myself and fought in the Iraqi War in the 2003 invasion. So it's a very interesting subject."

"Well, I don't know much about the Iraqi war, but the battle of Stalingrad," Kirilov started his story, "was one of the bloodiest battles of the twentieth century. This battle decided the fate of the entire Second World War. For the Soviet Union, it was a great moral victory and it showed that we could beat the Germans. The first day was the worst. After crossing the River Volga, we were attacked. We were constantly advancing and retreating, advancing and retreating. I was wounded three times. Death was everywhere. But then, later on, we got used to it: if someone got killed, well, everybody gets killed. If you got wounded, well, you were lucky. If I was to survive, then somebody in heaven liked me," Kirilov chuckled.

"How did you get used to seeing death constantly?" Anna asked quietly.

"Well, my dear, human beings can get used to anything," Kirilov replied. He paused for a moment and then added, "That's our nature."

Anna just shook her head, thinking of the carnage that brought about such morbid thinking.

"In November of 1942," Kirilov continued, "Our bunker got hit by a shell. Only two of the twelve of us survived. For two hours we sat in the rubble, waiting. Then we started digging ourselves out using our knives and canteen holders. Just when we had almost dug ourselves out, we got hit again. I lost consciousness. Luckily there were some troops passing through and I was pulled out by one of the soldiers. I was bleeding badly as well and was taken to a field hospital. I had no way of contacting Svetlana. In about three weeks' time my wound had healed, and I was attached to another unit. Meanwhile, the remaining soldiers from my previous unit had returned to the bunker and were digging it out so they could bury the dead and use the bunker again. They found my rucksack. Not giving it a second thought, they assumed that I was dead and a death certificate was sent to my wife."

Anna was moved, "That could've killed her."

"Well, it almost did, "continued Kirilov, "three months later, we won the battle of Stalingrad and captured thousands of German troops. It was then that I was finally able to send a note to Svetlana. I was stunned when I received the news from her that she was mourning my death. Even worse, she had arranged a funeral for me several months before. I was very happy to reassure her that I was alive and well. After Stalingrad, I participated in the liberation of Belarus, Ukraine and Poland. I was in Berlin when the war ended in May of 1945. Along with many of the Red Army soldiers, I left graffiti on the Reichstag wall in Berlin."

"Wow, that's quite a story," said Michael, his eyes wide.

"A German bullet is still lodged inside my brain," Kirilov suddenly added.

Both Michael and Anna looked at him in horror.

"No doctor is willing to take the risk to operate, but it's okay," chuckled Kirilov, "the bullet and I have bonded well together after so many years."

Kirilov's wife Svetlana walked into the living room carrying a tray with cups of coffee, milk and sugar.

"My wife told me that you two are interested in the Great Pyramid." There was a visible brightness in his eyes; this topic was his favorite.

"Yes, that's right," said Anna.

Kirilov sat at the desk as his wife set down the tray and disappeared back into the kitchen. Anna and Michael took their previous seats on the couch.

"Mister Kirilov," Anna began, "my father somehow knew you. I found your name inside his notebook."

"That's interesting," said Kirilov. "What is his name?"

"Günther Schulze."

"Hmmmm ... um ... Schulze?"

"He was German," added Anna.

"I see now. I'm sorry if I said anything bad about Germany in my war stories."

"Mr. Kirilov, I found your story fascinating. You fought bravely for your motherland and I admire that," she said respectfully.

"What was your father's last name again?" Kirilov asked.

"Schulze."

"Schulze, Schulze, Schulze," said Kirilov, thinking deeply. Several minutes passed. Anna and Michael tried to wait patiently.

Suddenly, Kirilov spoke, "Oh, yes, I remember him! He was in mail correspondence with me back in the 1980s when I was still developing my theory. Your father was one of many who were in touch with me. We were discussing different possible versions of the construction of the Great Pyramid in ancient Egypt. Your father was very much involved and giving possible accounts on how the Great Pyramid was erected."

"Wow, that's very interesting, I didn't know that. My father never mentioned that to me," said Anna. "So, how long was he in touch with you?" she asked.

"Oh, let's see here. About a year and then he lost an interest in my theory."

"Why, what happened?"

"Well, like many others your father thought it was too simple," said Kirilov. If I remember correctly, it was your father who delicately pointed out that it was *too good to be true*."

"When was the last time you had contact with him?" asked Anna.

"Well, let's see," Kirilov tried to concentrate. "Probably end of 1980s. That's the best I can remember."

"And he has never contacted you since?"

"No, never. I don't understand why you are asking me all these questions and not your father," asked Kirilov, surprised by Anna's questions.

"Mister Kirilov, I wish I could ask my father anything right now." Anna paused, tears in her eyes. "Unfortunately, I can't." She spoke quietly, "My father died last week inside the Great Pyramid."

"Dear Anna, I'm sorry. I did not know that," Kirilov replied sadly. As Anna began sobbing, Michael tried to calm her down by patting her arm. She found some tissues in her purse. After a couple of minutes, Anna was able to continue.

"What happened? How did he die?" asked Kirilov.

"He had a heart attack," Anna answered, looking askance at Michael. They had decided not to tell him that her father had possibly been poisoned. They did not want to scare Kirilov off.

"I'm really sorry," Kirilov said kindly. "May his soul rest in peace."

"Thank you so much," Anna said sadly. "Mister Kirilov, what's puzzling me is that your name was in my father's notebook. It was one that he had been using for about two years. So, why would he have your name if he had lost all interest in your theory?"

"Honestly, I don't know." Kirilov respectfully and quietly replied.

"OK, Mister Kirilov," Michael broke into their conversation. "Would you mind introducing us to your theory about Pharaoh Khufu and his Great Pyramid?"

"First, I'm curious. How did you even find me?" Kirilov asked.

"Are you familiar with a man named Rolf?" asked Michael.

"Yes, of course," Kirilov answered, stunned. "I met him on the train a while ago. But how do you know him?"

"The same way," Michael responded with a smile, "on the Berlin-Moscow train."

'Wow, it's a small world," exclaimed Kirilov.

"He mentioned your theory," said Anna.

"Do you really want to know?" asked Kirilov mysteriously, his glance shifting from Michael to Anna.

"Yes!" Michael and Anna both exclaimed.

"Oh, I have an enthusiastic audience here. I hope you are mentally prepared," said Kirilov with the big smile on his face, "because this mind-blowing journey is not for close-minded people."

# Chapter 32

Suschevskiy Val Street, Moscow, Russia
Saturday, September 23
12:38 p.m.

Asim sat in the taxi's backseat staring at the hotel building that Anna and the American had entered. As Seth chattered away with the driver, his mind returned to Germany and how the American had led him away from the angry mob.

Upon reaching the outdoor market, he unceremoniously hid under a table. When he was satisfied that the American was gone, he crept out and cautiously wandered around the unfamiliar square, trying to blend into the crowd. He kept nervously checking to make sure he was not being followed, while sometimes peering intently past the bright streetlights into the darkness for Seth's familiar Volvo. After some time passed, he turned to see Seth's Volvo several feet away.

As he approached the car, Asim glared into Seth's cowardly eyes. Yanking the door open and jumping inside, Asim was just about to unleash his full rage when Seth spoke first. While Asim seethed, Seth explained that he himself would have become a victim if he had tried to help Asim. He knew that the mob would have flipped over the Volvo and burned it with them inside. So by leaving the Medjay there on the street, Seth not only saved himself, but also managed to save his vehicle. According to Seth's twisted mind, he had made the right decision by leaving his partner to the mob.

But Asim was a Medjay warrior. He knew that Seth had abandoned him to the mercy of the intensely wild mob. Asim gave Seth a stare that if Seth had seen it, he would have been terrified to know what it meant. Deep in Asim's mind, he knew that he would pay Seth back in the same manner as he had been served. After taking some deep breaths, Asim commanded Seth to go back to the diner where he had encountered the American.

After parking outside, Asim directed Seth to look in the windows for the American and Anna. They knew Asim could not show his face and needed to hide behind the Volvo's tinted windows. Even though some time had passed, the crowd could still be looking for him.

Walking casually up and down the sidewalk, Seth scanned the diner through its windows. Then he smiled and walked back to the entrance, going inside. Asim remained quietly inside the Volvo, his head and body scrunched down. From time to time he dared to lift up his head to peek outside. After ten minutes Asim looked up to see Seth walking toward him, a grin filling his face.

Once inside Seth announced, "We're in luck." Seth had spotted an old girlfriend working as a waitress in the diner. She had noticed Anna and the American speaking English, peaking her natural curiosity. Pretending to be busy near their table, she listened in on their conversation. She clearly heard Anna announce, 'We're going to Russia!' and the American agree.

Asim looked in bewilderment at Seth, "Are you sure?"

"She heard them clearly say 'Moscow' several times during their conversation."

Back in the apartment, Seth found out that the next train to Moscow was leaving early the next morning from the Ostbahnhof railway station. Not anticipating this turn of events, Asim made a quick phone call to his chief and expressed to him that he wished he were back in Egypt with his beloved Medjay tribe. The Chief assured Asim of his blessing to continue his quest to any country in the world to find their missing stele. He also reassured Asim that he was not to worry about the money, as he would immediately make a money transfer under Seth's name.

"Asim, my fearless warrior," the Chief said, "you have my blessings and may the gods be with you."

Seth discovered that there were still plenty of seats available to Moscow. They packed and left immediately, hiding in the station to make sure Anna and her American friend were on that same train. To their undeniable excitement, they spotted their duo boarding the 5:04 a.m. train to Moscow.

While checking up on his prey during the long journey, Asim managed to escape the American's curiosity twice, almost compromising his entire clandestine mission. He was taking a smoke break in between the trains when he was startled to see the American approaching. Asim quickly climbed up and gripped the ceiling in an uncomfortable position for a few moments while the American unknowingly stood under him in the pitch-black darkness. When the American crouched down, Asim could barely keep from slipping onto the American's head. The second time, he miraculously saved detection by ducking down behind a group of families and pretending that he was looking for something.

Seth's elbow brought Asim back to Russia. He leaned forward and watched with interest as Anna and the American emerged from the hotel and got into a taxi. They followed the taxi inconspicuously until it pulled over next to a tall, blue building.

# Chapter 33

Voronezhskaya Street, Building 4, Moscow, Russia
Saturday, September 23
2:02 p.m.

"The Great Pyramid is shrouded in many veils of the great mysteries. To uncover at least some of them is the desire of many," Kirilov spoke calmly. "Based on my hypothesis, I can lead you to Pharaoh Khufu's true, final resting place. I would like to emphasize the word *true* because the well-known King's Chamber that contains a lidless, empty sarcophagus is, in reality a false burial place, designed by the chief architect HemIwno. This snare trapped, without exception, all of the tomb robbers, scientists and archeologists."

Michael looked at Kirilov in disbelief. In a record thirty-second's time, Kirilov had managed to make an accusation that questioned the very foundation of the official theory written and rewritten in every published scholarly book about Egypt. The King's Chamber was the place where the Pharaoh Khufu was buried. In fact, any history student beginning his studies of the Old Kingdom dynasties of ancient Egypt absorbed it without question.

*That's one of the most ridiculous claims I have ever heard.* Michael was already thinking that his trip to Moscow was turning out to be a big waste of time.

"Mr. Kirilov, I hope that you have proof," said Anna.

Michael noticed the same doubts on her face as he had. *Looks like I'm not the only one*, he thought.

"Listen, I will give you more than proof, trust me," Kirilov's tone remained calm. "Keep listening and ask questions anytime you are uncertain. Baghdad's Caliph Al-Mamun was the first to force entry into the Great Pyramid in his search for fabulous treasures. He quickly presumed that the Great Pyramid had been robbed in the ancient times and that there was nothing left. The explorers and archeologists that followed simply approved Al-Mamun's assumption, and nowadays it is accepted fact. The Great Pyramid was built by using 2.3 million limestone blocks set on top of each other. But, how exactly was it built?" Kirilov glanced each of them, patiently waiting for an answer.

"Well," Michael broke the silence first, "according to history, it was built by using long ramps. The blocks were dragged up the ramp to form the layers."

"What were the ramps made of?" asked Kirilov.

"As far as I recall … of mud brick, rubble and debris."

"You have a good memory," Kirilov grinned, "but let's think about that for a minute, shall we? You don't have to be an engineer to understand that a ramp made of mud brick would be impossible to lift up to immense heights and withstand tons of limestone blocks being transported across it. If the ramp was built out of stone, then its construction would not be easier than the pyramid itself."

Michael was startled.

Kirilov continued his explanation, "By analyzing the available descriptions, photographs and drawings of the Great Pyramid, I developed a theory based on a rather peculiar system of inner hollows. The functions of these hollows cannot be achieved without some additional conditions, which the Chief Architect HemIwno used in constructing the Great Pyramid. Inside the Great Pyramid, there is a natural cliff. Its presence not only determined the alignment of the pyramid, but also the plan for its construction, technology and engineering works around it. It also allowed the accomplishment of the most important task: making Pharaoh Khufu's final resting place unreachable."

Kirilov opened a lower desk drawer and removed an envelope. He opened it, removing some papers and a photo. "Michael, Anna," Kirilov gestured welcomingly toward them. "Here is a photo showing all of the major pyramids on the Giza Plateau," he said as Michael and Anna leaned in closer to him.

"The existence of natural cliffs on the Giza Plateau," continued Kirilov, "can be acknowledged by the Mokattam Hills residing nearby. The Great Sphinx was carved from a solid knoll of rock as well. It is evident that five thousand years ago there were the remains of an ancient alpine backbone. Four of its cliffs were used as foundations for the three large and the one small pyramid. The fifth cliff was used to carve the Sphinx."

*Cliffs?* Michael stared at the picture in disbelief.

Anna was visibly confused. "If there is a cliff at the base of the Great Pyramid, then how did the limestone blocks get enclosed around it?"

Michael glanced at Anna. *It's good to know that I'm not the only one who has doubts.*

Kirilov chuckled and reached into a side desk drawer and pulled out a piece of white paper. He drew a diagram on it as Anna and Michael carefully watched.

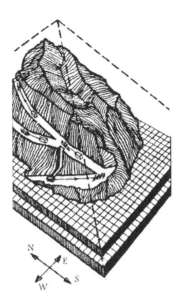

"What kind of technology was available to the ancient Egyptians in order to transport heavy limestone blocks?" Kirilov paused and then answered himself, "There is no secret about that: ropes, levers and sleds are widely known to archeologists. So, how did the ancient Egyptians manage to lift blocks weighing tons to the height of the construction site by using primitive technology?" Now he glanced at his visitors and waited for the answer.

Anna and Michael shook their heads in unity.

"I think you will agree with me that there needed to be a robust base in the form of a traditional inclined surface. Could an inclined surface be established on the sides of the pyramid?

"Well, that depends on the angle of the sides," Anna said, deep in thought.

"The angle is well known as fifty-one degrees and fifty-one minutes," Kirilov replied.

"Well, if the angle was steeper than forty-five degrees then the blocks would capsize," added Michael "unless they used levers behind the blocks in order to prop them."

Kirilov's face lit up. "I like the way you think," he complimented Michael, "but it is known that one block of limestone weighs roughly around three tons. Toward the apex of the Great Pyramid, there are blocks weighing sixty to seventy tons, if not more. No lever would ever support such an enormous weight. Besides, there was no space to fit the huge amount of workers needed in order to move such immense, heavily weighted blocks. Any questions?" Kirilov asked mysteriously. He looked like a math teacher who knew the answer.

"Of course we have questions!" Michael was fired up. "So, how were these enormous blocks transported?"

Seeing Michael's impatience, Kirilov decided not to torture him anymore. "There was only one way: levels inclined at an optimal angle that prevented the blocks from capsizing."

"Wait a second, are you referring to the angle of twenty-six degrees and thirty-four minutes?" Michael added, astonished. "Aren't the inclines of the Ascending and Descending Passages and the Grand Gallery at that angle?"

"You are a genius! Just like HemIwno himself!" Kirilov enthusiastically proclaimed.

Anna was astonished. "Michael," she asked curiously, "How did you know the angle of the inclines of those passages?"

"That's what I recall from studying the Great Pyramid. Those two passages and the Grand Gallery all have the same angle of incline, precisely equal to twenty-six degrees and thirty-four minutes."

"Michael is absolutely right," said Kirilov, searching through his papers. With a flourish, he put one in front of Michael and Anna. "In order to completely understand the function of all the inner hollows, I had to create a three-dimensional cross-section diagram of the Great Pyramid. Look at this:

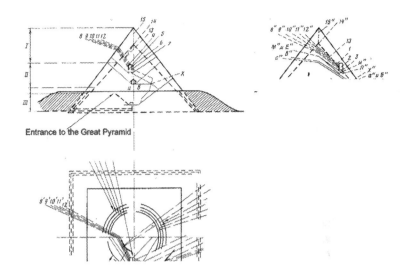

Entrance to the Great Pyramid

And here is another, closer look at it. You can look at this and follow along as we continue our discussion.

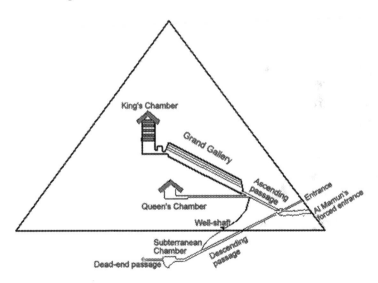

HemIwno's solution was very unique for the construction practices of the time. At the initial stage of the engineering preparation, straight pathways were carved into the slopes of the cliff. These pathways later functioned as passageways that were used to transport the limestone blocks. In addition, the large spaces that were carved-in acted like intermediary resting places, just like landings are used in a staircase. Preassembled granite slabs that later formed the King's Chamber and the Grand Gallery were placed ahead of time. As were the stone wedges, which tightly sealed the Ascending and Descending Passages."

"Excuse me," Michael interrupted, "it's all fascinating, but let's go back to the inclined levels. Even by using the optimal angle of twenty-six degrees and thirty-four minutes, transporting hundreds of tons of blocks in an upward direction would be a job suitable only for Superman."

"This task was accomplished without Superman's help," Kirilov gently replied. "There are even better examples. During the period of ancient Rome, the people, as you can imagine, were not much different than the ancient Egyptians. Their architectural engineering was not advanced that much further from Egyptian times, yet in the city of Baalbek, there are stone blocks weighing thousands of tons that were lifted up to heights exceeding twenty feet."

"Here, hold on one second," Kirilov got up from his chair and walked to a bookcase. He started shuffling through the books, selecting one. Returning to his desk, he looked through several pages and then read an excerpt from it:

*Baalbek, the town in the Bekaa Valley of Lebanon is famous for its exquisitely detailed, but monumentally scaled temple ruins of the Roman period. Baalbek, known as Heliopolis at that time, was one of the largest sanctuaries in the empire. The city was made a colony by the Roman Empire in fifteen BC and a legion was stationed there. The Roman buildings were constructed on top of earlier ruins. This involved the creation of an immense, raised plaza onto which the actual buildings were placed. The sloping terrain necessitated the creation of retaining walls on the north, south and west sides of the plaza. These walls are built of monoliths, which at their lowest level each weigh approximately 400 tons. The western and tallest retaining wall has a second course of monoliths containing the famous trilithon: a row of three stones each weighing in excess of a thousand tons. A fourth, still larger stone called "the stone of the south" or "the stone of the pregnant woman" lays unused in a nearby quarry. Had it been freed from the quarry, it would have been the largest stone ever moved, larger than the famous, unfinished obelisk in Aswan.*

"Questions?" asked Kirilov, putting the book aside.

"So, the stone blocks were first transported upward, right?" asked Anna.

"No," replied Kirilov, arching his brows. "Initially downward, toward the site that later became known as the Subterranean Chamber. Let me clarify that further," he added, seeing the surprised looks on Michael and Anna's faces. "The main quarry was situated on the east shore of the Nile River. Using the Nile, the carved blocks were hauled by boats to the bay beside the Sphinx. From there they were hauled to the roadway. According to Herodotus, it took ten years to make the causeway for the limestone block's conveyance. From there the blocks were carried to the east slope of the cliff and then downward along the inclined Hidden Passage, which has still not been found to this day."

"Would it possible to find that Hidden Passage?" Anna was intrigued.

"If you will be nice, then I can certainly provide you with some pointers," replied Kirilov mischievously.

Michael and Anna laughed.

"By the way," continued Kirilov, "today's line of the horizon is not the base of the Great Pyramid. In reality it lies deeper down at the level of the Subterranean Chamber. And beneath that chamber, deep down inside the cliff's cavity, Pharaoh Khufu's mummy quietly rests with his countless treasures."

"Wait a second," said Anna, glancing at Michael. "Khufu's mummy and his treasures are still inside the Great Pyramid?"

Kirilov nodded silently.

"Weren't they robbed like thousands of years ago?" she asked, her eyes widened.

Kirilov shook his head.

*If this theory proves to be real, then we are on the verge of the greatest discovery ever.* Michael was already imagining what the treasure chamber might contain.

"As the construction progressed," Kirilov continued, "those inclined levels were covered up from above, thus becoming passages bearing the constant upward transportation stream of the limestone blocks. From the inside of the pyramid these blocks were carried outside through the opening at the top of pyramid, which was sealed afterwards. As you can see, the erection of the pyramid or, in other words, the wrapping of the cliff served a double purpose: as the foundation and core of the pyramid, and as its transportation facility."

"OK, what was the purpose of the King's Chamber?" asked Anna, completely mesmerized by Kirilov's narrative.

"Obviously it wasn't the burial place, but rather a convenient accommodation for one of the working crews hauling the blocks along the Grand Gallery," Kirilov replied as he took a sip of his coffee. "Having executed the combined engineering and technological functions, the King's Chamber turned itself into a cenotaph."

"Cenotaph?" asked Anna.

"Cenotaph is a tomb erected in honor of a person whose remains were buried elsewhere. The sarcophagus installed earlier inside the King's Chamber further strengthened the illusion. Exactly the same intention was set for the Queen's Chamber, Subterranean Chamber and the open site of the north entrance of the Great Pyramid. The passageways served three functions during the construction of the Great Pyramid. First as transportation: aqueous lanes that carried the stream of rainwater toward the well inside the Subterranean Chamber. Next, they served as airshafts. Third, they were a part of the deception."

"So, Caliph Al-Mamun was the first one to get fooled by this sly snare, right?" suggested Michael.

"That's exactly right," Kirilov replied.

"Mr. Kirilov," Anna sat back in her seat. "Your theory is simple, and yet it covers all the aspects of the construction process. What I don't understand is how come your theory has never been proved or disproved?"

"When I developed my theory back in the 1980s, hardly anyone believed it because of its simplicity. Everybody was looking for something more, such as aliens, people from Atlantis and God's intervention." Kirilov's cheerful face was beginning to turn sad. "The fact of the matter is that the Great Pyramid was built by ordinary, but skilled Egyptian people and my theory proves it."

"What would be some of the ways to prove your theory?" Michael asked thoughtfully.

"The constant transportation of the heavy blocks atop the surface of the passages can be verified by a close, visual examination. The lower surfaces of the passages should be smoother than the surfaces of the other three sides because it sustained the continuous flow of the blocks. In addition, if you lifted up one of the floor blocks, the natural cliff would be seen."

Visibly amazed, Michael and Anna continued listening to Kirilov's explanation of his brilliant, yet simple hypothesis. At one point Svetlana brought in a tray of black bread and potato soup for them. The three new friends barely noticed as another two hours passed by quickly. Suddenly Svetlana surprised them all by walking into the living room and speaking, "Tolya, take a look at the time! It's late! They are tired, and you are tired as well. Tell them to come back tomorrow."

"We must be up early tomorrow because we are going to church to light our candles," Kirilov explained. "My health is not what it used to be. When I was younger I never even went to the doctor, but now the years are taking their toll."

"We are so sorry," Anna reassured him as they got up from the couch. "We were so fascinated that we lost track of time." They now noticed their host was looking a bit worn out from their conversation.

Kirilov got up from his desk chair and started down the hallway. "While you are putting your shoes on, I will tell you something else. Just don't interrupt me," he instructed. He rarely had any visitors lately and was trying to prolong their visit, even by a few extra minutes.

"Deep down inside the Subterranean Chamber, close to the center of its eastern wall, is a well. This well couldn't be positioned in the middle of the chamber because it would have been in the way of the movement of the blocks. If it were near the western wall, it would've increased the distance to the opposing side of the pyramid. Moreover, the exit from the water well was beneath the chamber's foundation and was probably destroyed after the pyramid's construction was complete.

213

By the way, this mysterious well has one peculiarity. Almost all of the explorers indicated the well to be about ten meters deep and assumed it had a dead end. In reality, it is blocked by a stone plug and should be an additional one to two meters deep. This is how the excess water was carried outside the pyramid. The position of the well is very important because it uncovers the connection of the well foundation with the existing water-carrying soil layer." With these words Kirilov held up a folded piece of notebook paper. "This is the schematic of the stone plug locking the dead-end of the well," he announced as he carefully unfolded it, showed it to them and then folded it back up, placing it in Michael's left hand.

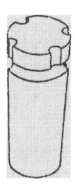

"Don't lose it," Kirilov added, grinning.

The sound of a throat clearing interrupted them. Svetlana was standing in the living room, her hands on her hips. Her look didn't require any translation: *let them go, now!*

"One last thing," said Kirilov, rushing his speech as his guests were putting on their coats. "The limestone blocks were introduced inside the pyramid through the entrance situated on its east side. The opening on the northern side in reality was not even an entrance, although it looked like a working site. Later on, the opening assumed the same role, just as the King's Chamber led potential robbers away from the true entrance to the Great Pyramid. By hiding the real entrance, HemIwno deprived potential robbers of access to the pharaoh's real chamber. The Great Pyramid became a creation that had neither an entrance nor an exit."

Michael and Anna thanked Svetlana for the meal and Kirilov for his time as he unlocked and opened the apartment door for them. They stepped into the hall and walked with Mr. Kirilov to the elevator. "Mr. Kirilov," Michael turned to address him, "I was touched by your fascinating story about how you survived that bunker during World War II. I myself was involved in a similar predicament during my deployment to Iraq in 2003." Michael had reached the elevator and pushed the button to summon it.

"What happened?" Kirilov asked.

"I was the gunner in a Humvee that was a part of a convoy making our way to Baghdad. Suddenly, whole hell broke loose. We got caught in what you would call a "kill zone." Rocket-propelled grenades hit several trucks and Humvees behind us. The Humvee driver steered us toward the enemy trench while I used my machine gun to destroy several enemy bunkers. Hundreds of enemy fighters poured out, shooting rocket-propelled grenades at us. We were getting hit left and right by AK-47 rounds. But thanks to our skilled driver, we still managed to avoid direct hits from the grenades. As our Humvee was steering away toward the big berm on the left side we got hit hard. One of the grenades hit the driver's side. I blacked out for a moment, but then I remember looking at our vehicle commander through a smoky haze. He was dead. When I looked over at the driver, his guts were falling out down his sides. But he was still alive. The Humvee was on fire, but I managed to free myself from my harness, crawl over to the driver and pull him out from the burning vehicle. As soon as I got him safely away from the vehicle, I observed several Marine Amphibious Assault Vehicles approaching our area. I blacked out again, and the next thing I remember, I was waking up in the Troop Medical Clinic with a third degree burn to my left leg."

"It's so good to meet a fellow veteran," said Kirilov, tears in his eyes. He leaned forward and heartily embraced Michael. "What happened to the driver?" Kirilov asked.

"Miraculously the driver survived, and I was credited with saving his life. I was surprised and deeply humbled when I was awarded the Bronze Star for my actions."

Kirilov embraced Michael again. "A guy like you pulled me out of that burning bunker and saved my life. All these years and up to this day I didn't know his name. But now I do."

"You do?" Anna asked quietly.

"Yes," said Kirilov, as tears rolled out from his eyes. "His name is Michael. What's your last name?" he asked.

"Doyle," Michael replied, slightly embarrassed.

"His name is Michael Doyle, and let's hope that there will be more loyal and brave fellows like him."

The elevator arrived, sliding its doors open.

"Mr. Kirilov," said Michael solemnly, "when I came back home from the war, I always imagined myself as a museum relic, sealed in a glass display case with the sign 'Break glass in case of war.'"

"No, Michael," Kirilov put his hand on Michael's shoulder "you are not the only one who thinks this way. For a very long time I couldn't understand why my life was spared. Why did so many of my comrades die, and why was I spared? But then I figured out the answer."

"You did?" asked Michael, enthralled. "That's the same question I keep asking myself over and over again."

"I was spared," Kirilov replied softly and proudly, "so I could uncover the secrets of the Great Pyramid. And guess what Michael, your life was spared … maybe exactly for the same reason."

"Thank you Mr. Kirilov for the lovely evening and the fascinating stories," said Anna, stepping inside the elevator as Michael shook Kirilov's hand.

Michael stepped into the elevator, and as the doors began to close, Kirilov spoke, "I'm proud to shake your hand."

"Likewise," replied Michael. The elevator doors then groaned shut and the elevator started its descent.

# Chapter 34

Voronezhskaya Street, Moscow, Russia
Saturday, September 23
8:05 p.m.

A gusty wind swirled toward Anna and Michael as they stepped out of the threadbare apartment building. Automatically zipping up their jackets, they strode past the lumbering buildings, deep in their own thoughts as the noise and screeches of Moscow's rush hour whirled around them. Their time with Kirilov had been moving, yet Michael had an uneasy feeling that Kirilov had left something out of their conversation. He thrust his chilled hands inside his pockets, appreciating the warmth. It was as if Kirilov had wanted to say something, but withheld it for some unknown reason. At the traffic light, they turned left onto another street, following the flow of pedestrians. They approached a brightly lit marketplace with small, open-air shops and sidewalk vendors.

The spell was broken when the first, small raindrops plopped onto their heads. Michael stopped and looked at Anna as a certain fact suddenly dawned on him. "I left my umbrella at Kirilov's apartment." The thought of having the perfect excuse to return to Kirilov's filled him with elation. Anna reassured Michael that she would enjoy poking around the market while he ran back. "I'll be right back," he promised as Anna happily waved Michael on and disappeared into the crowd. He turned and started running back to Kirilov's building, hoping he was still awake.

With the looming storm clouds it was getting darker and darker as Michael approached the building's entrance. The front door banged open and a man ran outside, almost clipping him. "Hey!" He barked at the rude stranger, the streetlights briefly illuminating the man's face. As he caught the door and entered the building, he realized that the stranger seemed familiar. But he was in the middle of Russia, miles and miles away from familiar faces and places, so he quickly dismissed that notion. After all, the lighting was rather inadequate, and he was tired. Once again, he entered the outdated elevator and pressed the button for the seventh floor.

When the elevator shuddered to a stop and opened its doors, he quickly approached Kirilov's door. To Michael's surprise, it was ajar. *Huh, Kirilov probably forgot to shut it.*

He knocked lightly on the slightly open door, calling, "Hello?" He was starting to feel a bit guilty about returning, as the elderly and sick Kirilov was probably asleep by now. Michael waited for a response. The apartment was quiet except for the beating of his heart in his ears. He pushed the door slightly: knocking a bit louder and longer. Michael peered inside, but could see nothing beyond the ambiguous, dark shape of coats stacked high on the coat rack.

"Hello? Mister Kirilov? Svetlana? Are you there?" Michael asked the dark apartment. Again, there was no response. Then he heard shuffling steps coming from inside the apartment. The dim hall light came on, and Svetlana's silhouette appeared.

"Michael, is that you?" she asked, her voice soft. She was still wearing her slippers and now had on a faded housecoat.

"Yes, ma'am," Michael replied, standing in the door's threshold.

"This is strange. Why is the door open?" she said, surprised.

"I left my umbrella here, so I came back," Michael replied softly, "When I got here, the front door was open."

Svetlana tsked tsked grumpily, "Tolya probably forgot." She sighed in exasperation, "He has this habit of forgetting to completely close the door."

"Oh, OK, I thought something had happened when I saw the door ajar."

"Not to worry," she said, smiling up at him in the dim light. "Tolya's asleep now."

"OK then, I'm just gonna get my umbrella and be on my way." Michael took a few steps into the hallway and looked around for his umbrella. Sometimes the hardest thing to do when you are flustered is to find exactly what you are looking for, especially if it is right in front of you. It took Michael several moments to notice the umbrella, almost in plain sight. Relived, he grabbed it and was shoving it into his backpack when he heard something heavily tumbling onto the living room floor. He quickly turned to look at Svetlana, but her facial expression remained unchanged; obviously she had not heard a thing.

"I heard a noise coming from your living room," Michael whispered in alarm.

"That noise was from my living room?" she asked, pleasantly surprised.

"Maybe the neighbors?" Assumed Michael.

"The walls are thick," she reassured him, "Tolya's asleep."

"I'm pretty sure the noise I heard came from your living room," Michael said cautiously.

"Go ahead," she chuckled, "you can check for yourself."

Confident he had heard something, Michael walked several steps and peeked around the corner. It was dark in the room with the curtains pulled, but there was a small bit of light coming from the kitchen and hallway. Michael's eyes landed on the couch where he and Anna had sat; it was now transformed into a bed. Startled, he strode to the couch looking intently at a fresh, dark stain on the bedding. Svetlana flipped on the overhead light, illuminating Kirilov lying in a heap on the floor. Donned only in his white trunks, bright red blood slowly pooled around his body. At first Michael feared Kirilov was dead, but as he rushed closer he heard a deep groan.

"He's hurt!" Michael shouted, turning to see Svetlana: her eyes large, her mouth open and her face completely white. "Call 9-1-1!" he shouted. Svetlana stood frozen and dazed. Frustrated with himself at instructing her to call 9-1-1, a command that made sense in the United States but nowhere else in the world, he changed tactics and shouted, "Call the ambulance!"

Svetlana rushed to the phone as Michael attended to Kirilov. Thinking that it was a gunshot wound, he immediately started searching for the exit wound, but could not find it. He looked closer and realized that Kirilov had not been shot, but stabbed. Kirilov moved a bit when he saw Michael kneeling next to him. Michael gently motioned for him to stay still.

"Quickly," he addressed Svetlana, who was gripping the telephone receiver to her ear. "I need a bit of sugar and a clean towel!"

Seeing the surprised look on her face and near-frozen stance, Michael called out to her, "Svetlana! Sugar and a clean towel!"

"What happened to my husband?" she managed to say.

"Did you call the ambulance?" he asked ignoring her question. "They will be here shortly." Her hand slowly took the telephone receiver from her ear down to the base. "What happened to my husband?"

"I don't know yet. So," he stopped, looking her steadily in the eyes so she would focus on his words, "I need you to bring me some granulated sugar, a bottle of vodka, some iodine and a clean towel."

"Sugar?" she asked, puzzled.

"Or honey."

"Vodka?" Svetlana thought she had misheard him.

"Come on, don't tell me you don't have a bottle of vodka," said Michael, visibly irritated. "Look, I don't always agree with stereotypes, but it's a dead giveaway that any respectable Russian would have some vodka stashed somewhere."

"I never said we didn't have vodka," scoffed Svetlana. Even though his request puzzled her, she complied. Shuffling as fast as she was able, Svetlana went into the kitchen.

Michael positioned Kirilov upright, propping him up with the bed pillow.

"We are out of honey," Svetlana announced as she returned with the vodka, a teacup filled with sugar, a towel and small bottle of iodine.

Michael carefully poured some sugar into his hand and then transferred a small amount to Kirilov's wound. He made sure the sugar granules were deeply inside the wound, under the skin. He grabbed the bottle of iodine, unscrewed the top and then, with a steady hand, proceeded to pour several drops of iodine solution into the wound. Without looking up from his work he explained, "This should enhance the wound healing."

Michael retrieved his wallet, pulling out a credit card. Grabbing the bottle of vodka, he quickly unscrewed the top and gently poured some vodka on the card. As Svetlana watched in amazement, he used the card's edge to seal the wound.

"This will stem the blood flow," he explained to Svetlana, who sat shaking on the edge of the bed. "Sugar or honey," continued Michael, "was used to treat the wounds of ancient Egyptian soldiers on the battlefield. As your husband would concur, the wounds were treated with a mixture of honey and lard applied daily." Kirilov nodded in agreement. Michael placed the towel carefully on the wound, applying a slight pressure on it.

"That should do it," Michael said, sitting next to Kirilov on the floor.

"How do you know this?" asked Svetlana, still visibly astounded. "Are you a doctor?"

"No, I'm not a doctor, but my grandfather was a combat medic in the Pacific during World War II. He taught me traditional remedies to cure cuts and bruises."

Kirilov moved slightly. Michael grabbed him gently, "What happened?" Outside the two-toned ambulance siren approached the building.

"It happened so quickly," Kirilov spoke slowly, visibly struggling to speak. "I probably forgot to close the door completely, and that's how he got inside," Kirilov paused, taking a rest. He took a deep breath and continued, "I was getting into bed when I heard the intruder's voice. He demanded that I give him the ancient artifact stolen from the Great Pyramid in Egypt."

Michael's heart sank. From the sound of siren outside, Michael concluded that the ambulance had arrived at the building and the paramedics were probably on their way up to the apartment.

"I told him I didn't know anything about that," Kirilov continued, "so he became very angry. We argued. Everything happened so fast that I didn't realize I had been stabbed. I wanted to scream, but couldn't. I felt the blood and collapsed onto my bed. The intruder walked around the living room and left. Then the next thing I remember, I was on the floor and you were kneeling next to me."

"What did he look like?" asked Michael.

"He was probably in his late twenties, wearing gold glasses, dressed in black. He spoke in English with a heavy Middle Eastern accent."

Michael suddenly had a flashback to the stranger who had run into him as he approached the building. *That was Seth! Anna's former boyfriend and the Medjay are here in Moscow?*

Michael groaned, "Anna."

Kirilov and Svetlana both looked puzzled at him.

"Anna is in danger," Michael said firmly. "I've gotta go, she's alone on the street where that creep could find her. Here," he motioned to Svetlana, "hold this towel." Svetlana took over pressing the towel to the wound.

Michael was getting up from the floor when Kirilov grabbed his hand.

"Wait a second," he said desperately, "grab my pants!"

Michael stared at him, confused as Kirilov gestured weakly toward the end table. "Just grab my pants and reach inside the right pocket," he commanded.

Groping inside Kirilov's pocket, Michael felt a small object and pulled it out. It was a small metal key. Michael looked over at Kirilov, puzzled.

"I think that's what that criminal was looking for," Kirilov assured him, nodding his head slightly.

"I don't understand."

"You will," Kirilov replied, attempting to apply a smirk to his face. "You are a smart guy and will figure it out," he said. He grasped Michael's hand and pulled. Michael leaned down as the elderly man whispered, "The storage box is inside the Kursky railway station, box number 57."

"The Kursky railway station, box number 57," Michael repeated.

"Thank you, Michael, for everything," said Kirilov as Michael stood back up, carefully secreting the key inside a zippered pocket inside his jacket. "Good luck to you in your adventures."

"Thank you so much Mister Kirilov," replied Michael. He could hear voices in the hallway. The paramedics must have arrived.

"Michael, you and I are very much alike. You are a soldier like me. We both have cheated death: you got out from that burning vehicle in Iraq, and I got out from that burning bunker in Stalingrad. You are my brother-in-arms," Kirilov said proudly, his voice weakening. Michael knelt down and embraced him. "Don't lose that key," Kirilov whispered. Michael nodded, smiling.

Suddenly the doorbell rang loudly, followed by heavy knocking.

"The paramedics!" Svetlana exclaimed. Michael ran and opened the front door to find two paramedics donned in white scrubs speaking in Russian.

Michael simply nodded his head and stepped aside to let the two men and their green gurney inside the apartment. Svetlana called out to them in Russian.

Michael grabbed his backpack, but turned when he heard Svetlana call out to him. Svetlana opened her arms out to him for a hug. He stepped over to her and was engulfed in her warm, strong embrace. "Thank you," she whispered and then, stepping back, she commanded, "Now, go! Go find Anna!"

"Good-bye!"

Outside, Michael opened his umbrella and literally dove under the pouring cold rain filling the street. He ran to the street market, dodging and leaping over puddles along the way. Reaching the market, he frantically started searching for Anna's familiar frame. Fearing the worst, Michael went back to the front and decided to start looking for her in the shops along the street. He was relieved to see Anna emerging from a military memorabilia store.

"It was dry in there," Anna said happily.

Without saying a word, Michael stepped forward and embraced her tightly.

Startled, she hugged him back. Breaking away from him, she looked at him curiously. "What took you so long?" she asked.

"It's a long story, but first we need to get out of here." They started walking along the street, Michael setting a fast pace. He looked behind them from time to time.

"You seem edgy," Anna commented. "Are we in danger?"

"Yes," Michael said firmly, increasing his pace.

"What do you mean?" She was starting to have trouble keeping up with him.

Michael jerked his thumb, pointing behind them, "That guy."

Anna looked back.

"Come on," Michael reached for her hand and pulled her forward. "We gotta get away from him."

"Who is that?" She was jogging now.

"Seth, your ex-boyfriend." Michael said calmly.

Anna's eyes widened. "What!?" She caught up with him, "He's here in Moscow?"

"Yes, he's here. He tried to kill Kirilov." Anna gasped and clamped her hand over her mouth in shock. Michael continued calmly, "So we need to get away from him as soon as possible and as far as possible." Michael grabbed her hand again firmly and ran toward a busy road intersection: Seth had started to gain on them.

Traditionally, cars are money in Russia, making it equivalent to power to the Russian citizen. In other words, a Russian can drive where he pleases. Even in the downtown areas, cars travel quickly, their speeds easily reaching one hundred kilometers per hour. If traffic has stopped, a driver will use the sidewalk. The pedestrian does not have the right of way, even on the sidewalks. In fact, if a pedestrian gets run over by a car, he will be at fault for interfering with a moving car. The safest way to cross a busy street in Moscow is through their underground passageways.

The dangers were obvious, and they had been warned to use the underground passageways to navigate the streets. However, as Seth's long stride brought him closer and closer, getting away quickly became their priority. Deciding to make a run for it, Michael squeezed Anna's hand tighter and instructed her to "Run!" They bolted though the busy intersection, weaving between the constant, swift flow of vehicles. As they made their daring way to the other side, car horns blared loudly and brakes screeched on the wet road as Michael and Anna managed to dodge the vehicles.

Despite the constant danger of being overrun, they were just a few feet from the other side when Anna abruptly fell, her right foot twisted inside a pothole. Her arms stretched outward, her chin on the wet pavement, she swiveled her eyes to see a minivan bearing down on her. Anna closed her eyes tightly.

Suddenly, she felt strong arms lifting her into the air. When Anna opened her eyes, she was on the sidewalk, safe and sound, inside Michael's arms. Stunned, Anna hugged her savior tightly as her tears mixed with the enormous raindrops that ran down her cheeks.

"It's OK," Michael murmured as he let go of her, "The worst is over." Suddenly, they were startled by the piercing, screeching sound of car brakes. They turned their heads as a large, rusty blue van barreled backwards toward them. As they turned and ran down the sidewalk, a long, haunting scream could be heard over the commotion.

The air filled with the smell and smoke of freshly burned tire rubber. When the cars stopped moving, Michael and Anna rushed back to the scene, along with other pedestrians who had scattered down the sidewalk with them. They coughed and choked on the smoke, even though it was dissipating in the rain.

As she drew closer, what Anna saw sent sparks of chills down her spine. For a moment she pictured herself as the one pinned between the black Ford Crown Victoria and the rusted, blue van. But, miraculously, it was not her body in the mangled mass but that of her ex-boyfriend, Seth. People were screaming in fear at the grisly sight. Both drivers were still inside their crumpled cars, visibly stunned by the scene trapped between them.

Seth was dead.

Seth had been attempting to cross the street following the same dangerous maneuver Michael and Anna had successfully completed. The driver of the black Ford Crown Victoria was racing down the street when a car cut him off in a desperate attempt to avoid Seth. Swerving in the driving rain, the driver had overcorrected and careened head on into the line of vehicles moving in the other direction.

The force and momentum with which the two heavy vehicles crashed was what had compressed Seth's body between them. The blue van was pushed onto the sidewalk with Seth's head and body crushed inside its front grill. The Ford's hood was completely crumpled by the impact that squeezed and mauled Seth's body beyond recognition against the van. The street was splashed with shattered glass, car and body parts, and blood.

"What a horrible death," said Michael, shaking his head as both drivers, obviously stunned and in shock, started climbing out of their cars. They were unharmed; saved by their seatbelts and deployed airbags. The crowd gathered closer to the gruesome scene.

"I used to love him," Anna said slowly.

"There is nothing we can do for him now."

"He slipped on the road the same way I did," Anna looked at Michael gratefully and continued, "but he didn't have a guardian angel to reach down and pull him out."

Michael kept quiet.

"Let's get out of here. I need to get away," Anna said softly, turning her face. They passed by an elderly man leaning on a cane, surveying the ghastly scene. He spoke to them in Russian. Although they did not understand the words, they understood their meaning. A two-tone ambulance siren filled the air as they nodded solemnly at the man and continued on their way.

# Chapter 35

"And just where do we find this storage locker?" asked Anna as their burgundy Soviet-built Volga GAZ-24 taxi sped through the streets. She felt overwhelmed trying to absorb everything: Seth's attempt to murder dear Kirilov and his own gruesome death.

"Kursky railway station," Michael repeated as he nervously glanced out the rear window. He dug into his jacket's interior zippered pocket and held up a small key with a red-painted top. "Box number fifty-seven," he said, carefully inserting it back inside. The Volga entered a four-lane highway and joined the constant, never-ending stream of vehicles. Soon they passed the magnificent Ostankino television center tower. Standing at 1,772 feet tall, it is currently the tallest freestanding structure in Europe and the seventh tallest in the world, surpassing even the Empire State Building in New York City. Michael did not notice. He twisted around and looked solemnly through the rear window. "I'm afraid someone is following us."

"What?" Anna turned her head to look through the rear window.

"There!" Michael pointed to a black BMW stridently pursuing them in the neighboring lane. "See the passenger? That's the Medjay."

Anna gasped in horror as she recognized the Medjay's familiar Afro-style hair. "Seth is dead, so he's out for revenge."

"Even if his partner-in-crime was alive, he would be pursuing us," Michael contradicted.

"How in the hell did he get a car equipped with a personal driver so quickly?" Anna asked as they both kept their eyes glued to the rear window.

"We just need to lose him," said Michael solemnly.

Knowing he was going to surprise his passengers by speaking in perfect English, the taxi driver could no longer hold his curiosity. "Is everything okay back there?"

Michael and Anna stared at each other and then turned in unison to stare at their driver. "You English is perfect!" Michael exclaimed, visibly stunned.

"Yes, I studied art in Chicago," he replied proudly. "I am an artist, but this is my family's taxi cab business."

"Wonderful!" Anna exclaimed in delight.

Michael leaned toward Anna and whispered in her ear, "We've gotta tell him something if we want get away from the Medjay." She nodded.

"Ummm ..." Anna started, not sure how to calmly explain the situation. "Do you see that black BMW a bit behind you?"

The driver looked in his rearview mirror and smiled, finally seeing what Anna and Michael were so obsessed with keeping in view. "Oh yes! It is a beautiful car."

"Yes ... well," Anna stopped and then plunged ahead, "The passenger, the man with the big hair, is trying to kill us."

The driver's grin instantly disappeared.

"Maybe he's not really going to kill us. Maybe he's just following us?" Michael wondered nervously, turning to glance out the rear window again.

"You saw what they did to Kirilov," Anna said reproachfully.

Michael nodded sadly.

Anna leaned forward, "How can we lose that BMW?"

"Are you kidding me?" exclaimed the driver. "This taxi is held together with baling wire and duct tape."

Michael groaned, "We're finished."

"Then we'll outsmart them," the driver offered, "we'll go through the side streets."

"That might just work," Anna agreed. She positioned herself so she could stare out the back window. She shivered and wrapped her arms around herself. Like a predator stalking its prey, the black BMW was getting closer and closer to their taxi.

"Hold on!" the driver warned. The taxi pulled out from the dense stream of vehicles and quickly jerked onto an exit, creaking from the spurt of speed. Moments later the pursuers performed the same maneuver. There was much less traffic on the side road, and soon the BMW was even closer.

"That was a really stupid move," murmured Michael, grinding his teeth.

"Sooner or later they will catch up with us," the driver retorted.

"What does he want from us?!" Michael was absolutely infuriated and turning beet red.

"To kill us! Like Seth tried to kill Kirilov!" Anna exclaimed irately.

"Then why does he always pick car chases?" Michael pounded his fist on the seat in frustration.

Anna was studying the BMW as it tailgated their cab. "Brake!" she suddenly shouted.

"What?" Michael exclaimed, staring at her curiously.

"Hey!" Anna reached up and tapped the driver's shoulder. "We're gonna duck down and you're gonna slam on the brakes!" she shouted. The driver obeyed, slamming on the brakes as Michael and Anna jumped down, curling into a fetal position. The steering wheel locked firmly in place, the tires screeching.

The BMW's driver, who obviously did not expect such maneuver, had no time to react and with a loud, metallic BANG the vehicles collided.

After their taxi came to a stop, Anna and Michael lifted their heads and peered out the rear window. The BMW's hood was smashed and the airbags had deployed.

"Now! Floor the gas pedal!" Anna commanded the driver, who was still in shock. Michael quickly ducked his head back down.

"You will be paying for the repairs!" The driver yelled angrily, but obeyed her order. The wrecked BMW remained behind.

A few minutes later, Michael heard Anna sigh with relief. "What, are we still alive?" He opened his eyes and looked around. Taking a deep breath, he looked down at his hands.

"Are you OK?" asked Anna. "How are your fingers?"

"What the worst that can happen? Besides putting them in a cast," he joked, carefully moving his fingers one by one. He looked over at

Anna, "At least it wasn't my head that got smashed." She grinned back at him.

Meanwhile, the driver pulled onto the nearest side road, then onto the next one and the next one.

"We're not gonna get lost now, are we?" Michael asked, looking up from his fingers.

"Who cares? The main thing is to lose them!" Anna exclaimed.

"Well," Michael said, looking at Anna with admiration, "that was amazing! I never knew you were an expert on street racing."

"You don't know a lot of things about me," she joked, "but no, that came from hours of watching NASCAR and, of course, the simple physics of braking distance," she explained. "I was an A student in school, and every fifth grader knows that the braking distance is the distance that a vehicle travels while slowing to a complete stop. So, obviously, the higher the speed of the vehicle, the longer it will take for it to stop. Simple."

"Simple indeed," replied Michael with a broad smile.

The driver turned onto another street, under an arch.

"Do you really think I play cat-and-mouse games every day?" the driver asked his passengers sternly. He drove across a courtyard, turned the corner and then discovered that the street was a dead end.

"Damn it!" the driver pounded his fist on the steering wheel in frustration, "We have to get out of here!" He put the car in reverse, slowly moving backwards.

At that precise moment, the black BMW with its smashed hood and steamy radiator appeared out of nowhere and parked right behind them. Their only escape route was blocked.

"He'll kill us!" Michael and Anna gasped as they looked out the rear window nervously; a trio of streetlights illuminated the scene.

"Not quite yet," stated the driver, to their surprise.

The BMW's passenger door swung open and the Medjay, with his bushy hair slightly waving in the breeze, jumped out of the damaged vehicle. His driver remained inside.

"Distract him," the taxi driver whispered to them, keeping his eyes on the BMW.

The Medjay swaggered toward the taxi. "Get out of the car!" he ordered menacingly in a heavy Middle Eastern accent.

Anna and Michael exchanged bewildered glances and looked discretely, but curiously at their driver as they got out.

"Well, we meet at last," the Medjay spoke to his captives with an evil grin. "I see you are a couple of brave ones."

"What do you want from us?" Anna demanded angrily.

The Medjay flipped back his cloak to reveal the handle of his long, silver sword. "You will go with me," he declared. "Get in the car!" he commanded, pointing his finger at the BMW, his eyes cold and intimidating.

"Let them go!" their taxi driver demanded from behind them. Michael and Anna whirled around to see him holding his left hand behind his back.

"What's this?" demanded the Medjay.

Anna looked at Michael in total bewilderment and saw that Michael was just as puzzled as her. As far as they were concerned, their driver should be running away.

"Hey, taxi driver," the Medjay shifted his attention to their cabbie, "You can take your taxi, and get out of here." The Medjay shifted his glance back to his captives. "Get moving!" he demanded. With a flourish, the Medjay pulled out his sword and started walking toward Michael.

"Let them go!" the taxi driver suddenly shouted again. Michael turned to see the driver leveling an enormous silver pistol at the Medjay. The Medjay stopped, stunned. He shouted something in Arabic.

Abruptly, an average-sized man, well into his 40s emerged from the BMW. This new man was dressed entirely in black, including his trench coat. His face was hard and thin with a thin scar running down his cheek. Michael's heart sank as he realized he was looking into the cold, sinister eyes of a mobster. They spoke in Arabic.

A window on the ground floor of the nearest building opened noisily. An old woman pushed her head out, calling out in Russian.

Anna turned and quietly asked the taxi driver what the woman had said.

"She is complaining about us waking her grandson," interpreted the driver with a small twitch of his face. Anna turned back to face her persecutors, realizing the driver had a clever plan in place.

The driver interchanged several phrases with the woman from the window, his voice unnaturally loud. While they were having their small discussion, the windows on the ten-story apartment building started lighting up like mushrooms after a spring rain.

"Now she is saying she will call the cops," the driver reported calmly from behind Anna and Michael.

Anna startled everyone by yelling, "Call the police! Help!" More and more windows opened up as the building's occupants were curious by the screaming and commotion. The Medjay took a threatening step toward Anna, his hand gripping his sword. The taxi driver shouted something again. Then Anna let loose with a disturbing scream that must have been heard for miles.

Suddenly the lady from the first window screamed hysterically herself, slamming her window shut.

The BMW driver spoke urgently to the Medjay; it sounded like an argument.

Staring down Anna and Michael, the Medjay threatened, "I will be seeing both of you real soon." He turned and jogged back to the crumpled BMW, stopping at the passenger door. "Consider yourselves lucky," he added angrily, his eyes icy cold.

The two-tone signal of the local police wafted through the twilight air. Both pursuers dove inside their vehicle. Tires squealing, the black BMW backed up quickly and dashed away.

"Thank you for saving our lives," Anna was breathless from screaming. She walked over to the taxi driver and hugged him.

"Thank you so much," Michael said, warmly shaking his hand.

"We don't even know your name," said Anna.

"Victor," said the driver, visibly overwhelmed.

"Victor, that was a quick thinking back there," said Michael.

"Well, I've been a taxi driver for the past five years on the mean streets of Moscow," he said proudly.

"And you did live in Chicago," Michael added as they both chuckled. "We need to figure out how much we owe you for the vehicle damage and everything else." Michael was mentally trying to figure out how much of a hit his credit card would take.

"Are you kidding me?" responded Victor, a broad grin spreading across his face. "I got at least 30 witnesses who will testify I was held at gun point by the two robbers who slammed their BMW into my taxi. You know how much insurance money I will get out of this?" he laughed out loud.

"I'm guessing it's gonna be a big amount," smiled Anna, relieved she was not going to be footing the bill.

"That's right," replied Victor, "I can buy myself a new taxi," he added with a huge smile.

"Victor, I just have one question for you," Michael was not able to fight his curiosity any longer. "What did you say to that woman in the window that made her so hysterical and shut her window?"

Victor smirked, "They have a gun." Anna and Michael burst into laughter. The driver leaned into his trunk, pulled his pistol out of his back pocket and carefully hid it under the spare tire. After he shut the trunk, he grabbed his radio and said, "Now, I'll call another cab for you."

The new taxi arrived quickly. In short time their new driver was pulling up to the stretched building of the Kursky railroad station. Michael noted that it still bore the official seal of the former, glorious USSR.

# Chapter 36

Kursky Railway Terminal, Moscow, Russia
Saturday, September 23
10:34 p.m.

The Kursky railway station, the largest railway station in Moscow, dates back to 1860 when the first building was constructed. Leo Tolstoy's immortal novel, "Anna Karenina," describes the character Vronsky as departing to war from there. Unfortunately, the building did not entirely survive to the present time. In 1972 the train terminal was rebuilt while retaining some of its old accommodations, including the colonnade and rich modeling inside. The building now has glass panels spanning the impressive fifty-foot high front that faces the station's square. It is covered with plicate roofing, an industrial modern style that is folded in a box-like fan configuration. The roof extends thirty feet past the roof like a visor, spanning the front of the station. The terminal's spacious halls can accommodate eleven thousand people simultaneously.

As soon as the taxi rolled up to the entrance, Michael and Anna ran inside, looking for the information booth. Even at this hour of the evening, there was a line. While they waited Anna pulled out her iPhone, tapped on her language app and typed, "Where are the storage lockers?" When they arrived at the window, the agent inside looked at them expectantly. When Anna held her iPhone up, the metallic Russian voice amused the man. Grinning, the agent pulled out a station map. Gesturing toward the escalators, he indicated they should ride it down to the lower level. Pointing to the map, he made a big "X" for the location of the lockers. When Anna's iPhone said, "Thank you," the agent laughed and nodded in response. Michael and Anna smiled back, grateful for this way of communicating. Michael took the map, and they found their way to the giant escalators, located in the center of the grand hall.

After their escalator ride they walked wearily to the lockers. When the rows of lockers came into view, however, they suddenly felt energized. Stepping up the pace, they hurriedly started checking the numbers and finding their way through the maze. Michael was walking rapidly down a row, counting off the numbers when Anna pointed at a rather ordinary looking box, crying out, "Here it is! Number fifty-seven."

"There it is," Michael replied, feeling relieved. He shuffled inside his pants pockets, and then pulled them inside out, visibly frustrated.

"What's wrong?" asked Anna, her smile fading.

"I think I've lost the key." He reached back and checked his back pockets.

"What?"

He shook his head as he frantically patted and checked his jacket pockets.

"Please don't tell me this," Anna groaned.

"Here it is!" Michael said slyly, holding up the key.

"Oh, come on Michael, that's not funny," Anna put her hand to her forehead. "I'm so tired."

"I know, I'm sorry. Just wanted to see your reaction, that's all."

She punched his arm as he laughed merrily at her. She grinned and started chuckling herself, shaking her head.

Michael slowly inserted the key inside the lock, and it was the perfect fit. Yet, no matter how hard he tried to turn the key in either direction, it remained in the upright position, despite all of his efforts.

"Maybe it's the wrong key?" he wondered out loud. He wiggled the key and pounded the door. "I could break this door open with no problem."

"Oh, really," said Anna sarcastically. "Look around you. You see those black domes on the ceiling? Those are called surveillance cameras. So, if you want to spend the rest of your vacation in the Gulag, then, please, break this lock."

"OK, so what do you suggest?"

"Hold on, I'll be right back," she turned and started striding down the aisle. In a few minutes she returned to Michael, visibly excited. "Hey! There was a nice couple from England a few rows down, newlyweds backpacking through Europe."

"Oh, I see," he said, chuckling, "I'll bet you've talked them into breaking into our locker. That for sure will spice up their honeymoon!"

"I'll bet that certainly would, or if you put some coins right here in this slot, then the key will magically turn."

Michael just looked at her, surprised.

"And, yes," Anna added with a smug smile, "The couple gave me some coins as well, so you're welcome."

"Ooohhhh." Michael could not believe he had missed the coin slot on the locker. He stepped aside as she inserted the coins. Michael turned the key and the door swung open. Reaching inside he retrieved a small wooden box.

"Wow," said Anna, stunned. "That's an old Cuban cigar box. My father used to smoke Cuban cigars just like these."

Michael looked closely at the box lid, which was held in place by black tape. Suddenly a family walked down their aisle.

Anna leaned forward, whispering, "Let's just take it back to our hotel room."

Michael nodded as he stuffed the box inside his backpack.

As soon as Michael and Anna emerged back on the street outside the station, a fresh, chill wind gently brushed their faces. It started raining. A train had recently arrived, and the passengers were crowding the square. It seemed as if every one of them needed a taxi. Every attempt Michael made to signal a taxi was simply in vain.

"Let's try over there," Anna suggested, pointing in the direction of a movie theater, about a hundred feet away. They started walking down the street. When they were almost to the movie theater, Anna suddenly pulled hard on Michael's left sleeve and clandestinely moved her head slightly toward the other side of the road.

"Don't say anything," she said whispering, not looking at him, "just carefully look across the street."

Michael scratched his head, turning slightly, spotting the man who gotten Anna's attention. He wore dark pants and a brown sweatshirt with a hood, which was up, covering his hair.

"Do you think it's him?" asked Michael.

"Of course it's him, who else might that be?"

"I mean, that could be him, but it's almost impossible to tell. There's a shadow across his face, and his hair is completely covered up."

"I'm telling you Michael, it is him. I have a gut feeling, trust me." At that same moment, a strong gust of wind blew across the road. The stranger's hood blew back, revealing his bushy Afro hair. Michael's heart sank. Looking ahead he saw a trolleybus approaching. "As soon as this trolleybus gets closer and he can't see us, we're gonna run, you got it?"

Anna nodded as she continued to look straight ahead. As soon as the approaching trolleybus interrupted their view of the Medjay, both Michael and Anna bolted to the entrance of the nearest subway station.

# Chapter 37

Kurskaya Subway station, Moscow, Russia
Saturday, September 23
11:04 p.m.

If subway commuters were asked whether they liked using the subway, it would sound like a trick question. To the many daily subway passengers who spend more than an hour traveling to work and then an hour to get back home, who do this while choked on every side by a dense crowd, who must run to make the connection from one subway line to another, who oftentimes are flying to cram themselves inside a crowded car, at the last moment, one arm holding the closing door open while using the other to squeeze inside the last few square inches of a tightly crammed space, this may seem like an inane question. This is how they travel day after day, year after year, for their everyday life. What can a subway passenger answer to this question? The same as the passengers of the Tokyo, London, Paris and Moscow subways, "Do we have a choice?"

Even after many years of daily riding the New York City MTA subway system with two-hour rides, Michael still had not lost that mystical and mysterious feeling of his first experience with the subway. When five-year-old Michael first opened the doors leading to the subway, an enchanted underground world was unlocked for him. The realm of the subway held a comfortable, lingering nostalgia of childhood for him, where, as is commonly believed, people were different, houses were different, and the subway was also, well, different. Those nostalgic feelings accompanied Michael throughout his life, and he always felt at home on the subway trains, even when compacted to a state of almost complete immobility in a crowded subway car. For some people the subway is just the usual part of the urban landscape or one of the types of its infrastructure. But for others, and Michael belonged with no doubt to this category, the subway was not just a mode of transportation, but something magical and special. As they dashed to the entrance and scrambled down the stairs, this was Michael and Anna's first time to use the famed Moscow subway system. Built during Stalin's rule, these metro stations were supposed to display the best of Soviet architecture and design in order to show off the privileged lifestyle of the Russian people. Often called "the people's palaces," they were elegantly designed with a lavish use of marble, mosaics, sculptures and chandeliers. During World War II the city's metro stations were used as air raid shelters. Many of the larger stations were used for important political and tactical meetings. Today the Metro system has grown into an enormous network of twelve interconnecting lines and over 185 stations, with new stations opening almost every year.

After whisking through the underground steps leading down into the subway, they experienced an initial, visual jolt. The contrast of Moscow's ostentatious subway to the bleak concrete walls of an ordinary subway back home was startling. Then Michael observed a familiar sight: the turnstiles. Leading the way, Michael bypassed the purchasing of tickets and jumped over the turnstile, a bad habit he had developed during his teenage years growing up in Brooklyn. Anna followed suit, as they raced to the nearest train, managing to jump inside as its doors closed. Michael and Anna sighed with relief when the train surged forward, but the moment was fleeting. As the train shuddered to a stop and opened its doors again, their anxious eyes met. "We gotta move, come on," Michael urged as he started making his way to the front of the train car.

As they dodged and squeezed around the late-night passengers, the doors closed shut and the train pulled forward, slowly departing from the Kurskaya station once again.

When they reached the door at the end of the train car, Michael spoke, "We gotta make it to the front car." Opening it, he stepped onto the short-end platform and carefully stepped over to the next car's platform. He extended his arms and as soon he felt Anna's hands, he squeezed them tight and pulled her to himself. It was in this manner that they managed to pass through all of the cars and reached the train's front car. The air conditioning system seemed to be out of order. As the train roared through the tunnel, the stale outside air rushed in through the open windows, cooling off their faces with a dry and dirty smell. Every time the train stopped at a station, however, the heat became unbearable, making them wish it would start moving again. In the middle of the car, Anna found a metal bar to lean against. Michael approached her saying, "Next stop we're getting off. I'm tired." As the doors shut and the train started pulling away from the station, he walked over to the front of the car.

Anna reached inside her purse and pulled out hair elastic. Moving quickly she smoothed and pulled her long reddish-brown hair into a ponytail. Her skin was starting to feel damp, so she started unzipping her jacket. Suddenly somebody's hand was squeezing her wrist tightly, something pointy pressed against her back. Above the subway noise, a male voice in her ear threatened, "I'll kill you if you scream."

The train lugged to a stop at the next station and the doors opened up, letting the passengers in and out. Michael started for the doors. "OK," he called out, turning toward Anna, "Let's go." He spotted her standing absolutely still with the Medjay right behind her, holding her tightly. Furious, Michael strode toward Anna. The tribesman was becoming more of a nuisance than a real threat. Then he noticed the Medjay's sword. He stopped.

"You make one move, and she is dead," the Medjay said ominously, his eyes red and bloody.

Meanwhile, the doors slammed shut and the train started moving again. The subway's roaring filled the car once again. Anna put her left hand onto the metal bar to steady herself as the train turned a corner, jerking them both to the side. Still, the Medjay kept his sword pressed hard against her back, and his large hand wrapped tightly around her right wrist.

"What do you want?" Michael demanded.

The lights went out and Michael instinctively jumped. The Medjay seemed to have anticipated the move and managed to avoid the initial blow to his head. Michael grabbed and twisted the Medjay's hoodie with his left hand while the other hand groped blindly for the Medjay's hand holding the sword. In the total darkness the subway noise seemed deafening.

"Anna, get away!" Michael screamed just as the lights flickered back on, blinking unevenly for a few moments until the car was fully lit. The train sped up into the curve, its wheels screeching, the car swaying. Still struggling, Michael finally managed to locate and then with his two hands tightly squeeze the Medjay's hand holding the sword. The car jerked, throwing them both forward. Michael's arms were stretched in front of him, pulling at the handle of the sword. The train jerked again, slamming Michael's full body weight on top of the Medjay's.

"Aaah," the Medjay cried out, but he managed to hold onto his sword as the train came out of the curve and the car stabilized.

The passengers in the car had slowly moved, positioning themselves away from the two men fighting on the floor. Michael could hear many voices talking, but could not make out a single word they were saying. The Medjay growled as he pushed away, managing to free himself from Michael's hands as he jumped back onto his feet, still holding onto his sword. Spotting Anna in the crowd, the Medjay leapt to her, throwing out his free arm and catching her in a chokehold. A tense cry rose up from the passengers, yet none made any attempt to intervene. After seeing the full extent and size of the Medjay's sword, Michael was not surprised.

"Leave her alone!" Michael commanded, jumping to his feet. The train started slowing down, jerking to a stop at a station. Amid the screeching noises and the doors sliding open, Michael could hear the crowd screaming and rushing out, their cries echoing through the underground station. Passengers waiting on the platform stepped away. The doors closed and the train began moving. They were alone with the terrifying Medjay.

Anna screamed, "What do you want from me?" In reply, the Medjay started dragging Anna to the door leading to the next train car. Michael followed them as the Medjay opened the door, glaring at him. "Please," Anna gasped, digging her fingers into the Medjay's arm, which was clenched around her neck. She could barely be heard above the thunderous noise of the moving train. "No, please, no," she whimpered as the Medjay, laughing wickedly, jerked her back and forth, pulling her onto the tiny platform that separated the two cars. Michael followed them, stepping onto the overcrowded platform.

"Do not come any closer or she is dead!" the Medjay shouted. "Give me the map."

"Who are you and why do you keep pursuing us?" asked Michael.

"I'm Asim from the Egyptian tribe of the Medjay warriors. Her father stole the stele from us and tried to sell it to smugglers to pay off his gambling debts."

"My father never gambled," cried Anna as she attempted to wrench out of his grasp. "He never even played cards."

"He hid the stele and mailed the map to her," continued Asim, ignoring her remarks.

"He didn't mail me any map," Anna screamed, struggling against him.

"That's a lie and I want that map right now," Asim demanded, brandishing the sword and bringing it to Anna's neck.

Suddenly the train shook violently and stuttered to a screeching, deafening halt. Michael grabbed one of the metal chains hanging loosely between the cars. White smoke from the brakes filled the surrounding area.

*Anna!* Michael thought, squinting hard to see through the thick smoke. He spotted her clinging to the edge of the platform with half of her body hanging off the platform. The Medjay had fallen as well, his feet almost touching the tracks as he held on to Anna.

"Anna, hold on!" Michael shouted, grabbing her arm. The train started pulling forward, slowly accelerating. He tried to pull her up but the Medjay held tightly on to her, unwilling to let her go. Anna tried to wrap her legs around the coupling mechanism of the interconnecting cars, but that also proved to be useless.

"Let her go!" Michael shouted. "I will pull her up and then will get you out."

The Medjay shook his head in disagreement.

"Trust me, I will not leave you."

The Medjay shook his head again.

"Remember Berlin? I saved you! Didn't I?" asked Michael.

"Her father is the thief. He stole the stele and I killed him. Now it's her turn!"

"Listen!" Michael screamed. "Your name is Asim, right?"

"Yes, Asim, the Protector."

"OK. Asim, her father didn't steal your tribe's stele. That's the lie."

"My chief informed me that he was the thief."

"Your chief was mistaken."

"Our Great Chief is never mistaken!" the Medjay thundered. "And now the daughter of the thief will die with me!" Asim started pulling Anna down.

"Nobody has to die!"

"Michael!" Anna screamed, pain and fear twisting through her voice. "I can't hold on any longer."

"Asim! No!"

"He's forcing me down," Anna screamed again, struggling as tears mixed with sweat ran down her cheeks.

"Last chance!" shouted Michael. "Asim, if you want to die today then it's your choice, but don't make that decision for her."

"We both will die today," Asim declared, forcing Anna's hands to release their hold.

"No," replied Michael firmly. "Only you."

Anna straightened her back, allowing Michael to squeeze in between her and the Medjay. With one hand holding Anna's arm and the other squeezing the metal security chains tightly, Michael managed to give his right leg a powerful thrust, striking the Medjay's face. The Medjay screamed but still held on to Anna. Michael pounded him several more times with his foot, unleashing all of his rage. He stopped and leaned toward the Medjay, breathing heavily. "Give up! Come on … I'll help you up!"

The Medjay growled.

"It doesn't have to end this way!" Michael pleaded.

"We will all die today!" the Medjay screamed and lunged, attempting to pull them both down with him. Holding on for dear life to Anna and the metal security chains, Michael snapped into position and in a wild rage started kicking the Medjay, now aiming for his throat. The Medjay's strength was waning. Anna felt his grip loosening as he feverishly struggled to hold on to her. Michael stopped to catch his breath and looked down at the filthy, sweaty, grunting Medjay warrior clinging to Anna.

Once again the wheels began their screeching noise and a white smoke started to plume up from below as the train started to slow down, pulling into the next station on the line. The Medjay's bloody and bulging eyes stared into Michael's. A moment later, they heard the thumping sound of his body being tossed against the wheels as the car jumped and swayed. The penetrating smell of burning ripped flesh filled the air.

Michael pulled Anna to the top of the platform between the trains. "Are you OK?"

"I'm alive!" Anna cried out, tears streaming from her eyes as she tightly embraced Michael.

"It's all over," Michael said, rubbing her back as they walked through the train. He picked up her purse and handed it to her. They were both shaking as they wearily stepped out onto the crowded station platform.

"Aahh!" A woman's shrieks pierced through the station, echoing through the magnificent hall. The screaming woman stumbled but was caught by several passengers as a crowd started to gather. People started flooding to that part of the station. The screaming woman was now silent, her face still portraying the horror she must have observed.

Michael and Anna started walking to the exit, but were pulled along by the gathering crowd. Passengers were looking down on the tracks and then desperately trying to get away from the sight. Some of the women screamed in terror or wept, while most people looked ill and disturbed by what curiosity had driven them to look at. This attracted more gawkers who pushed through the crowd to fill their eyes with what had caused the disturbance.

Peeking around various passengers, Michael and Anna finally managed to see what they already knew. Wedged between the train car and the platform was a man's head, ripped from his body. The man's disheveled Afro hair was still visible from one side of his head as the other side was severely burned. The one remaining eye, bloody and bulging, stared into the faces of the curious.

Anna and Michael quickly turned away. Several police officers were running to the scene, barking orders and directing everyone away. Michael and Anna held tightly onto each other as they walked away. Michael was not sure how he was able to walk, but knew that if he sat down he would not be able to get up again for a long, long time. Michael was surprised when he glanced up and read the name of the station. "Kurskaya? This is the same station we used to get inside the subway system."

"We probably made the full circle on that train," said Anna, pointing to the map of the Metro.

As they made their way to the exit, they admired the subway's rich designs that represented the essence of the long-gone Stalin era with its rich ostentatious design, communist slogans, chandeliers, loads of mosaics, gorgeous artwork and sculptures that once symbolized the victory of the Soviet people over poverty and starvation.

# Chapter 38

Café Алёнушка, Moscow, Russia
Sunday, September 24
12:05 a.m.

"This place looks okay," Anna said. Visibly exhausted, Michael and Anna stood in front of a small, but brightly lit diner. They were quite shaken up and troubled, the events on the subway train still fresh. "Yeah," Michael answered wearily. At this point, he was not going to be picky. He peeked inside; it was almost empty with only a few couples sitting at the tables.

As they walked inside, a sweet voice called out to them in Russian. They turned to see that the voice belonged to a young waitress.

"*Sprechen Sie Deutsches?*" Anna asked hopefully in German.

"Or English?" added Michael, observing the waitress shaking her head.

"English yes," the waitress responded with a heavy Russian accent, turning to Michael. "Please," she gestured for them to follow her to a corner table next to the window.

"My name is Tanya," she announced while Michael and Anna were making themselves comfortable. "Here is menu," Tanya handed them some menus and slowly walked away.

"Hey, Michael, look!" Anna exclaimed joyfully, "The menu has pictures!"

"Oh good." Michael opened his menu and scanned the pictures. "I'll have a beef stroganoff, what about you, Anna?"

"Beef stroganoff?" she asked, surprised.

"Beef stroganoff," Michael replied informatively, "A Russian dish of sautéed pieces of beef served in a sauce with sour cream. From its origins in nineteenth century Russia, it has become popular around the world, with considerable variations from the original recipe."

"Incredible!" exclaimed Anna, "You don't carry an Encyclopedia Britannica in your back pocket by chance, do you?"

Michael smiled and signaled their waitress. Tanya approached the table and shortly was on her way to the kitchen to place two orders of beef stroganoff.

Michael looked around. He could see two couples sitting at a table on the far side of the café. He turned to look out the window. Nobody was lurking outside. He pulled his backpack a little closer to himself and unzipped it, removing the Cuban cigar box.

Michael looked at Anna, "Shall we?"

"Sure, Michael, I can't even possibly imagine what could be inside this old cigar box."

"Me neither," said Michael as he stared glassy eyed at the old Cuban wooden box made around the 1970s when Cuba and Russia were still at the peak of their relationship. The label on the box read: Cuban Partagas Torpedo. At the bottom of the label was the word Habana. Michael carefully pulled back the black adhesive tape holding the lid down and dramatically opened it. Inside was an old folded piece of paper. He picked it up and saw that it was a piece of paper torn out of a daily planner, discolored yellow. He unfolded the paper as Anna watched.

At the top was the date: March 6, 1983. The paper was written in English, in very small print. When they examined the signature at the bottom, they were surprised to realize that Kirilov had written it.

\* \* \*

**Greek historian Herodotus who visited Egypt in the five B.C.:**

A hundred thousand men labored constantly on the construction of the Great Pyramid. They were relieved every three months by a fresh lot. It took ten year's oppression of the people to make the causeway for the conveyance of the stones. It is built of polished stone and covered with carvings of animals. To make it took ten years, or rather to make the causeway, the works on the mound where the pyramid stands, and the underground chambers, which the Pharaoh Cheops (Khufu) intended as vaults for his own use: these last were built on a <u>sort of</u> <u>island, surrounded by water introduced from the Nile by a canal.</u>

**Arabian doctor Abdallah Muhammed bin Abd ar-Rahim Al Kaisi:**
The pyramids all have four sides, whereas each side is a triangle. Opposite of Misr al-Fustat (Cairo) are three pyramids. The largest of them has a circumference of 2,000 ells, with 500 ells on each side, and a height of 500 ells. Every stone is thirty ells wide and ten ells thick and is prepared and fitted to the finest. Near the town of Pharaoh Joseph is a pyramid much larger than this one. Its circumference is 3,000 ells; its height is 700 ells. Each of the stones is fifty ells long. Near the city of the Pharaoh Moses are some pyramids even larger and mightier. One pyramid, called the pyramid of Maidum, is as large as a mountain. She consists of five layers. Al-Mamun has opened the large pyramid opposite of al-Fustat. I went into it and saw a large chamber, which was squared on the floor. In the middle of this chamber is a square well pit of ten ells depth. If one steps down there, one sees a door on any of its four sides. In the chamber is an opening that leads to a passage to the highest point of the pyramid, but there are no steps in it. It is five spans wide. It is said, that in the time of Al-Mamun they went up there and had reached a chamber where the corpse of a man was found.

\* \* \*

I'm pretty sure that Herodotus was absolutely right. The artificial canal was created in the rock bed of the Giza Plateau and is located at the height of the maximum level of the river Nile, which is eight meters and thirty-two centimeters. This canal begins at the foundation of (what I call) the baffling pyramid that was unearthed not long ago, and penetrates the underground burial of the Khufu pyramid on the same level at eight meters and thirty-two centimeters. The water introduced by the canal surrounds the artificial island where Pharaoh Khufu's sarcophagus was placed. Basically Khufu's chief architect HemIwno created the system of connected water containers that, complying with the laws of physics, provided a strictly set level and volume of clean constantly refreshed water inside Khufu's real burial place.

Each one of the following pathways leads to the artificial canal to the underground lake that surrounds the man-made island containing Khufu's sarcophagus:

1. The way used by the funeral procession through the temple located at the east side of the Great Pyramid and located at the distance of forty-four meters from the bisector of the pyramid and the depth of about five to seven meters.

2. A pathway that follows along the artificial canal situated deep inside the baffling pyramid.

3. The so-called "dead-ended" horizontal passage of the subterranean chamber of the Great Pyramid. In the middle of the sixteen-meter appendix on the ceiling of the passage there is a plug. And beyond the plug is an inclined passage that leads to the burial place.

4. The way from the Subterranean Chamber of the Great Pyramid through the foundation of the false well. This foundation is actually false and in reality is a stone plug, which has the following parameters: two meters wide, ten meters long and two meters filling thickness. Under this stone plug there is a continuation of the cylinder-shape opening about ten meters deep down.

* * *

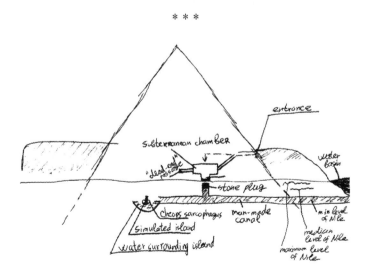

For the next several minutes Michael and Anna remained silent, trying to comprehend what they had just read. In the meantime, Tanya brought their meals.

"Do you remember what your father's dying words were?" Michael finally broke the silence.

"Sure," Anna replied. "He gave you my business card and told you to "find four ways" along with something else that was incomprehensible."

"Yes," Michael looked like he had won the lottery. "Four ways!"

"I don't get it," said Anna, confused.

"The number of the pathways in Kirilov's paper is that magic number four," Michael explained, pointing to the paper.

"Oh Michael, you are absolutely right. Do you think there is any connection between these numbers?"

"I think there is a direct connection. Your father and Kirilov might be speaking the same language after all."

Anna gave him a strange look.

"I mean they both speak the language of archeology," said Michael, grinning.

"If that's true, then we need to check this out," said Anna. "Are you still in?" she asked, holding out her right hand.

"We're in this together, whatever this is," Michael said proudly, bringing his hand up to shake Anna's. "But now I need to use the bathroom."

Michael returned to the table looking even more tired and sad.

Anna was finishing her warm dinner. "Is something the matter?" she asked.

"I've got bad news." Michael said, looking at the bill Tanya had dropped off. "I decided to call Kirilov's apartment. His nephew answered the phone and told me that Kirilov is unconscious in the Intensive Care Unit.

"Oh no! What should we do now?" asked Anna.

"You know what, we can't really help Kirilov, but let's go to the library in the morning to check out Herodotus' book, "The Histories." Maybe he will tell us something more," said Michael. He stashed Kirilov's letter inside the cigar box, sliding it back into his backpack and zipping it up. He pulled out his phone and calculated how much they needed to pay for the meal.

As they waited outside the café to catch a cab, Michael could see their waitress showing off the American dollars she had received from her customers. He smiled to himself.

A short time later they were safely at their hotel. As they entered the building, they were surprised to see many local couples patronizing the hotel at such a late hour. As they learned later, the hotel is popular among local couples that stay no longer than an hour in their rooms, since their apartments are small and often shared with extended families. This is the only privacy they can find for a small amount of their own private, happy time.

# Chapter 39

Memphis, Egypt
2583 B.C.

Khufu, the pharaoh of the fourth dynasty, the Lord of Egypt and beloved by Ra the sun god, sat on a high terrace gazing thoughtfully at the silent and lifeless desert known as the Land of the Dead. Upper and Lower Egypt were united by his predecessors, so his kingdom stretched thousands of miles along the Nile River. The taxes collected from the neighboring nations flowed like a shining golden river into his treasury. The greatness of the pharaoh, the living god, was commensurate with his dazzling wealth and solemn rituals. Only immortality, the highest goal of all human imaginations, remained his last mission.

All pharaohs were consumed with their life beyond the grave. Since the ancient times it was believed that at birth all human beings are endowed with Ba, the soul, and Ka, the person's twin. Ba, depicted as a bird with a human head, can be integrated with the body to become one, but also exist away from it. Depicted as raised hands, Ka seemed to be real, having flesh and able to consume food. At the same time, Ka was thought to live an eternal life apart from its body and act like its guardian angel. When a person dies, their Ba and Ka leave for a period of time, returning only if they recognize the body. If the body decomposes, its spiritual twin will die and the deceased will lose their chance for eternal life. To live for eternity, the body must retain its own image. This was made possible through the mummification process. The body was preserved with special solutions and wrapped with linen soaked in aromatic resins: no expense was spared.

In order to ensure its preservation, however, the mummy had to be hidden away from tomb robbers. Pre-dynastic rulers were buried inside secret wells in the far outskirts of the desert. These burial sites were often plundered. Later, huge royal tombs with mastabas, enormous flat rectangular roofs with outward sloping sides, were used. The first giant step-pyramid constructed was for Pharaoh Djoser. His architect, Imhotep, realized that in order to securely hide the needle there needed to be a haystack.

Getting away from the maddening crowds, Khufu found solace and peace on the Nile's left bank where the rocky spurs of the Mokattam plateau dissected the endless horizon of the Libyan Desert. The cliffs created the appearance of a notched barrier to the west beyond which stretched the silent desert. When he traveled around the imposing cliffs he never ceased to marvel; the peaks of the three cliffs captivated his imagination. An immense cliff located to the north and situated away from the others especially mesmerized Khufu. His priests related perplexing legends of the mysteries deep inside the cliff's womb. It was said to contain the treasury and sanctuary of the god Thoth, depicted as a man with the head of Ibis, the god of wisdom and numeracy, the keeper of the secrets of life and the protector of the dead. Thoth was the one who, together with the Goddess of the Truth, would someday escort him to eternal life.

From his first day Pharaoh Khufu had considered his eternal resting place. Countless pharaohs had gone into the realm of eternal darkness, but only the names of the most powerful and recently deceased stayed in human commemoration. The names of the others were erased by the ruthlessness of time. He might be doomed to be forgotten in some distant cave, his earthly traces gradually swept away by the squeaky sand. Reflected in these disturbing images, Pharaoh Khufu's sun-god earthly life seemed like a burden.

As he returned to his palace, Khufu stood on his solar boat looking back at the tallest cliff basking in the sundown rays of the sacred disc, Ra. As a farewell, a last greenish ray slashed along the cliff's crest. It was something marvelous, unearthly; a fragment of eternity that had swooped down and bonded with his immortal soul and mortal body. *I should place my eternal home here, next to Thoth's sanctuary, which stores the secret of our heavenly origin,* Khufu thought. Leaving the Mokattam cliffs behind, Khufu promised himself he would come back for good, for eternity.

Sailing briskly along the Nile, Khufu envisioned an edifice where no one would disturb his eternal rest, a pyramid engineered to be inaccessible to anyone who would ever dare to desecrate it. But who would be able to understand and implement his majestic plan? And where would he find somebody like Pharaoh Djoser's great architect Imhotep?

Back at his Memphis palace, Khufu walked to his mother's room. Queen Hetepheres eyes brightened at the sight of her son. Blonde with dark blue eyes, she sat proudly in her gold chair. Khufu bowed respectfully. After describing his plans and thoughts, she nodded, "You are the exalted pharaoh and your eternal tomb should be grand."

"But who can be trusted with constructing it?"

The queen sat quietly. Finally she answered, "I think you should invite our High Priest, HemIwno. He is experienced, energetic and loyal." Khufu meditated and shortly made his decision.

The High Priest, HemIwno, appeared at the appointed time and bowed low. As he raised his head, his cold eyes considered his ruler with an imperious gaze.

Khufu spoke, "It is time to think about my house of eternity. I'm appointing you to be Vizier, the Chief Architect, and entrusting you to engineer and build the greatest structure ever erected in our land. Everything will be at your disposal. If you accomplish it, you will be glorified for centuries to come."

The High Priest's eyes lit up at the thought of creating something unprecedented. After a long conversation, Khufu noted with satisfaction that by the grace of the gods his choice was successful; his mother always gave him good advice. HemIwno had asked for thirty days to come up with the plan's first outline and the preliminary calculations. Khufu grinned with anticipation.

The hoary head of the High Priest, and now Chief Architect, was reverently bowed as he went his way, deep in thought. He adored the grand beauty and craftsmanship of the pyramid for Pharaoh Djoser, who died nearly a hundred years before. Djoser's seven-step pyramid was the country's first stone building of that magnitude. If he accomplished his pharaoh's will, his name would be just as Imhotep's, glorified for the millenniums ahead. His stopped, gazing at the spiky ridges of the northern cliff. He needed to penetrate its secrets and find in its winding cracks the key to encasing it within a pyramid, a daunting task.

HemIwno strode through the gloomy temple where stone gods guarded the secrets of the priests. In his chambers he took out a roll of papyrus containing a record of external materials and tools, looked at it and threw it down in frustration. He needed something extraordinary. His eye caught the corner of the papyrus. Its acute vertex was ... HemIwno jumped. He realized the sacred structure should be shaped like the bent pyramid of Pharaoh Sneferu, the founder of the fourth dynasty and Pharaoh Khufu's father. Yet, it should be of slightly different proportions and unprecedented dimensions so it could encase the massive cliff. The ideas began flowing. The pyramid would be unadorned, its grandeur in its simplicity. The peak would draw the eye upward. The apex would rise above the valley and be the first to greet the morning light of the god Ra, long before its sunrays dispelled the darkness at the base of the pyramid. The Chief Architect began some preliminary calculations.

A few days later, his preliminary sketches were complete. An excellent designer, he had long tinkered with the calculations and, finally, after many efforts found it to be of unprecedented dimensions! He was overwhelmed by the resulting value and at the same time, proud of the novelty of his method. Using another papyrus, he designed the burial chamber. He provided ventilation channels that would pierce the masonry and emerge near the top. After much thought, he traced all false moves going up and down, and a preliminary schematic of treacherous traps with huge overhanging rocks that would crush anyone who dared to disturb the peace of his pharaoh. He felt ready to present it to Pharaoh Khufu. Yet, one thought haunted his mind.

At the palace, the high priest opened a scroll and began his presentation. Slightly on edge, he spoke passionately and persuasively. From the beginning, Khufu seemed to be skeptic and tensed as if preparing to jump into a fight. Toward the end of the presentation, however, the young pharaoh eased up, visibly satisfied.

"There is only one delicate issue that remains," HemIwno said, looking deeply concerned.

Khufu looked at him curiously.

"In order for the pyramid to retain its secrets, one of the workers has to be left behind. Someone has to set all the traps in motion, but no one must know the secret."

Pharaoh Khufu remained quiet for a while and finally nodded his approval. "Sacrifices have to be made for the greater good. The integrity of the pyramid cannot be compromised. May the god Thoth ease his sufferings and escort him peacefully to the underworld."

HemIwno bowed respectfully and asked for three months in order to finalize the project.

# Chapter 40

The Great Pyramid, Giza Plateau, Egypt
820 A.D.

H e could not believe his eyes: at his feet lay a dehydrated corpse. *A tomb robber?* But Al-Mamun, the son of the Caliph of Baghdad, was absolutely sure that nobody had ever been inside the Great Pyramid. They had thoroughly searched the Great Pyramid's exterior. Not even the slightest single aperture had been detected. Over the last several months his workers had been trying to crack open the colossal stone structure, spurred on by the knowledge that they would be the first ones inside!

But there was this corpse.

*Was it the pharaoh himself that somehow had fallen out of his own sarcophagus?* This seemed impossible. The ancient structure had been tightly sealed for centuries.

Once again, Al-Mamun circled the pyramid's hollows. He stopped inside the King's Chamber and leaned on the empty sarcophagus. Even if the corpse was indeed Pharaoh Khufu, then where was the lid to the sarcophagus? Even if some muscular robber had managed to lift it off, it would have been impossible to carry away: the passages were too narrow. Maybe the lid had been decorated with precious stones and metals. Could the burglar have broken the lid into pieces in order to carry it away? Then why was the sarcophagus made of only simple, dark granite without any decorations or carvings?

Al-Mamun looked around the empty room with its polished red-granite blocks; this room did not look like the burial place of one of the greatest pharaohs. Pharaoh Khufu had spent more than 30 years gathering people, money and treasures from all of his subordinated lands with the simple purpose of constructing his eternal abode. In 820 A.D. the young Caliph Al-Mamun, son of Harun Al-Rashid from the famed "Arabian Nights," had assembled a vast conglomeration of engineers, architects, builders and stonemasons in order to force entry into the Great Pyramid. Al-Mamun was diligently looking for the plate, which he had read about in Strabo's writings.

*On the side of the Great Pyramid there is a stone that can be moved, and if the stone is lifted open it will expose the winding passage leading to the grave.*

But all the stones were identical. To find only one out of thousands of twins was an impossible task. Al-Mamun ordered his workers make their own entrance, but the stones and calcareous shell were so hard that the cutters and chisels could not break them. They began splitting the stones by heating them up with fires and spraying them with cold vinegar. It was exhausting drudgery, but inch-by-inch the treasure hunters got deeper and deeper inside the pyramid. For over one hundred feet, they tunneled into the pyramid's solid core. They excavated a narrow passage that only became hotter, dustier and more constricted as they continued. Torches and candles consumed the precious oxygen and poisoned the air.

The legends of Queen Scheherazade in the famous "Arabian Nights" recalled that there were supposed to be "thirty underground chambers made of multicolored granite alongside the fabled Holy Gallery and filled to the top with precious stones, bountiful riches, exotic images and luxurious weapons that were greased by the fats cooked by using the ancient wisdom. And there exist glass that can be bent and does not break, and different miscellaneous potions and salutary waters." The treasures were not the only reason Caliph Al-Mamun was attracted to the Great Pyramid, he was also intrigued by the legends told by Herodotus and Strabo about the ancient steles with ancient knowledge written on them.

Al-Mamun was about to give up when one of the workers heard something heavy falling somewhere within the pyramid. Renewing their efforts and altering the direction of the bore, the workers managed to break into a hollow path. It was a passage three and a half feet wide by almost four feet high, sloping at a steep angle of twenty-six degrees. It was the entrance Strabo had mentioned in his writings.

Next, his workers moved in the opposite direction: down. This course led them into an empty cave with jagged, rough-hewn walls. On one wall they discovered a blackened, horizontal entrance to a passage. The workers followed the path, but after about fifty feet it was a dead-end. When the workers followed the path in the other direction, they found that after another thirty feet it ended with a well dug into the cave floor.

Yet, Al-Mamun continued searching. He carefully examined the entrance tunnel and found a granite plug that covered the opening of yet another passage, which had never been mentioned before. Al-Mamun figured he had stumbled onto a secret, hidden passage.

The workers tried to chip away at the granite plug, but it was tightly wedged, of indeterminate length and evidently weighed several tons. Spurred by the prospect of a new passage leading to some hidden treasure chamber, Al-Mamun ordered his men to cut around the plug through the softer limestone blocks of the surrounding walls. Even this turned out to be a huge job. After boring beyond the first granite plug, the workers encountered another granite plug, equally as hard and equally as tightly wedged. Beyond it laid yet another, third plug. Beyond the third granite plug they came upon a passage filled with a limestone plug that could be cracked with chisels and removed piece by piece.

On their hands and knees and holding their torches low, Al-Mamun and his men were obliged to crawl through roughly 150 feet of a dark passage, at the same steep slope of twenty-six degrees before they could raise their heads and stand on a level spot.

In front of them stretched another low horizontal passage, no higher than the one they had just ascended. At the end of this passage, they found themselves in a rectangular limestone room with a rough floor and a gabled limestone roof. Because of the Arab custom of placing their women in tombs with gabled ceilings (as opposed to flat ones for the men), this room became known as the Queen's Chamber.

The bare room was eighteen feet long and had an empty niche in the east wall, large enough for a life-sized statue. Thinking the niche might conceal the entrance to a second chamber, the Arabs hacked their way into its solid masonry for another yard before giving up.

Retracing their steps back to the low Ascending Passage, the Arabs raised their torches to get a better look at the ominous void above them. They discovered joist holes in the walls indicating that the floor of the Ascending Passage had continued upwards, blocking and hiding the low passage to the Queen's Chamber.

Climbing on the top of each other, Al-Mamun's workers found themselves at the bottom of a grandiose gallery, later known as the Grand Gallery. It was about twenty-eight feet high and appeared to stretch upward at the same steep slope into the mysterious heart of the Great Pyramid. The center of this new passage was very slippery, but on either side were narrow ramps slotted at regular intervals; they afforded a better foothold.

Holding their torches high, the workers proceeded to climb these ramps. At the end of another 150-foot climb, they came upon a huge solid stone, raised three feet from the floor. They scaled the stone and reached the platform located on the top of the Grand Gallery. Beyond the platform the floor was level, but the ceiling fell to a mere forty-one inches, forming a sort of portcullis entrance to a small antechamber. Past the portcullis, Al-Mamun's men were again obliged to stoop along a short passage that led to yet another chamber. Their torches revealed a great and well-proportioned room; the walls, floor and ceiling were all of beautifully wrought and polished red-granite blocks, squared and extremely finely jointed. Because of its flat ceiling, the Arabs named it the King's Chamber.

Al-Mamun's men frantically searched the chamber's every cranny, but could find nothing of interest or value. There was no sign of any treasure besides an empty, lidless, granite sarcophagus with a broken corner: no treasure or papyruses with ancient writing were found. The workers started angrily striking the walls with their hammers, attempting to find another passage. But it was all in vain: the walls responded back with the lifeless sound of intact rock. It appeared that the whole place had already been looted. It was hard to imagine though, considering the enormous number of stones they had been obliged to break in order to gain the entrance.

Al-Mamun's caravan of camels moved slowly through the Libyan Desert dunes on its way back to Baghdad. Alongside his cheerful workers, the Great Caliph kept silently to himself, analyzing the events of the last few months.

# Chapter 41

Russian State Library, Moscow, Russia
Sunday, September 24
11:45 a.m.

The edifice of the Russian State Library would take anybody's breath away. Surrounded by enormous steps and columns, the Library complex has five grand buildings connected in an elaborate system around several courtyards.

Inside the Grand Hall entrance, Michael and Anna stood staring at the columns, art and sculptures. A sweeping marble staircase led to many halls. Anna nodded toward a glass-enclosed desk with an attendant inside. Once at the front of the line, Michael spoke, "Excuse me, sir, but do you speak English?"

"Yes, how may I help you?" The man spoke English well, enunciating each word with a British accent.

Michael grinned, "We are looking for *The Histories* book by Herodotus. Of course, we need it in the English translation."

"Certainly, just a moment while I find someone to man this desk." The man walked away, disappearing behind a door. Michael expected to hear exasperated sighs and comments from the people behind him in line. Amazingly, there was just the usual sound of general conversation that a line seemed to generate. Michael supposed everyone was simply used to lines and waiting patiently. It reminded him of being in the Army: lines and more lines.

The man returned with a lady who stepped up to the desk and took charge. The man motioned to them. Anna and Michael joined him in walking through the gorgeous hallways and up palatial steps. Noticing they were intrigued by the art and sculptures, their guide eagerly lectured on the various world-famous Russians depicted and their accomplishments. Anna and Michael were wide-eyed at his depth of knowledge. Eventually they ended up in an enormous room filled with card catalogs. He turned, saying, "*The Histories* book by Herodotus?" Upon their nodded approval, he quickly made his way to a certain card catalogue and started searching the nameplates on the front of the boxes. Abruptly, he pulled one out and started flipping through the cards. He pulled out a small notepad and pencil out of his suit jacket, quickly writing down the reference. Pushing the box back into place, he turned, saying, "Let's go find it now."

"We really appreciate you are doing it for us," Anna gushed with a huge smile.

The Russian man looked uncomfortable, "You're welcome," he bowed slightly. "Now, please follow me."

Anna looked at Michael, confused. "Yikes," she whispered, "I didn't mean to overdo it." Michael just shrugged his shoulders; the Russian culture was a mystery to him.

After more stairs, rooms and corridors, Michael whispered mischievously to Anna, "I wish we had some bread crumbs or pebbles to lead us back to the entrance." Anna just grinned and shushed him.

Their guide suddenly stopped and said, "We will find the book in here." They were standing at the entrance of yet another grand room with high ceilings and bookshelves that soared above them. Quickly walking past the rows, their guide turned down an aisle. He stopped, his finger pointing in the air, his eyes searching. "Aha!" He cried softly, as he put his fingers around the edge of a rather large book and pulled it out gently. Michael and Anna leaned forward and looked at the book. "This is the first of the volumes, translated into English by George Rawlinson," the librarian continued. "Which story are you looking for?"

After taking the book into their own hands, Michael and Anna decided they needed Volume IV. "Please return it to that cart when you are finished," the librarian instructed, gesturing toward a cart. "You may find the next room over a good place to sit and look at your book."

Michael reached out and shook hands with the librarian. "Again, thank you for your assistance," he said solemnly.

"It was my pleasure," the librarian replied. He nodded at Anna, turned and departed.

"I guess he would have rather spoken with you," Anna pouted a little, a bit embarrassed that she had spoken up so enthusiastically before.

Michael smiled, "I think their custom is that the men speak and the ladies do not." They walked to the reading room the librarian had indicated. As they entered, several people looked up at them and returned quickly to their books.

"Have you noticed that no one smiles around here either?" Anna frowned a little.

"We are in an entirely different culture here. At least when they do smile, their smiles are genuine."

"True," Anna sighed.

They found an empty table and sat down. Anna opened *The Histories* and started reading. For a period of time, Michael just looked around the enormous reading room. Then he reached down into his backpack and pulled out Kirilov's cigar box. Pulling away the adhesive tape, he opened it and pulled out the paper. He began rereading and examining it.

"Michael," Anna whispered, closing *The Histories*, "there isn't much here besides what Kirilov already told us or mentioned in his diary. So, what about that corpse?" she asked.

"You mean the corpse mentioned in Kirilov's notes by the Arabian doctor, Al Kaisi?"

She nodded.

"You know what, the more I think about it, the more sense it makes."

Anna looked puzzled.

"OK, let me try to explain it to you," said Michael. "You see, HemIwno and the builders of the Great Pyramid were humans and thus capable of making mistakes. I think that the corpse found by Al-Mamun was the result of HemIwno's unintentional mistake."

"Let's hope it was his fatal mistake!" Anna said eagerly. "And that mistake will help us uncover what he tried to hide so diligently."

"OK, do you remember what Kirilov mentioned about the debris and rubble found inside the King's Chamber?" asked Michael.

Anna shook her head.

Michael said, "I'll be back," as he got up from the table, strode across the enormous room and disappeared into the next. After about ten minute's time, Michael returned holding another book. He quickly opened it up to the necessary page and read a short passage from there.

*The crypt was sealed off carefully. At its entrance the granite slabs of the portcullis were lowered down. The workers remaining inside the pyramid used the special well to get down to the underground level and from there by the inclined passage climbed outside. Later this passage was filled with stones. The true entrance to the pyramid was closed off and covered by the outer casing and nothing indicated its location.*

Michael shuffled several pages until the diagram of the cross section of the Great Pyramid appeared.

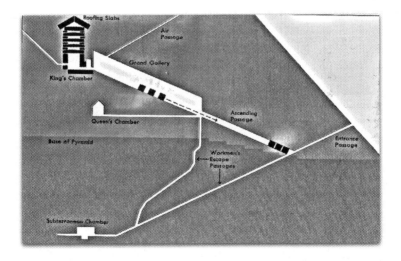

"OK, so according to Kirilov's statement, the corpse was found somewhere between the Grand Gallery and the King's Chamber's entrance."

"So what kind of evil plan was that? Did they purposely leave the last worker behind to die?" asked Anna, visibly outraged.

"I would like to think that was an unintentional mistake," Michael said quietly. "However, taking into account the customs of that period, the death of the ... hmmm ... let's call him 'the janitor' was well suited with Chief Architect HemIwno's plan."

"I still can't understand why HemIwno needed to leave a person who would ultimately die and decompose inside this sacred place next to Pharaoh Khufu's mummified body." Anna remained persistent.

"Well, there could be two reasons for such a devilish plan," Michael calmly continued. "One reason would be to seal off the Ascending passage that was used as the conveyor in order to transport limestone blocks toward the Grand Gallery. The second reason would be that he served as a decoy for the first tomb robbers penetrating the pyramid. Think about it for a moment," Michael gently touched Anna's hand, trying to distract her from her fuming, "A corpse discovered at the footsteps of the Grand Gallery or, even better, inside the King's Chamber was like a sign shouting to your face that *you are not the first one here* and as further proof to that testimonial, the robbers were to find nothing except the empty chipped sarcophagus. And as we already know, that's exactly what Al-Mamun encountered."

"OK, wait," said Anna, putting her hands to her forehead, "I don't understand how it was possible that the Great Pharaoh Khufu's burial ceremony was conducted inside a dirty chamber filled with rubble. And if the stone plug was sealed off before the Pharaoh's burial, then it means that besides the janitor, nobody else remained inside the pyramid."

A minute or two passed until Michael said a word. His suddenly straightened up in his chair. "Do you even realize what you just said?" he asked.

"What do you mean?"

"You just proved that Pharaoh Khufu's mummy was never buried inside the King's Chamber," Michael said, his mind whirling with the idea, "The King's Chamber never contained Pharaoh Khufu's mummy!"

"So, Pharaoh Khufu was buried in an entirely different place?"

"That's exactly right," said Michael.

"Michael, do you think the janitor could've known about his destiny? Did he ever suspect anything?" asked Anna, her eyes filled with sadness.

"I don't think he did. Most likely he hoped to use so-called transportation passage. He probably knew the plan was to go through the opening inside the Grand Gallery and climb outside the pyramid. But while performing the final touches to the Ascending passage, he was intentionally blocked inside."

"You're absolutely right," Anna declared softly, "However, based on Kirilov's theory, the plug located at the intersection of the Workmen's and Descending Passages is one of the secrets of the pyramid."

"And it's not hard to imagine that anybody familiar with this secret should die. Therefore, nobody could compromise the integrity of the pyramid."

"So, basically the poor janitor became HemIwno's sacrifice," continued Anna. "He was the last witness and had to die."

"I guess HemIwno had no other choice." Michael was shaking his head sadly.

"But Michael, that is really sad and outrageous. I hope HemIwno is burning in hell."

"I think we can avenge the poor janitor's death."

"How?"

"How? Hmmm. Good question. Basically, HemIwno wanted to improve his decoy design by adding an extra element: the corpse. That's exactly where HemIwno messed up. Instead of further mystifying the King's Chamber's real purpose, he unwillingly revealed its secret. And I think that the corpse is the weakest link in HemIwno's Great Pyramid project," said Michael triumphantly.

"Michael, I'm proud to say you just avenged the janitor!"

"Well, Anna, you can give yourself credit as well. It was you who made the ingenious realization about the impossibility of the pharaoh and the janitor sharing the same quarters."

"And now we know that the real burial place was nowhere near the King's Chamber," Anna said proudly.

"Yes, we now know HemIwno's secret. And I'm pretty sure Kirilov uncovered it as well. He just didn't have a chance to let us know."

"No, remember the 'four ways' in Kirilov's paper in the cigar box?"

"You're right!" exclaimed Michael, quietly pounding his fist on the desk.

"Michael, we need to establish our next plan of action," said Anna, looking mischievously at him as she picked up her iPhone.

# Chapter 42

EgyptAir Moscow-to-Cairo
Monday, September 25
8:20 a.m.

Most of the passengers on Flight 32S EgyptAir were asleep, as the flight had left early that morning from Moscow. Giving up on sleep, Anna finished up her juice and put her can on Michael's tray. Michael reached inside his jacket and pulled out the pencil rubbing made by Anna's father. *Why did he make this? Where is that stele now?* Questions on top of questions were just piling up inside his brain, and Michael could not come up with any possible explanation for Schulze's actions. His mind was back inside the Great Pyramid where he knelt next to the dying Schulze. His heart filled with guilt. *He was dying and I couldn't do a damn thing to keep him alive. If I had approached him the first time he screamed for help, then maybe he would still be alive today.* The pain was not getting any easier.

"Anna," Michael suddenly said. "Remember those 'four ways' your father mentioned and wrote down in his notebook?"

"Yes," Anna replied sadly. "Do you think is there the slightest chance we can explore any of these ways?"

"I don't think so. The Egyptian Supreme Council of Antiquities has banned all excavations on the Giza Plateau, around any of the pyramids and especially inside the Great Pyramid. In fact, they installed closed-circuit TVs and enclosed the pyramids with a wall."

"Yeah, that's what I was afraid of."

"What do you mean?" asked Michael.

"To explore any one of the four ways we will need to use an intrusive method to get to that underground canal. The Egyptian

Antiquities department wouldn't let us dig there unless..." Anna paused for a moment.

"Unless what?" Michael asked, curious.

"Unless we show them the stele from which my father made that etching. I'm almost positive this stele will answer many, if not all, of our questions."

"But how are we going to find that stele? We don't even know whether it exists for sure. Maybe with your father dying, the stele is lost forever."

"Yes, but let's stay on the positive side. When we get to Cairo, we'll use all of our efforts to find the answers.

"You can count on me, Anna. We're in this together," Michael said proudly, shaking her hand.

The flight attendants made their final rounds around the cabin. Anna was glued to the window watching as the airplane dipped below the clouds. She could not help but scream a little bit with excitement as soon as she saw the peaks of the three majestic pyramids slowly appearing.

"Let's summarize what we know so far from Kirilov's theory, OK? And if I miss something then you just remind me," Michael winked.

"Sounds good."

"The Great Pyramid was built using a cliff, with the height of the cliff at about 390 to 410 feet. The well located in the Subterranean Chamber did not collect rainwater, but redirected it outside the pyramid. All of the internal passages, such as the Descending, Ascending and Horizontal Passages, served as transportation lanes, drainage channels and ventilation ducts. The dead-end Subterranean Chamber, the Queen's Chamber, the King's Chamber, as well as the Grand Gallery served as working chambers assisting in the transportation and raising of the building blocks. And last, but not least, the masonry of the pyramid was constructed by a bottom-to-top method, while the encasing of the pyramid was done by using a top-to-bottom method," concluded Michael. "Did I miss anything?"

"No, I think you touched on all the main points."

"So, what kind of treasures are we going to find inside the Great Pyramid?" he asked.

"We're not even there yet, and you're already dreaming of treasure?"

Michael grinned.

"OK, let's see," said Anna, flipping through the pages in her book until she found the right page. "Obviously Pharaoh Khufu hasn't been audited yet," she frowned comically at him, "but we can estimate. From Tutankhamun's tomb located in the Valley of the Kings, Howard Carter pulled out twelve quintals of gold, not including jewels and ceramics. But the young Pharaoh Tutankhamun was a 'poor' boy in comparison with the great pharaohs of the Old Kingdom." Anna fumbled through several pages, "Then, from the tomb of Khufu's mother, Queen Hetepheres, was found a canopy bed, two armchairs, a carrying chair, and several chests, all covered in gold. The legs of the beds and chairs were in the form of lions' paws and showed accurate anatomical features including the muscles and blood vessels pulsating under the skin. In addition, twenty bracelets made of an alloy of gold and silver, and decorated with turquoise and azure stones were found. All these were in a small sized tomb. Now, imagine the assortment of riches that would be in the thirty chambers of her son, Pharaoh Khufu."

"Thirty chambers?"

"Thirty chambers of parti-colored syenite, full of precious gems and treasures galore, and rare images and utensils and costly weapons, which are anointed with egromantic unguents, so that they may not rust until the day of Resurrection. Therein, also, are vessels of glass, which bend and break not, containing various kinds of compound drugs and sympathetic waters."

"Whence such accuracy?"

"That's what Queen Scheherazade says in the story of 'The Caliph Al-Mamun and the Pyramids of Egypt' from the famed stories, *One Thousand and One Arabian Nights*."

Michael rubbed his hands with pleasure and grinned at Anna.

"You are not afraid of Pharaoh Khufu's revenge?" Anna suddenly asked.

"What do you mean? He's been dead for a while."

"I mean the Curse of the Pharaohs. You know, anyone who disturbs the peace of the pharaohs?"

"Blah blah blah. No, I'm not afraid. I do not believe in simple coincidences. Everything is happening for a reason. Kirilov uncovered the Great Pyramid's secret and advanced the time of uncovering the great mysteries. That is what may change the fate of our civilization."

The instant the wheels touched the runway, the passengers of the plane erupted in applause. Michael smiled at Anna, "Welcome to Egypt!"

# Chapter 43

Cairo International Airport, Egypt
Monday, September 25
11:17 a.m.

As the plane made its way to the terminal, Anna pondered about stepping foot in the mysterious country where her father had been murdered, realizing for the first time that she felt nervous. *What am I doing here?* After her experiences with Seth and the Medjay, she knew she simply feared the unknown. Who would be watching for her? Who would be chasing her?

The flight attendant's kind voice, speaking in Egyptian, startled Anna. She turned and looked at the flight attendant, who nodded at her. Looking around in confusion, Anna realized that the last few passengers were disembarking the aircraft. Michael must have gotten in line thinking she was behind him.

"Thank you," she muttered sheepishly. She stepped to the aisle and grabbed her small bag from the overhead bin.

*So, the main thing now is to look down,* she thought, *otherwise, the tears rolling down my face will make it difficult to see the steps. I don't want to fall down.* As if in a daze, she moved slowly along the cabin toward the exit in the hopes of waking up in her own bed in her family home in Germany. She could hear her mom, chastising her father, scolding him about spending so much time at work. If only she knew back then where her father was really spending his evenings.

The bright sunlight almost blinded Anna as she approached the exit door of the plane. Michael's smiling face was sneaking in from the top of the ladder. He reached up for her bag and descended ahead of her. Blocking the sunlight with one hand as her other hand firmly grasped the railing; she slowly descended the stairs.

As soon as they stepped inside the Cairo airport, the chaos and apparent lack of organization gave them an appropriate introduction to the country. Michael had gone through customs before, so the process was far speedier than it would have been if she had been on her own. But the bedlam, disorder and inefficiency going through customs gave Anna a brand new appreciation for German's orderliness and efficiency.

Anna and Michael picked up their luggage and made their way out of the terminal building. English-speaking touts, middlemen who make a commission for walking customers out to a taxi driver, swarmed them. While Michael was negotiating the price with one of the touts, Anna heard her name.

"Anna!" a male voice cheerfully exclaimed. Startled, she looked around, wondering who could be calling her name.

"Anna!" The voice was familiar. This time, she spotted a heavy-set man wearing glasses with grey hair bristling in different directions. When he saw her looking, he started smiling and waving as he strode quickly towards her. He wore an old, white T-shirt with a faded red lion, Dusseldorf's mascot. The long shirt almost hid his gray linen shorts, which were soiled in several spots. He exclaimed in German, "Anna, I'm so pleased to see you!" Suddenly he was embracing her in a tight, bear hug: his small backpack bumping into her.

Confused, Anna took a step back. She had not anticipated the man's sweaty hug, despite his familiar voice. The stranger held onto her shoulders and smiled familiarly at her.

After fending off several touts, Michael approached them. "Is everything all right?" he asked confused, looking at Anna.

"Ummm," said Anna, staring at the disheveled man.

The man stepped back scowling, "I should have known I wouldn't get a warm welcome from you," the stranger said, visibly disappointed.

Suddenly she remembered the voice. "Karl-Heinz?" She asked, as memories of her dad's old friend and partner flooded her mind.

"*Ja!*" The man replied enthusiastically. His smile seemed odd to her.

*Of course, Karl-Heinz,* she thought. He used to come to their apartment often, but it had been about three years since she had last seen him. She remembered him as being taller with bright brown eyes. She had always considered him to be an elegant man, who even at his age always dressed with taste. Apparently a lot had changed since those memorable times. His signature, elegant style had disappeared without a trace. He had put on a great deal of weight as well.

"Karl-Heinz Fischer?" She was surprised to see him in Cairo, of all places.

He smiled oddly at her and declared, "Well, who else?"

"Well, it's been a long time," Anna stuttered. "I'm sorry; I'm just surprised to see you here." She turned to Michael, switching to English, "Michael, please meet my father's old friend, Karl-Heinz Fischer."

"Nice to meet you Mister Fischer. I'm Michael Doyle," he said shaking his hand.

"Oh, please," said Fischer, switching to English, "you can call me Karl and the pleasure is mine."

"Karl, Michael is American and he is my friend," said Anna. "So what are you doing here in Cairo? Did you hear about my father's death?"

"Yes, I was so shocked," said Fischer, solemn now and embracing her with one arm, "He was my colleague here. We were restoring the Great Pyramid."

"That's exactly the place where he was poisoned."

"Poisoned?" Fisher removed his arm and stepped back, "He wasn't poisoned; he died of a heart attack."

"Well, that's not entirely true," Michael broke into the conversation, noticing that Fischer looked at him in a strange, unfriendly way. "I was with him inside the Great Pyramid when he told me he was poisoned."

"Well, he must've been confused," said Fischer, "I saw the hospital report."

"Karl," said Anna, "I don't know what to believe anymore. But how did you find me?"

"I called your mother and she told me that you were on your way to Egypt after making a short stop in Russia. What were you doing in Russia?"

"Well," Anna started, glancing at Michael as he barely-noticeably shook his head to stop her, "we met one man who had a very interesting theory about the Great Pyramid."

275

Michael dropped his shoulders in frustration.

"Wow, really?" asked Fischer in amazement. "Anna, where is the map your father mailed to you?"

"What?" Anna exclaimed, bewildered. "How could you possibly know that?"

"I know everything," said Fischer, slowly grinning.

Anna's heart sank. "He didn't send me a map!" She scoffed. "What are you talking about?"

"Don't lie to me!" Fischer snapped, his face turning a bright red color. He stepped closer to her and threatened, "You will give me that map and tell me what I need to know!"

Some of the touts started watching the three white people with interest. Cab drivers leaning on their cars were watching as well.

"Hey!" Michael barked, "Take it easy, man! She doesn't have a map."

"Oh, so then you have the map?"

"No, I don't."

"Then where is it?" Fischer's voice was a harnessed growl.

"Karl, please," Anna pleaded, taking a step backwards, "you're acting really weird." She noticed the small crowd watching them closely.

"Oh, you think I'm acting weird? No, that's not acting weird," his face was curled into a snarl. Keeping his eyes riveted on hers, he reached inside his backpack. He pulled out a hand-held six-shot silver revolver, hefting it up into the palm of his hand so that it reflected the brilliant sunlight. "This is what acting weird looks like," he snapped, brandishing the revolver. The crowd scattered. Fischer pointed his revolver at Anna, and Michael made a quick move to shield her.

Fischer growled, "I want that map."

"Karl, we really do not have a map," said Anna, trying to remain calm, "My father didn't send me any map. What are you talking about?"

"The map to the location of the stele!" Fischer shouted angrily.

"How do you know about the stele?" asked Anna, finally coming to her senses.

"It was my stele! I found it, and your father stole it from me, and now I want it back! I will give you one minute! If you don't give me that map, I'll shoot you both!"

"Karl, please calm down! My father didn't send me a map."

"Thirty seconds," Fischer warned.

"Mister Fischer," Michael implored, "we can do this together. You, Anna and me: we all can try to find the stele. You don't need to do this."

"Time's up," Fischer announced coldly.

"Look," Michael announced, standing his ground. "I have the map! Leave Anna out of it! I stole the map from the package her father sent her."

Anna was shocked, because she was the one who had opened the package. Then it dawned on her that Michael was bluffing.

"Now you will die," Fischer snarled, pointing the gun at Michael.

BAM! Anna's whole body shook and quavered when she heard the nerve-wrenching sound of the bullet blast. She closed her eyes as her heart raced to astronomical speeds. There was no sound. Then arms were embracing her in a strong hug. She looked up to see Michael, unharmed.

"It's over," Michael whispered in her ear.

"But how?" she asked in bewilderment. Anna looked in Fischer's direction. He was now lying on the ground, blood pooling under his hip. A group of local policemen surrounded him; one was putting handcuffs on him. Suddenly, all the noise of her surroundings rushed at her. She could hear the bellows of Fischer in pain, the roar of the nearby airplanes and distant traffic, and the murmurings of the crowd. As they lifted Fischer up and walked him away, one of the policemen, a middle-aged, balding man, approached them.

"Detective Hussein, right?" asked Michael.

"Yes, Detective Ashraf Hussein," the detective replied with a heavy Middle Eastern accent.

"Michael, you know this man?" Anna asked, her voice rising.

"Yes," Michael said calmly, "we met during my first visit to Egypt."

"Mister Doyle," the detective said pleasantly, "my Inspector and I would like to have a word with you and your lady friend sometime later this evening."

"Yes, of course. This is Anna and she is Schulze's daughter."

"Madam, nice to meet you," said detective. He winked at Michael, "and we know who she is." He pulled out a small notebook and pen, "Where will you be staying?"

"The Windsor Hotel," said Michael. "The very hotel her father, Mr. Schulze, was staying at."

"Thank you for saving our lives," said Anna, shaking.

"That's our job," the detective replied modestly. "We've been watching Fischer for the past few days, and thanks to the Almighty Allah, we arrived on time today. Plus we witnessed Fischer's confession. That will put him in jail for a long time."

"Thanks again detective," said Michael, shaking the detective's hand.

"Don't leave the hotel. The Inspector and I will stop by around six o'clock," the detective said as he walked away. Michael and Anna waved good-bye and turned to find a taxicab, this time without any help from the touts.

# Chapter 44

Cairo, Egypt
Monday, September 25
1:30 p.m.

Egypt is essentially sand, rocks and sand again. Its only "strip of life" is the narrow Nile Valley, which gave birth to the Egyptian civilization. The whole truth about the current Egypt lies in its past, which literally feeds the country today.

With a population of about ninety million people, Egypt consists of several ethnic groups: the Arabs who speak the Egyptian dialect of Arabic, the dark-skinned Nubians in the South and the many Greeks in Alexandria. The Arabs were not always an ethnic component of Egypt. Up until the seventh century there lived a very different kind of people who built thousands of wonderful monuments such as the pyramids of Giza and Saqqara, the temples of Luxor and the tombs of the pharaohs' treasures. Some of these monuments have been found, while many have not.

Remembering his previous taxicab rides, Michael advised Anna that riding in a taxi in Cairo would be the Egyptian equivalent of Russian roulette and recommended that either she closed her eyes or have nerves of steel. Anna breezily ignored his remarks as their taxi sputtered and wheezed through the gridlocked traffic. But when a gap suddenly opened up, the driver raced through it as they clutched their seat with a death grip. When the taxi slowed down, Anna simply said, "Wow," as Michael chuckled. Meanwhile the cab driver smoked non-stop, jabbered on his phone and occasionally leaned out the window to abuse other drivers. It was then that Anna realized Michael had given prophetic advice. But, in the meantime, she enjoyed the views of Cairo slowly opening up in front of her. As traffic stopped and started, the city began to reveal itself layer by layer. Anna gazed in awe, eager to experience this distant and enigmatic land.

Founded in the year 969, Cairo grew until it had absorbed all the neighboring cities and spread across the Nile. It is difficult to describe a third world country to someone who has never visited. Although full of modern technology, Egypt remains rich with tradition, culture and pharaoh-related superstitions. Cairo's composition is like a patchwork quilt, composed of Muslim, Mamluk, Turkish, Coptic, Egyptian, English, French and modern Arab neighborhoods. A metropolis with sixteen million people, it is a chaotic city that truly never sleeps.

As their cab entered Cairo's downtown area, Anna was glued to the window, staring in amazement as hundreds of people walked along the road. Amidst all of this activity and people traffic, Anna was dumbfounded to see a camel carcass lying flat in the dirt, just skin and bones, and the people simply walking around it.

Anna grabbed Michael's attention, asking, "Why doesn't anyone remove it?"

"Camels are indeed beasts of burden in Egypt," replied Michael, shaking his head in disbelief.

Soon they were driving through Tahrir Square on its wide and busy traffic circle. They passed by the Mogamma, a fourteen-story governmental administrative office building, rumored to be a gift from the Soviet state after World War II. The roar of engines, however, drew their attention as a convoy of dark green armored trucks swarmed around the square, lining up around its entire perimeter. Anna and Michael gasped as Egyptian SWAT teams leapt onto the street armed with riot gear and automatic weapons. More armored trucks filled the side streets as the military readied itself to disperse the day's planned protests and demonstrations.

After they passed through the busy square, traffic began to recede. Ten minutes later, the cab zipped up next to the Windsor Hotel, an elegant building featuring colonial-style architecture. Built at the turn of the last century to serve as baths for the Egyptian royal family, the hotel also served as a colonial British officer's club for many years before being turned into a hotel. At the turn of the nineteenth century the hotel held exquisite balls. There were beautiful dinners by candlelight after which the Arabs could dance with real European women, an unprecedented occurrence in Cairo at that time. Michael noticed that it was located just steps away from a market known as the Khan El Khalili Bazaar.

Still shaking, Anna stepped out of the taxicab. "Anna," Michael called out to her, grinning widely as he retrieved their luggage, "now you can cross off 'surviving a Cairo taxicab ride in one piece' from your bucket list."

She ignored his comment and inhaled a life-affirming breath. Instead, her lungs were filled with exhaust fumes, a souvenir from their taxicab speeding away. She coughed and took in another breath, this time of the exotic smells surrounding her. As she was deciphering the mysterious smells, her ears were filled with the seemingly nonstop car horn blares and sounds of the nearby crowd. Over all of this chaos, the evening call to prayer sounded, as loud as thunder amid the clear skies.

Anna looked over at Michael only to find him heading to the hotel entrance. The hotel seemed to have been frozen in time in the late nineteenth century, providing a unique opportunity to enjoy the dusty old flavor of a bygone era. Once inside they were immediately welcomed by the hotel staff and offered complimentary drinks. A pretty lady named Ramla was stationed at an old, dark wooden receptionist desk. Speaking in excellent English, Ramla politely informed Anna that the room in which her father stayed was currently unoccupied and available to her. She sincerely offered her deepest condolences in the death of Mister Schulze who, in her words "was very friendly with the hotel staff and the center of the livelihood of the hotel." Anna nodded her head, her eyes brimming with tears. Ramla added that the police had retrieved all of Mister Schulze's belongings.

Michael did not require any help with carrying the luggage as it only consisted of his old faded green duffle bag and Anna's pink suitcase, which easily rolled around on its wheels. Nevertheless, Ramla insisted, in the good memory of Anna's father, that one of the concierges be dispatched to accompany them to their room and deliver their luggage.

The guestroom retained an ambience of faded grandeur and old world charm with its original wood furnishings combined with all the modern necessities of today's world. Michael was pleasantly surprised to discover a plasma screen television, small refrigerator, complimentary wireless Internet connection and a modern bathroom. Anna did not notice these fine amenities until later, as the second she walked inside the room her eyes were fixated on the two queen beds. On top of each bed were bathroom towels folded in a heart shape, surrounded by fresh, colorful flower petals. After he dropped off their luggage, the concierge politely refused Michael's tip, bowed slightly and then left, closing the door behind him.

"Wow, I can't believe my father stayed in this very room," Anna remarked as she walked slowly across the room. "Only a week ago he was alive and restoring the Great Pyramid."

"Well, I'm not deeply religious, but based on my own experience, G-d always takes the good ones first."

"He was a very good father," said Anna as she sat on a bed. "He was the kind of dad every kid wishes to have." She paused and took a deep breath. "And even though later in my life he betrayed my mom, he still remained a great dad."

"That's true. He will always be your dad. Nobody can take that away from you," Michael replied gently.

"Thanks, Michael," Anna said, looking up at him with a small smile.

"Oh, look at the time," Michael groaned, pointing to the digital clock on the nightstand. "The Inspector and detective will be here in about an hour. I would like to take a quick shower and change, and then the bathroom will be all yours."

While Michael was digging in his duffle bag for his clothes, Anna grabbed her purse and started searching through it for her hairbrush. When she dumped the contents out, her lipstick fell off the bed and rolled underneath. She sighed and crouched down on the floor to get it.

"Michael!" she called out. "Michael!"

"Yes!" Michael said, "What happened?" He walked toward her, "Are you all right?"

"My lipstick is somewhere under this bed, but I can't find it."

"Lipstick?" he asked. "Wow! I thought somebody was trying to kidnap you."

Anna gave him a look.

"OK, OK," he replied, grinning. "Move aside, please." He crouched down and stretched his hand under the bed. In a few short seconds he had triumphantly retrieved her lipstick along with a piece of notebook paper.

"Ta da!" Michael announced as he handed the lipstick over. She reached out with her other hand and grabbed the paper from his hand.

"By the way, if you are such a lipstick fanatic, then you should know that during the French Revolution wearing lipstick of any kind was taken as a sign that you sympathized with the aristocracy. It could get you sent to the guillotine."

"Oh really? Wise ass," she replied in dismay as she looked over the paper Michael had retrieved with the lipstick.

"Yep, and I'm proud to say that this ended the era of men wearing lipstick," he smirked, but Anna was already too deep in her thoughts to hear.

"Hello? Are you OK?" he asked, seeing her expression.

"You are not going to believe this, but this paper was my father's," she finally managed to utter.

"Really?" this time it was Michael's turn to be astonished. "Let me see it," he asked, holding out his hand.

The paper was obviously torn from a notebook. It had a skillful sketch of a military tank that included various small details. There were some words handwritten underneath the sketch in an unfamiliar language.

**Die Allgemeine versengt die Erde in dem Dorf zwei Flaggen,
wo zwei große Schlachten einmal gewonnen wurden**

"That's my father's handwriting," Anna said sadly. "At least I now have something that belonged to him," she added, as tears rolled to her eyes.

"The police probably missed it," Michael suggested, handing it back. "I'm almost sure this tank is an American Sherman tank. But I think the last time it was used was during World War II."

"Well, my father loved sketching. That was his passion."

"I can tell you more about this unusual tank," said Michael.

"Unusual?" asked Anna.

"Well, as you can clearly see on this sketch, this tank has fenders," Michael pointed to the panel covering the tank's tracks. "The American models didn't use fenders, because they were easier to maintain that way. But the British forces attached fenders. So, this American tank was used by the British forces during World War II," Michael concluded.

"Wow, Michael, you continue to surprise me."

"OK, but what does this phrase say in German?" asked Michael, ignoring her remark. "Your father wrote it, right?"

"Yes, he wrote it, but I'm kind of lost."

"What do you mean?"

"Well, roughly translating, it means something like 'the General scorched the earth in the village of two flags where two great battles once were won.'"

"What's that supposed to mean?"

"I don't know," Anna answered, shaking her head.

Suddenly the room phone rang loudly. Michael reached for the receiver. "Michael Doyle," he announced into the phone. "Oh, Inspector Suliman. Yes, we are in room number five. OK, see you in a minute." As he hung up the phone, he turned and looked at Anna, "They're here. Hide the paper and don't say anything about it."

Anna nodded and rolled up the paper, putting it inside her purse. She threw the rest of her stuff back inside.

They heard a knock. Michael walked over and opened the door. "Hello, Inspector, nice to see you again," he said, shaking the Inspector's hand. The Inspector solemnly walked inside the room followed by his seemingly inseparable detective. "I would like to introduce you to my friend, Anna Schulze."

"Miss Schulze," said the Inspector, bowing slightly, "Inspector Suliman."

"Nice to meet you Inspector."

"I believe you already met Detective Hussein back at the airport, right?" asked the Inspector.

"Yes, sir, he saved our lives, and we're grateful for that, but my father—"

"Miss Schulze," the Inspector gently interrupted her, "let me first offer my sincere apologies to Mister Doyle and specifically to you."

Anna and Michael looked at each other in complete shock.

"Your father," continued the Inspector "is not a thief as we initially thought when we first received this case. We now have the real thief in our custody."

"Wonderful!" Anna exclaimed, embracing Michael joyfully. "I knew it all along!"

"I'm so relieved!" Michael said, tightly embracing Anna as tears of joy welled up in her beautiful eyes.

"Even though we suspected your father stole the ancient stele," continued the Inspector, "during our investigation we encountered a very peculiar twist in this case. The real criminal was another German engineer working for the same company, AirCo. I'm pretty sure by now you know who that might be."

"Fischer!" Anna exclaimed.

"Yes," sighed the Inspector. "Fisher was the one who found the stele, which, by the way, belonged to the ancestral tribe of the ancient Egyptian Medjay warriors," said the Inspector, pausing to look at them closely. "Have you ever heard of them?" he asked.

"No," Michael replied immediately, looking frankly at Anna. The Inspector looked at Anna. "What about you?" he asked.

"Never heard of them," Anna firmly replied, shaking her head.

"Now, Fischer found the stele hidden inside the Great Pyramid and tried to sell it to smugglers. He needed the money to pay off some gambling debts. But, luckily, your father intervened and the sale never took place. At first Fisher denied all the accusations and blamed everything on your father, Miss. But then we showed him the footage taken from several surveillance cameras, which clearly showed that the real thief was Fisher himself. He begged for mercy and revealed that one night Schulze came to his hotel room in Alexandria, and they had gotten really drunk together. He blacked out, but when he woke up the following morning, the stele had vanished. He thinks that Schulze drugged him while they were drinking and took the stele. Detective, can you please tell them what we have found out so far?"

"Yes," said Detective Hussein, "we reviewed the hotel surveillance cameras where Fischer was staying and confirmed that Schulze left the hotel at midnight carrying something heavy wrapped in a cloth. He put it in the trunk of his rental car and drove away. The next footage showed him coming back at five o'clock in the morning with nothing in his hands."

"Well, that doesn't prove anything," said Michael, "he probably wanted to protect the stele from Fischer."

"We are not excluding that option, but the stele is still missing. Unfortunately, the only person who knows its location was your father, Miss.

"Did Fischer kill my father?" asked Anna.

"Unlikely," this time the Inspector replied.

"But he didn't die of a heart attack, did he?" The Inspector glanced at the Detective. "Please, tell me the truth!" Anna cried.

"Miss, your father was poisoned," the Inspector said quietly.
"I knew it!" exclaimed Michael. "He told me he'd been poisoned. I knew he hadn't been hallucinating. So, Fischer poisoned him?"
"No," the detective said, "Someone else."
"Who then?" asked Anna, furrowing her brows.
The Detective and the Inspector looked at each other. "It's still under investigation," the Detective replied firmly.
"Now," said the Inspector. "Do you happen to know an Egyptian by the name of Asim?"
"Inspector," Michael stated carefully, "you and Detective Hussein are the only Egyptians we know."
"Do you always reply for Miss Schulze as well?"
"Inspector, this is Anna's first visit to Egypt."
"I'm well aware of that, but I'm investigating this man's disappearance from about three days ago …"
"Inspector," Michael interrupted him, "three days ago we weren't in this country. You know all too well that we just arrived in Egypt this afternoon."
The Inspector looked angry, but continued calmly, "Three days ago the Medjay warrior Asim disappeared in Moscow, Russia. Before he traveled to Russia, he was in Berlin, Germany." The Inspector paused and looked directly at each of them before continuing, "I know you two were in Berlin and traveled to Moscow before flying to Egypt. We have Fischer's signed confession." He looked at Anna, "Your mother told him your whereabouts."
"Inspector," Anna said calmly, although her heart was racing, "you're absolutely right. We were in Berlin because it's my hometown. We did travel to Russia to meet one of my old college friends, but I never met any Egyptians there."
The Inspector turned to the detective, "Show them the photograph." The detective opened up his briefcase and quickly retrieved a photograph.
"He's a hard one to miss," said the detective, displaying the photograph. They both looked studiously at the picture.
"No sir," Michael said with an assured tone of voice.
"No," concurred Anna.

"Very well," said the Inspector. "Before we leave I want to let you know that the stele has not been found yet. And even though your father," the Inspector turned to Anna, "wasn't the one who stole it, he certainly was the one who hid it. So I'm going to ask you one last question." He looked directly into her eyes. "Do you possess any information that could help us find the stele?"

Anna thought and shook her head. "No, I'm sorry."

"OK, very well, we are not going to waste any more of your time, but keep in mind that you didn't get shot today only because we intervened. Your luck could run out if you know something and don't disclose it to us." Anna and Michael nodded solemnly. Satisfied, the Inspector walked to the door.

Michael walked over and opened the door. "Good night, Inspector," he said as they briskly walked out the door. "Have a good evening detective," he added.

The Inspector reached into his shirt pocket and handed Michael a card, "Here is my contact information. If you need me, give me a call."

Michael took the card, thanked them and shut the door. He stood there for a moment, listening. Then, he locked the door and turned back to Anna, whispering, "We've gotta find that stele and clear your father's name." He walked over and sat on the bed next to her. "First thing tomorrow morning, we'll head over to the Great Pyramid."

"Right," Anna replied. "This way we can check Kirilov's theory and maybe find a clue to where the stele is located. Maybe he put it back inside the Great Pyramid."

"I hope you're right. But we have to be careful; the Inspector knows about the Medjay."

"Do you think the Inspector sent him to kill us?" asked Anna, getting the shivers.

"Doubtfully, but who knows?"

After sitting in silence for a few moments, Michael perked up, "Enough of that! Right now, I would like to invite you to the famous Barrel Bar on the next floor. I hope you're hungry."

"Starving!" Anna laughed, jumping up from the bed and walking to the bathroom. "I'll be ready in a minute."

# Chapter 45

Windsor Hotel, Cairo, Egypt
Monday, September 25
6:48 p.m.

As Inspector Suliman and Detective Hussein stepped out of the ancient elevator and into the elegant lobby, the Inspector's phone rang. "Inspector Suliman."

"Hello, Inspector."

The hoarse voice of his old friend, the Chief of the Medjay warrior tribe was impossible to confuse with anybody else's. "Chief Jibade, glad to hear from you!"

"Inspector, I hear you had a peculiar twist in the search for our missing stele."

Surprised, the Inspector paused. He replied, "Yes, the German Schulze was not the thief, and the real thief is another German by the name of Fischer."

"That news already reached me."

*How*? The Inspector wondered, saying, "Oh?"

"Did you find the stele?" asked the Chief, impatience creeping into his voice. "My people are getting a bit suspicious. It will be difficult for me to keep this from them for much longer. I hope you won't let me down, old friend."

The Inspector walked away from the lobby, hoping for a bit more privacy. "Chief, we're getting closer. Give me three more days."

"Fine. But after three days I will have no other choice but to go to the media. You will have a national scandal on your hands. In fact, this case could end up in more authoritative ones ... such as Inspector Moustafa."

"Chief, you know I need this case ... please."

"Three days," the Chief stated sternly. "And one more thing, did you ask the American and Schulze's daughter about the disappearance of my fearless warrior, Asim, in Moscow?"

"I showed them the picture, but they claim they didn't know him."

"Inspector, I thought that you had sophisticated ways of persuading people to talk," said the Chief, chuckling quietly.

Startled, the Inspector spoke tensely, "I will not interrogate German and especially not American nationals and have an international incident on my hands in return. I told you: three days and you will get your stele back."

"Fine."

"And one more thing, Chief," the Inspector's voice became sharper, "if you sent one of your Medjay killers to follow those two, then whatever happened to him lies on you! It's your hands that are stained with his blood. And let me remind you that here in Egypt, I'm the law. I intend to protect the lives of every foreign national who comes to visit. Tourism is our country's main livelihood."

"Don't forget our deadline," said the Chief, abruptly hanging up.

Frustrated and concerned about the Chief's motives, the Inspector turned to Detective Hussein. "Detective Hussein, I want your men following our guests' every move. If something comes up, I want to be personally informed immediately!"

"Yes, Inspector," said the Detective. He removed his police radio and started barking several orders into it. The Inspector was deep in thought. The Detective nodded at his Inspector.

As they walked outside, the Inspector said, "Detective, please gather all the possible information you can find on the Medjay tribe activities and especially Chief Jibade."

"Yes, Inspector."

"Something is not right here. Chief Jibade knows certain details that he couldn't possibly know. I want to know his source."

"Inspector, do you really expect Schulze's daughter and the American to call you?"

"Oh, I'm sure of that. Knowing the tactics my friend Jibade uses, it won't be long." After making his dire prediction, the Inspector got inside his police vehicle and sped away from the hotel.

# Chapter 46

Windsor Hotel, Cairo, Egypt
Tuesday, September 26
5:00 a.m.

At precisely five o'clock the next morning, Michael was abruptly awakened. Sleepy and dazed, he lifted his head from the pillow. The alarming sound of the muezzin, the one appointed to call the faithful to prayer, blared from a nearby minaret and seemed to be echoing over the entire city. Two hours and a brief continental breakfast later, Michael and Anna were boarding the tour bus, "Sakkara Tours."

On the way to the pyramids, their delightful tour guide, Hatima, educated her thirty tourists about the Great Pyramid's known facts with her soft, soothing voice. Everyone listened with genuine interest as Hatima reported the standard information on which modern Egyptology stands today: the Great Pyramid was ransacked in ancient times of which you can personally be convinced after glancing at the empty lidless sarcophagus; it was constructed with the aid of the mounds or by supplying the blocks on the steps of the already constructed part; the Great Pyramid was built by using 2.3 million limestone blocks; the mentioning by the Father of History, Herodotus, of an underground island, on which allegedly stands the sarcophagus with the mummy of the Pharaoh Khufu, is nothing more than a fairy tale.

On his first trip to Egypt, Michael had been completely satisfied with the tour guide's information. But that was last week. Now things were different. "Can you believe it?" Michael whispered to Anna, visibly frustrated. "I heard that same nonsense last week and it hasn't changed a bit."

"Michael," said Anna, looking directly into his eyes, "you are forgetting that we are the only ones who know the real story, which nobody is going to believe unless we find solid evidence about what we heard from Kirilov."

"Yeah, you're right," Michael agreed, sighing. The tour bus pulled over in front of the northeastern side of the pyramid site. "Give me a minute, I want to speak to our tour guide."

"Don't do it, Michael," Anna said as he got up. As she passed him on her way out, Anna murmured, "She's not gonna believe you anyway."

Michael started describing to Hatima just a small part of what he had heard from Kirilov. Halima displayed polite interest; however, she doubted Michael's intention of visually verifying something inside the Great Pyramid.

"Let's be realistic," Hatima said doubtfully. "After Caliph Al-Mamun broke into the inner hollows of the Great Pyramid, it was repeatedly rummaged in all possible ways. Millions of tourists come here every year, stepping on the same passages as millions prior to them. If there was something out of the ordinary, I'm pretty sure somebody from the crowd of tourists, guides, scientists and Egyptologists would notice something, right?" she paused, staring skeptically at Michael.

Michael noticed the skepticism in her voice. But her point definitely made sense. Millions and millions of people had visited the Great Pyramid throughout time, extensively in the last two centuries. Any realistic person would definitely agree that if there was something hidden inside the Great Pyramid, it would have been found already. Michael decided there was no point in arguing, at least, not yet. He thanked the tour guide and soon caught up to Anna.

"How did it go?" she asked with a snicker.

"Well, pretty much the way you predicted," he replied gloomily. "And I know what you wanna say."

Anna slowed down and gazed at him. "Really?"

"I told you so," said Michael, mimicking Anna's voice.

Anna chuckled.

"Well, at least she told me the magic word," Michael commented as they continued walking toward the three big pyramids.

"What's that?"

"She helped me come up with a reasonable amount of *baksheesh* to offer in negotiations with the pyramid's guards."

"Backsplash?" Anna asked, smiling.

"No, silly," Michael grinned, "we are not trying to remodel your kitchen here. Baksheesh is an Arabic word meaning a tip or a little extra payment for exceptional service. Hatima explained to me that Egyptians are very proud people, so they refuse to beg. Instead, they operate under a powerful concept called baksheesh, which loosely translated means, 'share the wealth.'"

"Basically, it's a bribe, right?"

"Well, more like an aggressive form of tipping. Kind of like, you've got it and I don't, so give some of whatever you got to me. Hatima told me that baksheesh could be taken to ridiculous heights. For example, if you ask directions from someone on the street, chances are that person will expect baksheesh. Since nobody begs, the idea of a welfare system seems insulting to Egyptians. They earn their money, no matter how little the money or the work. I wish that idea existed back home in the States."

"So how is baksheesh going to help us?"

"Hopefully it will unlock some tightly closed doors," Michael answered mysteriously.

At the ticket office they stood in line and purchased their coveted tickets, as only 300 tourists are allowed in the Great Pyramid each day. As they walked away from the lines, Michael said, "From now on, I will go alone. I'll have a better chance to negotiate with the security guard," he said pointing to the guard who stood in front of the gated entrance.

"I understand," Anna said quietly. "I'll be waiting for you here in the shade."

"Excellent."

"Just promise me something." Anna paused as her eyes filled with tears.

"Anything, just name it."

"Promise me that you'll show me where my father died."

"Dear Anna," Michael tenderly placed his hand on Anna's shoulder. "I will take you there, I promise."

Anna nodded her head and turned to find a seat in the shade. Michael looked at the Great Pyramid looming above him in the morning sun and started walking.

"Be careful!" she shouted as Michael started climbing the stairs.

"I will!" Michael called back to her.

There are two entrances almost next to each other on the northern side of the Great Pyramid: Al-Mamun's and the original entrance. In 820 A.D. Caliph Al-Mamun's workers dug the entrance where tourists are allowed to enter today. This tunnel is aptly named the 'Robber's Tunnel.' The pyramid's original entrance is located higher and to the left of Al-Mamun's.

When Michael arrived at the top of the stairs at the Robber's Tunnel, he was greeted by the sight of a sleepy ticket collector donned in a mustard-colored *galabeya*, a traditional Islamic shirt lengthened all the way to the feet. Michael handed the man his ticket and took a deep breath before diving into the millennial gloom.

It was his second journey inside the Great Pyramid within a week's period, but this time was different. Instead of blindly stepping over the beaten path, Michael took baby steps as he ran his palms along the tunnel's walls in a pat-down motion.

After about ninety feet the tunnel turned sharply left, where it met some stones that blocked its continuation. Al-Mamun's workers had been unable to move the stones, so they had dug around them. This passageway continued toward the Ascending Passage. It is at this point where the Descending Passage connects with the Ascending Passage. The original entrance leading into the Descending Passage is blocked. The ticket purchased in the kiosk does not give the visitor the right to enter the Descending Passage leading to the grotto. It only allows the purchaser to go upward to the King's and Queen's chambers.

Al-Mamun's passage was rough as it twisted like a snake-shaped tunnel into the interior of the pyramid. It was in complete contrast with the smooth passages of the rest of the pyramid. Michael decided to crawl under the low arches of Al-Mamun's passage in order to completely perceive the contrast. *What a bonanza that I returned here,* he thought as he suddenly noticed one additional and very important difference between the two passages. The walls and ceiling of Al-Mamun's passage were coarse from the forceful use of chisels and hammers. Michael turned and looked at the two passages that almost converged near the end of Al-Mamun's hacked entrance.

The walls and the ceilings of the Descending and Ascending Passages seemed virtually polished in comparison to Al-Mamun's. Looking closely, Michael was able to observe the surface of the original passages. He noticed some distinguished notches and small chippings, but they were strikingly different from Al-Mamun's as there was only some trifling roughness.

*What does this difference signify?* Al-Mamun's workers revealed what could be achieved by digging through the thickness of the limestone even though their chisels and hammers were made of the finest Damascus steel. The builders of the Great Pyramid, however, used primitive copper and granite tools. If they were digging in the limestone in the same manner as Al-Mamun's workers, they would have been unable to attain the smooth surface finish.

For a second, Michael imagined himself back inside Kirilov's apartment surrounded by Kirilov's comforting voice. "Remember, the ancient Egyptians cut their future passages on the exposed surface of the limestone rock. During the construction stages of the Great Pyramid these passages served as inclined flat surfaces in order to transport multi-ton limestone blocks in the upward direction."

Michael pondered the skepticism he had met back at the tour bus with the tour guide. Yes, it went against common sense to think that more could possibly be found after millions had passed here before him. But Michael was the first one armed with Kirilov's hypothesis and it worked perfectly.

*Well, now what? Upward, according to the purchased tickets or downward where the way is shielded by the locked iron gate?* He did not hesitate. Squaring his shoulders he commenced climbing to the entrance currently barred to the general public.

The guard watching over the Descending Passage saw Michael and winked understandably several times, signaling for him to wait. A group of tourists from Italy came through and then disappeared past the turning point. When the guard and Michael were alone at last, the guard whispered the magic word, "Baksheesh."

"How much?" Michael asked quickly.

"100 Egyptian pounds."

Michael shook his head and started to turn, as if to go back to the Ascending Passage.

The guard grabbed Michael's hand, "OK, agreed, seventy-five pounds."

"No."

Their bargaining ceased as they heard steps approaching from above. The guard signaled Michael to quickly get inside Al-Mamun's passage as another guard passed by. After the second guard walked away, the guard called Michael back. As Michael approached the guard, he discretely displayed a fifty-pound banknote.

As the tour guide had explained earlier, if he were to bribe the guard with 1,000 American dollars, it would instantly raise suspicions. The guard would be hesitant to let a stranger pass to the closed area in fear of some elaborate scheme. By offering the guard a relatively small amount of money and pretending that he was just a curious tourist, he would not raise the guard's suspicions.

The guard grabbed the bill, tucked it away and reached out to help Michael climb over the gate. Michael could see the steps leading downward in the half-darkness. As it was necessary to step carefully inside the tiny grooves alongside the stairs, the guard carefully placed Michael's foot inside the first one.

"Quickly!" the guard commanded when Michael was only a few feet away. Michael nodded, although he knew his journey would be anything but quick. As soon as he passed behind the turning point, the seemingly infinite Descending Passage opened up in front of him, faintly illuminated by a smooth garland of electric lamps attached to one side. Michael spun back around to take a final look back toward the entrance of the pyramid. Through the gaps in the iron gate he could see the celestial blue sky. That was the exact point from where it was possible to observe the Polar Star according to Piazzi Smyth, or the North Star Alpha Draconis according to the astronomer Richard Proctor.

Bending down into a duck-walking position, Michael began his descent. About 130 feet down the passage Michael suddenly found himself able to stand up straight. *Hmmm, I don't remember any book mentioning this.* The unknown *cocoon*, as Michael decided to call it, was unfortunately located in a dark niche between the lights. As he reached up, his hands rubbed against the ceiling's friable clay. The cocoon soon became narrow both overhead and along the sides of the passage.

Finally, the descent was over. At this point, Michael was underground where the horizontal passage of the Subterranean Chamber began. Michael estimated it was about twenty feet to the Lesser Subterranean Chamber. He was halfway there when ...

Blackout!

The few seconds that passed by felt like an eternity. Inside the vast abyss of darkness Michael felt the gloom enveloping him.

"Quickly!" the guard shouted from above.

That meant Michael's fifty Egyptian pounds had run its course already. *I want to get to the well. I might not get a second chance.* He kept quiet, thinking that the guard would not force him to climb back up in the darkness.

The lights turned back on.

Michael rejoiced and continued his journey until he noticed a visible crack, approximately four inches wide, running all the way across the floor, walls and the ceiling. It was entirely filled in with clay-like material. *With mountains of books written about the Great Pyramid, why was this crack never mentioned?* As he admired the crack encircling him, his mind returned to Kirilov's cozy apartment.

"It is rather strange," said Kirilov, "that Egyptologists were never puzzled by the fact that one of the horizontal sections of the Subterranean Chamber is shorter than the other. It is widely known that the ancient Egyptian's way of rationalization was based on symmetry. However, if you look closely at the diagram of the internal hollows of the Great Pyramid, the Subterranean Chamber was situated at about the axis of symmetry. If we were to continue the Descending Passage until it intersected with the well, then this line would to lead us to the plug. Now from this point on, continuing at the same angle of twenty-six degrees and thirty-four minutes, mentally picture the line extending to the opposite side. It would cross the horizontal passage of the Subterranean Chamber exactly in the middle, leaving the remaining section of the chamber to be twenty-six feet long. In this exact point, on the ceiling of the Dead-end Passage, must be a well-hidden plug closing off the other, undiscovered Inclined Passage. This hidden,

Inclined Passage would lead upward until it intersected with the former road coming off the water basin. At this point is the beginning of the original path that leads to Pharaoh Khufu's tomb. Obviously, it is hidden from the eyes."

Michael walked the next several feet while running both of his hands slowly across the ceiling. He knew exactly what he was looking for as Kirilov had mentioned more than once the importance of the barely-noticeable and seemingly useless seam. Several feet down the passage, to his excitement, was a shallow joint as thick as his pinky. It intersected the passage, not across its perimeter, but across the ceiling and the left eastern wall of the Subterranean Chamber.

"This smooth joint has an equal thickness throughout its length," Kirilov explained as both Anna and Michael studied his 3-D diagram of a cross-section of the Great Pyramid, "and although it was created with great technical difficulties, it still seems rather pointless and peculiar at the same time. If the tunnel was lit well, then you might see something. Namely, the other seams; barely noticeable, they blend in with the joints of the walls, floor and the ceiling. The now-hidden and sealed shaft in the ceiling of the horizontal passage was the beginning of the now-hidden passage, which I would call the Inclined Passage. This hidden Inclined Passage intersects with the Dead-end Passage. The builders of the Great Pyramid thoroughly sealed the ceiling opening of the horizontal Dead-end Passage. HemIwno, the chief architect knew rather well that the Dead-end Passage he created was the key to unlocking the greatest secret of the Great Pyramid. In order to avoid this, HemIwno extended the Dead-end Passage about thirteen feet further. The logic behind it was to lure potential robbers slightly forward and away from barely noticeable seams."

"Mr. Kirilov," Anna asked carefully, "what was the purpose of the Inclined Passage, if the mummy of the Pharaoh Khufu, as you mentioned earlier, was brought into his tomb through an entirely different way?"

"That's a very good question," said Kirilov, visibly impressed. "Try to imagine how the pyramid builders made these passages. Iron tools were not invented for another twelve hundred years, so their arsenal consisted only of copper tools, right?"

"Yes, of course."

"The sizes of the passages illustrate that only one stonemason could work inside it at a time. He would be working in a kneeling position, completely surrounded by darkness. They couldn't use torches because of the rapidly depleting oxygen. The working conditions were diabolical. Imagine striking a stone against other stone and dodging pieces of rock. In order to throw away the dislodged stones, the worker had to climb outside."

"But," Michael interrupted Kirilov, "then thousands of stonemasons would not have been able to complete the Great Pyramid within a hundred years' time."

"That's true. However, they built it in a span of thirty years. There is no reason not to trust Herodotus. So, it means HemIwno found a solution, which I finally figured out!" exclaimed Kirilov, beaming with pride.

"What was it?" Michael asked.

"HemIwno's wisdom consisted in the fact," Kirilov continued in his calm voice, "that the creation of the passages occurred not only from top to bottom, but also from bottom to top at the same time, in both directions. This method made it possible to expedite the construction process. Hammering into the rocky soil of the created passage, stonemasons were getting rid of discarded stones by throwing them down, thus never leaving the passage. Along the Inclined Passage these discarded stones were carried outside. The Inclined and Dead-end Passages were intersected at an angle, thus functioning as a continuous assembly line. The Inclined Passage joined the Descending Passage outside in the base of the rock. HemIwno was a genius."

Suddenly the lights went off again. Michael quickly crawled into the Lesser Subterranean Chamber and then continued toward the cave-like room known as the Subterranean Chamber as the lights were turned on again. He noticed it was becoming a real challenge to breathe.

According to Kirilov, this chamber was surrounded on all sides by the pyramid's rocky ground cliff. It had functioned as a major transportation link in the continuous movement of the limestone blocks. Hidden and safeguarded, the Subterranean Chamber successfully provided the transportation of the large number of building blocks toward the upper sections. The Subterranean Chamber itself did not need to be reinforced by the granite slabs, as the use of them in these conditions was not possible. Therefore, this Subterranean Chamber at the end of the construction had acquired the uneven shape of the cave because it was not meant for viewing or for future use.

Below Michael's feet was the well. It was the key technological aperture of the Great Pyramid and used as a drain during the construction work. When the pyramid was complete, the workers plugged the well by wedging a conical stone inside and burying it in seven feet of sand. Beneath the plug, the thirty-two feet deep well leads into the secret artificial canal, which connects the Nile River with the underground artificial lake. It is in the middle of this artificial lake where the sarcophagus containing Pharaoh Khufu's mummy rests. For a moment, Michael was able to visualize a piece of Kirilov's hypothesis.

Contemporary Egyptology does not mention the plug, the well, the artificial underground canal, the underground lake or the island with the sarcophagus. In fact, it alleges that those features were a fantasy dreamt up by Herodotus. All that is known about the inside of the Subterranean Chamber is that there is a seven-foot Dead-end Passage filled with rubble leading to nowhere.

The lights started blinking irritably. Michael took a final glance toward the Dead-end Passage at the end of the Subterranean Chamber. There was no way to get back there because it was barred by a fence and had no lights.

The ascent took considerably longer than the descent. Michael had to stop several times and hold onto the railing in order not to slip downward. With the air shortage, he felt suffocated. Everything seemed to ripple. Limiting access to the Descending Passage made perfect sense, as it would be technically impossible to provide ventilation without damaging the Descending Passage and especially the Subterranean Chamber. If somebody started to feel ill, it would not be easy to send help down there because it was so narrow. If he had found Schulze in the Descending Passage, there would have been no way to assist him.

At the intersection of the Descending, Ascending and Al-Mamun's Passages the guard asked him to be quiet and squat for a moment while he checked on the entrance. After a few moments, he returned and asked Michael to say nothing about going down below.

Before moving upward, toward the main hollows of the Great Pyramid, Michael looked closely at the very peculiar place where the two main passages, the Ascending and Descending, converged. In order to get inside the Ascending Passage, visitors have to start from the platform where the guard on duty is seated. However, to walk upward directly from the Descending Passage would be physically impossible as the point of the intersection of the two main passages is blocked by an enormous granite plug.

"Michael, remember the granite plug that Caliph Al-Mamun stumbled upon at the end of the Descending Passage inside the Great Pyramid? It looks like this plug was hiding the Ascending Passage behind it. All of the attempts to remove or destroy the plug were unsuccessful."

"So, what was the purpose of this enormous piece of granite?"

"When I examined the photos and diagrams of that plug," Kirilov continued, "I realized that it's not a plug at all. It's a piece of the engineering. If this granite block did not exist, neither could the Great Pyramid with its underground burial of the Pharaoh Khufu exist. In order to create the pyramid, the builders used a rock protrusion as the base for its construction. However, the height of the rock base of the pyramid made it possible to create one more passage for further transportation of the building blocks to even higher altitudes. When Hemlwno created this passage, it was subsequently named as the Ascending Passage. Since the rock base of the pyramid consisted of soft limestone, it was necessary to use granite. The enormous durability of the granite block ensured the reliability of the transportation of the limestone blocks. The granite block not only withstood the resistance of the blocks, but also the sleds filled with building blocks that moved higher and higher."

"So you think the purpose of this granite block," Anna interrupted Kirilov's thoughts for a moment, "was to hide the Ascending Passage?"

"No," Kirilov answered. "Egyptologists still do not know its prime designation, even today. They continue to assert that the plug was simply to hide the Ascending Passage. On the contrary, being located in plain sight at the end of the Descending Passage, it attracted attention, instigating a natural desire to explore what lay behind it. It teased and invited the unwanted, but expected, robbers to penetrate the pyramid further."

"That's exactly what Al-Mamun did," said Anna.

"That's right," continued Kirilov. "Al-Mamun's workers couldn't break the granite, had to dig around it and found the Ascending Passage. This passage eventually led them to the upper sections of the Great Pyramid."

\* \* \* \* \*

"I couldn't sit outside any longer. So, how was it? Did you find any proof to Kirilov's theory?"

"Anna, you can't even imagine!" Michael whispered excitedly, his eyes shining in the semi-darkness. "Right now, I need some fresh air."

Anna realized at that moment that they were standing at the doorway of the greatest discovery.

# Chapter 47

The Great Pyramid, Giza Plateau, Egypt
Tuesday, September 26
10:25 a.m.

"An ancient Arab proverb says, 'Man fears time, but time fears the pyramids,'" Michael remarked to Anna as they sat in the shade, taking a water break. "Once you hear it, don't you feel a whiff of eternity?"

Anna nodded thoughtfully, looking around and taking her time to fully enjoy the view.

"You see, nowadays pyramids have the desert all around them," said Michael, adjusting his sunglasses. "But don't let that fool you. In ancient times, palaces, temples and other tombs surrounded them. Barks and boats stood anchored at the pier on the Nile River. Priests and artisans lived nearby in crowded neighborhoods."

Anna paused, admiring the breathtaking view as the brilliant morning sun warmed her face. On one hand, the man-made mountains, created by the supremacy of human ingenuity on the bare yellow plateau, impressed her with their grandeur. On the other hand, she was stunned by the Herculean human effort that employed only simple tools to lift up countless massive stones and assemble them in a surprisingly harmonic structure. The Great Pyramid was especially amazing and beautiful in the morning's rays of light. It seemed that it peaked at the top of the bright blue sky, while its surface blended with the desert sand.

"OK, it's time for us to go in," Michael said abruptly, nudging her. "Come on, let's go!"

"Wait, what's the sudden hurry?" asked Anna, surprised.

"I just saw the Inspector spying on us." He paused to finish up his third bottle of water. "Come on, let's get inside the pyramid."

As they started making their way to the Great Pyramid, Anna thought sadly, *I'm not sure if I'm ready for this.* Her head started whirling with superstitious thoughts about the curse of the pharaohs. They reached the Great Pyramid, and as Michael started climbing up the outer carved stairs, Anna paused to rest. She vividly recalled the inscription on one of the tombs: "anyone who would harm this tomb will be struck twice by the goddess Hathor, cursed by the gods and torn apart by a crocodile, hippo and a lion." Anna looked up at Michael climbing the stairs and decided; *I have to do this in memory of my father.* She caught up to Michael as he was presenting their tickets to the ticket collector.

"Shall we?" he asked, with a smile for her.

She nodded and pushed past her fears, bravely stepping inside the 4,500 year old masonry. Once inside they started by walking around the granite plug, just as Al-Mamun's workers had done back in the ninth century. Anna admired Al-Mamun's persistence as they passed through the limestone tunnel. Slightly bending their heads down, they headed up the steep twenty-six degree and thirty-four minute angle of the Ascending Passage. Soon it split into two routes. One route continued going up to the larger, open area of the Grand Gallery, where Anna's father had collapsed, and the King's Chamber. The other route continued in a horizontal direction through the lower passage and ended in the Queen's Chamber. As they knew from Kirilov's explanations, these were conventional names given to the chambers since neither ever contained royal mummies. Michael suggested they first explore the horizontal passage that led to the Queen's Chamber.

The lower horizontal passage starts at the junction of the Ascending Passage and the Grand Gallery. It continues south through a vertical wall that increases in height via a stepped floor prior to entering the Queen's Chamber. The Queen's Chamber is the first large accommodation in the pyramid and positioned in the center of the pyramid itself. Michael gauged it to be roughly thirteen feet high. The relieving blocks transmitted the pressure of the superincumbent stones on the walls, shaping the ceiling in the form of a tent.

"Look at the walls," Michael said, scrutinizing the walls.

"What are we looking for again?"

"Evidence of a cliff, remember?"

"A flashlight and a magnifying glass would be nice," Anna commented as she frowned and squinted in the semi-darkness. Michael did not hear her as he was completely consumed with combing the walls of the chamber. Suddenly, he stopped. He looked fixedly at the deepening on one of the walls.

"Anna, come here! Michael exclaimed. Anna went over to him. "Look!" Rapturously he pointed at the eastern wall located outside the chamber not far from the niche. "That's the piece of the mainland cliff!"

Anna squinted and looked hard at what he was talking about, trying to get accustomed to the chamber's artificial lamplight. Finally, she noticed that an entire ten-foot section of the wall did not have one single joint between the wall blocks.

"That has to be a part of the cliff!" Michael announced happily.

"Well, if it was located to the right of the entrance, as part of the western wall of the Queen's Chamber, then it would be clear that this was precisely the part of the natural supportive cliff. But on the left side there is supposed to be the casing of the pyramid. So, maybe this piece of the rock is something like the wall of the inner cave within the cliff."

"Well, it's impossible to assume that the pyramid's builders dragged this giant piece of rock upwards. It must weigh tens of tons," said Michael, puzzled.

"Well," said Anna, pausing for a moment. "I would assume that this chamber is nothing more than a natural deepening in the cliff. It's basically a cave coated by limestone blocks over its three sides. The internal cliff certainly did not have a correct geometric form but had bulges and caves. So, it's logical to assume that the chamber built into the cliff was constructed taking into the account its natural unevenness."

"How did you know that?" he asked, flabbergasted.

"I went back over the notes I took in Kirilov's apartment," Anna explained, smiling calmly.

Michael's mind pulled him back in time to Kirilov's cozy Russian apartment. "Richard Pocoke was an Englishman traveling in Egypt in the middle of the eighteenth century. He was the first one to assume that a cliff was the basis of the Great Pyramid," Kirilov said, getting up from his armchair and walking to his bookcase. Grabbing one of the books, he continued. "In his book, *Description of the East and Some Other Countries,*" Kirilov held the book up, "he wrote about the traditional centuries-old custom of covering the mountains to convert them into pharaohs' tombs. Pocoke assumed that the Great Pyramid covered a two-headed cliff," added Kirilov, after placing the book on the dining table. "And in 1986 the French firm EDF obtained all of the necessary permits to perform a special kind of work inside the Great Pyramid. They drilled three openings into the left wall of the horizontal passage leading to the Queen's Chamber. They were testing the theory that there was a hidden chamber behind the west wall. The holes revealed a large cavity filled with unusually fine sand, which turned out to be quartz sand. It is believed that the volume of the cavity amounted to about fifteen to twenty percent of the whole volume of the Great Pyramid. This discovery gave birth to quasi-scientific explanations with the absurd conclusion that the Great Pyramid is just an empty shell filled with sand. But, if we recall that this is an enclosed natural cliff with all its disproportions, then the Frenchmen merely stumbled onto one of its hollows."

Michael and Anna located the set of square airshafts that were a sensation back in the 1990s. "Back at Kirilov's apartment, you mentioned that your father participated in the *Upuaut* Project to explore these airshafts," said Michael.

"That's right. The other set of airshafts are located in the King's Chamber. Back in 1993, after getting their expedition cleared through enormous amounts of red tape, some German scientists sent micro-robots through these airshafts. My father assisted them. At the end of the first shaft, the micro-robots stumbled against a smooth stone slab with two copper fittings."

"Do you happen to recall what Kirilov mentioned about the function of these shafts?" asked Michael.

"All four had the same purpose. They ensured effective air circulation by using the force of a breeze, which ensured the necessary atmosphere inside during the construction of the Great Pyramid. It was obvious that the robot could not move beyond the surface of the rock soil of the cliff."

"And what about the stone slab with two copper fittings?"

"They drilled through that and a robot pushed a camera inside," Anna replied with a grin. "It led to another stone slab door."

The last ascent led Michael and Anna to the Grand Gallery. At its top, the Ascending Passage suddenly opened up into what is always described as the most magnificent example of architecture in the ancient world. The Grand Gallery was a 153-foot long, twenty-eight-foot high passage that continued upward, at the same angle of twenty-six degrees and thirty-four minutes as the rest of the passages. The Grand Gallery consisted of a narrow, channeled floor situated between two high ramps and corbelled walls that reduced its seven-foot width just above the ramps to less than four feet at the stepped ceiling. Halfway up the sidewalls, and for the full length of the Gallery, small grooves ran parallel to the corbelling. Where the base of each wall met the ramps, twenty-eight sets of angled depressions and stone inserts divided the Grand Gallery at equal intervals.

Anna's eyes were busy searching for the spot where her father collapsed a mere week before. This was the second time Michael had been inside the Grand Gallery. During his first visit he was performing CPR on a dying German engineer. And now for his second visit, he was with the man's daughter.

"It happened here," Michael said quietly, pointing to the spot in the middle of the Grand Gallery.

"I need to be alone," Anna murmured.

Michael nodded his head and continued his ascent to the top of the Grand Gallery. Later Anna joined him. "Are you going to be all right?" he asked, watching her dab at her eyes with a tissue.

She nodded and blew her nose.

"I'm so sorry," said Michael. "I tried to revive him."

"I know you did everything you could. I'm glad it was you who was there."

Michael hugged her gently. From their vantage point at the top, they looked back at the breathtaking view of the Grand Gallery stretching in front of their eyes. They stood silently, listening to their own thoughts.

"So, what was the Grand Gallery's purpose?"

"Well, according to Kirilov, the Grand Gallery was mainly used to transport the heaviest blocks, including the granite blocks, which weighed more than fifty tons. Take a look at that ditch in the middle of the gallery."

"Oh, that's right, the ditch was built with the height of workers' shoulder level in mind. It was necessary for the sleds that were filled up with heavy blocks to advance toward the upper chamber."

"Yes, and I think it made perfect, practical sense. So, are you ready to go inside the King's Chamber?" Michael asked gently.

Anna nodded.

Soon they were ascending up the walkway to the antechamber, which was lined with large grooves that once housed the large granite portcullis blocks. These blocks had been lowered halfway in order to seal off the King's Chamber from intruders. The King's Chamber was the main and most spacious accommodation of the Great Pyramid. Near the right wall was an enormous granite sarcophagus without a lid and with a broken corner. Michael approached the sarcophagus and stood silently, looking between the entryway and sarcophagus itself.

"Look, this sarcophagus obviously was not brought in through that narrow passageway."

"That's right," said Anna, looking carefully at the sarcophagus' dimensions. "That means it was placed in here prior to the casing of this chamber."

"This is proof that this so-called King's Chamber was not cut into the thick rock, but was built first and then covered up by the granite blocks."

"So," continued Anna, "according to Kirilov's theory, this chamber served as a working accommodation for the transit of the blocks. The blocks were skidded inside the chamber along the inclined surface of the Ascending Passage and the Grand Gallery respectfully. From there, they were glided upward and conveyed from within the pyramid toward its outer casing."

Michael paused to consider her words. "Precisely," he said. "At the end of the construction process, the Ascending Passage, the Grand Gallery and this chamber began to serve another purpose: deceiving the pyramid's visitors."

"You know, many people are still convinced that the pharaoh's tomb was ransacked."

"Imagine what would happen if they found out the real purpose of this chamber," said Michael, grinning. "But anyway, let's look closely at the walls. Maybe we'll get lucky and find something interesting."

The smooth walls were coated by bare black granite with no writings or hieroglyphics whatsoever. On the southern wall were the two square airshafts that exited up through the pyramid and into the open air.

"Look at those stairs on the right side of the sarcophagus."

"Why are they are closed off with the fence going downward?"

"I don't know. Where do you think they lead to?" asked Michael, his mind swirling with curiosity.

"Unfortunately, we can't check it out right now," said Anna, looking at a group of French tourists and their tour guide who were noisily making their way inside the chamber.

"Let's go back," said Michael. "I feel like I just ran a marathon."

Going back alongside the Grand Gallery, Anna noticed two additional openings. But these openings are well known. One is located on the ceiling in the upper part of the Grand Gallery. About two hundred years ago, Nathaniel Davison, a British official climbed up there and discovered a relieving chamber. This chamber later became known as Davison's Chamber, in honor of its first discoverer. Later on, in the same spot, an Italian explorer, Giovanni Caviglia, used gunpowder at the end of the Davison's Chamber. By doing so, he laid a tunnel bearing his name and caused a crack in the granite plate, which lies above the King's Chamber.

Another opening is located at the lower end of the Grand Gallery and fenced off. That is the exact location where Caliph Al -Mamun in 820 A.D. found the corpse. He mistakenly thought that the corpse was the remains of Pharaoh Khufu. In reality, it was the remains of the "janitor," the last person left inside the pyramid. The pyramid's designer needed someone inside the pyramid to seal off one of the passages leading to the real final resting place of Pharaoh Khufu.

Michael and Anna emerged from the pyramid, squinting in the sunlight. "Anna, what you see today is not how the pyramid was intended to be seen," Michael commented as they walked away. "It had casing stones made of fine-grained sandstone, which were removed back in the fourteenth century. At that time, some French travelers wrote that they were stunned by the activity around the Great Pyramid. Workers swarmed like ants as they stripped it of its polished casing stones. The stones were sent to build the palaces of the Mamluk sultans and the mosques in Cairo."

"I can only imagine," said Anna sipping from a warm bottle of water.

Michael continued, "The pyramids' white exteriors shone in the sun. Their peaks were covered with thin gold plates and probably blinded people's eyes. Only Pharaoh Khafre's pyramid still has a portion of its outer casing intact, near the apex."

They stood at the southern tip of the rocky Giza Plateau, on the top of which the three biggest pyramids stretched smoothly from west to east. In the early morning hours, a serenity and tranquility had reigned here. But as the day slowly unfolded, buses filled with tourists had arrived non-stop.

The crowds stepping out from their buses encountered an army of vendors with souvenirs and camels. The vendors, including many youngsters, shoved all sorts of trinkets, such as greeting cards, key chains and ornaments with images of the elegant beauty Queen Nefertiti and sacred scarabs, in the tourists' hands. The camel owners called out to the tourists, guiding the crowds to their camels. Once payment was made, the camels would get down on their knees and the riders would climb onto a velvet saddle. Known as the "ships of the desert" for their ability to glide across the desert sands, the camels are an iconic feature.

The pyramids looked particularly majestic: like a mirage floating in hot air. Anna could not imagine looking at them from the valley they were so immensely huge.

"In the book I read on the plane, it said that one of the researchers assumed that the Great Pyramid was not an architectural structure, but a giant sculpture, carved out of the mountain range," Anna said.

"Well, he was not far from reality and hopefully soon we can finally shine a ray of light inside that mysterious darkness," Michael replied.

# Chapter 48

Cairo, Egypt
Tuesday, September 26
4:20 p.m.

The electronic, melancholy sounds of Arabic pop music drifted longingly out the taxi window as Michael and Anna wearily got into the back seat. After giving the taxi driver the name of their hotel, they settled back to watch the scenery go by their windows. The taxi driver, taking advantage of his captive audience, showed them a big smile along with a bag full of trinkets. After glimpsing the driver's pictures of his family with six small children, Anna bought a few trinkets to help him. As she sat back in her seat, Anna could not help but think that these people were only trying to scratch out a living. To them, Americans are beyond wealthy. When the taxi driver asked Michael what kind of car he drove, he did not have the heart to tell him that most American families own at least two cars.

In the downtown area they got stuck in the famous Cairo traffic. After a while, Anna could not take it anymore and suggested they walk to their hotel. Soon they were walking along the streets of ancient Cairo with the constant honking surrounding them.

Even though Egypt is predominantly Muslim, it is a moderate country, so fundamentalist practices are not overtly evident. They observed as a man greeted another man with a kiss on the cheek, a common scene that is an expression of friendship and kindness.

They stopped at a coffee shop, a place where men traditionally go after hours to play backgammon and dominos and to smoke hookahs. One of the most wonderful smells in the world comes from *mu'assel*, which translated from Arabic means "honeyed." Mu'assel is tobacco mixed with molasses and vegetable glycerol; it creates a syrupy mix, which is burned inside a hookah or water pipe. The smell of the burning mu'assel was so strong that later in the evening, as Michael sat in the hotel's roof garden sipping a glass of exquisite wine, he was still getting whiffs of its unforgettable aroma, diligently making its way six floors up.

They arrived at their hotel and took the short ride up in the elevator. Anna went into the bathroom to make up a cool washcloth for her neck, as she was hot and tired from their day in the desert. She started to lie down when something occurred to her. She sat up and quickly opened up her purse. "Michael!" she exclaimed, the excitement rising in her voice. "I just remembered my father's sketch. I think we might be able to figure out his riddle."

"Let me see it again," said Michael, stretching out comfortably on the armchair next to the table as Anna handed him the paper.

"Roughly translated from German, it says something like, 'The General scorched the earth in the village of two flags where two great battles once were won.'"

"Hmm," Michael thought hard. "You've never seen this phrase before, right?"

Anna shook her head.

"You know what, let's use that free WI-FI the hotel offers and see what Google says. Meanwhile, I think we need to get out of this stuffy room." Michael stood up from the chair and handed Anna the sketch. "How about we go up to the rooftop garden and relax?"

"Oh, yes! That sounds nice."

They left the room, took the elevator to the top floor and followed the signs down the hallway. Opening the door, a slight breeze and the gentle rays of the Egyptian sun greeted them. They stepped out onto the terrace where they admired the view of Cairo's downtown and beyond. They quickly found some cushioned chairs and pulled them away from the other tourists enjoying themselves in the glowing evening sun. After settling in and giving their wine order to the waiter, Anna retrieved her iPhone. "Should I input the whole phrase?" she asked.

"No, let's divide it into parts first. OK, first, type in 'scorched earth.'"

"Found it." Anna read it out loud for him:

> *A scorched earth policy is a military strategy that involves destroying anything that might be useful to the enemy while advancing through or withdrawing from an area.*

Michael held out his hand for her iPhone and Anna handed it to him. Michael scanned the page by scrolling down. He suddenly stopped, visibly surprised, and started reading out loud:

> *General Sherman most famously used the scorched earth method against the South in the American Civil War.*

Handing back the phone to Anna he said, "Hmm … The Sherman tank is named after a Civil War general. Can you search for 'General Sherman' now, please?"

Anna typed the two words in the search box and in less than a second read out loud from the screen:

> *William Tecumseh Sherman (February 8, 1820 – February 14, 1891) served as a General in the Union Army during the American Civil War (1861–65), for which he received recognition for his outstanding command of military strategy as well as criticism for the harshness of the "scorched earth" policies that he implemented in conducting total war against the Confederate States.*

"OK," said Michael, satisfied. "Now Google 'Sherman tank.'" After a few short keystrokes, Anna started reading out loud again:

> *In the United Kingdom, the M4 is an American-made tank. It was named after the Union's General William Tecumseh Sherman, following the British practice of naming their American-built tanks after famous*

*American Civil War generals. Subsequently, the tank's
British name found its way into common use in the
United States.*

Anna exclaimed, "Wow! You were absolutely right; it is the Sherman tank!"

"Right," said Michael, grinning.

"But why would my father make a sketch of this tank? He wasn't a military fanatic."

"Hopefully … eventually, we will find the answer to this question. But for now, let's concentrate on the tank." Anna nodded in agreement with Michael. The waiter appeared by their side with their wine. After a bit of small talk about the scenery, one of the other guests called out to the waiter who then bowed and excused himself.

Michael continued, "OK, the Sherman tank. We know that the tank in your father's sketch was used by the British forces because it has fenders, as I explained to you before."

Anna nodded in agreement, taking a small sip of her delicious wine.

"So, the tank is British and it was used during World War II. Let's find out where the British forces won two battles during World War II." Michael chuckled, "Make your iPhone useful again."

"How would I do the search?" asked Anna.

Michael thought for a few minutes. "Well, according to our hotel's pamphlet, during World War II this was a British military's officer's club. So the British were stationed here in Egypt. Check to see if any of those battles were fought here in Egypt."

"Well, what do you know," Anna announced shortly. "The battle of El Alamein was fought in Egypt," she said, her eyes sparkling with excitement.

"Really?"

"And that's not all! Not one, but two battles were fought here in Egypt during World War II."

"Let me see it," said Michael, setting down his glass and taking her iPhone. He started reading to her:

*There were two battles of El Alamein in Egypt during
World War II. The El Alamein Battlefield was the site*

*of a major victory by the Allied forces. The site is in and around the area named after a railway stop called El Alamein. Known as the First and the Second Battle of El-Alamein, both were fought in 1942 to prevent Germans from capturing Alexandria and the Suez Canal. The First Battle of El Alamein saw the Allies stall the progress of Italian and German armies. However, it was the Second Battle of El Alamein that changed the fortunes of the Allies as it forced the Axis out of Egypt and safeguarded the vital route of the Suez Canal. The victory at the El Alamein Battlefield was a vital turning point for the Allies. Winston Churchill summarized it succinctly by saying, "It may almost be said, before Alamein we never had a victory, and after Alamein we never had a defeat.*

Michael handed the iPhone back to Anna exclaiming, "Excellent!" Anna smiled and nodded at him. He instructed, "Now Google 'El Alamein.'"

Anna quickly found it and started reading:

*El Alamein, Arabic: literally, 'the two flags.'*

"Wow! Michael, here are the two flags from my father's riddle."

"You are absolutely right! Congratulations."

"For what? We solved the riddle, but didn't actually solve anything. What does this El Alamein have to do with anything? I'm completely lost."

"OK, you're still in Egypt, still in this marvelous hotel and still sitting in the roof garden having drinks with me."

"That's not funny," Anna replied, pretending to pout as she took a sip.

"I apologize," Michael grinned at her. "On a serious note now, check and see if El Alamein has some kind of World War II museum."

"First, let me finish what it said about El Alamein." Anna continued with her reading:

315

*El Alamein is a town in the northern Matrouh Governorate of Egypt. Located on the Mediterranean Sea, it lies sixty-six miles west of Alexandria and 149 miles northwest of Cairo.*

Anna paused, "OK, let's see if there is a World War II museum there." She concentrated on her iPhone. Looking up, she smiled, saying, "Oh, you bet they do."

But Michael was ignoring her. His eyes were closed as the sun caressed his face, the mu'assel drifted into his brain and the wine warmed his insides. "Just read it to me, lady."

Anna laughed and started reading to him:

*The El Alamein Military Museum houses a series of exhibitions about the Battles of El Alamein, a crucial Allied victory during World War II in which the Italian and German armies were forced out of Egypt. Housing a collection of uniforms, armed vehicles and weaponry, the El Alamein War Museum provides an insight into the 1942 battle which has since been labeled a turning point in the war. The museum is located close to the main El Alamein Battlefield.*

"Hey! Armed vehicles?" Michael opened his eyes and sat up, looking excited. "Inspector Suliman mentioned that the hotel surveillance video showed your father with the stele leaving the hotel in Alexandria at midnight and returning early in the morning, right?"

"Yes."

"And since El Alamein is a mere sixty-six miles away from Alexandria, then he had plenty of time to drive all the way to El Alamein and stash that stele somewhere in that area."

"My God, Michael," Anna sighed deeply. "How are we going to find that stele in El Alamein? It's a huge museum filled with military artifacts! It's like looking for a needle in a haystack."

Michael concentrated his thoughts for a moment. His mind traveled back to his Rockland Community College economics class, when his wise professor gave the class an explanation of the whole concept of a needle-in-a-haystack dilemma.

"A needle in a haystack," the professor had lectured, "presents difficulty when the correct answer is almost impossible to figure out in advance. But it's easy to recognize if someone points it out to you. Faced with a big haystack, it's hard to find the needle; but if someone points out where the needle is located, it's easy to verify that they're right."

"So, what's the best solution when you are faced with one of those needle-in-a-haystack problems?" Michael had asked, mesmerized, as if he had foreseen that he would ever face this type of task.

"It's rather simple," the professor had replied mischievously. "Maximize the size of the needle or reduce the size of the haystack."

"So, Michael, how are we going to find this needle in the haystack?" Anna asked impatiently.

"Reduce the size of the haystack."

"Huh?" she asked, puzzled.

"There is only one way to find out," Michael said mysteriously. "So, first thing tomorrow morning we're heading there."

# Chapter 49

Village of El Alamein, Egypt
Wednesday, September 27
10:05 a.m.

Although it is one of those places everybody has heard about, El Alamein can be found only on a very detailed map. In 1942 the Germans and the Allies battled for dominance of North Africa here. The Allies won, thus taking control of the Suez Canal, much of the Middle East and the sea route from the Mediterranean to the Indian Ocean. Previously a small Bedouin village, El Alamein is a resort now.

After a three-hour trip, Michael and Anna stepped out of the taxicab. The unrelenting sun and suffocating heat nearly took their breath away. The atmosphere, mixed with beige sand, barbed wire, military vehicles and unexploded mines brought back distant memories of the World War II documentaries Michael had seen on the History channel. On one side was the vast blue expanse of the Mediterranean Sea. On the other side were the endless beige sands of the Sahara desert. World War II had ended more than seventy years ago, but the evidence of it was still everywhere.

The museum, originally opened in 1956 to commemorate the World War II battles, was renewed and reopened in 1992. As Anna and Michael slowly walked through the cool air-conditioned halls, they admired the murals depicting the weapons, equipment and experiences of the British, Commonwealth, German and Italian forces during the conflict. A simple but enormous map display showed the troop movements during the battles of El Alamein.

The moment they stepped outside into the courtyard, Anna and Michael were surrounded by various vehicles and large weaponry mounted on enormous stone pedestals. The vehicles and tanks appeared to be in the condition in which they were recovered from the battlefields. One truck, filled with rations of food and weapons, was discovered near the Libyan border in 1996. The driver's decayed body was still in his seat. It was towed back, rewired and given some oil. And after sitting in the desert for over fifty years, the Ford truck started.

Michael stopped at each tank pedestal with Anna's father's sketch in hand.

After walking slowly between the pedestals for a good twenty minutes, Anna asked, "How are we going to find the stele among these relics?"

"I told you, by reducing the size of the haystack," answered Michael slyly. "Patience, my dear Anna, patience," he added, quoting his favorite childhood hero, the great detective Sherlock Holmes.

The sun beat down on them ferociously as it always did over El Alamein where the World War II soldiers fought not only their enemies, but also the inhumane heat, sand and dust conditions. Anna took a break in the shadow of one of the pedestals.

Michael ran over to her. "Come here," he called excitedly before jogging away.

As she approached where he was standing, she looked at tank on the pedestal. "That's the tank!" she exclaimed.

"It sure is," he replied happily.

"Do you think the stele is under the tank?"

"I would hope so," replied Michael as he knelt down and peeked under the tank's shadow. He walked around the tank, kneeling down to check under it from each possible location. "Not here," he said each time he got up.

Anna sighed deeply. She was starting to lose hope as the sun's rays beat down on her burning head.

"Eureka!" Michael exclaimed the famous exclamation attributed to the ancient Greek scholar, Archimedes. In ancient Greece, Archimedes had been tasked with finding out if the local goldsmith was secretly inserting cheap silver into his gold coins. According to the ancient story, when Archimedes stepped inside a communal bathtub filled with water, he discovered or realized the principle of mass displacing water. Having figured out the best possible way to investigate the gold coins' purity, he leapt out of the bathtub and ran through the streets of the city naked shouting "I've found it! (Eureka!)"

"What?" asked Anna, "Did you actually find it?"

Michael had a big grin. "Our survey says ... Correct! Ding! Ding! Ding!"

"Are you kidding me or is it true?" asked Anna, losing her patience.

Michael glanced around. "Watch," he announced as he carefully put his hand inside the tank's front left caterpillar wheel. He cautiously dragged out a plastic bag. Anna crouched down next to him, watching, holding her breath. Slowly he opened up the bag and removed a heavy object wrapped in a green blanket with a hotel logo on it. He carefully unwrapped it.

Anna leaned closer as they marveled at the stone slab, sixteen inches high and eleven inches wide. They both carefully brushed their fingers against the nearly polished front side of the stele, in awe that it could easily be three thousand years old.

The round-topped limestone stele was inscribed on the front side in shallow relief. The middle portion of the stele had a register in the shape of a rectangle. This rectangle was divided into twenty smaller squares: four rectangular rows of five squares, one on the top of another. An identical image was placed either at the beginning or the end of each row. This image depicted a person holding a stick with one of his arms outstretched, pointing to a specific direction. On each side of the bigger rectangle were images of inclining steps toward a body of bright blue water. One each side of the bigger rectangle was an image of the god of wisdom, Thoth. Thoth was depicted as a human being using his writing tools to make an inscription, its head was an ibis-stork and on top of this stork head was a half moon. The stele had a visible crack in its lower right portion that was repaired and cleaned.

"You still have that pencil rubbing your father sent to you, right?" asked Michael, still mesmerized.

"Of course," she replied, pulling the bag out of her purse. Sitting in the tank's shadow, Michael placed it over the stele. It was a perfect match.

Michael spoke quietly, "Do you have a pencil?" Anna found a pencil in her purse and gave it to Michael. "Here, hold this down while I trace it." Anna pressed the paper tightly against the stele as Michael made a pencil rubbing of the remainder of the image.

"Why are you doing this?" asked Anna, slightly confused. "I mean, after all, we have the stele now."

"I just wanted to finish the task your father started. He probably got spooked by somebody and couldn't finish it."

"Thank you, Michael," said Anna, touched by his gesture. "My father would definitely appreciate this. The only thing I don't understand is how he had time to make a sketch of this tank at night and in total darkness. The most puzzling thing to me is how did he get inside this courtyard at night when the museum was closed?"

"Well, I'm pretty sure he planned that in advance. He definitely was here before that night when he sneaked out of the hotel in Alexandria. He obviously made the sketch of the tank in broad daylight as you can see from the tiny details he included. That's when he spotted the perfect hiding place for the stele. I'm guessing he didn't know whom to trust and decided that the best course of action would be to hide it. He probably knew Fischer would make another attempt to sell it. As for the pencil rubbing, he made it the night he hid the stele. As you can see, he was in a hurry and missed some important attributes of the whole top design."

"Who might have spooked him here at night? I mean these artifacts are valuable historically, but nobody would try to steal them, right?"

"Well, not here in the courtyard, but the museum has quite a few showpieces inside the building. They probably have at least one guard here at night just in case something does happen," said Michael as he handed Anna back her pencil. He carefully wrapped the stele back in its blanket, placed it in the plastic bag and then put the entire package inside his backpack. He folded the completed pencil rubbing of the stele and tucked it inside his jeans pocket.

As they walked toward the museum, Anna tried to imagine what it would be like to be stuck inside one of the chunks of metal during a broiling hot day like today. She could not imagine it. Even donned in just a T-shirt and skirt, she felt drops of sweat on her skin. Never mind the fact that she was constantly getting hydrated. In fact, she was just finishing up her third bottle of water. What would happen if she were placed inside one of those war relics donned in a full military uniform complete with helmet? The only possible outcome she could imagine was a hardboiled egg.

Back inside the chill of the museum and away from the boiling sun of the open-air courtyard, they walked back through the halls. After their long walk under the scorching sun, Anna felt relieved to be inside the coolness of the museum. They spent some more time checking out the weapons, uniforms and other artifacts of the soldiers of that era.

When Anna and Michael walked out of the museum, their taxicab was waiting for them at the same spot. The driver even waved his hands just to be sure they would find their way back to his cab, as there were several other taxis parked by the curb. The driver happily greeted them as they climbed inside. Michael took off his backpack and set it on the floor. As they started back for Cairo, Anna leaned on Michael's shoulder and closed her eyes. In anticipation of the three-hour drive back, Michael stretched back and closed his eyes as well.

After about fifteen minutes, the cab stopped with a mighty jerk of the brakes. If Michael had not automatically stretched his arms out and broken their fall, they both would have easily been thrown into the front seat or worse.

As the dust cleared, Michael looked through the windshield. For a moment thought he was seeing a ghost. Asim, the Medjay warrior, stood a few yards away. The man had the same bushy Afro hair, the same white cotton cloak and even the same tan. If Michael had not personally observed Asim getting hit by a 400-ton train inside the Moscow Metro subway, he would be certain that Asim was standing in front of him. And Asim looked too real to be a ghost. Michael glanced at Anna and saw the same expression on her face: amazement mixed with doubt.

"Michael, are you seeing what I'm seeing?" she finally managed to whisper.

"Well, I've heard that traumatic experiences can alter your perception, but is it possible we're both seeing it?"

"We both went through the traumatic experience, right?"

Michael nodded. "But what about the taxi driver?" he asked as their driver opened his door, slammed it shut and started walking toward the Medjay.

"Maybe he is a psychic," suggested Anna.

"Come on Anna! This guy looks too real to be a ghost, he—"

"Oh Michael, look," Anna interrupted him, pointing to a nearby palm tree. "There's another one." Another Asim emerged from behind the tree and walked to the first Asim.

"OK, these two guys are not the ghosts of Asim," said Michael firmly. "I mean, come on, look at them, the guy on the left is darker and at least five inches shorter than real Asim. And the guy on the right has a facial tattoo on his right cheek that Asim definitely didn't have." Michael absentmindedly reached up and wiped the sweat from his forehead.

"Oh good," replied Anna. "The last thing I need to see here in Egypt is a ghost, or worse, two ghosts."

Michael started looking around. "It's really hot in here." He peered into the front seat, "The driver not only turned off the engine, but he also removed the key from the ignition." Michael turned and tried to open his side door. "And he locked the doors!" he exclaimed nervously.

"Maybe he stopped to see his old friends?" Anna suggested.

"Or maybe we're here because they want revenge for their killed tribesman, or worse, their brother."

"Oh, come on, you can't be serious, how they could possibly know?"

Anna's door jerked open, "Out of the car!" the taxi driver commanded. Michael and Anna turned their heads to see their taxi driver with the two ferocious Medjay warriors by his side.

"What's the meaning of this?" Anna asked angrily. "What is going on? We paid you for a round trip! If you want more money then let us know!"

"It's not just about the money," said the driver, speaking normally now, sounding almost sorrowful. "I'm sorry. I'm just a middleman who needs to feed my family. They will kill me if I don't obey them."

"And what now?" asked Michael, his voice rising. "They're just gonna kidnap us and ask for a ransom? Is that what's this is about? Hey, why don't they men up and just say it for themselves?"

"They don't speak English. Sorry, you better follow them to their car, otherwise ..."

"Otherwise what?" asked Michael, furious.

"Otherwise they will kill you and take away what you have in your backpack."

"Oh, OK, I see. So I guess you told them about us going to the El Alamein museum, right?" asked Anna.

"It's not just me. They have other informants. They've been following you this whole time. You are just naïve tourists who don't even know what you are up against here." The driver leaned into the car and warned them, whispering, "They can make you disappear just like that!" He snapped his fingers.

Suddenly, one of the Medjay's barked something and pulled out his crusader-type sword with his right hand. He pushed the taxi driver to the side and with his left hand grabbed Anna's wrist, forcibly yanking her out of the vehicle. She screamed in fear as he threw her to the ground, while the other Medjay rolled her on her stomach and tied a rope tightly around her wrists. Horrified, Michael pushed himself out of the car and rushed toward Anna, knocking the driver and one of the Medjay in the process. A huge blow to his back knocked him to the ground. He grappled for several minutes with the shorter Medjay, and after a few rolls on the ground overpowered him by a few elbow blows. Claiming the victory, Michael was about to get up when the taller Medjay knocked him to the ground. He quickly found himself facing the Medjay's sword blade pressed tightly against his neck.

"OK, OK," said Michael as he allowed his hands to be pulled behind his back while the other Medjay tied them tightly with a rope.

The taller Medjay reached inside the taxicab and grabbed Michael's backpack. After peering inside, he appeared satisfied. Then the two warriors pulled Michael and Anna off the ground and pushed them toward the bushes.

"Oh, you've got to be kidding me!" exclaimed Anna when a vehicle came into view. "That piece of junk runs?"

Behind the bushes was parked a 1950 Club Coupe Oldsmobile that had definitely seen better days. It obviously had been in several, terrible accidents and had holes where its original black paint had peeled off and rusted out. The smashed front bumper was tied to the body of the car with ropes.

As Michael and Anna were pushed inside the ratty backseat of the 1950s relic, they joined a driver dressed in regular clothes, awaiting the Medjays' instructions. Michael observed as the shorter Medjay gave their taxicab driver a wad of cash while the taller one watched. Michael quickly looked down as they strode over to the car. The shorter Medjay opened the front passenger door and sat in the front seat, Michael's backpack in his hands. The taller Medjay opened up the back door and sat in the backseat next to Michael. He produced two small black bags and used them as blindfolds, wrapping and tying them around Michael and Anna's heads accordingly. After he was satisfied that they could not see, he spoke sharply. The driver revved the ignition and they sped off in an unknown direction.

# Chapter 50

Medjay Tribe, Sahara Desert, Egypt
Wednesday, September 27
2:25 p.m.

Throughout his life Chief Jibade loyally followed his tribe's ancient customs and traditions, which dated back to the glorious Old Kingdom. Increasingly he felt he violated every conceivable rule—especially in recent days.

Chief Jibade prayed the Medjay creed over and over as he studied the sky so blue that it seemed to be painted on top of the ocher sand dunes. The September Egyptian sun still burned skin literally to the bone. Deep shadows ran along the slabs of the ancient tombs. He chanted the ancient words, "Medjay are those who defend the land of Egypt from the age-old evil. Medjay are those who learn from their mistakes. Medjay are people of destiny." The words, older than the tombs, pierced the afternoon haze. He pressed his forehead against the red-hot stones, biting his wind-scorched lips until he tasted blood.

Heavy thoughts assailed him. Although deterred by the naive and superstitious Medjay guarding the ancient places, what kept the criminals away were a fear of the gods and the horror of punishments in the afterlife. The pharaohs carved warnings to those who would rob or destroy any part of their tombs and temples, threatening severe punishment, such as being eaten by the crocodile and bitten by the poisonous snake. *That was then*, thought Jibade. Then the day came when the guards were let go, leaving the ancient places completely vulnerable. During those chaotic, unsupervised times, powerful organized gangs disregarded the ancient threats, looting and plundering at will.

The Chief gazed upon the stretch of desert with the tents of his fellow tribesman. Two weeks had passed since their sacred stele was stolen. He sent his most fearless warrior to Germany, personally instructing him on how to obtain the map sent by that low life Schulze to his daughter. Four days ago his loyal warrior strangely and suddenly vanished in Moscow. As had Seth, their point of contact in Germany and Asim's escort to Moscow. The situation seemed strange: something was not right.

Then his old friend, Police Inspector Suliman, informed him that the real thief was not Schulze, but a different German: Fischer. His warrior had followed the wrong lead. The great Chief walked back inside his tent, sat in his chair and bowed his head on the table.

Moments later, he heard footsteps outside. "Great Chief Jibade," said the bodyguard. "The gods were great to us today. Our guards managed to recover our sacred stele and kidnap those who wanted to steal it."

"What? Where is the stele?" he asked, not sure if he was dreaming.

The two Medjay silently walked forward and handed Michael's backpack to the Chief. Stunned, he carefully received the backpack and pulled out the blanket wrapped object. Slowly and cautiously, he unwrapped the stele as tears of joy sprang into his eyes.

"The holy stele has been safely returned! Thanks to our gods!" he exclaimed, laughing and crying at the same time.

On the other side of the tribal grounds, Anna and Michael were locked inside a stable. Once the car arrived at the camp, the two Medjay warriors brutally pulled Anna and Michael out of the car, marched them across the blazing sand and pushed them inside.

Even though their blindfolds were removed, they were still bound with their hands behind their backs. Anna cursed loudly and went into hysterics demanding that her hands be set free. Michael furtively told her to pretend to faint. As soon as Anna's body fell to the floor in slow motion, their guards seemed to be worried. As he watched the Medjay untie her rope, Michael figured that their orders were to secure the stele and not to harm them. *At least not yet,* he guessed. The Medjay untied Michael's rope and stepped out, locking the stable door behind him. A new Medjay, dressed in the same outfit and hair, was left to guard them.

"Are you OK?" Michael asked quietly.

"Yes, I'm fine," she chuckled slightly.

"I'm glad."

She shook her head in frustration. "I can't believe they took away my father's stele after what we had to go through to find it."

"Well, in reality, the stele is theirs. That bastard Fischer either stole it from them or stumbled on it by accident. Obviously he unleashed the fury of these Medjay, who I guess were its protectors. I wonder if it's been in their possession since ancient times."

"Michael, you're probably right, but we're not the bad guys and neither was my father."

"Yes, your father wanted to protect the stele and that's why he hid it."

"So, our kidnapping is just big misunderstanding, that's all, right?" she asked.

"Who knows? They caught us red-handed with their stele. As far as they are concerned, we are the thieves. And we're certainly not in police custody."

"What? We found that stele and pretty much handed it to them on a silver platter."

"Again it proves to them that we're the thieves. They even sent one of their friends to Germany and Moscow to follow our every step, thinking that your father mailed a map to you."

"Well, technically speaking, he did send me a type of map, which took us a week to decode."

"I'm proud we figured it out," said Michael.

"We sure did!"

"But, I'm still puzzled by the stele," said Michael.

"What do you mean?"

"The message in the pictures."

"Oh Michael, I wish David, my father's friend from the Archaeological Institute, was here," Anna said wistfully. "He could crack that message easily."

"Yeah, but I don't think David would appreciate being locked up in a stable and sitting on hay," Michael said grinning.

Anna chuckled in agreement.

"Let's see if we can crack it ourselves," said Michael, pulling the paper from his jeans pocket. He unfolded the pencil rubbing and started studying it. Anna moved closer.

"OK," said Michael after a short while. "Each row of smaller rectangles has the same image placed either at the beginning of each row or at the end. It's a person holding a stick with an outstretched arm pointing to a specific direction."

Anna nodded.

"It looks like we have four short journeys leading somewhere, but where?"

"Look!" exclaimed Anna. "All of these journeys have the same end; they finish up at a water reservoir with an island, with some kind of sarcophagus on top of it."

"I see it! It looks like a royal sarcophagus."

"That has to be Pharaoh Khufu's! His sarcophagus must be located on some sort of island surrounded by a river."

Anna, please tell me you still have that page from Kirilov's cigar box."

"Well, they took my iPhone, but I still have my purse," said Anna as she rummaged through it. "Here it is," she said happily, pulling out a folded paper and handing it over.

"OK, look at the third row from the top," said Michael as he carefully read Kirilov's page and then looked at the rubbing.

"The second way to get to Khufu's burial place is to follow an artificial canal inside the baffling pyramid. And here is the pyramid."

"Oh," said Anna, visibly amazed. "OK, let me see that paper. That first row shows the first way to get to Khufu, according to Kirilov. The funeral procession went through the temple located at the east side of the Great Pyramid. It's located at forty-four meters from the bisector of the pyramid and at a depth of about five to seven meters."

"Great," said Michael. "Now, if you look at the second row, it actually shows Kirilov's fourth way. It goes from the Great Pyramid's Subterranean Chamber through the foundation of the false well. In reality, the foundation is a stone plug with the following parameters: two meters wide, ten meters in length and two meter filling thickness. Under this stone plug there is a cylinder-shaped opening about ten meters deep down."

"So," said Anna, "here is the last row. According to Kirilov, it is in the horizontal so-called Dead-end Passage of the pyramid's Subterranean Chamber. In the middle of the sixteen-meter appendix on the ceiling of the passage there is a plug and from there an inclined passage leads to the burial place."

"Wait a second," said Michael, mesmerized as he sat back, concentrating. "What we have here is a three to four thousand year old stele showing Kirilov's four ways."

"Wow!" exclaimed Anna. "We have concrete proof the Kirilov's theory is 100 percent right. We need to get this information to the right people so he will be recognized."

"If we get out of here alive," Michael added sarcastically.

"We've gotta tell these Medjay. They've had this stele for the past several thousand years and had no clue that they had a treasure map in their hands the entire time."

"Let's first find out what they are planning to do with us. The information on the stele will be our leverage if something goes wrong."

"What do you mean if something goes wrong?"

They heard a key jiggling in the lock, and the door swung wide open. The same duo that kidnapped them entered. Suddenly, another man emerged from behind them and stepped forward, carrying himself with confidence and authority. His high forehead and black eyebrows set off his dark eyes, shining with intellect and slyness. High cheekbones and a square jaw line intensified the masculinity of his looks. He wore a long, white cotton cloak like the other men. Unlike the others, he wore earrings; silver wire formed into hoops with overlapping ends. He turned slightly and spoke authoritatively to the two Medjay in their native language. Michael and Anna watched as the guards instantly turned around and walked out of the stable.

"I'm Chief Jibade of the Medjay tribe." To Michael and Anna's surprise, the man spoke English well. "We've been guarding our sacred stele for the past three thousand years and now—"

"Chief," Michael interrupted. "We didn't steal the stele, we—"

The chief raised his hands, "I know that you didn't steal the stele."

"Really?" Michael said, amazed.

"Yes, I do," said the chief, turning to face Anna. "And I also happen to know that your father didn't steal it either," he finished solemnly.

"I am so very glad to hear that," said Anna, relieved.

"From the beginning, we suspected your father to be the thief. In our effort to try to locate the stele, one of my warriors went too far. I deeply regret that. Anna, please accept my deepest condolences in the death of your father. That slimy Fischer was the thief and tried to sell it to smugglers on the black market. Thanks to your father's efforts, the stele was saved. The only thing we didn't know was where your father hid it. So, I had my men follow you. As soon as they spotted you with the stele at El Alamein, they followed my orders and brought you here."

"Well, Chief," said Anna, "you've got some harsh methods of welcoming people." Anna held her wrists out, displaying the red marks on her skin left from the ropes used to bind her.

"I am so very sorry for the actions of my people. Our way of life teaches us to be cautious. But you are not prisoners here anymore," said the chief, smiling broadly. "You are my guests." He held his arm out, indicating they should leave the stable.

"What's the meaning of the stele?" asked Michael.

"It has been passed from one generation to the next, but the ancient meaning of the stele has been lost. It is used in numerous ceremonies, as well as in the Rite of Passage for our people."

Michael and Anna glanced at each other.

"Is anything the matter?" asked the Chief, seeing their faces.

"No, I'm just glad that no more confusion remains on both our sides," responded Anna.

"I have one question," said the Chief. "What happened to my warrior Asim and his companion Seth? They both disappeared in Moscow the day before your arrival in Egypt."

"Well," Anna spoke carefully. "Seth was involved in a terrible car accident on one of the busiest streets in Moscow."

"We saw it happen, unfortunately," Michael concurred, grimacing.

"And Asim?" asked the Chief, his voice rising. "What about my fearless warrior?"

"He was fearless, all right," said Anna. "Moscow is ..."

"A mysterious place," Michael said, shaking his head grimly.

The Chief gave him a strange look, but did not say a word as they walked outside into the scorching afternoon sun, the guards right behind them.

# Chapter 51

Cairo, Egypt
Thursday, September 28
7:15 a.m.

Cairo's Police Inspector Suliman woke up early inside his two-bedroom apartment located in Doqqi, a largely residential area of Cairo west of the River Nile, and began his morning ritual. Ready for the day, he relaxed with a mug of strong coffee and his breakfast while watching the news. Looking at his watch, he got up from the table, turned off the television and washed his dishes. Then, checking his watch once more to make sure that 9 a.m. had come, he retrieved his mobile phone, checked for his ID, holstered his service weapon and left his tidy apartment. As he walked down the stairs, his mobile phone rang. Sighing heavily, he answered the call.

"Inspector Suliman," he answered with his familiar greeting. With every passing moment that he listened, his face grew darker and darker. He grimly stated, "I'll be there soon," and turned off the phone. The morning's calmness and tranquility had disappeared rapidly.

Striding out of his apartment building into the sizzling sun, the Inspector hurried to his car. Silently cursing, he started the car and sped away. The car flew over the familiar route, but today everything was different. He gripped the steering wheel and tried to concentrate on the road, but disturbing thoughts haunted him. *Why they didn't call me immediately like I instructed?*

The last time had ended up so tragically. The kidnapping of the tourist group from France was still fresh on his mind. Local Bedouins had demanded one of their men be released from prison in exchange for the French tourists. The Inspector did everything he could, but as the SWAT team set up, the Bedouins murdered one of the tourists.

And now this damn call from the Medjay Chief Jibade! The Inspector's office was still investigating the suspicious heart attack of a German national as a possible homicide and now this. His old friend had called to inform him that his men had kidnapped the American and German nationals, as calm as if he was asking the Inspector to have lunch with him. The ghost of the slaughtered French tourist still haunted him, and now this call summoned memories of those dark days. He thought he had buried them somewhere deep where they could never escape, but today they resurfaced yet again.

The Inspector dodged traffic by way of back streets and alleys, slamming on the brakes as he pulled up to the familiar apartment building, honking his horn. Chief Detective Hussein was already waiting for his boss and quickly stepped out of the lobby. As he entered the car's cool interior, he greeted his boss cheerfully. The Inspector nodded silently and quickly zipped away from the curb.

Chief Detective Hussein knew right away something was wrong with his Inspector, whom he had known for the past five years. Normally a cheerful and talkative man, the Inspector was now eerily silent. Hussein felt uncomfortable interrupting the prolonged pause. Occasionally he glanced at the Inspector. Ten minutes later, when the air inside the car was literally resonating with tense silence, he could not tolerate it any longer. "My Inspector, can you explain to me what is happening?"

"I'm sure you remember Mr. Doyle, the American, and Anna, the German Schulze's daughter, whom we both meet the other day."

The Detective nodded.

"This morning I received a call from Chief Jibade. His men have kidnapped them."

"Where is the SWAT team? They could take that whole tribe out in a few minutes!"

"Right, they will take the whole tribe out along with the lives of two foreign nationals. Don't you remember when the Bedouin village kidnapped those French tourists? The life of that Frenchman was in our hands and we blew it. That man never had a chance after the SWAT team moved in. If we had allowed more time for negotiations, then the outcome would have been different."

"My Inspector, I'm with you, however you wish to resolve the situation."

"I promised to guard the lives of Mr. Doyle and Miss Schulze, and I intend on keeping that promise. Too many lives have been wasted already." His eyes full of pain, the Inspector looked at his companion, "Will you help me, my dear partner and friend?"

"Of course I will help you," detective said softly, "but why don't we call the SWAT team, just in case the negotiations don't go anywhere? If the Medjay kill those poor Westerners then the media will blame everything on you. That will be the end of your career."

"The Medjay Chief told me that he will kill the Westerners if he sees any sign of the police force present. I gave him my word that it would only be us," the Inspector said quietly, sighing deeply.

They rode the rest of the way in silence, lost in their own thoughts of that nightmarish night when they found the Frenchman's mangled corpse inside the Bedouin village. The Inspector often replayed and pondered that fateful night in his mind. *Why didn't I continue negotiations? Why did I give in to the pressure mounted by the media?*

An hour and a half later, they were driving inside the Medjay tribe's compound. The Inspector and his Chief Detective stared in astonishment. For the first time that morning, the Inspector smiled. Michael was hugging Anna as they stood in the middle of the meadow. Next to them was the grinning Chief of the Medjay tribe himself.

"How is this possible?" the Inspector asked incredulously. He quickly stopped the car and jumped out. He was immediately greeted by his old friend, who informed him that he wanted to see the face of his dear old friend the moment he saw that not only was police action not necessary, but also that the hostages were safe and sound.

As the Inspector and Detective listened, the Chief eloquently expressed his sincere gratitude for all the work Michael and Anna had done to safely return the sacred stele back to the tribe. Anna and Michael kept looking from the Medjay Chief to the Inspector, not able to figure out which one of them beamed with a pride more.

# Chapter 52

Windsor Hotel, Cairo, Egypt
Friday, September 29
8:00 a.m.

The sun streamed through the curtain edges as the woman stretched reluctantly, hoping the brightness would disappear behind some clouds. Someone pounded on the door. She turned over, but the sun and the pounding remained relentless. She sighed and glanced at the clock. "Michael!" she shouted. "Are you asleep?" No answer: just continued pounding.

*Just who could that be? Housekeeping?* Anna reluctantly stretched out in the soft embrace of her comforter, forcing herself to sit up. She fumbled on her robe and headed for the door. As she unlocked and yanked the door open, her eyes flew open at the sight.

"Michael? You're on the wrong side of the door." He grinned at her, a chuckle escaping. "Oh!" Anna exclaimed, folding her arms across her chest. "And now you're checking me out? Are you drunk?"

"No, of course not! Come on, I only had one beer," he said in jest, unable to look away from such a beautiful, sleepy woman. "Hey, it's time to get ready."

"Where are we going?" Anna raised her eyebrows at him. He seemed strangely excited.

"Well, I couldn't sleep, so I decided to go through some of the notes I took in Kirilov's apartment. I went to the roof garden, but when I came back I realized I had forgotten the door key. It was still really early, and I was thinking about Kirilov anyways, so I decided to call Moscow." He stopped and looked sadly at her.

"And?"

337

"Kirilov passed away two days ago."

"Oh no!" Anna exclaimed.

"Yeah, his body was frail even before that bastard Seth stabbed him. Plus, remember he's had that bullet stuck in his head for the past sixty something years."

"He didn't have a chance," Anna said sorrowfully.

"Before he died, Kirilov instructed his wife to remind us about the baffling pyramid."

"Yeah, I remember him mentioning that."

"Exactly, and she also asked me for our hotel's fax number."

"Why?"

"To fax this," said Michael, holding up the fax he had picked up minutes earlier at the hotel's front desk. Anna looked at it curiously.

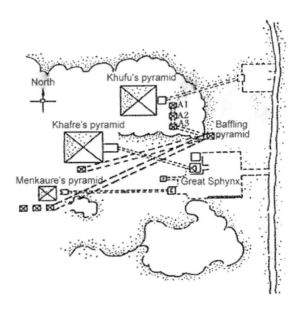

"Wait a second!" Anna exclaimed. "I saw this diagram in Kirilov's apartment."

"You're absolutely right, so let's not lose any more time. We're going on our next adventure, which hopefully will bring us closer to Pharaoh Khufu's mummy and the treasures." He paused, staring at her, "Well, are you gonna let me in?"

"Of course, come on in," Anna stepped aside with a mocking flourish.

Michael stooped down to pick up a large paper bag. "And I hope you will don something a little less transparent than that robe, otherwise I can't guarantee your safety," he joked.

"OK, just give me a few minutes," she replied with a faint smile, shutting the door while Michael walked over and sat down on the couch. Anna opened the closet and went through her clothes for a couple of minutes. She went into the bathroom to dress, put on her makeup and brush out her long hair. She emerged wearing a knee-length light brown skirt with a floral design and a light creamy blouse with a wide neck that fell becomingly from the shoulders, slightly baring them. She playfully twirled in front of the large mirror, observing herself appreciatively. She turned and looked expectantly at Michael.

Michael looked up and needed a moment to come to his senses.

"Well?" she asked, tilting her head and tossing her hair back lightly.

"Well, what?" Michael asked, realizing the absurdity of the whole situation. Just moments before, he had literally pounded on the door to hurry her up, and now he was sitting quietly on the couch unable to move. This elegant woman with her stylish appearance had forced him to forget everything.

"Well, where are we going?" asked Anna, breaking the awkward silence.

"Anna, you look fantastic and I would consider myself to be the luckiest man on earth walking next to you, but –"

"But what?"

"I bought you something at the street market this morning. It's a bit more conservative," Michael said, smiling mischievously as he opened up his paper bag and pulled out something large and black. "This is called a *jilbāb*," he explained, indicating the black, high-necked traditional Muslim robe he was holding up for her to see. He laid it down and pulled out something blue from the bag. "And this is called a *shaylah*." He held up a blue scarf that would cover all but the face. He set it down and pulled something light grey out of the paper bag. "Those two are for you. And as for me, I will be wearing a *gallibaya*," Michael held up his ankle-length robe with long sleeves. Reaching down with one hand he pulled out a white cloth, "and this turban, which is a draped headscarf."

Anna frowned.

"Relax," Michael said, chuckling. "It's all a part of my plan –"

Anna interrupted him, her voice rising, "What plan? Are you converting into a Muslim and dragging me into it?"

"Of course not! We're going to put these on and head out incognito, just in case our friends from the police department or the Medjay tribe are still spying on us."

"Oh, so I take it we're looking for that baffling pyramid?"

"Yes, the water-intake pyramid."

"And you think you know where to find it?"

"We have Kirilov's diagram of the necropolis right here."

It took them a good twenty minutes and the use of Anna's iPhone to more or less properly dress themselves in the traditional Islamic clothes. Carefully examining each other, they concluded that even their own mothers would not recognize them.

"OK, let's go," he said merrily.

"How is this going to work?"

He steered her out the door. "Just trust me!" When they reached the lobby, Michael started walking slowly. Anna looked down as she walked beside him. They left the hotel unnoticed.

Once outside the front door, they turned left and started walking quickly. Although it was September, the sun burned through their outfits. After several blocks Anna was sweltering in her dark costume. Soon Michael spotted a building with an entrance that seemed to be deserted. They cautiously stepped inside the cool, empty foyer and removed their disguises. Michael carefully folded and placed them inside his backpack. A few minutes later, they were sitting in a taxi speeding away to the Giza Plateau.

Michael gazed through the side window at the three biggest pyramids gradually appearing and disappearing in the horizon. He secretly wished that he could see the baffling pyramid from the taxi. Although the baffling pyramid was tiny compared to the three giants, it definitely did not diminish her importance and functionality. Michael imagined that the baffling pyramid looked like Gulliver in the land of Brobdingnag, the land occupied by giants who were twelve times taller than Gulliver from the famous book "Gulliver's Travels," written by Jonathan Swift in the eighteenth century. In Kirilov's words, "without the existence of this small baffling pyramid, the existence of the three biggest pyramids would not be possible."

"Michael, Anna," said Kirilov, showing them one of the diagrams. "Here is a map of the Giza necropolis. Besides the three big pyramids, you can see seven small pyramids known as the Mokattam Formation. One of the small pyramids is located at the foot of Khafre's pyramid. The next three pyramids are to the south of Menkaure's pyramid. The last three pyramids are to the southeast of the Great Pyramid. Renowned Egyptologists assume that these small pyramids were intended to be the burial places of the pharaoh's queens, sons and daughters."

"That's what I thought as well," said Anna.

"It is strange that Pharaoh Khufu's son, the hereditary Prince Ka-Wab, who died before his father, was buried in a mastaba," Kirilov commented. "The mastaba was a rectangular tomb that had a flat roof with walls that inclined toward the center. The others were buried inside the small pyramids. That is odd, don't you think?" asked Kirilov, looking at Anna.

"Yes, I would say so."

"Good. This diagram clearly demonstrates that all the small pyramids are identical in size and closely located to the larger pyramid's bases. Furthermore, they are not coated, but instead have a unique form of laying blocks, which is different from the outer layer of the large pyramids. Is it pure coincidence that six of the seven small pyramids were constructed in a straight line?"

"Well," Michael started, but was quickly interrupted by Kirilov.

"Once I looked at old photographs of the Great Pyramid, I was stunned. On one of the photographs, taken from the side of the Sphinx, an unknown pyramid is visible in the foreground. It had a broken off edge and was sunk in the low place of the very curb of the road that runs toward the Great Pyramid. Its form and location in the low place, next to the road, on the outskirts of the eastern side of the plateau was bewildering. After several years of studying it, I understood that without the existence of this mysterious, or as I call it baffling pyramid, the existence of the three biggest pyramids would not be possible. The idea of the pharaoh's burial under the Great Pyramid, in the cave and on an island required raising very pure Nile water and directing it to a special water basin. The volume of the water in the cave had to be constant at all times."

"So, the Nile and the cave's pond were directly connected through an artificial canal, right?" asked Michael.

"No, Michael, your assumption is erroneous. This direct connection couldn't be possible because the inlet of the artificial canal is physically lower than the lower level of the Nile. Therefore, water densely saturated by silt would have to pass through the canal. In just a few years sediment would clog up the canal and the water basin itself. Using contaminated *dead* water to flood the burial chamber was inadmissible. On the other hand, clean *live* water could only be obtained from the upper layer of the Nile waters. In addition, the artificial canal could not directly open up to the Nile River because in periods of low tides it would reveal the entrance to the tomb, thus revealing the main secret of the Great Pyramid."

"I guess you came to a dead end, right?" Anna asked.

"Not really," Kirilov paused as if he was expecting this very question. "This contradiction was resolved by the Chief Architect HemIwno quite cleverly. Take a look again at the plan of the necropolis."

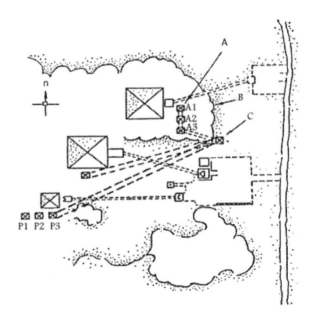

"The baffling pyramid is marked by the letter C. It has an artificial canal underneath it that travels north towards the other three small pyramids marked as A3, A2 and A1. Do you see how canal C-A1 passes horizontally along the Nile River? The Nile River is sixteen ancient Egyptian cubits in height. One Egyptian cubit is about fifty-two centimeters, which means the water was raised up to eight meters and thirty-two centimeters. When the river reached its maximum water level, the necessary quantity of *living* water was removed from the highest level of the tidal wave. Then gravity directed this living water along the artificial C-A1 canal to the water basin located beneath the Subterranean Chamber of the Great Pyramid."

"But in practice, how exactly that was happening?" asked Anna. "I still find it hard to imagine the whole picture."

"I used to be as lost as you are right now," said Kirilov, smiling. "Then I read Nancy Jenkins' book, 'The Boat Beneath the Pyramid: King Cheops' Royal Ship.'" Kirilov reached over and grabbed the book from the bookshelf. He opened it up, flipped through some pages and started reading:

> *As recently as fifty years ago the Nile in flood reached to the village of Kfar es-Sammân just under the pyramid plateau and the imposing bulk of the monument was mirrored in the placid surface of the Nile floodwaters.*

He stopped to show his two pupils a picture. "This is how the Giza Plateau looked in the 1920s. You can see how different this entire area looks today."

"Definitely," said Michael. "I don't remember seeing the Nile River so close to the Giza Plateau."

"When the Aswan High Dam was constructed in 1970, the Nile River was diverted away from the Giza Plateau. The village of Kfar es-Sammân, which Nancy Jenkins mentions in her book, is called the town of Nazlet el-Samman nowadays. This town and the baffling pyramid are both located at the edge of the plateau. Here you can see where the wavy line marks the edge of the plateau. The baffling pyramid is the key. If you follow the diagram, the modestly sized pyramid is situated on the necropolis' edge and in its lowest place, next to the road curb. When the Nile was in its flood stage, this pyramid would fill up with the cleanest water from the Nile surface," Kirilov paused to see if they understood. He continued slowly, "Because it was never coated, it always appeared unattractive and even doomed. Therefore, this pyramid has fooled all of the treasure seekers, compelling them to go around it: Chief Architect HemIwno's exact intent. But, if we were to dig at least thirty-two feet into its northern side, we would reach the artificial canal carved in the rock that allowed the pyramid to constantly pass water through itself. Once inside, we could crawl all the way to the water basin and the artificial island located beneath the Subterranean Chamber of the Great Pyramid."

"Hey, wake up!" Anna's shouts brought Michael back from Moscow to the taxi in Cairo. The driver, who had been nodding off, was suddenly fully awake and aware that he was on the opposite side of the road. Everyone in the taxi screamed as an old truck barreled down into their faces. The taxi driver jerked the steering wheel and the two vehicles darted past each other, with only a few inches to spare.

Still slightly shaking, Michael glanced through the windshield and saw the unforgettable outlines of the Giza Plateau located only a few miles south of Cairo where a limestone cliff rose abruptly from the other side of a sandy desert plateau. The ancient Egyptians called Giza "kher neter," meaning the necropolis. Shortly thereafter, at the far edge of the Giza Plateau, Michael observed the outlines of one of the oldest towns in Egypt beneath which supposedly lies the Valley Temple of the Great Pyramid's complex.

"Nazlet el-Samman," announced the driver as he pulled up to their destination in a cloud of dust. He hoped that his passengers' near-death experience would not prevent them from forgetting to leave a tip. After all, death-defying experiences made you more resilient and proved that what did not kill you, made you stronger.

# Chapter 53

Nazlet el-Samman, Egypt
Thursday, September 28
9:05 a.m.

The town of Nazlet el-Samman was in the shadows of the pyramids, located between the Giza Plateau and the western edge of Cairo. The ancient ruins were separated from the town's modern residents by a solid concrete wall topped with a chain link fence. Photos of its residents can be found in family albums all over the world as they provide tourists with horse and camel rides. Unfortunately, the town has been badly affected by the Egyptian revolution. In their desperation, the town's residents waged the Battle of the Camel, taking their camels and horses over to Tahrir Square to trample and beat the growing demonstration that ultimately toppled the Mubarak regime after thirty years in power.

It was still relatively early when Anna and Michael got out of their taxi. As they walked in the dusty morning rays of sunshine, life in the village was already bustling. Children were rushing to school and tour guides were attending to their animals. Michael and Anna wandered around looking at the local features that tourists often do not get a chance to see.

They decided to catch a ride on a *tok tok*, a motorized tricycle with a small cabin. It may look awkward, but is maneuverable through the winding, dusty streets lined with mud huts and small buildings. They got out near the concrete wall that separates the town from the pyramids. Looking beyond the concrete wall, Michael and Anna admired the view of the three pyramids. They appeared to be a stone's throw away and looked magnificent in the shimmering sun.

They walked beside the concrete wall, trying to find the town's entrance to the desert. A half an hour later, after a fruitless search along the wall, they decided that it was time to explore the desert behind it. Propping up the trunk of an old tree against the concrete wall, Michael managed to scale it with Anna following after him. They looked around to see if anyone had noticed, but no one was in the vicinity. Michael climbed up and over the sturdy chain link fence. Once he was on the other side, he coached Anna as she climbed up it. As he was assisting her in climbing over the top of the fence, a policeman suddenly appeared out of nowhere, calling after them in Arabic. It was obvious that he did not want them to climb the wall, but Anna and Michael pretended they did not hear him. Anna quickly finished climbing down the other side of the chain link fence. Turning their backs and ignoring not only the shouting policeman, but also their thundering hearts, they carefully held onto the concrete wall and slid down it, dropping down onto the desert floor. Once outside the wall, they walked far away to a quiet spot and stood against the cool concrete wall. They gazed at the pyramids in their stark beauty. From their perspective, it really looked as if they were alone in the desert.

Down below them stretched the Sphinx, a huge stone structure with a colossal gateway that may have been the entrance to the ancient necropolis. They had a good overview of the ancient workmen's village. This is where archaeologists discovered the bakeries, breweries, houses and the burial places of the population who built and maintained the pyramids.

Then they started exploring by looking at the Kirilov's necropolis map and walking through the Mokattam, an area defined by a low range of hills. The eastern part of the Mokattam Formation had undergone significant changes as a result of the construction activity. They wandered in different directions to find the location of the baffling pyramid marked on their map. There was a multitude of different elevations made of the same limestone, which made it almost impossible to determine the real age of its abandoned pieces and structures. In the intersection of two old roads, however, Michael managed to find several rows of masonry covered partially in sand.

"These are the remains of the baffling pyramid," he announced, an unmasked glow in his eyes. "Beneath this rubble is supposed to be an artificial canal made of carved rock. This pyramid served as the water pump, bringing the stream of fresh water along the artificial canal," he added, deep in his thoughts.

"So, hypothetically speaking," said Anna, perched on Kirilov's comfortable couch, "if we were to dig into the northern side of this baffling pyramid about thirty-two feet, then we would reach this artificial canal, right?"

"No, unfortunately, we can't," he paused and sighed deeply. "The baffling pyramid doesn't exist anymore."

"What?" both Anna and Michael exclaimed, shocked.

Kirilov sighed. "This so-called auxiliary pyramid was leveled to the ground some time ago. It had been labeled as an unnecessary and useless construction."

"But by doing so, it prevented the access of the living water into the burial scene located underneath the Great Pyramid," said Michael in astonishment.

"Exactly," Kirilov said grimly. "All seven of the small pyramids, plus this baffling pyramid located on the side of the road, played a vital role for the necropolis as a whole. As it remained uncoated and was built with special masonry stone blocks, it allowed an adequate amount of air inside the burial site. It functioned as the lungs of the burials: the three big pyramids were breathing through the smaller eight pyramids. At the base of each of the eight small pyramids were basically sumps, which served as drainage reservoirs to better dilute the accumulating pollutants in the Nile River's tidal water. But it was almost impossible to completely purify the water, and some small amounts of impurities still came through the purification process. It was known that these impurities would lead to their degradation and the formation of gases. Over time, the burial site could become a hotbed of germs and toxic gases. The only possible solution was to provide permanent, effective air ventilation. This could be done by using the gallery, through which Khufu's mummy was brought into the crypt."

"But after the burial ritual, the gallery was covered with masonry and casing stones," said Michael.

"Exactly right," said Kirilov, his eyes shining at his understanding. "And that's the secret: this masonry was unusual. It had the ability to pass the air, released from the pyramid's underground, through itself.

The local residents used to say that at night the air was illuminated at the foot of the pyramids in some places. The glowing air seen at the foot of the pyramids is the gas that once poisoned the tourists inside Khafre's pyramid. In April of 1984, fifteen tourists inside the pyramid complained of eye irritation and difficulty in breathing and rushed outside. Because it happened during the daytime, no one noticed the air glow. Recently, the glow has disappeared completely. The reason is simple. The foolish keepers of the necropolis at Giza discovered some "shaky" stones in the masonry of the pyramids and decided to strengthen them. Not selectively, but all of them, including the blocks that passed bad air out of the underground chamber. In order to seal the cracks and crevices in the stone blocks, they used stainless steel fittings. When I heard the news, I was horrified. The curators of the ancient pyramids truly have no idea what they have done. By depriving the underground chamber of the inflow of fresh water and air, they have transformed the crypts into putrid foci. The ecology of the tombs is now broken." Kirilov shook his head solemnly, "The pharaohs do not forgive those who disturb their peace."

"We have to get into the underground chamber and restore the ecology inside of it," said Anna, bringing Michael back from his thoughts. "If we could remove all this sand, then we could find the artificial canal leading west to Pharaoh Khufu's burial place."

"Yeah, if only we could get a permission to dig around here," said Michael, looking over the vast land of sand dunes.

"Well," said Anna. "I know what we have to do."

"I think I know what you have in mind," said Michael.

It was already mid-afternoon and the heat was becoming oppressive. They decided to walk toward the bedlam, into the plateau's multitude of tourists and peddlers.

After their long walk, lunch and a couple of bottles of water each, it luckily only took them a few minutes to find a taxi. They were glad to find a driver who agreed to take them to their hotel for only sixty Egyptian pounds, a bargain considering it was a journey of about an hour at that time of day. During the ride Michael and Anna quietly discussed what they should do next.

"The stele belongs to the guardians, the Medjay, but the Egyptian heritage belongs to Egypt," Michael spoke softly as he searched his backpack for the hotel envelope and pencil rubbing he had put in there that morning.

"But, we are not gonna make it easy for them," said Anna, grinning. She got out her iPhone and started searching for the Egyptian Department of Antiquities address. Michael leaned forward and tapped on the driver's shoulder, asking him to stop at a post office. After the driver turned down his haunting, electronic music and understood Michael's request, he was willing to make the extra stop, but only for an additional ten Egyptian pounds. Michael grinned at Anna as he took another ten pounds out of his wallet. She smiled and shrugged back at him. Satisfied, the driver accepted his fee and turned his music back up, now singing along. Anna found a pen in her purse and carefully addressed the envelope as the taxi stopped and started in the Cairo traffic.

Soon, the driver pulled up to an ancient building and stopped, turning around in his seat, nodding his head and pointing to the building. As Michael took the envelope from her and started to exit the taxi, Anna smiled, saying, "Now it's up to them to decipher the real and final resting place of Pharaoh Khufu."

Later that evening, Anna and Michael took a Nile River dining cruise aboard a pharaoh-style barge. As they glided past Cairo's illuminated skyline, Anna and Michael dined on Lebanese cuisine. Then they sat back, relaxed and watched the colorful belly-dancing show and the unforgettable Sufi men, who performed their *tanoura* spin, in keeping with Egypt's whirling dervishes' tradition.

Later, they walked up to the upper deck of the boat and sat there, chatting and whiling away the hours until midnight. From their seats they could look down and watch Cairo's trendy young set dancing. Soon they were looking upward and watching the bright stars. Above them was the prominent constellation of the Big Dipper, or Big Bear as it is sometimes called, which is featured as part of the Alaskan flag. The seven stars, sparkling in the velvet black sky, were like guardian angels looking down on Anna and Michael in their journey. They laughed and joked as the cruise boat sailed toward the famous Cairo tower. They stopped speaking as it came closer into view. Shaped like the iconic ancient lotus plant of the Pharaoh's, it was spectacularly illuminated in different shades of colors: a breathtaking masterpiece of structural art.

The next day the Egyptian Department of Antiquities got a letter in the mail. The director could not believe his eyes.

# Chapter 54

The Great Pyramid, Giza Plateau, Egypt
Friday, September 29
8:45 p.m.

A lmost five thousand years have passed since the pharaohs of
the Fourth Dynasty walked the earth, but tonight they appeared
again. Every night, as the sun sets on the bustling city of Cairo and
the last gentle rays fall behind the pyramids on the Giza Plateau, the
pharaohs reawaken during the magnificent Sound and Light Show held
at the foot of the three enormous pyramids. Michael and Anna sat as
old friends in the hushed crowd, completely immersed in the thrilling
program about ancient Egypt's history. Their eyes could hardly contain
the splendid effects.

"This is incredible," Anna whispered. Suddenly, thanks to a clever
projection, the face of the Sphinx came alive and the audience could
hear the words spoken by a long-dead pharaoh.

"Yeah," Michael answered, his eyes never leaving the Sphinx.
"This is amazing."

Shortly after the show, with the dunes of the Libyan Desert
disappearing into the Egyptian twilight, they walked away from the
Giza Plateau along the twisting road. They repeatedly looked back as
the pyramids fell into the backlit exposure, becoming simple, black
triangles with rough edges: silent, black silhouettes against the red
dusk sky.

Gradually they were pulled into Cairo's vigorous, busy crowds.
The myriad calls from souvenir lots, the wild honking of nearby traffic
and the voices of many languages swarmed the air as they made their
way through the dusty streets.

They stopped a few times to admire the little trinkets being sold, which proudly carried the names of almost all of the pharaohs that existed during all thirty dynasties. They watched as camels proudly sashayed to their stables as cars screeched and halted right up next to them. Involuntarily enveloped by the sweetish and stupefying hazes from the street hookahs, they slowly strolled past the eternally relaxed habitués relaxing on small benches outside the shops. Mesmerized, they walked deeper inside the city, unaware of their purpose and destination.

The duo strolled past tiny shops with so many trinkets, baubles and sundry items that they were literally stacked, piled and pouring out of the doorways onto the sidewalk. The merchants themselves were annoying as flies, offering their unnecessary trinkets with cloying "dear American friend" appeals and offers of their bitter Arabian coffee.

Michael and Anna continued to look back at the pyramids from time to time. Twilight obliterated the features of their surroundings and with the upward direction of the highway as its multiple-colored garland; the two biggest pyramids flickered like Christmas trees. These were entirely different pyramids without their secrets and ancient mysteries, now merely amusing accessories of the nightlife.

The last time they glanced backward, the pyramids appeared again through the tiniest opening between some buildings, as if saying goodbye. The final glimpse lasted a mere split-second, as the pyramids surrendered to the pressure of space and darkness, fading away into the impenetrable shroud of Cairo's smog.

Michael was enchanted by this mysterious city and could not comprehend how anyone would not fall in love with this ancient land, its pyramids and its people. As he walked, he pondered the famed tales of "Thousand and One Arabian Nights." He caught Anna's eye, and to her delight he quoted, "He who hath not seen Cairo hath not seen the world: her soil is gold, her Nile is a marvel; her women are like the black-eyed hours of Paradise; her houses are palaces; and her air is soft, more odorous than aloes-wood, rejoicing the heart. And how can Cairo be otherwise when she is the Mother of the World?"

There was much about Egypt, Cairo in particular, that Michael had come to love. Cairo is a city full of contrary images, where it was not unusual to see the latest luxury sedan sharing the road with a donkey-drawn cart. It has a bustling public transportation system with taxis and minibuses hustling along its many streets and overpasses that swoop through the ever-moving city. Cairo even boasts a subway, the only one that exists in the Arabian world.

Cairo is a city with many traditional and filling foods. The fragrance of the streets is the *shwarma*, a traditional meat sandwich. Meat is skewered on a metal stick and roasted slowly on a spit, rotating in front of an open flame for hours. When it is dripping off the stick a small amount is shaved off and, together with vegetables and dressing, rolled up in a *lavash* flatbread. The city's aroma is a textured world of fried corns, fruit, coffee, sweets and the heavenly evening hookahs.

Cairo is a city exploding with sounds. From the morning shout of the roosters strutting on their balconies to the discordant hubbub of a multitude of automobile horns to the ever present calls-to-prayer echoing throughout the city, Cairo is never still or silent.

Cairo is a city with unexpected color alongside the blowing desert sands, piling trash and grey, concrete buildings. It is found in the blossoming acacia plant, the brightly colored rugs on the camels and the lush greenery thriving along the Nile. The buildings constructed in English colonial style and the marvelous pyramids themselves are splashes of beauty in the Middle Eastern monotony.

Almost everything about Michael's two visits to Egypt was now familiar to him. The famous Cairo traffic where cars dodged past families in horse-drawn carts was becoming unremarkable. He had gotten used to hearing donkeys braying, horse hoofs on the pavement as well as the man who loudly called for his friend Kasim every single night.

Egypt and its world famous pyramids had been a part of Michael's passion for the longest part of his life. After arriving, leaving and coming back, Michael was sad to realize that the time had come for him to leave again. He knew what was ahead of him: the long security checks in the airport, the long hours in the air and the jarring immersion into western culture. Soon he would be dully riding the morning commute on the Metro-North commuter train. He was not eager to put Egypt and the Great Pyramid in his rearview mirror and head back to life as usual.

The events of the past almost two weeks had been a life-changing vacation-turned-quest. His trip had been consumed with his adventure in puzzling out Schulze's dying words to him: to find four ways. He had raced across Egypt, Germany and Russia and back again to Egypt to uncover one of history's long-forgotten secrets, while being chased by a fiercely skilled Medjay warrior, who seemed to be eerily resurrected from ancient times. He had witnessed first-hand things that at first had saddened him, then infuriated him, intrigued him, frightened him, bewildered him and, finally, surprised him. His endeavor to uncover one of the secrets of the Great Pyramid had come to its finale. He marveled that he had ever thought that he could uncover one of the Great Pyramids' secrets. She was yet masked in her dark secrets and ancient mysteries.

"You know, Michael, the saying 'we'll meet again' is entirely different than saying goodbye, right?" Anna suddenly asked, tears slowly escaping her beautiful, green eyes.

"Of course," Michael replied. He reached for Anna and embraced her saying, "The pyramids will always remain in my heart."

"I wasn't just talking about the pyramids," Anna said, her voice muffled against his shirt.

"Neither was I," replied Michael, chuckling. He leaned down to plant a long kiss on her beautiful lips. "The pyramids," said Michael, as they continued walking, their arms around each other, "helped me to encounter three remarkable people in my life. You," he kissed Anna again, "your father and Kirilov."

"My father helped to preserve a great discovery, and Kirilov helped the Great Pyramid expose its secret and thus prolong its immortality," Anna spoke reverently. Michael nodded solemnly in agreement. "Blessed Kirilov," she continued, "who never saw the Great Pyramid in person, yet dedicated his life to uncovering her secrets. They each in their own small steps made a huge leap in bringing humanity closer to uncovering one of the greatest secrets of all time. This may bring about the answers to such questions as who we are, why we are here and where we are going."

"I think those who never visit the Great Pyramid will never know the world," Michael replied, embracing Anna as they continued their stroll through the mysterious alleys of ancient Cairo.

Back at the hotel, Anna excused herself to take a shower. Michael took off his shoes and socks and sat down in the comfortable lounge chair. He picked up the remote, turning on the television and flipping through several channels. He watched with some amusement at the shows clicking past until he stumbled on the evening news. The announcer was reporting.

> *Sky News. An ancient stele, dating back at least four thousand five hundred years and bearing the seal of Pharaoh Khufu of the Fourth Dynasty, the builder of the last remaining wonder of the Ancient World, The Great Pyramid, was discovered earlier this week in Egypt.*

"Anna!" Michael shouted. "Anna! You might wanna see this."

> *The Minister of State for Antiquities, Dr. Mohamed Jamal, made the finding public today at The Museum of Egyptian Antiquities in Cairo. The Cairo Police Department's Inspector Setkufy Suliman accompanied him.*

The bathroom door opened. Anna appeared in the doorway, a towel wrapped around her, "What happened?"

"Look at this!" Michael exclaimed, turning the volume higher and pointing to the television set.

> *The origin of the stele is a mystery, and its owner has asked to remain anonymous. Dr. Jamal has shown a traced copy of the stele to only a small circle of experts in Egyptology and hieroglyph linguistics, who concluded that it is most likely not a forgery. Dr. Jamal and his collaborators said they are eager for more scholars to weigh in and support their conclusions. If proven to be authentic, the discovery of such importance and magnitude could reignite the debate over whether Pharaoh Khufu was really the*

*builder of the Great Pyramid. Until this discovery, the only justification for attributing the Great Pyramid to the Pharaoh Khufu was a stenciled cartouche bearing Pharaoh Khufu's name, which was found in a crawl space over the King's chamber in the nineteenth century by the British Egyptologist Howard Vyse.*

*Dr. Jamal gave an interview and displayed the ancient stele, encased in glass, to reporters from* The New York Times *and* The Daily Telegraph. *"The discovery is sensational," said Dr. Jamal, "because it provides further evidence that the Great Pyramid was indeed built by the Pharaoh Khufu of the Old Kingdom of the Fourth Dynasty. I can't express enough words of gratitude toward Inspector Suliman who successfully recovered this ancient stele from the hands of organized crime."*

*Cairo Police Inspector Suliman was praised in the recovery of the stele and keeping it out of the hands of smugglers of the antiquities. "One German national and three locals have been arrested as the result of the ongoing investigation," said the Inspector. This is Sky News, reporting from Cairo, I am Mike Whitters.*

"Wow," said Michael chuckling. "Did you see that big ol' cheesy smile on the Inspector's face?"

"Sure, and why wouldn't he smile?" Anna replied sarcastically. "He took all the credit for discovering the stele without even mentioning my father's name. He'll probably get a promotion."

"One day we'll correct this injustice," Michael said, winking at Anna. "Let the Inspector relish his fame and bask in his glory for now. Our glory days are on their way."

# Epilogue

The sun's rays were leaking through the window drapes when the phone rang. The man sleeping under the disheveled bed sheets did not stir. The phone continued to trill like a school bell on a summer morning. Finally a sigh could be heard, followed by a hand making its way out from under the sheets and abruptly grabbing the phone.

"Yes," the man spoke softly into the receiver.

After talking for a few minutes, the man hung up the phone. He quietly got out of bed, trying to not wake up the gorgeous naked woman lying next to him. He strolled to the bathroom and started the shower. Soon he came out, a towel wrapped around his muscular torso, and walked across the room.

He reached for the balcony door and as soon as it opened, Cairo exploded inside the room like a trumpet blast: car horns, street vendors and eager boys selling newspapers. The sleeping woman groaned and buried her head under a pillow. The man stepped out onto the balcony and leaned on the forged bars. In the following days he would be back to running for work, paying the bills and catching up. The man threw his head back with pleasure, exposing his face to the invigorating morning rays. He thought of nothing, but simply enjoyed the moment.

Soon the sounds crowding inside the room were overwhelmed by the savory smell of the morning street: freshly brewed coffee, grilled shwarma meat and the dusty aroma of sand and smoke. The enveloping sounds and smells from the street filled and penetrated every part of the room, every nook and cranny.

The light movements of the woman joining him on the balcony brought the man back to reality. She had donned his buttoned shirt and now casually leaned against him. As they wrapped their arms around each other, she planted a long, luxurious kiss on his lips. The man looked at her closely; the woman's eyes trusted him, despite the fact that her recent boyfriend had betrayed her, kidnapped her, stalked her and attempted to kill her in the span of the past ten days. After a few moments, the man went inside to get dressed. While he rummaged through the closet to find a clean polo shirt and khakis, she sauntered back inside and sat in a chair, posing seductively. He smiled, purposely attempting to ignore her. She watched him with a straight face, dressed only in his shirt. Soon the man had buckled his watch on his wrist and shoved his wallet in his back pocket. He walked over to her, bent down and kissed her tenderly.

She looked up at him. "Where do you think you going?"

The man looked at her compassionately, melting away her worries. He quickly kissed her and ran out the door. The pillow that was meant to strike him only bumped against the door and fell to the floor. The woman frowned.

A few seconds later, the door opened up slightly to the man's face. "Dear, sweet Anna, the Medjay Chief Jibade called. He's sending one of his tribesmen to meet me in the lobby. He wishes to bestow a token of his appreciation to us for safely returning their stele."

"I thought that you were leaving Egypt without saying goodbye."

"Really? Come on!" he laughed. "I'll be right back, OK?"

Anna smiled. "Hurry back!" she shouted as Michael shut the door.

Whistling, Michael skipped the elevator and hurried down the stairs. When he reached the lobby he looked around and found the familiar face of the Medjay warrior he had met two days earlier. The warrior ceremoniously held out an object wrapped with thick green paper. Michael held out his hands and accepted it. Without saying a word, the Medjay warrior bowed, slowly turned and walked away.

Curious, he walked over to a corner and glanced around, making sure nobody was watching him. He carefully unwrapped the gift and was awed by the metal object lying in his hands. It was a crusader-type sword; just like those he had seen slung behind every Medjay's back. Quickly he wrapped it back up.

He casually wandered over to the elevator. Two men wearing suits and carrying computer bags joined him. As they waited, the men discussed the progress of the computer technologies they were developing. As someone with a career in the computer industry, Michael's interest was peaked.

"I definitely need to test that software program again," said the guy wearing the dark blue suit.

"Don't forget to check all the bugs before presenting the final version at Monday's presentation," his colleague reminded him.

"Don't worry, I will debug everything out."

The elevator finally arrived and the little group stepped inside. The two businessmen were deep in conversation as the elevator started its struggle upward. Michael was lost in thought, envisioning himself back in his cubicle working to debug a program's coding.

When the elevator finally stopped on his floor, Michael was so deep inside his head that he almost missed it. Startled, he jumped and stuck his arm out to stop the doors from gliding together. As he stepped out the two men with him never stopped their conversation.

He walked down the hallway, stopping short a few feet away from his room.

*Computer program, software bug, debugging ... can this be it? How could have I missed that in the first place?*

When Michael opened the door, Anna was standing next to the open window blow-drying her glossy, long hair. She smiled as he absent-mindedly sat down on the couch. He sat still, concentrating on something that fully consumed his mind. Anna turned off the hair dryer and picked up her brush.

Michael emerged from his thoughts, "Anna, do you know what a computer software bug is?"

"Not exactly," Anna hesitated, as she made her living working with legal documents in the German court system.

"Have I mentioned to you that I work in the software testing industry?"

"Oh yeah, sure," answered Anna as she walked over to Michael and took a seat next to him.

"OK, by definition, a software bug is an error in a computer program that prevents it from behaving as intended. In other words, when you use a computer program, a bug produces an incorrect result. Most bugs arise from people who make errors when writing a program's source code or its design. Some bugs have only a subtle effect on the program's functionality and might lay undetected for a long time. Usually bugs are a consequence of the nature of the programming task. Some bugs arise from simple oversights made when computer programmers write source code carelessly or transcribe data incorrectly. Having an undetected bug in the system can lead to disasters." Michael paused. He tried to be aware that English was her second language. She nodded at him, indicating that she understood his explanation.

He continued, "For example, in the 1960s the NASA Mariner 1 went off course during its launch due to a missing 'bar' in its software. The famous 2003 North American blackout was triggered by a local outage that went undetected due to a bug in the monitoring software."

"That's really fascinating, but why are you telling me all this?" asked Anna.

"Because that's what I do in my everyday job." Michael paused. "And it made me realize that the Chief Architect of the Great Pyramid, HemIwno was just like a computer programmer. In fact, we could call him the first computer programmer in history."

"What?" Anna was chuckling at the thought.

"Well, he designed the program that everyone believed was Pharaoh Khufu's final resting place. All the chambers, passageways and the Grand Gallery are parts of his cunning program. The King's Chamber had a false purpose: a lure, simply speaking. The more obvious the obstacles, the greater were the wishes to overcome them. The place where the Ascending and Descending Passages intersect was blocked by the heavy, granite plug, remember?" Michael looked at Anna.

She nodded.

"That plug was so obvious that it tempted its visitors to get behind it. And as you recall, Caliph Al-Mamun, who broke into the Great Pyramid in the ninth century, got so excited and intrigued when he saw the first plug that he ordered his men to cut around it until they broke into the Ascending Passage, an agonizing and painstakingly difficult task. Ahead of them, at the end of the Grand Gallery, they found the doorway, the so-called 'antechamber,' leading to the King's Chamber. Then these unwelcomed but expected guests were led to the disappointing grand finale. As they reached the threshold of the King's Chamber, they encountered a sliding door that was strangely left half-shut, thus allowing them to get inside. That opening drove them to search further. The fact that it was not left completely shut was not a sign of the builders' forgetfulness but a lure! In fact, it was so well thought out that a corpse was found inside, as if shouting to every new visitor, 'You are not the first one here!' And what did they find inside the King's Chamber? A single, empty sarcophagus! It was the obvious, logical proof of that statement." He looked at Anna who was listening with eager fascination.

He continued, "The cherry on top was the broken corner on the empty sarcophagus. It seemed obvious that someone else had been in there and had broken it in their haste to rob the pyramid. Don't you see? The Chief Architect HemIwno implemented a bug in the design of the program called 'The Great Pyramid.' Basically, it behaved in such a way that it provided false pathways for its user. The false pathways led them to discover Khufu's phony burial site and thus prevented them from using one of the four true ways leading to the Khufu's real and final resting place. Caliph Al-Mamun unwittingly was the first user of that program."

"Looks like somebody did his homework," Anna said, smiling broadly. Michael slightly smirked. "So Al-Mamun's doubtful fame as a burglar provided the greatest gift to Khufu's tranquility in future centuries. It guaranteed that those following would use the same bogus pathways leading to nowhere."

"Sure," Michael replied. "Al-Mamun unwittingly convinced all future visitors that searching inside the Great Pyramid would lead to fruitless results. As you well know, pyramids were robbed in ancient times! Every single author of every single book written about the pyramids makes this conclusion."

"Michael Doyle, a simple computer software engineer, understood the great architect HemIwno, the first computer programmer, who designed a program known as 'The Great Pyramid.' This program had a bug designed to lead its users, those who penetrated and explored the pyramid, to the incorrect finale," Anna concluded.

Michael remained silent.

Printed in the United States
By Bookmasters